To the Follow[illegible]

The Dream is Not Dead

By Summer C. Marshall

Acknowledgements

Thank you, Jesus Christ of Nazareth for saving my life! Thank you for choosing me and calling my name. I will do your will. Come Lord Jesus! Your, Kingdom come, Your will be done on earth as it is in Heaven.

Introduction

I never could have imagined that a dream would change the course of my life and my family's lives. I have been having dreams since I was a little girl, and I remember those dreams being very dark when I was 16 years old. In the dreams, I kept falling into darkness, but every time I called Jesus' name in the dreams, He rescued me. As a matter of fact, He always saved me. Interestingly enough, and I know it was not happenstance, the year 2016, was "The Year of the Dream' and the year a very special dream I had of my mother (who passed away in 1995) which came true on Sunday, Christmas Day, December 25, 2016. It was during a play I participated in called the 'Story of a Man'. In the dream I was standing on a stage, surrounded by family and friends and my mother's bright spirit was hovering over and in the dream, I thanked her for introducing me to Jesus. That year was a turning point in my life as I had made a decision that I would only live a life that was pleasing to God (true transformation) and I was determined to walk in my purpose in all areas of my life. And on the very last day of that year, Wednesday, December 31, 2016, God said, "Write the Book!"

Dedication

I would like to thank my beautiful family and loved ones who were patient with me during this process. Writing these books was very challenging because I was writing about my life in real time. Major events were taking place in my life and in the world at the same time and it was really challenging focusing my time on anyone or anything else other than the Lord God Almighty and His word. Thank you for allowing me time to do what God told me to do and not making me feel guilty about it. I love you for that. Thank you for understanding. John 8:33 (14)

Foreword

Jesus returned to the Mount of Olives, but early the next morning he was back again at the Temple. A crowd soon gathered, and he sat down and taught them. As he was speaking, the teachers of religious law and the Pharisees brought a woman who had been caught in the act of adultery. They put her in front of the crowd. “Teacher,” they said to Jesus, “this woman was caught in the act of adultery. The law of Moses says to stone her. What do you say?” They were trying to trap him into saying something they could use against him, but Jesus stooped down and wrote in the dust with his finger. They kept demanding an answer, so he stood up again and said, “All right, but let the one who has never sinned throw the first stone!”

Then he stooped down again and wrote in the dust. When the accusers heard this, they slipped away one by one, beginning with the oldest, until only Jesus was left in the middle of the crowd with the woman. Then Jesus stood up again and said to the woman, “Where are your accusers? Didn’t even one of them condemn you?” “No, Lord,” she said. And Jesus said, “Neither do I. Go and sin no more.” John 8:1-11 (11)

On this ancient day, the Awesome One, Jesus Christ of Nazareth rewrote both history and His story. The end is only the beginning.

Introduction

“Then Adam and Eve entered the cave, and stood praying, in their own tongue, unknown to us, but which they knew well. And as they prayed, Adam raised his eyes, and saw the rock and the roof of the cave that covered [him] overhead, so that he could see neither heaven, nor God’s creatures. So, he wept and smote heavily upon his breast, until he dropped, and was as dead. And Eve sat weeping; for she believed he was dead.

Then she arose, spread her hands towards God, suing Him for mercy and pity, and said, “O God, forgive me my sin, [the sin] which I committed, and remember it not against me. For I alone caused Thy servant to fall from the garden into this lost estate from light unto this darkness, and from the abode of joy into this prison. O’God, look upon this Thy servant thus fallen and raise him from his death, that he may weep and repent of his transgression which he committed through me.

Take not away his soul this once; but let him [live] that he may stand after this measure of his repentance, and do Thy will, as before his death. But if Thou do not raise him up, then, O God, take away my own soul, [that I be] like him; and leave me not in this dungeon, one and alone; for I could not stand alone in this world, but with him [only]. For Thou, O God, didst cause a slumber to come upon him, and didst take a bone from his side, and didst restore the flesh in the place of it, by Thy divine power.

And Thou didst take me, the bone, and make a woman, bright like him, with heart, reason, and speech; and in flesh, like unto his own; and Thou didst make me after the likeness of his countenance, by Thy mercy and power. O, Lord, I, and he are one, Thou, O God, art our Creator, thou art [He] who made us both in one day. Therefore, O God, give him life, that he may be with me in this strange land, while we dwell in it on account of our transgression. But if Thou wilt not give him life, then take me, even me, like him; that we both may die the same day.” And Eve wept bitterly, and fell upon our father Adam, from her great sorrow. But God looked upon them; for they had killed themselves through great sorrow. But He would raise them and comfort them. He, therefore, sent His word unto them; that they should stand and be raised forthwith.

“…For I am God the Creator, who, when I created My creatures, did not intend to destroy them. But after they had sorely roused My anger, I punished them with grievous plagues, until they repent. But if on the contrary, they still continue hardened in their transgression, they shall be under a curse forever.” – The Book of Adam and Eve, Page 7-8

Preface

God reveals His mysteries to His children. The dreams given to me by God have revealed that I am His daughter and His special possession and the Lord Himself is my treasure. I had no idea who I was until I started writing the book God told me to write. This book is about my life and how my dreams and visions and the word of God opened a door to an exciting world, supernatural experiences, and the journey of a lifetime. I am the dreamer and the dream. This is a continuation of my first book, 'God Said Write the Book – the Second Beginning' and it details the beginning of my journey with the Lord. Jesus has watched over me from Heaven, never left me alone and has now come back to help the descendants of Abraham and it appears, I am one of them. I live in the Town of the Queen of Angels, and with this writing the Spirit and the bride say, "Come." Revelations 22:17 (12)

Prologue

"On April 24, as I was standing on the bank of the great Tigris River, I looked up and saw a man dressed in linen clothing, with a belt of pure gold around his waist. His body looked like a precious gem. His face flashed like lightning, and his eyes flamed like torches. His arms and feet shone like polished bronze, and his voice roared like a vast multitude of people. Only I, Daniel, saw this vision." – Daniel 10:4-7 (11)

A female tiger is called a tiger, or a tigress and a lioness.

Chapter 1: The Dream is Not Dead

"A woman in the crowd had suffered for twelve years with constant bleeding [having spent everything she had on doctors] and she could find no cure. Coming up behind Jesus, she touched the fringe of his robe. Immediately, the bleeding stopped. "Who touched me?" Jesus asked. Everyone denied it, and Peter said, "Master, this whole crowd is pressing up against you." But Jesus said, "Someone deliberately touched me, for I felt healing power go out from me." When the woman realized that she could not stay hidden, she began to tremble and fell to her knees in front of him. The whole crowd heard her explain why she had touched him and that she had been immediately healed. "Daughter," he said to her, "your faith has made you well. Go in peace." Luke 8:43-48

It was midday in the spring of April, 2014. I was laying down taking a nap. While lying in my bed, I had an out of body experience and a strange vision. I saw myself floating above my lifeless, still body and I was terrified, but I wasn't alone. I felt another presence beside me, though I was the only person in the house. I began to weep and while floating there, I saw an image, a figure wrapped in linen clothes inching towards me like it was coming from an ancient time and it touched me on the forehead and I heard a man's voice say, "Wake up!" I sat straight up and began wondering, who touched me? I was home alone and I became very afraid. After this encounter, I began attending church, hoping that God will give me the answers. I hadn't heard the Lord speak to me in a long time. I used to go to church and get a word and I knew it was God speaking directly to me. I mean, I knew deep down it was God, but why now? I believe this supernatural encounter was a sign of an awakening of God's chosen children. I wrote this note in my journal on July 19, 2014. "Before you help someone, you have to first help yourself. Meaning, you have to have your stuff in order."

Fast forward to May of 2016, I had a dream about my mother. It was significant because I hadn't dreamed about her in a minute. She passed away in 1995 of breast cancer and as she was dying, she made a point to tell me not to blame God for her sickness because it wasn't His fault. She warned me to go to the hospital, take pharmaceutical drugs or get surgery. She told me that the doctor's were merely practicing medicine. She wrote me letters, encouraging me to stay close to the Lord and to teach my children about Him, implying that we would need Jesus in his generation. I often dreamed about her, but oddly she never spoke in the dreams until that faithful Saturday night. In the dream, I was in an unfamiliar place, surrounded by a room full of people - most of which I didn't know.

In the dream, I was transported to a stage, facing an audience and my family and friends were there, waiting for me to sing. When I looked towards the back of the room, there was a bright light and my mother was hovering there, looking beautiful with a warm smile on her face. As I went to tell her "thank you for introducing me to Jesus," she spoke and said, "I saw you." The next morning, I went to church to hear the Pastor say three times during the service, "God told me to tell you, I see you." The Pastor acknowledge that he didn't know who it was for, however it was that very moment, I was for certain that God was again speaking to me and I didn't think it a coincidence that we were in 'The Year of the Dream'. I started attending every church service I could from that moment on, in hopes of getting the answers I was seeking from God. That would also be the year God said, "Write the Book."

As I began attending church more regularly, I learned that the year of transformation was necessary in order to prosper by way of dream. As I was transforming, I realized that I didn't have to keep changing. I was told that the dream that was inside of me, was ahead of me. I was learning that faith was an action word. I had to do something and at the time, it was to write down the things that God was saying to me, however my journey was filled with obstacles. Though, the Lord was encouraging me every step of the way not to be afraid of what God had put inside of me. It was a must that I begin to live God's word so that I could be transformed, even though I didn't know I hadn't recognized the seasons.

I was working on my spiritual man, renewing my mind so that God could be my strength. I was learning that fear was a hinderance to my faith. God was telling me that he was preparing me to help the women. He was telling me that He had something better for me than what I had been used to. You can't believe negative and positive at the same time. I was holding on to a past that was causing my dream to be stagnant and making decisions based on emotions, but God wanted to show me a better way. I had to learn that obedience was my willful compliance and I wanted to do it. I was learning to believe and trust God no matter what I saw with my natural eyes, and somehow I knew I had become the watcher. The Bible says, "When the watchman sees the enemy coming, he sounds the alarm to warn the people." (Ezekiel 33:3)

God was telling me that the dream was not dead and that all of the dreams He had been giving me over the years had and have meaning and would play a vital role in the end times, but that puzzled me because in my mind, I was a nobody. "I will climb up to my watchtower and stand at my guardpost. There I will wait to see what the Lord says and how he [I] will answer my complaint. Then the Lord said to me, "Write my answer plainly on tablets, so that a runner can carry the correct message to others. This vision is for a future time. It describes the end, and it will be fulfilled. If it seems slow in coming, wait for it will surely take place. It will not be delayed. Look at the proud! They trust in themselves, and their lives are crooked. But the righteous will live by their faithfulness to God. Wealth is treacherous, and the arrogant are never at rest. They open their mouths as wide as the grave, and like death, they are never satisfied. In their greed they have gathered up many nations and swallowed many peoples. But soon their captives will taunt them. They will mock them, saying, "What sorrow awaits you thieves! Now you will get what you deserve! You've become rich by extortion, but how much longer can this go on?" Suddenly, your debtors will take action. They will turn on you and take all you have, while you stand troubling and helpless. Because you have plundered many nations, now all the survivors will plunder you." Habakkuk 2:1-8

Chapter 2: God Appointed

"Moses himself told the people of Israel, 'God will raise up for you a Prophet like me from among your own people'. Moses was with our ancestors, the assembly of God's people in the wilderness, when the angel spoke to him at Mount Sinai. And there Moses received life-giving words to pass on to us [you]." Acts of the Apostles 7:37-38

On this journey, I've learned that a dream or intuition is God's way of speaking to you. The dream is an inward witness and how He relays information to you. I learned in 2016, that satisfaction and fulfillment in my life would only come from walking in my purpose but, I didn't know what my purpose was. However, the bible tells me He knew before I was in my mother's womb as it says in Jeremiah 29:11. God knew and that's why I believe He began giving me the dreams to help me along. Jesus appeared as a man in human form so that He could show us how to be free and his earthly ministry is written in the Bible so that we would have an example of the correct way. This is why Jesus' followers were called, 'Followers of the Way'. Afterall, in John 14:6, Jesus said, "I am the way, the truth, and the life. No one can come to the Father except through me." By the way, the number 14 is symbolic for salvation and the number 6 represents the creation of man.

Jesus operated as a man, even though He was filled with the Holy Spirit. Jesus was given a position of entitlement as God's Son. "So you see, just as death came into the world through a man, now the resurrection from the dead has begun through another man. Just as everyone dies because we all belong to Adam, everyone who belongs to Christ will be given new life. But there is an order to this resurrection: Christ was raised as the first of the harvest; then all who belong to Christ will be raised when he comes back. After that the end will come, when he will turn the Kingdom over to God the Father, having destroyed every ruler and authority and power. For Christ must reign until he humbles all his enemies beneath his feet. And the last enemy to be destroyed is death. For the Scriptures say, "God has put all things under his authority. [Psalms 8:6]' (Of course, when it says, "all things are under his authority," that does not include God himself, who gave Christ his authority.) Then, when all things are under his authority, the Son will put himself under God's authority, so that God, who gave his Son authority over all things, will be utterly supreme over everything everywhere." (1 Corinthians 15:21-28) Hallelujah! The scripture is clear, and it says Christ was given authority over everything, everywhere!

He was the advocate for humanity, teaching us through the things that he suffered and helping us learn lessons from the suffering. I had to learn to stop bowing to the devil and stop compromising my integrity for temporary pleasure. The Holy Spirit lead me into the trial so that I could learn my identity. Jesus learned obedience in the wilderness. I had to stop sinning, and commit my life to God and I had to do this by not allowing the enemy to play with my mind, which is why both hearing and knowing the Word of God are so very important in these last days. I got really distracted with life and had fallen asleep until that angel woke me up in 2014. I had dropped my dream, but it was time to pick it back up again. Moving to the valley in 2009 was definitely God's direction. "Then the Lord took hold of me, and I was carried away by the Spirit of the Lord to a valley filled with bones. He led me all around among the bones that covered the valley floor. They were scattered everywhere across the ground and were completely dried out.

Then he asked me, "Son of man, can these bones become living people again?" "O Sovereign Lord," I replied, "You alone know the answer to that." Then he said to me, "Speak a prophetic message to these bones and say, 'Dry bones listen to the word of the Lord! This is what the Sovereign Lord says: Look! I am going to put breath into you and make you live again! I will put flesh and muscles on you and cover you with skin. I will put breath into you, and you will come to life. Then you will know that I am the Lord.'" (Ezekiel 37:1-6) Then he said to me, "Speak a prophetic message to the winds, son of man. Speak a prophetic message and say, 'This is what the Sovereign Lord says: Come, O breath, from the four winds! [Matthew, Mark, Luke and John] Breathe into these dead bodies so they may live again.'" So I spoke the message as he commanded me, and breath came into their bodies. They all came to life and stood up on their feet – a great army.

Then he said to me, "Son of man, these bones represent the people of Israel. They are saying, 'We have become old, dry bones – all hope is gone. Our nation is finished.' Therefore, prophesy to them and say, 'This is what the Sovereign Lord says: O my people, I will open your graves of exile and cause you to rise again. Then I will bring you back to the land of Israel. When this happens, O my people, you will know that I am the Lord. I will put my Spirit in you, and you will live again and return home to your own land. Then you will know that I, the Lord, have spoken, and I have done what I said. Yes, the Lord has spoken!'" (Ezekiel 37:9-14) I wrote this in my journal on July 28, 2016: Before Moses was chosen to show the people they could go into the promised land, he was a murderer and had a speech impediment but God was still faithful because Moses didn't give up. Jesus also fought through the process. Focus on God only: 1) submit myself to the process, be disciplined and stay in the word. 2) Obey the word of God (do not be in unity with unbelievers). 3) Only believe – God is able. 4) Pray and confess by faith.

I said this prayer: "I thank you Father God for helping me with publishing this book. I thank you Father God for putting me in touch with the right people. There is nobody better than You. Thank you for giving me this dream. You are causing me to prosper and be a person of favor. Thank you Father for turning the King's heart to my favor. Thank you for allowing me to go boldly and gracefully to the throne as you are a God of your word, trustworthy, faithful and true. In Jesus name, Amen." Free your mind. Don't allow your old nature, Satan and the world systems to cause you to detour away from the dreams that God has given you. The world is trying to push certain agendas. Do not turn away from who God destined you to be. Take your broken pieces to God and ask Him to mend you.

This dream wouldn't be a reality if it wasn't for Jesus. I am becoming a better person when I submit myself to the dream process. It's not about me, it's for other people. I was told I was going to experience heaven so that I could rule and reign with the Lord in the earth realm. God gave me the dreams and visions and in doing so appointed me as prophet to the nations. The dream is God's purpose, and the enemy wants to defeat that purpose. I had to continue to press so that I could receive the supernatural help on the other side because afterall we are in a war and that's why the Lord gave me the dreams to help me navigate through the rough, spiritual terrain. I am His vehicle. "And we know that God causes everything to work together for the good of those who love God and are called according to his purpose for them." (Romans 8:28)

Chapter 3: The Battle Over Our Souls

"For we are not fighting against flesh-and-blood enemies, but against evil rulers and authorities of the unseen world, against mighty powers in this dark world, and against evil spirits in the heavenly places." Ephesians 6:12

The year 2017, was the Year of Implementation and a year I purposed to learn all I could about the Lord and the Word of God. What I learned is that I am just the clay. God is the Master Potter. I had to learn the Word and get it deep into my heart because I needed to be made honorable so the Lord could use me. I had to be crushed like grapes. "Throughout the earth the story is the same – only a remnant is left, like the stray olives left on the tree or the few grapes left on the vine after harvest." (Isaiah 24:13). As I said in an earlier chapter, an angel of the Lord touched me in 2014 and told me to wake up. I experienced heartbreak that shook me to my core in 1995, with the loss of my mother and so in 2015 when I began going through a pruning and separation, I felt that same mournful spirit, but God! As I began to heal, I started dreaming again in 2016.

As my dreams began to come true in 2016, I began to discover that I was born with a purpose, possibly a watcher and more likely than not, a messenger for my generation "X". I became anxious to find out what it was the Lord had purposed for me to do. "The Lord gave another message to Jeremiah. He said, "Go down to the potter's shop [before the throne – the alter], and I will speak to you there." So I did as he told me and found the potter working at his wheel. But the jar he was making did not turn out as he had hoped, so he crushed it into a lump of clay again and started over. Then the Lord gave me this message: "O Israel, can I not do to you as this potter has done to his clay? As the clay is in the potter's hand, so are you in my hand. If I announce that a certain nation or kingdom is to be uprooted, torn down, and destroyed, but then that nation renounces its evil ways, I will not destroy it as I had planned. And if I announce that I will plant and build up a certain nation or kingdom, but then that nation turns to evil and refuses to obey me, I will not bless it as I said I would.

Therefore, Jeremiah, go and warn all Judah and Jerusalem. Say to them, 'This is what the Lord says: I am planning disaster for you instead of good. So, turn from your evil ways, each of you, and do what is right.'" Jeremiah 18:1-11 (21) I was crushed in 1995 when my mother passed away at 46. I was crushed when my father and my grandfather passed away in 1998. But, what I didn't know is that I was Israel! In doing my ancestry, I discovered that more of my family members who were veterans and seniors passed away in 1998. When I experienced my heartbreak in 2015, I felt as if I was in mourning again, but this relationship was doomed from the start because he was not a believer – so I was unequally yoked.

I went into a deep depression, and then God sent a bird, but not any old bird – he sent a baby boy dove as a signal to go down to the potter's house and receive His Word. In following the Holy Spirit, the Lord brought me back to Himself. "He is the Potter, and he is certainly greater than you, the clay! Should the created thing say of the one who made it, "He didn't make me?" Does a jar ever say, "The potter who made me is stupid?" Soon and it will not be very long – the forests of Lebanon will become a fertile field, and the fertile field will yield bountiful crops. In that day the deaf will hear words read from a book, and the blind will see through the gloom and darkness. The humble will be filled with fresh joy from the Lord. The poor will rejoice in the Holy One of Israel." (Isaiah 29:16-19) (28) Hallelujah!

I began to realize that God was talking to me and that the words in the Bible weren't just words, but God was speaking directly to me through those words. His voice was becoming very clear and the Words were beginning to come to life. A real live Christmas story. For once in my life, I was beginning to feel alive! The Word was guiding me into my purpose. In 2014, the skies were changing. In 2015 the climate was changing. Then in 2016 the culture began drastically changing and it seemed that everything that was evil and opposed God was in and Jesus was being pushed out. God began giving me some serious messages. I felt I had become the watcher. "What sorrow awaits those who argue with their Creator. Does a clay pot argue with its maker? Does the clay dispute with the one who shapes it, saying, 'Stop, you're doing it wrong!' Does the pot exclaim, 'How clumsy can you be?' How terrible it would be if a newborn baby said to its father, 'Why was I born?' or if it said to its mother, 'Why did you make me this way?'"

This is what the Lord says – the Holy One of Israel and your Creator: "Do you question what I do for my children? Do you give me orders about the work of my hands? I am the one who made the earth and created people to live on it. With my hands I stretched out the heavens. All the stars are at my command. I will raise up Cyrus to fulfill my righteous purpose, and I will guide his actions. He will restore my city and free my captive people – without seeking a reward! I, the Lord of Heaven's Armies, have spoken!" This is what the Lord says: "You will rule the Egyptians, the Ethiopians [Hebrew Cushites] and the Sabeans. They will come to you with all their merchandise, and it will be all yours. They will follow you as prisoners in chains. They will fall to their knees in front of you and say, 'God is with you, and he is the only God. There is no other. Truly, O God of Israel, our Savior, you work in mysterious ways." Isaiah 45:9-15

During the year of Implementation, I believe the Lord was calling back His chosen people and who are we to argue with God? "But the Lord said to Samuel, "Don't judge by his appearance or height, for I have rejected him. The Lord doesn't see things the way you see them. People judge by outward appearance, but the Lord looks at the heart." I had to separate myself from contaminating influences and I truly believe this is why I experienced so much heartbreak in my life because God was going to use all of it. I wasn't like everyone else. I had to live holy. I always wanted to be liked, because I love people and I just wanted the same love. I suppose that's how God feels, He loved us so much He sent us His Son to help us and we rejected him because He was different. But He was different in a good way. He didn't sin. Through it all, I've not ever blamed God or turned away from Him, because I've always believed that He was. I just had to get to know Him. "The Lord will work out his plans for my life – for your faithful love, O Lord, endures forever. Don't abandon me, for you made me." (Psalms 138:8) I began to truly believe that the Lord was with me, because I could see the evidence. My faith was increasing by leaps and bounds. It was both an exciting and scary time.

I was learning that I could love people, as Jesus commanded me to do, but I couldn't just go along with or accept people's lifestyle if it wasn't holy and didn't line up with the Word of God. If I did what they did, then I was bowing to the enemy and going against my Creator, the One in whom I believed and worshipped. To bow is to worship. I had to live by God's principles and live the thing I was talking about. I had to leave my old way of living. I couldn't operate in my old ways, working in my new place. I learned to speak different and walk different. I learned to speak to my future, so I could put it into my present and I didn't know it at the time, but I was prophesying.

I had to make better choices. I had to learn not to sin in my anger when people hurt me which is very difficult to do and I'm still working on it. Afterall, I am flesh. I am not Jesus, he was the only perfect One. God didn't give me permission to curse people who've hurt me, He said that vengeance belongs to Him. The blessing was on me, so I had to learn to be more compassionate and forgiving and judge not. I had to learn to walk away from people or situations that may cause me to come out of my character and sin. I felt something major was ahead of us so strong that forgiveness was going to have to be preached more than anything else. "And 'don't sin by letting anger control you.' Don't let the sun go down while you are still angry, for anger gives a foothold to the devil." Ephesians 4:26-27

In 2017, I learned God speaks to you in certain ways – visions and dreams. God was showing me things that were to come. I always had dreams, but I hadn't experienced the visions yet. On October 1, 2017, the Lord gave me this word: "Stay true to what God shows you. The evidence is inside of you. The thing God told you is more real than the situation you are in right now. Don't let others rob you of it or let the weight of it cause you to walk away. When it's from God, it's not going to leave you alone. God is doing new things still. You have to complete the season you are in before you go to the next season. Don't stay in a season too long. Some of your relationships are just for a season. Some people have to leave people behind in their season. Have the faith to believe God no matter what season you are in, for the results He's trying to produce in you for that season are completion and fulfillment of the new things. Obedience to the instruction God gives you can't be altered. Stay on the right track. Don't be moved by what's going on. Have patience to be steadfast while you are in the process and you will win. Everything takes process to be established. You are significant. You matter. Be present in your greatness and in your gift to minister to others. God didn't' plant fruit trees to eat their own fruit. It's for others to enjoy. It's necessary to encourage people, they need you. Stop robbing people, they need what you have. Say yes to God and try something new. No weapons formed against you shall prosper."

I wrote: I'm in transition and I'm about to shift to my next. I will have nothing attached to me that separates me from my purpose. Everyone on my path should be serving God's purpose in my life. I saw that we were coming into a season where we were going to preach the Word more, but not to the Gentiles, but the believers. "If you see a fellow believer sinning in a way that does not lead to death, you should pray, and God will give that person life. But there is a sin that leads to death, and I am not saying you should pray for those who commit it. All wicked actions are sin, but not every sin leads to death. We know that God's children do not make a practice of sinning, for God's Son holds them securely, and the evil one cannot touch them. We know that we are children of God and the world around us is under the control of the evil one. And we know that the Son of God has come, and he has given us understanding so that we can know the true God [the one who is true]. And now we live in fellowship with the true God because we live in fellowship with his Son, Jesus Christ. He is the only true God, and he is eternal life. Dear children, keep away from anything that might take God's place in your hearts [keep yourselves from idols]. In 2017, I dedicated my entire life to Christ and committed myself to learning God's Word and His ways.

This as also the year that we had miraculous signs in heaven, like September 23, 2017, when the planets aligned perfectly and Revelations 12 happened. We had massive fires. Then, on Friday, December 22, 2017, SpaceX's Falcon 9 rocket delivered the fourth set of 10 Iridium NEXT satellites in a series of 75 total satellites to low-Earth orbit for Iridium, a global leader in mobile voice and data satellite communications. December 22, just so happened to be the day I got married in 1999. As it flew across the night sky, it had everyone thinking it was the end, but it was just the beginning of the end. The end of the world as we have known it to be. "If you try to hang on to your life, you will lose it. But if you give up your life for my sake and for the sake of the Good News, you will save it." (Mark 8:35) A spiritual battle is on the horizon, a battle for our souls. In December 2017, I was told to pay attention to God's voice, He would direct my path towards my purpose.

Chapter 4 – The Feast of Trumpets

"Our Father in heaven may Your name always be kept holy. May Your Kingdom come soon! May Your will be done on earth, as it is in heaven. Give us today the food we need [give us today our food for tomorrow] and forgive us our sins, as we have forgiven those who sin against us. And don't let us yield to temptation but rescue us from the evil one [or from evil]." (Matthew 6:10)

In the year 2018, my whole entire life changed. I discovered that the words in the Bible weren't just simply words on a page, but God's actual voice was speaking to me through those very words. I know I sound like a broken record, but it's the truth! God is speaking, now. Psalms 19 says, "The heavens proclaim the glory of God. The skies display his craftsmanship. Day after day they make him known. They speak without a sound or word; their voice is never heard [or there is no speech or language where their voice is not heard]. Yet their message has gone throughout the earth, and their words to all the world." God has made a home in the heavens for the sun." (Psalms 19:1-4) This is the year I began having day and night visions. It was as if heaven had invaded earth. I began having supernatural encounters with God. I have always been a dreamer, however now I was having waking visions to go along with the dreams and clearly seeing the Word come to life through His creations. All of nature and science began communicating with me and I could see with my natural eyes that angels, the Holy Spirit, and the Lord Jesus Christ were real. I was seeing things manifest in the natural from the Spirit. The Holy Spirit was communicating with me;

and giving me very important messages from the Lord God Almighty. Something was going on in heaven to where God was trying to get my attention in the earth. Reverse that, something was going on in the earth realm, to where Heaven was trying to get my attention. I needed to be alert.

Birds were bringing me messages and it seemed like every time I read the Bible or listened to an inspirational message; I heard from Yah. The message was always directly connected to what I was experiencing in real life. It was like something I had never experienced before in my life. All of these experiences were accompanied by signs in the heavens and on the earth. The moon was shining brighter than ever before, the clouds were heavenly, and stars were blinking. We were having fires, volcano eruptions, earthquakes, and hailstorms. I wondered, why would the Lord tell us to pray that God's will be done on earth, as it is in heaven? What was going on in heaven that it should be brought down to earth? I'm learning that we bring heaven to earth, according to God's timetable AND we bring to earth that which exist in heaven. Today is September 23, 2019, exactly two years to the date of the Revelation 12 sign that took place in the heavens in 2017. It's also the actual start date of the Fall Holy Days or what the Jews call the Feast of Trumpets..

I was discovering Yahweh speaks during certain seasons and cycles which just so happened to coincide with the Jewish festivals and their annual celebrations. I'm thinking that's why He wanted us to celebrate these festivals so that we could be looking for His return. The Ram's horn announces God's coming down to the earth and revealing Himself to mankind. I heard the sound of the ram's horn on the morning of March 23, 2018, the morning the Lord revealed Himself to me. That sound was something I had never heard before and it literally made me leap out of the bed and look out of my window in terror. I never told anyone this, but I had a dream in 2014, before the angel of the Lord touched me. I dreamt that nuclear bombs were coming from Russia. They didn't make it to the US physically, but we saw them coming on television. It was a weird dream, but it was the number of bombs that concerned me. This encounter can be found in the first book, 'God Said Write the Book – the Second Beginning'. The number was 300. I always pay attention to the numbers in my dreams as they are important.

The Meaning of Numbers: The Number 300: Although the meaning of the number 300 is not entirely clear from the Bible, it does have a relationship with several well-known people in God's word. Samson, angry that the father of a Philistine woman he married gave her to someone else (Judges 15:1 - 2), decides to get revenge. He catches 300 foxes and then, in pairs, ties their tails, along with a small torch, together with a cord. This is symbolic of Jeremiah 23 and Revelation 9. I believe the Lord was showing me what was ahead; that He was going to be dealing with false teachers, false prophets and false doctrine. He then lets them loose among Philistine farmland. This causes not only the recently harvested crops, but also that which was yet to be harvested, to be consumed by fire (verse 5)! I believe that fire will be a Holy Ghost fire or the latter rain/reign! Enoch, representing the seventh generation of patriarch on the earth, was 65 years old when he gave birth to his firstborn son Methuselah (Genesis 5:21). Scripture states he walked with God another three hundred years after this event until he was taken to another location on the earth (verses 22 - 24). Enoch and Elijah, and their apparent disappearance, mystifies many readers of God's word. Some believe they are evidence proving those who die righteously will go to heaven. So, what does the Bible really say happened to these two men?

Although the prophet Elijah is referenced 69 (creation of man, God's movement and judgement) times in the KJV Bible, only two places discuss Enoch by name. "Enoch lived 365 years, walking in close fellowship with God. Then one day he disappeared, because God took him." (Genesis 5:24) I believe this is symbolic of the rapture and the Holy Spirit's movement. "It was by faith that Enoch was taken up to heaven without dying – "he disappeared, because God took him. For before he was taken up, he was known as a person who pleased God." (Hebrews 11:5). I believe this scripture also is symbolic of the resurrection and being caught up with the Lord, not physically dying, but dying to the flesh. Concerning the reference in Genesis, various translations state that he walked with God and that he took him (KJV, NKJV, NIV, HCSB, and NRSV). The NAB says he "was no longer here."

Appearances of the number three hundred: Joseph, sold into slavery by his brothers, ends up as the second most powerful person in the Egyptian Empire (Genesis 41, 45:8 - 9). Since 2017, I've been saying that I AM, Joseph hidden in plain sight. After an emotional revealing of his true identity to his brothers (Genesis 45), he sends them back to Canaan. Remember Canaan is the land promised to Abraham and his descendants. The purpose of the journey is bring Jacob (Israel), and the rest of the family, back to Egypt to avoid famine. I think the Lord showed me this so that I could indeed warn people to come out of the world. Before his brothers leave, however, Joseph has a tearful reunion with his youngest brother Benjamin and gives him a special gift of 300 pieces of silver (Genesis 45:22).

The REAL 300! The movie "300," released in 2007, was a fictionalize account of the battle of Thermopylae. The historic battle, which took place over land and sea in 480 B.C., pitted a Greek force against the mighty Persian Empire. The Greeks, on land, were able to hold off the Persians for seven days. Their remaining force, however, of roughly 1,400 men (the Spartans also had 1,100 others fighting with them) was then decimated. More than 650 years earlier, however, the original battle of "three hundred" took place in the great battlefield of Palestine known as the valley of Jezreel! It is here that Gideon, who is called by God to free the Israelites from oppression, fought against the Midianites and was victorious. I do believe this is symbolic of Armageddon and the final great battle between good and evil, between the heavenly hosts and Satan and his evil army. It's a spiritual war.

How awesome was Gideon's victory? Modern research states the Greeks, at Thermopylae, had an army of 7,000 men while the Persians, at most, fielded 300,000 troops (Battle of Thermopylae, Encyclopedia Britannica). This means the Greeks had a force 43 times smaller than Persia. Gideon's army of 300, however, went up against a 135,000 strong Midian led army that was 450 times bigger than it was and still won the war (Judges 8:10, 28)! "Yet we know that a person is made right with God by faith in Jesus Christ, not by obeying the law. And we have believed in Christ Jesus, so that we might be made right with God because of our faith in Christ, not because we have obeyed the law. For no one will ever be made right with God by obeying the law [some translators hold that the quotation extends through verse 14; others through verse 16; and still others through verse 21]." (Galatians

2:16) I am really blown away by the numbers in the verses because they match the years that I have had and apparently will have supernatural encounters with the Creator of the Universe. Amazing!

Additional info on Biblical Meaning of 300: A woman in Bethany, just before Jesus' death, anoints him with precious oil. Some of the disciples who see this complain that the ointment could have been sold for over three hundred silver coins and the money given to the poor (Mark 14:3 - 7). Jesus gently chides the disciples for their criticism of the woman's good work. I believe that this is symbolic of the Lord pouring out heavily on the daughters more so than the men because we were warned at during the last days that men's hearts would be far from God and that they would be lovers of money and all things that oppose the very nature and essence of God and His word. How is the number 300 related to Solomon's incredible wealth? He could afford the creation of three hundred golden full body shields with an estimated value, in today's money, of $66,000 each (1Kings 10:17). He also could afford seven hundred wives, and three hundred concubines, who sadly turned his heart from God and led him to worshipping false deities (1Kings 11:1 - 6).

The dimensions of Noah's Ark, mandated by God, was 300 cubits long, 50 cubits wide and 30 cubits high. A cubit was considered the distance between a man's elbow and the top of his middle finger. Biblical commentaries place the length of a cubit anywhere from 17.5 to 21.5 inches (44.4 to 54.6 centimeters). Interestingly enough, 2017, was the year that the book of Daniel opened up for me and my family and we were able to see Yahweh's words coming true. I was also 44 when the angel of the Lord touched me on the forehead and told me to wake up. It's becoming clearer with each passing day that I am hearing alarms ringing and feeling an urgency to warn people to live holy and come out of the world. I kept telling all the people in my circle who would listen, that He's coming back sooner than they thought. We must recognize the signs of His coming by things that are happening in the earth AND in the heavens. I had a habit of always looking up at the sky, I kept my head in the clouds. However, after seeing a movie about a comet hitting the earth, my days of looking up was cut short and I'm beginning to think now that this was the reason for movies like these, to make people afraid to look up; and to instill fear in people.

After I was touched by the angel of the Lord, my brother's Pastor reminded me to look up because he said, "the skies are changing" and they were. The society we live in today acts as if it has no fear of God but instead has become a world full of self and pleasure seekers and many little gods. Everyone wants to be famous and worshipped and for inconsequential and immoral things. The internet has made many people an overnight sensation, but they add no good to our world. When did man create the earth, sun, moon, or stars? Like Nipsey Hussle said, "Last time that I checked", he didn't. God created the earth and everything above and in it. The spiritual climate of the times we live in seem to describe the last days per 2 Timothy 3:1-2, "You should know this, Timothy, that in the last days there will be very difficult times. For people will love only themselves and their money. They will be boastful and proud, scoffing at God, disobedient to their parents, and ungrateful. They will consider nothing sacred." I hear the Holy Spirit telling me that Jesus is returning very soon, and He keeps telling me He's near to me and to not to be afraid. I don't exactly understand it, but I know He will reveal it to me when the time is right. I'm trying not to be afraid, but God is so BIG it's scary. We are talking about the Creator of the Universe, of human life and all things!

So, join me as I take a quick look back at some events that occurred two years ago after the Revelation 12 sign. These are things most people don't know because they weren't paying attention. On December 6, 2017, President Trump announced the United States recognition of Jerusalem as the capital of Israel and ordered the planning of the relocation of the U.S. Embassy in Israel from Tel Aviv to Jerusalem. Trump's decision to recognize Jerusalem as Israel's capital was rejected by most world leaders. Why? All of America should have been questioning this – what do we have to do with foreign affairs? If these are the true people of God, why did the other world leaders take an issue with it? People of God live righteous, pure, holy, and are non-violently and do not advocate for war, but peace. Their weapon is the word of God. We will get into this in later chapters. "Then he said to me, "This is what the Lord says to Zerubbabel. It is not by force nor by strength, but my Spirit, says the Lord of Heaven's Armies." (Zechariah 4:6)

The United Nations Security Council held an emergency meeting on December 7, (this date will be significant later), where 14 [represents salvation] out of 15 [represents rest] members condemned Trump's decision, but the motion was vetoed by the United States. Why do we have this much power over other countries? Something is out of order because all of these people do not serve the Lord God Almighty, Yahweh is His name. Britain, France, Sweden, Italy, and Japan were among the countries who criticized Trump's decision at the emergency meeting. So, all of these countries listed were against Trump's decision. However, Paraguay, Czech Republic, Romania, and Honduras said that they were considering relocation. The European Union's foreign policy chief said that all governments of EU member states were united on the issue of Jerusalem and reaffirmed their commitment to a Palestinian State with East Jerusalem as its capital. Representatives from 32 countries were present at the opening of the embassy, including EU members Austria, Czech Republic, and Romania. President Trump made some historic decisions by recognizing Jerusalem as Israel's capital, transferring the US Embassy from Tel Aviv to Jerusalem, recognizing Israel's sovereignty in Golan Heights, and shifting US policy to no longer consider the establishment of Israeli settlements in the West Bank as illegal. But that was an incorrect decision because they are illegal because they claim sovereignty when they are not! But I digress.

My question now becomes, what about the real Jews, the remnant that are mostly in the United States, but scattered all over the world? There are Jews all over the world, the real children and chosen people of God, not Jewish but Jews who don't live in Israel and Jerusalem. Though maybe his alliance has something to do with who his daughter married or his ties to Epstein. All I know is since this man has become President, it's become like hell on earth. He is President of the United States, not a world leader! I don't know where this title of 'Leader of the Free World' came from, but it's not an accurate title for the President of the United States because everyone in the United States isn't free, let alone the world. People have long said that whoever is the President of the United States is the ruler of the world, and that statement may very well be the problem. Presidents don't govern, governors do. He has been protecting the wrong Israel.

Israel is a nation, a people, a city, a place and an individual. Israel is wherever and whomever the Lord God Almighty chooses it or them to be. God decides. Isaac was the seed and Jacob was Israel. The Bible says the Lord would return to Mount Zion and wherever He returned, it would be the New Jerusalem and the capital of the world. "You have not come to a physical mountain [to something that can be touched], to a place of flaming fire, darkness, gloom, and whirlwind, as the Israelites did at Mount Sinai. For they heard an awesome trumpet blast and a voice so terrible that they begged God to stop speaking. They staggered back under God's command. "If even an animal touches the mountain, it must be stoned to death [Exodus 19:13]." Moses himself was so frightened at the sight he said, "I am terrified and trembling [Deut 9:19]." No, you have come to Mount Zion, to the city of the living God, the heavenly Jerusalem, and to countless thousands of angels in a joyful gathering. You have come to the assembly of God's firstborn children, whose names are written in heaven. You have come to God himself, who is the judge over all things.

You have come to the spirits of the righteous ones in heaven who have now been made perfect. You have come to Jesus, the one who mediates the new covenant between God and people, and to the sprinkled blood, which speaks of forgiveness instead of crying out for vengeance like the blood of Abel. Be careful that you do not refuse to listen to the One who is speaking. For if the people of Israel did not escape when they refused to listen to Moses, the earthly messenger, we will certainly not escape if we reject the One who speaks to us from heaven!" (Hebrews 12:18-25) Something else I found interesting in my conversations with God is that the numbers of the scriptures most time lined up with the years. The chosen children of God are the followers of the ways of Jesus Christ, because the Christian church became Israel under the new blood covenant and Mount Zion and the New Jerusalem is wherever you find the bride of Christ.

The definition of the word Jew is a person chosen by God and not the other way around. When Jesus died for the sins of the world, this began the new blood covenant from Judaism to Christianity, but Christianity is not as most think that it is today. We've witnessed many calling themselves Christians, but they don't act like, it's all lip service. In fact, they weren't called Christians, they were called followers of the way. These priests were merely wolves in sheep's clothing. The Bible says in the last days, men will have a form of godliness. Godliness was important to God, and more than just a form of it. "As for you, if you will follow me with integrity and godliness, as David your father did, obeying all my commands, decrees, and regulations, then I will establish the throne of your dynasty over Israel forever. For I made this promise to your father; David: 'One of your descendants will always sit on the throne of Israel.'" (1 Kings 9:4-5) The descendant that forever sits on the throne of Israel is Jesus Christ of Nazareth. "Godliness makes a nation great, but sin is a disgrace to any people." (Proverbs 14:34) The earliest evidence of human habitation on the Golan dates to the Upper Paleolithic period. According to the Bible, an Amorite (meaning talkers) Kingdom in Bashan (meaning soft fertile land sown with wheat or wheat land) was conquered by Israelites during the reign of King Og. Throughout the biblical period, the Golan was "the focus of a power struggle between the kings of Israel and the Aramaeans who were based near modern-day Damascus." Jesus was a Jew, Hebrew and man of color and we will get into that later as well.

Paul, was also a Jew himself, on the way to persecute Christians while on the road to Damascus when he saw the light of Jesus. Afterall, it was Jews who made the plan to kill Jesus, and the Gentile and Romans helped them carry it out. The devil was all in the details. The Bible says, "Meanwhile, Saul was uttering threats with every breath and was eager to kill the Lord's followers [disciples]. So, he went to the high priest. He requested letters addressed to the synagogues [of Satan] in Damascus, asking for their cooperation in the arrest of any followers of the Way he found there. He wanted to bring them – both men and women – back to Jerusalem in chains. As he was approaching Damascus on this mission, a light from heaven suddenly shone down around him. He fell to the ground and heard a voice saying to him, "Saul, Saul! Why are you persecuting me?" "Who are you, lord?" Saul asked. And the voice replied, "I am Jesus, the one you are persecuting! Now get up and go into the city; and you will be told what you must do." The men with Saul stood speechless, for they heard the sound of someone's voice but saw no one! – Acts of the Apostles 9:1-7" This is how I felt when I heard my dad's voice call my name. I sat straight up and the message that came after was "time to boot up! Time to put your boots on." This term of booting up or putting them on means you'll need to be wise in a tricky situation. Basically, time to boot up for war, rough terrain ahead.

Who were these Amorites who lived in Damascus? Genesis 10 gives the account of the families of Shem, Ham, and Japheth, the three sons of Noah. In my last book, I touch on how Noah named his children, and their names were specific to their skin color, thanks to a great teaching I heard by way of Gateway church. According to Genesis 10:16, the Amorites are descendants of Canaan, a son of Ham, who is a son of Noah. The Amorites are mentioned in all kinds of very early, non-Biblical material. According to the Abarim Publications website, although the Bible doesn't mention it, they readily assumed that the name Amorite comes from the name Amor (the Latin word *amor*, meaning love), which in Hebrew means to speak or say. "God said," is mentioned 9 times (9 represents God's movement and judgement) and "God called," is mentioned 3 times (3 represents The Holy Triune God) in Genesis, Chapter 1. "God called the space "sky." (Genesis 1:8) "God called the dry ground "land" and the waters "seas." And God saw that it was good." (Genesis 1:10) (18) All of this was showing me that the Lord was gathering His people. He had been watching and He saw things getting progressively worse and He saw who was worshipping Him in spirit and truth and those who were not.

The number 18 represents bondage and slavery and that is spiritual in nature and I believe that's why I'm so closely tied to Joseph. Believers are in spiritual bondage. In March of 2018, the Holy Spirit showed me we were in the halftime. "For there will be greater anguish than at any time since the world began. And it will never be so great again. In fact, unless that time of calamity is shortened, not a single person will survive. But it will be shortened for the sake of God's chosen ones." (Matthew 24:21-22) We are in spiritual battle and bonded to sin because under the current law, we are still considered slaves. This is why all the changing of the laws, and removing God and replacing it with evil and wickedness. The 14th Amendment was never ratified. To confirm what I just wrote, I am including a paper written by Thomas J. DiLorenzo, entitled 'The 14th Amendment Was NOT Ratified.

He wrote: “Gene Healy has made a powerful argument in favor of abolishing the Fourteenth Amendment to the US Constitution. When a fair vote was taken on it in 1865, in the aftermath of the War for Southern Independence, it was rejected by the Southern states and all the border states. Failing to secure the necessary three-fourths of the states, the Republican party, which controlled Congress, passed the Reconstruction Act of 1867 which placed the entire South under military rule. The purpose of this, according to one Republican congressman, was to coerce Southern legislators to vote for the amendment "at the point of a bayonet." President Andrew Johnson called this tactic "absolute despotism," the likes of which had not been exercised by any British monarch "for more than 500 years." For his outspokenness Johnson was impeached by the Republican Congress. The South eventually voted to ratify the amendment, after which two Northern states-Ohio and New Jersey-withdrew support because of their disgust with Republican party tyranny.

The Republicans just ignored this and declared the amendment valid despite their failure to secure the constitutionally-required three-fourths majority. The Cato Institute's Roger Pilon, who is a supporter of the Fourteenth Amendment, has defended the way in which the amendment was adopted on the grounds that after the war some Southern states had enacted the "notorious Black Codes" (Liberty Magazine, Feb. 2000). "What should Congress have done," Pilon asked, "turn a blind eye to what was going on?" The notion that a racially-enlightened and benevolent Republican Congress unconstitutionally imposed the Fourteenth Amendment on the nation because it was motivated primarily (if not solely) out of concern with racial discrimination in the South is childishly naive and a historical. The fact is, Northern states pioneered viciously discriminatory "black codes" long before they existed in any Southern state, and these codes were supported by many of the same Northern politicians who voted for the Fourteenth Amendment.

The Revised Code of Indiana stated in 1862 that "Negroes and mulattos are not allowed to come into the state;" forbade the consummation of legal contracts with "Negroes and mulattos;" imposed a $500 fine on anyone who employed a black person; forbade interracial marriage; and forbade blacks from testifying in court against white persons. Illinois-the "land of Lincoln"-added almost identical restrictions in 1848, as did Oregon in 1857. Most Northern states in the 1860s did not permit immigration by blacks or, if they did, required them to post a $1,000 bond that would be confiscated if they behaved "improperly." Senator Lyman Trimball of Illinois, a close confidant of Lincoln's, stated that "our people want nothing to do with the Negro" and was a strong supporter of Illinois' "black codes." Northern newspapers were often just as racist as the Northern black codes were. The Philadelphia Daily News editorialized on November 22, 1860, that "the African is naturally the inferior race."

The Daily Chicago Times wrote on December 7, 1860, that "nothing but evil" has come from the idea of Abolition and urged everyone to return any escaped slave "to his master where he belongs." The 14th Amendment Was NOT Ratified On January 22, 1861, the New York Times announced that slavery would indeed be a "very tolerable system" if only slaves were allowed to legally marry, be taught to read, and to invest their savings. In short, the cartoonish notion that the Republican party was so incensed over racial discrimination in the South after the war that, in a fit of moral outrage, it trashed all constitutional precepts to dictatorially adopt the Fourteenth Amendment, should not be taken seriously. As Alexis de Tocqueville wrote in Democracy in America, it was obvious to all that racial prejudice was stronger in the North than it was in the South. "The prejudice of race," wrote Tocqueville, "appears to be stronger in the states that have abolished slavery than in those where it still exists."

If the Republican party was so sensitive about racial discrimination in the post-war era it would not have sent General Sherman out west just three months after the war ended to commence a campaign of genocide against the Plains Indians. The very same army that had recently conquered and occupied the Southern states-led by Generals Grant, Sherman, and Sheridan-mass murdered Indian men, women, and children during the winters, when families would be together, with massive Gatling gun and artillery fire. In a letter to his son a year before he died (1889), Sherman expressed his regret that his armies did not murder every last Indian in North America. The Fourteenth Amendment has had precisely the effect that its nineteenth-century Republican party supporters intended it to have: it has greatly centralized power in Washington, D.C., and has subjected Americans to the kind of judicial tyranny that Thomas Jefferson warned about when he described federal judges as those who would be "constantly working underground to undermine the foundations of our confederated fabric." It's time for all Americans to reexamine the official history of the "Civil War" and its aftermath as taught by paid government propagandists in the "public" schools for the past 135 years. -- Thomas J. DiLorenzo is professor of economics at Loyola College and an adjunct scholar of the Mises Institute.

Furthermore, I found this little gem, 'King Alfred Plan'. The King Alfred Plan is a supposed CIA-led scheme supporting an international effort to eliminate people of African descent, invented by author John A. Williams in his novel, 'The Man Who Cried I Am.' People need to ask themselves, why would they want to kill of an entire ethnicity or nation of people? The answer I believe, because God chose them! Williams described it as a government plan to deal with the threat of a black uprising in the United States by cordoning off black people into concentration camps in the event of a major racial incident. What are they afraid of? The truth, perhaps? Interesting tidbit, it was revealed that a second CIA headquarters operates under the Denver airport which many know to be a very racist place. Look at the mural in their airport that predicts the end times, very evil stuff.

In my first book, I speak about how names and numbers have a lot of meaning. God uses all of His creations. The Bible says when God created the earth, 1) He created, 2) He spoke, 3) He saw [looked down] ,4) He separated [set us apart], 5) He called, 6) He made [born again – new creation in Christ] and 7) He numbered [marked and stamped]. It's what's happening now. "Let this be recorded for future generations, so that a people not yet born will praise the Lord. Tell them the Lord looked down from his heavenly sanctuary. He looked down to earth from heaven to hear the groans of the prisoners, to release those condemned to die. And so the Lord's fame will be celebrated in Zion, his praises in Jerusalem, when multitudes gather together and kingdoms come to worship the Lord. He broke my strength in midlife, cutting short my days. But I cried to him, "O my God, who lives forever, don't take my life while I am so young! Long ago you laid the foundation of the earth and made the heavens with your hands. They will perish, but you remain forever;

they will wear out like old clothing. You will change them like a garment and discard them. But you are always the same; you will live forever. The children of your people will live in security. Their children's children will thrive in your presence." (Psalms 102:18-28)

I believe this is where the scriptures Revelation 2:9 and 3:9 came from. Jesus said, "I know about your suffering and your poverty – but you are rich! I know the blasphemy of those opposing you. They say they are Jews, but they are not, because their synagogue belongs to Satan." "Look, I will force those who belong to Satan's synagogue – those liars who say they are Jews but are not – to come and bow down at your feet. They will acknowledge that you are the ones I love." There are names that were strategically put in the Bible because they mean something for us who live in this current age. The Lord used symbolism, after all the prophets saw visions of things that were not only not in existence, but things that were to happen in the future – an unknown time. The Lord could not reveal his full plan back then because he understood and witnessed firsthand the wickedness of man's heart and He knew they would again try to kill the seed and the root. This is why some of the prophets were asked to seal up their prophecies until the end. Now is the end and time for them to be revealed and time for them to be fulfilled. Even I could not reveal certain things that the Lord was revealing to me in my dreams because I too experienced hate, persecution, mocking and even theft of the words the Lord had spoken onto me. It was my Joseph experience. It was my King David experience. I had to learn to use discernment and trust only God and the Holy Spirit for everything. We have reached the end of days and the world as we know it.

God saw how the world was going and He saw me earnestly trying to live holy and righteous. He saw my heart and He communicated that message to me through a dream He gave me of my mother in May, 2016 which came true on the day the world celebrates Christmas, December 25. I believe my mother was a representation of the Holy Spirit in the dream because she lived what she believed. In the dream she said "I saw you." God is indeed speaking and the Holy Spirit is pouring out on the children of Israel – the true chosen ones. God is watching. As far as the word Amorite, there is more. In Hebrew the latter is identical to the verb אמר (*'amar*), meaning to speak or say: The ubiquitous verb (amar) means to talk or say and may even mean to promise or command. God told me that all of my dreams were going to come true and they have been. It's no coincidence that the word Amorite would have the Hebrew meaning to speak or say because it's just confirmation that the word of God is alive. It's also confirmation that the Jews, God's special treasure are people of color. The promise to Abraham was the land that he was a foreigner in and that was Canaan. The people of Canaan, were essentially Negroes. And let's talk about that word real quick. Niger was the name of a place, and the people from that place were people of color, but more interestingly the word Niger was also used the same way as the word Christian. So when they called Niger or niggers, it was a negative way of calling them followers of the way. Few people know this.

I believe the Lord is going to speak to and through the Amorite, the descendants of Noah. "For the word of God is alive and powerful. It is *sharper than* the sharpest *two-edged sword*, cutting between soul and spirit, between joint and marrow. It exposes our innermost thoughts and desires." (Hebrews 4:12) I just said above that God separated, and it was the fourth thing He did. The number four represents the physical creation. That the Lord would choose these people as His special treasure and possession and then speak to them through the Holy Spirit at the end times, I believe is directly connected to the promise and the inheritance because I believe it's highly possible that I am a descendant of Noah, but because I don't know my true history or genealogy – there's no way to tell. Though my DNA speaks to it as well as the Holy Spirit. My DNA puts me on the map of places I've only seen on television. Our DNA is our genealogy, our ancestry and our represents our family bloodline.

The root nouns of the word Amorite (omer) and (ma'amar) mean speech, word, promise or command. The metaphorical noun refers to the leafy and fruit bearing "crown" of a tree. The bible says, "God blesses those who patiently endure testing and temptation. Afterward they will receive the crown of life that God has promised to those who love him." (James 1:12) "He also released a dove to see if the water had receded and it could find dry ground. But the dove could find no place because the water still covered the ground. So, it returned to the boat, and Noah held out his hand and drew the dove back inside. After waiting another seven days, Noah released the dove again. This time the dove returned to him the evening with a fresh olive leaf in its beak. Then Noah knew that the floodwaters were almost gone. – Genesis 8:8-11" I believe this is symbolic of the halftime.

The Holy Spirit is pouring out, but as the scripture says, God is speaking and no one hears it, because they aren't listening. The Holy Spirit goes forth but needs somewhere to land. Wow! Now I know that Noah sent the dove on that faithful spring day of April 10, 2016. Praise God I was ready at the time of my visitation! It was crying so loud, and it would not leave the doorpost and that was the morning I went to church and the prophetess gave me this word, "But Moses protested, "If I go to the people of Israel and tell them, 'The God of your ancestors has sent me to you,' they will ask me, 'What is his name?' Then what should I tell them?" God replied to Moses, "I AM WHO I AM [OR I WILL BE WHAT I WILL BE]. Say this to the people of Israel: I AM has sent me to you." God also said to Moses, "Say this to the people of Israel: Yahweh [YHWH or Jehovah], the God of your ancestors – the God of Abraham, the God of Isaac, and the God of Jacob – has sent me to you. This is my eternal name, my name to remember for all generations.

Now go and call together all the elders of Israel. Tell them, 'Yahweh, the God of your ancestors – the God of Abraham, Isaac, and Jacob – has appeared to me. He told me, "I have been watching closely…" (Exodus 3:12-16) On that faithful morning, the Lord told me, "I am ALL that you need!" And it was the answer to a prayer from the previous night. I cried out to God that I was tired of being on this earth alone and I needed to hear His voice and I needed Him to hold me. He answered in supreme style! God truly is attentive to the prayers of the righteous as it says in Psalms 34. Jesus' return is woven all throughout the history of the Bible. He designed it this way, and the reason will be revealed later. All that from the word Amorite. So, if I'm reading this history in correlation with the bible scriptures, President Obama was actually correct in not moving the capital of Jerusalem from Tel Aviv, however it fulfilled prophesy – the actions of both presidents have.

Again, I ask the question: "Why are we involved in foreign affairs and policies of governing other countries when the affairs of our country are in complete and utter disarray?" Shame on America!!! Shame on the American government, politics and all the politicians! After Assyrian (meaning straight or level) and Babylonian (meaning confused) rule, Persia (meaning Land of the horses) dominated the region of Golan (a city east of the Jordan) and allowed it to be resettled by returning "Jews" from the Babylonian Captivity. The Bible is real history. The Itureans, a province of Nineveh, settled there in the 2nd century BCE and remained until the end of the Byzantine period. Gamla (meaning the camel), the capital of Jewish Galaunitis (Galatians), would play a major role in the Jewish-Roman wars, and came to house the earliest known "urban" synagogue from the Hasmonean/Herodian realm.

Remember in the earlier scripture, the Lord said the word "dynasty." The Hasmonean dynasty was a ruling dynasty of Judea and surrounding regions during classical antiquity. These were people of color and they were royalty, but you don't hear anything about this in the history books, nor is it being taught in America's education curriculum. The only things you hear about in connection with people of color in America is slavery, gun violence, drugs, murder, oppression, and injustice and what's sad is that the men and women of color are usually the ones on the receiving end of this evil and most times are defending themselves and not the other way around. In the Bible, the problem with the Galatians was an issue regarding the law. We can see the nature of the Galatian problem in the first few verses of Chapter 3. "Oh, foolish Galatians! Who has cast an evil spell on you? For the meaning of Jesus Christ's death was made as clear to you as if you had seen a picture of his death on the cross. Let me ask you this one question: Did you receive the Holy Spirit by obeying the law of Moses?

Of course not! You received the Spirit because you believed the message you heard about Christ. How foolish can you be? After starting your Christian lives in the Spirit, why are you now trying to become perfect by your own human effort? " Paul was making it as plain as he could, showing them that something had changed among the Christians of Galatia and although they had begun their walk with the Lord in the power of the Holy Spirit, they were now seeking to complete their salvation by means of the flesh and religious practices. This has happened with the churches in America. Most churches are clueless to what's going on because their hearts are far from God. Most churches don't even acknowledge the Judaism foundation of the Bible nor do they understand the reason why living holy, or why the Levitical way was so important. Instead the churches today teach the abuse of grace. The Holy Spirit is not welcomed in the churches because they deny it's power by their unbelief even though the word clearly says, "Do not stifle the Holy Spirit." (1 Thessalonians 5:19) In addition, it also says, "Do not scoff at prophecies." (1 Thessalonians 5:20) Unless the people receive a word for their itching ears, giving them a word of monetary blessing, they don't want to hear it and that's sad.

This contrast between the Holy Spirit and the flesh is very important for Paul, especially in this letter. The word "flesh" is appropriate because of the Judaizers' who were insisting the Gentiles had to be circumcised to be included, but it also suggests the weakness of human nature and thus our inability to please God. In our own strength, we can do nothing! We need God! The circumcision thing is the same as people saying you have to be physically baptized when John the Baptist said that Jesus would come baptizing people in the

Holy Spirit. This is why it was bad to separate church and state because God is the head of the church and therefore the head of the state, without Him it's utter and complete chaos because people want to go by their feelings, opinions and thoughts and you can't trust these things because they are not sound, truth or eternal but merely temporary. Read Romans 8. The separation of church and state was for the purpose of the government not getting involved the church's business because by doing so, they were able to take over the Temple fortress. The government getting involved in the church, weakened the church because it caused them to compromise their core beliefs and conform to the ways of the world.

At the end of chapter 4 Paul uses the same two terms to contrast the birth of Ishmael (by natural human abilities) with that of Isaac (the seed, by the supernatural power of the spirit in fulfillment of the promise), which is symbolism for the antichrist, the birth of Christ and the Second Coming of Christ. Accordingly, the term "flesh" becomes shorthand to describe the character of the present evil world, that is, everything that is opposite the world to come, which is the Kingdom of God, which in turn is represented by the Holy Spirit. "Seek the Kingdom of God above all else, and he will give you everything you need." (Luke 12:31) Jesus was asked about the Kingdom of God many times and this is the most important of all his answers in my opinions because it deals with believing. Then Jesus said, "What is the Kingdom of God like? How can I illustrate it? It is like a tiny mustard seed that a man planted in a garden; it grows and becomes a tree, and the birds make nests in its branches." (Luke 13:18-19) A mustard seed is very tiny, like a spec of pepper, but once planted, you cannot stop it from growing. It takes over! All you gotta do is believe!

The world of the Spirit, however, is a world of faith, not of works of the law. Continuing with history, between c. 140 and c. 116 BCE the dynasty ruled Judea semi-autonomously from the Seleucids. From 110 BCE, with the Seleucid Empire disintegrating, the dynasty became fully independent, expanded into the neighboring regions of Samaria, Galilee, Ituraea, Perea, and Idumea, and the rulers took the title "basileus". ***Basileus*** (Greek: βασιλεύς) is a Greek term and title that has signified various types of monarchs in history. In the English-speaking world it is perhaps most widely understood to mean "king" or "emperor". The Lord spoke to David about a dynasty, I'm thinking all of this related to Israel. The title was used by "sovereigns" and other persons of authority in ancient Greece, the Byzantine emperors, and the kings of modern Greece. The feminine forms are basileia, basilis, basilissa, or the archaic basilinna, meaning "queen" or "empress". The meaning of these words keeps blowing my mind.

This organized Jewish settlement in the region came to an end in 636 CE when it was conquered by Arabs under Umar ibn al-Khattāb. In the 16th century, the Golan was conquered by the Ottoman Empire and was part of the Vilayet of Damascus until it was transferred to French mandate in 1918. This date 1918 came up a lot in my last book. The Holy Spirit keeps leading me back to the events of 1917, 1918 and 1919. When the mandate terminated in 1946, it became part of the newly independent Syrian Republic. These years are very significant as it relates to prophecy. While I was reviewing this chapter, I found that in 1991 an Israeli settlement called Brukhim (Indians) was established on the land of the future Trump Heights. The government of Israel convened on June 16, 2019, at the planned location in the abandoned settlement of Brukhim, very close to Kela Alon in the north-west of the Golan Heights, and declared the establishment of the new settlement as gratitude to Donald Trump for support for Israel and recognition of Israeli sovereignty over the Golan Heights. "In appreciation of the work of the 45th President of the United States, President Donald Trump, on behalf of the State of Israel in a wide range of fields and out of gratitude for the American recognition of Jerusalem as the capital of Israel and the recognition of Israeli sovereignty on the Golan Heights, it was decided to initiate the establishment of a new community settlement in the Golan Heights called *Trump Heights*." I wonder if this gift, especially considering the name of the place they met being called Indians was some sort of payment for keeping the "Indians" in line or far worse, planning the eradication of the African American or all people of color, no matter nationality.

In the first stage, 110 housing units are planned. On August 6, 2019, the National Planning and Building Council approved the establishment of the new settlement. This is a conflict of interest and should have been considered bribery. It is the first community in Israel and Israeli-occupied territories named after a sitting American president since Kfar Truman. As of June 2020, the site remained deserted and all, but two letters of the entrance sign had been stolen by vandals. The US Embassy was officially opened in Jerusalem on May 14, 2018, coinciding with the 70th Anniversary of the Israeli Declaration of Independence. Bible prophecy "fulfilled" as it would seem for the Northern Tribe, but not so. I think the baby being born in the sky and in the clouds and visions the Lord gave me have something to do with Jerusalem, Israel, and myself.

When the planets aligned perfectly in 2017, the star was directly over Jerusalem. You may ask why all this matters? "So, when the apostles were with Jesus, they kept asking him, "Lord, has the time come for you to free Israel and restore our kingdom?" He replied, "The Father alone has the authority to set those dates and times, and they are not for you to know. But you will receive power when the Holy Spirit comes upon you. And you will be my witnesses, telling people about me everywhere – in Jerusalem, throughout Judea, in Samaria, and to the ends of the earth." Acts of the Apostles 1:6-8 (6,7,8) These numbers represent the creation of man, God's perfect number and resurrection, regeneration, and abundance with no lack. They are also the same sequence of numbers as the days in August when the Lord showed me what was to come. Notice also, the date above, August 6, 2019, when they established a new settlement for #45 in Israel. They gifted him land, wow! This could very well be considered a payback or bribe as a favor for him moving the embassy and a much darker plan in the future.

This sign took place over Israel on September 23, 2017, which is the first day of the libra astrological sign and it's the only sign with an inanimate object as it's symbol and it just so happens to be a "scale". Often under Libra, we see 'Lady Liberty' holding the scales of justice, her eyes blindfolded (no color seen), representing impartiality, the ideal that justice must be applied without regard to wealth, power, ethnicity, or any other status. I believe God uses everything that He created to reveal His mysteries. He told us He would show us signs in the sun, moon, and stars. Nostradamus predicted this day as the end of the world, and I believe he gave a correct prediction – only it was the beginning of the end of the Gentile Age. "Here comes the dreamer!" they said. (Genesis 37:19) When the Holy Spirit gave me the dream in February of 2018, that all of my dreams would come true and not to be afraid, I believe the Lord was preparing me for 2020! Afterall, the 20th generation from Adam was Abraham's generation and Jesus said He was coming back to help the descendants of Abraham, of which I am one of them! Praise God!

Chapter 5: Calling All the Stars

"He counts the stars and calls them all by name." Psalms 147:4

I believe the Lord is gathering the scattered children of Israel. I believe He's calling for the dry hearts and bones to wake up, arise and shine bright for Jesus because judgement seems to be ahead for the world. When Noah sent the dove out, it couldn't find dry ground and I believe this was symbolism for the Holy Spirit needing a place to land and giving life to the dry bones. It was also the 7th month on the Hebrew lunar calendar, which just so happens to be considered the Second Beginning and year 5777. In the Bible the number 7 is represented as the symbol of perfection and completion. Number 7 is repeated three times in number 777, which means that 777 is a perfect number. It represents the perfect trinity of God – God the Father, God the Son, and God the Holy Spirit, the three Godheads in One. Think about it this way, you have a body, a soul and a spirit and you need all three to operate in the earth.

I'm not sure why some find it hard to believe in the Holy Trinity or the three Godheads. I understand it perfectly in that they all have different functions, but they all work together like your body. I heard the Lord say, "It's going to be a second beginning." I felt the Holy Spirit prompting me to go back to the beginning, go back to Genesis. In Israel, the Hebrew lunar calendar is used for religious purposes, provides a time frame for agriculture (Farmers) and is an official calendar for civil purposes. A farmer is a person who owns or manages a farm. Jesus used agriculture, vegetation and farmers to describe the Kingdom of God. "The farmer plants seed by taking God's word to others." (Mark 4:14) I explained in my first book how both my mother and grandfather's names meant 'farmer' and 'tiller of the soil'. "Now listen to the explanation of the parable about the farmer planting seeds: The seed that fell on the footpath represents those who hear the message about the Kingdom and don't understand it. Then the evil one comes and snatches away the seed that was planted in their hearts. The seed on the rocky soil represents those who hear the message and immediately receive it with joy. But since they don't have deep roots, they don't last long. They fall away as soon as they have problems or are persecuted for believing God's word. The seed that fell among the thorns represents those who hear God's word, but all to quickly the message is crowded out by the worries of this life and the lure of wealth, so no fruit is produced. The seed that fell on good soil represents those who truly hear and understand God's word and produce a harvest of thirty, sixty, or even a hundred times as much as had been planted!" (Matthew 13:18-23) I believe the seed of the word fell on good ground as far as it goes with me. I received it with pleasure.

Now I don't think it any coincidence that the numbers of the verses in the above scriptures coincide with the actual dates of the week in March that the Lord began making the words leap off of the page, March 17-23, 2018. "Jesus replied, "The Son of Man is the farmer who plants the good seed. The field is the world, and the good seed represents the people of the Kingdom. The weeds are the people who belong to the evil one. The enemy who planted the weeds among the wheat is the devil. The harvest is the end of the world [or the age], and the harvesters are the angels." (Matthew 13:37-39) The calendar also determines the dates for Jewish holidays, the appropriate public reading of certain dates to commemorate the death of a relative, daily Psalms readings and many ceremonials uses. For example, the day that Billy Graham died, February 21, 2018, was a day that the Jews read the scriptures of Moses aloud. "Jesus also said, "The Kingdom of God is like a farmer who scatters seed on the ground. Night and day, while he's asleep or awake, the seed sprouts and grows, but he does not understand how it happens. The earth produces the crops on its own. First a leaf blade pushes through, then the heads of wheat are formed, and finally the grain ripens. And as soon as the grain is ready, the farmer comes and harvests it with a sickle, for the harvest time has come." (Mark 4:26-29)

One more thing interesting about the number 777 is Lamech (meaning pauper – Cainite) died when he was 777 years old. Now Lamech is a person in Cain's genealogy referenced in the fourth chapter of the Book of Genesis. Lots of pastors in 2019 were comparing this dispensation of time or the season we are currently living in as the days of Cain who we know killed his brother, Able out of jealousy and spite. Lamech is a sixth-generation descendant of Cain; his father was named Methushael, and he was responsible for the "Song of the Sword," and noted as one of the first polygamist mentioned in the Bible for taking two wives. "Cain had sexual relations with his wife, and she became pregnant and gave birth to Enoch. Then Cain founded a city, which he named Enoch, after his son. Enoch had a son named Irad. Irad became the father of (or the ancestor of) Mehujael. Mehujael became the father of Methushael. Methushael became the father of Lamech. Lamech married two women. The first was named Adah (ornament), and the second was Zillah (shadow). Adah gave birth to Jabal (meaning stream of water) who was the first of those who raise livestock and live in tents. His brother's name was Jubal, the first of all who play the harp and flute. Lamech's other wife, Zillah, gave birth to a son named Tubal-cain. He became an expert in forging tools of bronze and iron. Tubal-cain (meaning he who spices the craft of cain) had a sister named Naamah (meaning pleasant, sweet, delightful).

One day Lamech said to his wives, "Adah and Zillah, hear my voice; listen to me, you wives of Lamech. I have killed a man who attacked me, a young man who wounded me. If someone who kills Cain is punished seven times, then the one who kills me will be punished seventy-seven times!" Adam had sexual relations with his wife again, and she gave birth to another son. She named him Seth (means granted and appointed) for she said, "God had granted me another son in place of Abel, whom Cain killed." When Seth grew up, he had a son and named him Enosh. At that time people first began to worship the LORD by name. – Genesis 4:19-26" I believe we are in the time of Tubal-cain, because it is said that his people would be front and center in the end times, and be used as the sword and usher in both war and peace and help in establishing heaven on earth. In order to accomplish this monumental task, Tubal Cain and his descendants were instructed by God in Matthew 10:34, "Don't imagine that I came to bring peace to the earth! I came not to bring peace, but a sword." Tubal Cain is the widow's son who originally was "a sharpener"—one who whets or sharpens instruments.

In more modern times such as in the most recent translations of the Bible we find that he morphs from being one who sharpens instruments for example; a sword, to becoming the "forger of all instruments of bronze and iron" (ESV), or an "instructor of every artificer in brass and iron" (KJV). Hence, he is the Supreme Hierophant or High Priest of commerce, war and materialism which currently rules this 6th Age. This sounds exactly like the world in which we currently reside. Josephus in 'The Antiquities of the Jews', says that "Tubal exceeded all men in strength, and was very expert and famous in martial performances, … and first of all invented the art of working brass." Josephus in the Antiquities of the Jews, A.D. 93; even while Adam was alive, it came to pass that the posterity of Cain became exceedingly wicked, every one successively dying one after the other, more wicked than the former. They were intolerable in war, and vehement in robberies; and if anyone were slow to murder people, but he was bold in his behavior, in acting unjustly, and doing injury for gain. Tubal is said to be the last soul-survivor of the race of Cain after the flood. The Sons of Tubal Cain, his descendants are first recorded in the inscriptions of Tiglath-Pileser I, by the King of Assyria in approximately the year 1100 BC. I know the Lord was with all of these people and that He sent His word along with the Lord's angels each and every time to rescue them. The Lord steps in and out of time. "And they were singing the song of Moses, the servant of God, and the song of the Lamb: "Great and marvelous are your works, O Lord God, the Almighty. Just and true are your ways, O King of the nations. – Revelation 15:3"

I thought about the honeycomb dream and the scriptures about honey and wisdom, which brought to mind Maya Angelou's poem – In and Out of Time. I know that the Lord was with Maya when she wrote: The sun [Son] has come. The mist [tears] has gone. We see in the distance...our long way home [the promised land]. I was always yours to have. You were always mine. We have loved each other in and out of time. When the first stone looked up at the blazing sun and the first tree struggled up from the forest floor, I had always loved you more. You freed your braids [surrendered to God] ...gave your hair [broke the chains] to the breeze. It hummed [sang and praised] like a hive of honeybees. I reached in the mass for the sweet honeycomb there.... Mmmm...God how I love your hair. You saw me bludgeoned by circumstance. Lost, injured, hurt by chance. I screamed to the heavens.... loudly screamed.... Trying to change our nightmares into dreams...The sun [Son] has come. The mist [clouds and tears] has gone. We see in the distance our long way home [The Promised Land]. I was always yours to have [Jerusalem/Mount Zion]. You were always mine (Israel). We have loved each other in and out, in and out, in and out of time."

Jesus has stepped in and out of time. He is the Alpha (the beginning), the Mesis (in the middle of) and the Omega (the end). His Holy Spirit allows Him to do as He pleases and in itself is a reason to sing, shout and praise God! He truly won the victory! That scripture that says He gave himself to the universe, it describes the Holy Spirit. The Holy Spirit is the Lord Jesus Christ. I'm finding that God does things symbolically, metaphorically, and literally and though He uses symbolism, again it's symbolic of real events, people, places, and things to come. He not only gives us a warning of what's to come but enough time to prepare for it, now that's real love! God has shown Himself to be trustworthy. He has kept His word time and time again, even when we haven't kept ours, and even in our sin and rebellion because He alone is good and just. Jesus warned us to keep watch and pray. We prayed, but most of us, including myself stopped watching and became caught up in this world and these government systems. We were being blinded by science and tricked by lying tongues. It took the angel of the Lord to show me myself and to wake me from my slumber and right in the nick of time, hallelujah! Praise God!

Also, on September 23, 2017, the moon was in a waxing crescent phase. Why is this information important? A waxing crescent is the first phase after the new moon, this is connected to the lunar Hebrew calendar as well. "You made the moon to mark the seasons, and the sun knows when to set." (Psalms 104:19) We forget there was a time before this technological age where people had to look up at the sky and stars and the moon for signs and know the season they were in and it was by this that the dates were set. Our eyes were taken off of God's creations and we started worshipping the creature. This event also occurred in the sky on the Sabbath. "And there will be strange signs in the sun, moon, and stars. And here on earth the nations will be in turmoil, perplexed by the roaring seas and strange tides," Luke 21:25. While I do believe that horoscopes, reading palms, tarot cards and things of this nature - practiced by psychics is witchcraft and demonic and a sin in the eyes of God, I also believe that astronomy is not a sin, especially since He told us in His word to look at His creations because they mark the seasons – He did not tell us to worship them. "You alone are the Lord. You made the skies and the heavens and all the stars. You made the earth and the seas and everything in them. You preserve them all, and the angels of heaven worship you." Nehemiah 9:6.

Furthermore, I have found He uses His creations, the stars, the constellations, the moon phases and the sun to communicate important information to His children and that is not witchcraft, because witches don't have the ability to communicate with the Holy Spirit because darkness has no fellowship with the light and therefore has no knowledge of future things that can only be determined by the Lord God Almighty Himself. "Indeed, the Sovereign Lord never does anything until he reveals his plans to his servants the prophets." (Amos 3:7) And maybe this is what the government is afraid of, why they try to make people believe that there is no God, it's because they can't hear from God because they are evil. Additionally, there is a whole book in the Bible entitled Numbers. This is God's system. God is the only one who determines when you are born and when you die, man has no control over this although he likes to think he does. It is according to what God allows. "Remember the things I have done in the past. For I alone am God! I am God, and there is none like me. Only I can tell you the future before it even happens. Everything I plan will come to pass, for I do whatever I wish. I will call a swift bird of prey from the east – a leader from a distant land to come and do my bidding. I have said what I would do, and I will do it. Listen to me, your stubborn people who are so far from doing right. For I am ready to set things right, not in the distant future, but right now! I am ready to save Jerusalem and show my glory to Israel," Isaiah 46:9-13.

This would have been a scripture given to me in 2016, I was 46 years old. My mother was 46 years old when she went to heaven. In my last book I talk about the 10 Commandments and how they were written on two tablets, four commandments on one and six on the other. Four represents the physical creation and 6 the creation of man. This is what makes the 10 Commandments one of the two witnesses that stand before the Lord. Moses was inspired by the Holy Spirit when he wrote them. I posted on my social media back in 2011 that if Trump gets into the oval office, we were in the last days. I went so far as to say that he was the beast or the antichrist, one of the two. President Trump came on the scene with a bold move, making Jerusalem the capital of Israel and I believe this fulfilled scripture and set the stage for the second coming of Christ. Fast forward to present day, September 23, 2019, President Trump became the first President of the United States to host a meeting at the United Nations on religious freedom. He was standing up for human rights and against dictators. Approximately 80 percent of the world's population live in countries where religious liberty is threatened, restricted, or even banned. Though it should be noted that he was fighting for religious liberty for all religions and that is the same as fighting for all gods and I would like to state for the record that I do not believe in a universal, nameless god, nor any other false god, nor any wooden or ceramic idol formed with human hands which the Father considers graven images; nor do I believe all religions lead to the Yahweh.

I believe in and serve the One and only True and Living God of Abraham, Isaac, and Jacob, Yahweh is His name as He revealed it to Moses, and He created the heavens and the earth and everything in it. I believe in the same Lord God Almighty who created man in His image (The Father, Son and Holy Spirit) and breathed life into us. Scripture says, "Jesus told him, "I am the way, the truth, and the life. No one can come to the Father except through me," John 14:6. At the meeting, President Trump highlighted specifically the fact that "11 Christians are being killed a day for their faith and belief in Christ Jesus." He said that he didn't think it was an accurate number and so he had them go back and check the numbers. Now I'm wondering if he asked for the count because it was such a low number? I don't trust any man, and certainly not a politician who has deep pockets. "For God watches how people live; he sees everything they do," Job 34:21. I don't think it's any coincidence that the very next day, the Democrats called for his impeachment.

That's what I meant when I said in an earlier chapter that the Democratic party seems to stand for things that are blatantly and directly against God and I'm wondering why? What am I talking about? What might those things be you ask? Let's see: abortion, homosexuality, legalized prostitution, allowing strip clubs to operate, pornography, planned parenthood and the like. I start feeling the need to get extremely close to the Lord so that I didn't miss anything that He was trying to communicate to me. I encouraged my family and those in my immediate circle to celebrate the Fall Feasts. I took a break from serving in all the ministries and increased my time in the word and spent more time with my family. Some of the people I served with at the church seem to take offence at me taking this time, but I knew what I heard the Lord say. He told me to stay close, get the word in my heart, worship and pray. We had the blood moons, the moons with Halos around them, the perfect alignment with the planets, blinking stars and that was enough for me to start paying extra close attention to everything going on all over the world, not just in the United States. I had become the watcher, for real.

According to Brother Daniel, the Feast of the Tabernacles was the copy and shadow of the second coming of Jesus and the only one of the types and shadows that had not yet been fulfilled. Rabbi kept saying, "Beloved, Jesus is coming soon." I was finding that the teachings of Rabbi were in sync with the visions and dreams that the Father God was giving me. It's as if I was hearing instructions directly from the Father God. Hebrews 9 talks about old rules about worship. "That first covenant between God and Israel had regulations for worship and a place of worship here on earth. There were two rooms in that Tabernacle [or tent]. In the first room were a lampstand, a table, and sacred loaves of bread on the table.

This room was called the Holy Place. Then there was a curtain, and behind the curtain was the second room [second tent] called the Most Holy Place. In that room were a gold incense altar and a wooden chest called the Ark of the Covenant, which was covered with gold on all sides. This is symbolism for the new Ark of the Covenant, where the Holy Spirit is hidden inside of us.

Inside the Ark were a gold jar containing manna [the word of God], Aaron's staff that sprouted leaves [wood and leaves] and the stone tablets of the covenant [the living stones]. Above the Ark were the cherubim [angels] of divine glory, whose wings stretched out over the Ark's cover, the place of atonement. But we cannot explain these things in detail now. When these things were all in place, the priests regularly entered the first room [first tent] as they performed their religious duties. But only the high priest ever entered the Most Holy Place, and only once a year. And he always offered blood for his own sins and for the sins the people had committed in ignorance [symbolism of Jesus death on the tree]. By these regulations, the Holy Spirit revealed that the entrance to the Most Holy Place was not freely open as long as the Tabernacle [or the first tent – Jesus] and the system it represented were still in use. (So, this is why the Lord had to die because He was the first tent and it's the only way He could send the Holy Spirit and be universal.)

This is an illustration pointing to the present time. For the gifts and sacrifices that the priests offer is NOT able to cleanse the consciences of the people who bring them. For that old system deals only with food and drink and various cleansing ceremonies – physical regulations that were in effect only until a better system could be established. So, Christ has now become the High Priest over all the good things that have come [that are about to come]. He has entered that greater, more perfect Tabernacle in heaven, which was not made by human hands and is not part of this created world. With his own blood – not the blood of goats and calves – he entered the Most Holy Place once for all time and secured our redemption forever. Under the old system, the blood of goats and bulls and the ashes of a heifer could cleanse people's bodies from ceremonial impurity. Just think how much more the blood of Christ will purify our consciences from sinful deeds [from dead works] so that we can worship the living God. For by the power of the eternal Spirit, Christ offered himself to God as a perfect sacrifice for our sins. That is why he is the one who mediates a new covenant between God and people, so that all who are called can receive the eternal inheritance God has promised them. For Christ died to set them free from the penalty of the sins they had committed under that first covenant. Now when someone leaves a will [or covenant], it is necessary to prove that the person who made it is dead [meaning it is necessary to ratify it with the death of a sacrifice].(Maybe this is why my mother wrote me the letter giving me Jesus for Christmas. I'm thinking maybe they knew who I was. My grandmother Ruby also gave me a yellow dress when I was 18 years old, sadly I don't have it anymore. But I later found out that yellow is a color that represents anointing.)

The will goes into effect only after the person's death. While the person who made it is still alive, the will cannot be put into effect. That is why even the first covenant was put into effect with the blood of an animal. For after Moses had read each of God's commandments to all the people, he took the blood of calves and goats, along with water, and sprinkled both the book of God's law and all the people, using hyssop branches and scarlet wool. Then he said, "This blood confirms the covenant God has made with you (Exodus 24:8)." And in the same way, he sprinkled blood on the Tabernacle and on everything used for worship. In fact, according to the law of Moses, nearly everything was purified with blood. For without the shedding of blood, there is no forgiveness.

That is why the Tabernacle and everything in it, which were copies of things in heaven, had to be purified by the blood of animals. But the real things in heaven had to be purified with a far better sacrifice than the blood of animals. For Christ did not enter into a holy place made with human hands, which was only a copy of the true one in heaven. He entered into heaven itself to appear now before God on our behalf. And he did not enter heaven to offer himself again and again, like the high priest here on earth who enters the Most Holy Place year after year with the blood of an animal. If that had been necessary, Christ would have had to die again and again, ever since the world began. But now, once for all time, he has appeared at the end of the age [Greek the ages] to remove sin by his own death as a sacrifice. And just as each person is destined to die once and after that comes judgement, so also Christ was offered once for all time as a sacrifice to take away the sins of many people. He will come again, not to deal with our sins, but to bring salvation to all who are eagerly waiting for him. – Hebrews 9:1-27"

Remember I asked in an earlier chapter, what is in heaven that needs to be brought down to earth? The answer, the word of God, God's grace, and salvation!

Jesus is salvation and because of Him we have grace. Jesus was the word in the flesh that dwelt among us and He will do it again. Seeing that there were 27 verses in the chapter, I looked up the biblical meaning of the number 27. The number 27 derives its meaning from being the cube of 3 (3 x 3 x 3), that's 4, 3's – the Father, The Son, The Holy Spirit, and The Word of God. Of the top ten occurring names in God's word, the name Abraham appears in 27 Books. The Old Testament phrases 'mercy seat' and 'the candlestick' occurs twenty-seven times. The New Testament contains twenty-seven separate books that, along with the Old Testament's 39, makes 66 books total and there are 66 books in the bible as well as 66 chapters in the book of Isaiah. We need God's word here on earth, now! Your Kingdom Come Soon Lord. The Lord is calling the dry hearts and bones to come alive! He's calling all the stars to rise and shine for Him! This Kingdom draws near.

Chapter 6: Build on the Rock

"Anyone who listens to my teaching and follows it is wise, like a person who builds a house on solid rock." – Matthew 7:24

In the silent years, I learned to recognize the voice of God and I learned what it truly means to walk with Jesus and follow the guidance of the Holy Spirit. However, I am human and while on this journey to discovering my purpose, I allowed my own selfish desires to distract me and take me off course, but God! He didn't let me get too far and now that I'm listening, obeying and walking on this holy path – I hear the Lord speaking clearly and I'm for certain all the words have meaning. "Listen to me, O royal daughter; take to heart what I say. Forget your people and your family far away. For your royal husband delights in your beauty; honor him, for he is your lord." (Psalms 45:101) Sheep depend on their shepherd. The Lord has shown me that He is my Shepherd. He has continued to pursue me with dreams, visions, knocking, calling my name, communicating with me through his beautiful creations, clouds, birds and animals; as well as signs in the stars, the moon, the sun and with earthquakes and more. "I am the good shepherd; I know my own sheep, and they know me, just as my Father knows me and I know the Father. So, I sacrifice my life for the sheep. I have other sheep, too, that are not in this sheepfold. I must bring them also. They will listen to my voice, and there will be one flock with one shepherd." (John 10:14-16) I think these other sheep are those scattered around the world and in other countries.

I must admit, it hasn't been a very popular lifestyle. I've lost quite a few "friends", but can I really call them friends if I lost them? People don't really want to hear a lot about the word of God in these seemingly last days, even those who call themselves believers which makes me think about the scripture that says they will have "a form of godliness." I've been blocked, looked at strangely, mocked, persecuted, called out of my name, gossiped and whispered about by some who at one time called me sister. I know now that the Lord was preparing me and He was protecting me. "But it is no shame to suffer for being a Christian. Praise God for the privilege of being called by his name!" (1 Peter 4:16) "Dear brothers and sisters, when troubles of any kind come your way, consider it an opportunity for great joy. For you know that when your faith is tested, your endurance has a chance to grow." James 1:2-3 Oh, have I been growing!

I was excited to go to church on Sunday, November 3. I woke up that morning and I was reading in Matthew 26. God showed me today how Peter told Jesus He would die for Him and not deny Him. Peter was so excited to be with Jesus once He got the revelation, must like myself. Peter would go on to deny Jesus three times just as Jesus said he would, and Peter ran but I read the words "he followed" Jesus STILL, even after his denials, failures, and shame. Even after his sin. After Jesus resurrected, He came back and called out and made Himself known, singling out Peter and calling him to Himself. That blew my mind. He then asked Peter to feed and take care of His sheep. I can identify with Peter in this moment. I fell in love with Jesus. After he sent me to that church, I started following, became celibate, cleaned up, put on my white robe, my joy was restored, my feet were back on the path of righteousness for His name sake and then I fell AGAIN into sexual immorality. I was so angry with myself because I know the sacrifice my Savior made for me and I knew now just how very real he was. Peter walked with Jesus, He knew the man was God in the flesh and he too, still denied Him.

I denied Him in my disobedience, and YET and still He showed me mercy and continued to pursue me. He still forgave me. He still loved me and protected me and showed me compassion because that's what GRACE does. He didn't leave me. He came every time I called for Him. Grace is the gift that Jesus gave us with His LIFE! He gave His life for me so that I can be free from shame and guilt when I fall because He was the only one that was perfect. He died for us because he knew that without Him, and His Holy Spirit – we could nothing. I denied Him in my flesh and Jesus reconciled with me! He spoke to me! He revealed His mysteries to me! And is still revealing them and I can't understand why? I don't deserve this, but one thing I do, I believe! I love Jesus! I know He is now, He was, and He is still to come, and He will be, forever. My stomach was all in knots and I couldn't stop crying.

I was so honored and grateful and so humbled to know that the God of the universe is a loving and forgiving God. He could have said, enough! He could have cut my life short, but He didn't leave me. He's a good God! That's what I saw with Peter when I read the book of John, Chapter 21. Though Peter denied Jesus three times, Jesus still asked Peter to feed His sheep. He still asked Peter to preach the Good News! He knew Peter wasn't perfect and he would not ever be, but Peter believed Jesus was the Messiah. He believed that Jesus was the One that God sent to deliver the Good News and that the Father God is going to give us one more opportunity to accept Him. To acknowledge Yahweh as the Creator. He saw all of Jesus' words come true. The Word of God is true.

"After breakfast Jesus asked Simon Peter, "Simon son of John [Yohanon], do you love me more than these [or more than these others do]? "Yes, Lord," Peter replied, "you know I love you." "Then feed my lambs," Jesus told him. Jesus repeated the question: "Simone son of John, do you love me?" "Yes, Lord," Peter said, "you know I love you." "Then take care of my sheep." Jesus said. A third time he asked him, "Simon son of John, do you love me?" Peter was hurt that Jesus asked the question a third time. He said, "Lord, you know everything. You know that I love you." Jesus said, "Then feed my sheep. I tell you the truth, when you were young, you were able to do as you liked; you dressed yourself and went wherever you wanted to go. But when you are old, you will stretch out your hands, and others [another one] will dress you and take you where you don't want to go." Jesus said this to let him know by what kind of death he would glorify God. Then Jesus told him, "Follow me." – John 21:16-19

Jesus gave Peter some pretty simple instructions, He said feed his lambs [sisters], take care of His sheep [brothers] and feed His sheep [the church]. Notice Jesus asked Him to feed the lambs first. Jesus wasn't talking about natural food either, He was talking about sharing the word of God with His chosen. Now I'm understanding why the tiny pebbles rained on me and the tiny pebble symbolism. Peter's spirit must be here with me as well as John. Jesus didn't give up on Peter. He didn't give up on me. I cried for about an hour before getting to church, and I looked forward with anticipation to the prophetic word the Lord was going to speak through the Pastors. "God blesses those who are persecuted for doing right, for the Kingdom of Heaven is theirs." Matthew 5:10 "You love justice and hate evil. Therefore God, your God, has anointed you, pouring out the oil of joy on you more than on anyone else." Psalms 45:7 "I tell you the truth, wherever the Good News is preached throughout the world, this woman's deed will be remembered and discussed." Matthew 26:10-11, 13

Towards the end of the service, the prophetic word came forth and this is what the Lord said: "Sometime this month and maybe several times this month you will experience an encounter or breakthrough. God starts a deliverance process from the inside out. There is a breakthrough coming and He's going to use force to break it down. To stop something or somebody. You are too worried about the lies. If you would hold on to God and pursuing God's purpose and keep focused on His word, He will let them live long enough to see your victory. Stay on point with God. Stay in obedience. God did not give up on you. You do not have to start over. Get back in line." I received all these words, and I knew that the Lord was speaking directly to me. Something else was said in the service that I didn't take personally, but I made a mental note. The Pastor said that someone in the congregation was under strong demonic attack and called people up for prayer, but I didn't go up because I didn't think it was me.

That evening there was a believer's night meeting that was going to be held at our sister church, but I really didn't feel up to going. I was emotionally exhausted. I had been caught up in the spirit of the word and all of the things that the Lord was revealing to me; but a dear friend asked if I would meet her there so that she could tell me about her dream afterward. I agreed to go to the meeting but only for her. The worship was amazing, and I was able to pour my heart out in song to the Lord. More prophetic words flowed from the young Pastor over the service that evening. The following was said: "Out of a year and into a new dimension – you want to be ready for it. Freedom was declared! Your situation is already worked out! God is the master of the breakthrough. I made a declaration "God do a significant thing in my life!" The breakout, break away, break off, break loose and break down. There will be a sudden solution to the problem. Escape from control. A situation turned sour and you can't release yourself. Captured and could not walk away. I feel a detachment coming. God is breaking you loose. Spiritual activity against you. Demonic opposition. Warfare in your mind. Exodus 400 years! I made a declaration, "Breakdown – the wall of Jericho!" I heard the Lord say, "I'm bringing you out of your prison. This is last season you will be bound. Any devil that secretly came into the room trying to defray your blessing is being seared and chased out!"

Revelation 12 was mentioned during the service (The Woman and the Dragon). 1 Chronicles 14:8 was given which says, "And if the bugler doesn't sound a clear call, how will the soldiers know they are being called to battle?" Well, I've been sounding the alarm, no one is listening and it's probably because I'm so far in the background, because I don't have "the look" but God! He has a purpose, a time, and a season. (David anointed as King) (I had dreams where I saw a four headed dragon slayed in a foreign land, a place I had never been before.) Israel is being persecuted because Jesus came from Israel and is returning to Israel, but which Israel? The seeds are those that keep the commandments of God and have the testimony of Jesus Christ. The Pastor said, "If he (the devil) can give you enough pain – he can distract you in the natural and keep you from your purpose."

Heaven was cleansed by the blood of Christ. God does everything spiritually first. The earth is here to aid us in our deliverance. We've been called to be servants of the Lord and in doing so we usher in the Lord's righteousness on the earth. Elijah, Joshua, and Moses were all God's chosen leaders. (My ears were wide open) In Exodus 14, God told Moses what to do. God gives you what you need in the dark place – take that authority and ability and you speak to your sea – it shall be opened – God is opening the sea for His people. Use your mantle! It doesn't matter what you are going through, it only matters whose taking you there! Romans 8:19, "For all creation is waiting eagerly for that future day when God will reveal who his children really are." He said, "If it's in His plan, it's already done." I'm for certain that I am definitely a child of the Highest God, the One that no other is above!

After the word was spoken, the young Pastor called everyone who wanted prayer to the middle aisle of the church. Actually, he just said, "Get to the middle aisle," and I got in line. During the service, this Pastor was very dramatic. He was running all over the stage and putting his hands up to his cheeks and opening his mouth wide. He was very eccentric and moving a lot, acting almost like the eagle in my dream, but I didn't recognize it at the time. I stood in a line that had been formed down the center aisle of the church and as I was drawing nearer to the front for the Pastor's to pray for me. I noticed the ushers were choosing who was going to pray for whom. In my flesh, I didn't want the young Pastor to pray for me. He was doing the most, but that's not to discredit him because I believe that the Lord speaks to and through him, again the rocks will cry out if we don't.

I just wanted my Pastor's to pray for me, but God knows what's best for us and He had other plans. I didn't have a choice in who would pray for me and the usher sent me right in the young Pastor's direction. As I stood there waiting for him to pray for me, while he was standing up on the stage, he was staring at me intently, almost like the eagle at the top of the steeple. He rushed off the stage towards me like a soaring bird, blowing like a mighty wind as he placed one hand on my stomach and one on my head, he began to pray in the spirit. Then he spoke these words in my ears, "God is taking the yokes off you. You have two yokes on you. God is about to break the yokes off you, and you are about to rise up in power!" Then he shouted, "Double for your trouble!" I began to cry because I had a dream of a judge from on high, that I couldn't see his face, but I heard him say, "Double for your trouble," and this dream had not yet come true. He then said I would be "leaping" in it. I couldn't make this stuff up if I wanted to. God is real! I just read about 2020 being a leap year.

Then he said, I would be "Quantum leaping out of this dimension into my next dimension where I won't look like myself." Whoa. I truly believe that people are going to be looking for Jesus in the body of a man, but He will not be. This is my 2020 breakthrough! I went back to my seat a complete mess. My friend had also gone up for prayer but when she returned to her seat – she was not only crying but, appeared to be distraught. I asked her if she was ready to leave and she was. We went to sit in her car so she could tell me about her dream. On the way to the car she expressed that she was crying because she didn't usually let people touch on her and she, like myself, didn't want to go to the young Pastor. That part was funny.

We served together in the prison ministry and she had been complaining about this strange pain in her side during our visits. Funny thing is, I too was experiencing this same pain, like a sticking in the side. We were both believing for our healing. Anyway, when she went up for healing, the young Pastor didn't say anything – he just kept touching her in that spot where she was feeling the pain and instantly her faith had increased so much so that she was now desiring to have the gift of speaking in the heavenly language, so I told her to pray and ask God. We talked for a little while and then she talked to me about her dream. She told me that she had the dream about three years prior before getting married, and the dream was her hitting it big at the slots with the numbers 777. Those numbers stuck out with her and she always wondered what it meant. I told her that I would pray about it and get back to her.

If you remember in the earlier chapters I talked about 777 being God's perfect number, but specifically 5777, the Hebrew year that the perfect alignment happened in the heavens. When I prayed about it, the Lord revealed that He was calling her, and she would be saved, and it had more meaning as it pertained to her. See, she had the dream before she met her husband, who by the way was a Christian man at the time she met him, and by her admission to me, she was not. Her husband being a member of my church is actually how she and I met, serving the homeless community. We became good friends which is also how I got involved in the Prison ministry because of what the Lord had delivered her from. I was grateful that she shared her dream with me as it gave me some revelation and insight as to the seasons that were ahead.

Her dream took me back to my days of fasting, day 37 of 40 back in 2018. During those days of fasting, I ate daily from the book of life. My day usually flowed with the verse of the day and then I'd spend the rest of day looking back at previous notes and listening to the word and jotting down whatever scriptures the Holy Spirit lead me to. "You will show me the way of life, granting me the joy of your presence and the pleasures of living with you forever," Psalm 16:11. God is all powerful. "Jesus looked at them and said, "With man this is impossible, but with God all things are possible." Matthew 19:26 NIV "I know that you can do all things; no purpose of yours can be thwarted." Job 42:2 "Is anything too hard for the Lord? I will return to you at the appointed time next year, and Sarah will have a son." Genesis 18:14 NIV "He made the earth by his power; he founded the world by his wisdom and stretched out the heavens by his understanding." Jeremiah 51:15 NIV The Lord and the Holy Spirit are writing this book! I'm simply the vessel that was chosen. I had to live holy to be able to have a relationship, so that I could both see and hear with clarity, what was being communicated to me.

Looking over my notes for that time period, I found the following: "Moses and crossing the Jordan – the Old Testament is significant to the New Testament. There is something hidden behind the Jordan river and something extraordinary about John the baptizer. A place for people and a divine presence. People, place, and divine presence. Matthew 3: significant person and significant place and a divine presence – same river – confessing their sins and preparing the way for the Messiah – same river – Jesus has scandalous grace! God sees the heart and we shouldn't be resistant to someone who was deep in sin but now changed – there is nothing God can't forgive and completely purify you from, except for blasphemy which we covered in an earlier chapter. God forgives completely, and anything that becomes fruit is a seed first and has to grow – there is fruit of repentance – keep praying and there will be an outpouring of grace. Hallelujah!

I needed to review these notes right at that moment because I was still feeling a little hurt behind the rejection from my past, feeling as if the person had no remorse for his actions or how he hurt me. I'm learning to give every single thing and I mean everything completely over to God even when the enemy tries to remind me of it. There is nothing God can't handle. I know this is coming up right now, because there is going to be a great need ahead for the people to forgive and extend mercy and compassion. "I have forgiven him and have moved on – I won't allow the enemy to judge me, condemn me or make me feel ashamed (this is a message from the year before 2018 – wow). I understand that because he wasn't living according to the Word of God, he was available for the enemy to use. I take full responsibility because I should not have opened the door and been casting my pearls before swine. Moving on in God's grace and his mercy which is available and new every morning." Thank you, Jesus!

Then I received a text that day with the 7 promises of God. Here I am researching the triple 7 and I get 7 more blessings. The Lord told me, "1. I will be with you. 2. I will protect you. 3. I will be your strength. 4. I will answer you. 5. I will provide for you. 6. I will give you peace, and last but certainly more important than all the others, 7. I will always love you." When you see anything related to number 37 (and its reverse 73) think about number 777, perfection, sanctification, consecration, truth, and Jesus. Thirty-seven can be seen like three sevens – 777 – which has similar meaning. The 3700th verse of the Bible finds the Lord selecting the Levites to be the tribe of Priests who are to be holy and set apart for serving God – not coincidentally, this is also the 3rd chapter and 7th verse (37) of the book of Numbers. This is just one of the Bible's many examples showing how number 37 is related to being saved/raised up or being holy, perfect or something to do with God's will.

Like all God's numbers, opposite meanings can also be found associated with them, so with #37 you will also find themes of not being saved or being defeated/destroyed. One very compelling example of the consistent theme association with number 37 are the contents of the (7) seven chapters with (37) thirty-sevens chapters in the Bible. Each of these (7) seven chapters speak of being saved, made perfect, lifted, or opposite themes such as being thrown down or not being saved. It seems no coincidence there happen to be seven, chapter thirty-sevens: In the book of Genesis, Chapter 37 – Joseph is thrown into a pit but is lifted out of it (saved). (Joseph's life keeps coming before me as an example because I am a dreamer). In the book of Exodus, Chapter 37 – It involves the perfection of furniture in the tabernacle – things of Pure Gold, made perfect, and anointing oil. In the book of Job, Chapter 37, God comes down from heaven and we cannot comprehend a perfect God. Also, the 13,777th Bible verse is Job 37:7 where God seals the hand of every man. In the book of Psalms, Chapter 37 – The Lord will save his people. Psalm 37:37 says, "Mark the blameless man" (saved).

In the book of Isaiah, Chapter 37, it covers God saving Jerusalem and the 733rd verse of Isaiah is 37:35 "For I will defend this city to save it for My own sake and for My servant David's sake.'" In the book of Jeremiah, Chapter 37, Jerusalem was saved when the siege was lifted, and Jeremiah was also saved from death. In Jeremiah, 37:21, King Zedekiah commanded – they commit Jeremiah to the court of the guardhouse and gave him a loaf of bread daily (interesting c37 x v21 = 777 and both numbers reflect 3 sevens). In the book of Ezekiel, Chapter 37, the dry bones vision of Israel is the discussion and asks the question, who will be saved? Ezekiel 37:28 says, "And the nations will know that I am the LORD who sanctifies Israel, when My sanctuary is in their midst forever."

I know how impossible this all sounds but consider in the 777th Bible chapter Jeremiah 32:27 says "Behold, I am the LORD, the God of all flesh; is anything too difficult for Me?", and the 37th verse of Luke (1:37) says, "For nothing will be impossible with God." Don't be surprised when you see that God has done the impossible. Like God, his numbers and the Bible's perfection, they are far beyond our comprehension. You cannot figure God out, you just must follow, and listen and do what He says. Looking back allowed me to see that all of what God spoke to me in the silent years, was a prediction of future events to come in 2020 as they pertained to my purpose, but I got distracted. I also begin to notice that every time the guy would pop up and I would resist the temptation or try to make good of the situation handling it God's way, I would receive more in way of a blessing of wisdom, knowledge, revelation and in some cases, the Lord blessed monetarily.

The 777 also lead me once again to Lamech who is a person in Cain's genealogy in the fourth chapter of the Book of Genesis. Lamech was the 8th generation descendant of Adam (Genesis 5:25), the son of Methuselah, and the father of Noah (Genesis 5:29), in the genealogy of Seth in Genesis 5. In Genesis 5:12-25, Lamech was a son of Methuselah, who was a grandson of Jared, who was a grandson of Kenan descended from Adam. Noah was the 8th man, wow. We seem to be in the Cain generation. Brothers are dying. "When the Son of man returns, it will be like it was in Noah's day." Matthew 24:37 This brings us to the conclusion of my notes from 2018 regarding the subject of the number 777.

I keep saying that Jesus is coming back, and I am running out of ways to say it. He keeps telling me He's very close to me. I'm screaming it from the rooftops and even the believers don't believe. We've seen the signs, in the sun, the moon and the stars – Revelation 12 has happened. There have been many earthquakes. Many strange weather happenings. Volcanos erupting all over the world. We see the signs in men becoming lovers of men, the same sex marriage I believe ushered in the antichrist. We have been having an unusual number of earthquakes all over the world and unusual weather. We have had more fires within the last few years than ever before, not to mention the fires in Australia that were still burning at the time of this writing. There is also the locusts that came out of Africa and went into China and it was the worst and largest number of locusts in decades. There were a billion animals killed in the Australian fires, that sounds like a burnt offering. Then we had the painted "ladies" which is a monarch or butterfly of a royal nature, migrating towards the north in spring when they usually have migrated during summer/autumn. How many signs do you need??? But the more important question is, what has you so busy that you missed all of it?

"In my desperation I prayed, and the Lord listened; he saved me from all my troubles. For the angel of the Lord is a guard; he surrounds and defends all who fear him. Taste and see that the Lord is good. Oh, the joys of those who take refuge in him!" Psalms 34:6-8 It was becoming clear what God wanted me to do. "This was John's testimony when the Jewish leaders sent priests and Temple assistants from Jerusalem to ask John, "Who are you?" He came right out and said, "I am not the Messiah." "Well then, who are you?" they asked. "Are you Elijah?" "No," he replied. "Are you the Prophet we are expecting?" "No." "Then who are you? We need an answer for those who sent us. What do you have to say about yourself?" John replied in the words of the prophet Isaiah: "I am a voice shouting in the wilderness, 'Clear the way for the Lord's coming!" John 1:19-23 That's me! It's sad that every man that I try to share the Good News with, the first thing they ask me is if I'm Jesus and I tell them, the Lord is dwelling with me, but I am not him. I am Kandake. I do not claim to be Jesus or the Messiah, but I do claim to be God's Daughter and Jesus' sister as well as his servant and his queen.

"Say to them, 'This is what the Sovereign Lord says: I will take Ephraim and the northern tribes and join them to Judah. I will make them one piece of wood [one tribe all colors) in my hand.' "Then hold out the piece of wood in my hand.' "then hold out the pieces of wood you have inscribed, so the people can see them. And give them this message from the Sovereign Lord: I will gather the people of Israel from among the nations. I will bring them home to their own land from the places where they have been scattered. I will unify them into one nation on the mountains of Israel. One king [Yeshua] will rule them all; no longer will they be divided into two nations or into two kingdoms. They will never again pollute themselves with their idols and vile images and rebellion, for I will save them from their sinful apostasy. I will cleanse them. Then they will truly be my people, and I will be their god.

"My servant David will be their king, and they will have only one shepherd. They will obey my regulations and be careful to keep my decrees. They will live in the land I gave my servant Jacob, the land where their ancestors lived. They and their children and their grandchildren after them will live there forever, generation after generation. And my servant David will be their prince forever. And I will make a covenant of peace with them, an everlasting covenant. I will give them their land and increase their numbers, and I will put my Temple among them forever. I will make my home among them. I will be their God, and they will be my people. And when my Temple is among them forever, the nations will know that I am the Lord, who makes Israel holy." Ezekiel 37:19-28. Israel is the name of a person; a nation and the term 'Israel' refers to different entities.

Paul calls the body of Messiah "the Israel of God." "As for me, may I never boast about anything except the cross of our Lord Jesus Christ. Because of that cross (or because of Him), my interest in this world has been crucified, and the world's interest in me has also died. It doesn't matter whether we have been circumcised or not. What counts is whether we have been transformed into a new creation. May God's peace and mercy be upon all who live by his principle; they are the new people of God [this principle and upon the Israel of God]. From now on, don't let anyone trouble me with these things. For I bear on my body the scars that show I belong to Jesus. Dear brothers and sisters may the grace of our Lord Jesus Christ be with your spirit. Amen. (Galatians 6:14-18) The ecclesia (Greek word for collective congregation, assembly, or church) is the continuation of chosen Israel, but now under the New Covenant. The Christian church is the new Israel.

This verse, along with Revelation 7:4, are the only two times in the New Testament (out of 79 references to Israel) where the followers of Yeshua are clearly addressed as Israel. The Number 79 represents the Congregation and Testimony. This is why I said, I am Israel. Mind you, all of this revelation because of one dream. The Congregation and Testimony is this "Each tribe of Israel will camp in a designated area with its own family banner. But the Levites will camp around the Tabernacle of the Covenant to protect the community of Israel from the Lord's anger. The Levites are responsible to stand guard around the Tabernacle. So, the Israelites did everything just as the Lord had commanded Moses. – Numbers 1:52-53"

In my first book I covered the importance of numbers and also the importance of the Levites. The Levites were responsible for carrying the Tabernacle because they were the most holy tribe. Their tribe consisted of the royal priests, singers, and musicians and they were responsible to carry the covenant because they lived holy lives and according to God's laws. Also, they could not drink strong drink. I am a follower of Christ; therefore, I am Israel. I would also be considered a Levite because I seem to be a priestess, a psalmist, a worshipper, a teacher, preacher, a seer and I have visions and dreams and I'm able to interpret them – the Holy Spirit has bestowed upon me many gifts for which I am grateful. Maybe the reason God kept references to the church being Israel to a minimum was that He didn't want the Gentiles to think they had replaced the Jewish nation. The fact is the Jews retained sole possession to the title 'Israel' even though they rejected Yeshua as Messiah. Paul tells us "a partial hardening has happened to Israel (meaning the original Jews) until the fullness of the Gentiles has come in." And again, a Gentile is an unbeliever. "I want you to understand this mystery, dear brothers and sisters, so that you will not feel proud about yourselves. Some of the people of Israel have hard hearts, but this will last only until the full number of Gentiles comes to Christ. And so, all Israel will be saved.

As the Scriptures say, "The one who rescues will come from Jerusalem [Greek from Zion] and he will turn Israel [Greek Jacob] away from ungodliness. And this is my covenant with them, that I will take away their sins (Isaiah 59:20-21; 27:9) - Romans 11:25-27. So, we see in the next sentence he informs us that when all the "Gentiles" that is "all the unbelievers" come in, that is when "all Israel will be saved." Here the name "Israel" has been expanded to mean the whole nation – not just the Jews! I heard the Rabbi say recently, "I believe there is a day coming, and coming soon, when all the confusion over who or what is Israel will suddenly disappear. The whole world will see the Israel of God revealed in glory as both one nation and one person in Jesus!" Rabbi said this. He said, "one nation and one person in Jesus!" "God reigns above the nations, sitting on his holy throne." (Psalms 47:8) The angels in heaven shouted for joy when God created the world. Jesus had joy in His heart which he wanted us all to share. The disciples were filled with joy at the coming of the Holy Spirit. God delights in us and He wants us to delight in Him. This is exciting because it means that He didn't forget about us! He didn't leave us! He is trustworthy!

There was a time in my life, before the angel of the Lord touched me in 2014, that I thought I had gotten beyond saving. I had given up hope. I wasn't even sure I wanted to live anymore, but I just couldn't leave my children and I kept thinking about the things my mother and father had said to me in my youth. Understanding now that 14 represents salvation, as well as the triple 777, I'm for certain now that the Lord is returning to help the descendants of Abraham, to be free! In fact, I believe He had already returned at Pentecost when He sent His Holy Spirit. "People who have no hope are easy to control and whoever has the control, has the power." That was a quote from one of my favorite childhood movies, The Neverending Story. Had I lost my hope, the devil would have taken control of my mind and the direction of my life. Giving up hope is the same as putting your destiny in the enemy's hands. I had to hope that better days were ahead of me. I had to think about the things that the Lord had in mind when He created me. "For I know the plans I have for you," says the Lord. "They are plans for good and not for disaster, to give you a future and a hope." – Jeremiah 29:11 This hope is a strong and trustworthy anchor for our souls. It leads us through the curtain into God's inner sanctuary." Hebrews 6:19 "And this hope will not lead to disappointment. For we know how dearly God loves us, because he has given us the Holy Spirit to fill our hearts with his love." Romans 5:5

I'm so very thankful that the Lord sent His Word and He did not leave me wallowing in my misery and let me die in my sin. Something about these supernatural things happening and people speaking words to me about my situation, and they didn't even know me or my story and that caused me to be more sensitive to the Holy Spirit, my surroundings and the people and things I was giving my time and attention to. People who have never met me, were somehow speaking directly into my heart and it woke me up. Now that I was listening with intent, I knew instantly, I was forgiven. It was just like He said, He was still going forward with the plan, I just had to get back in "line" or get in "alignment" which is what 9/11 is all about. I am a sinner saved by Grace; I just don't abuse grace. I am a fleshly human being, but I lean on the Lord when I'm weak and I seek His help in guiding my desires to be in His will. I knew that all my sins – past, present, and future – were covered under the blood of Jesus Christ and I know I am saved by His grace – otherwise, He wouldn't be talking to me. When I was reading the Book of Life, I was noticing that whenever Adam and Eve repented and gave an offering to show their repentant heart, God always sent His Word and angels to comfort and give them a Word and a blessing.

My life has meaning and purpose, but exactly what God has planned for me is starting to unfold. I was becoming wiser and He made it perfectly clear that I could not save myself. This was about my salvation, but not just mines, the salvation of His people. No human can save themselves. Jesus saves us. I was born in sin and I am a human being and I'm going to stumble and fall from time to time – because I will never be perfect and so I need God. We all need God! So, I give thanks daily for His mercy and His marvelous grace. I know without a doubt that my God forgives and He restores; it is the very heart of the Gospel message, the cry of Jesus from the cross – "Father, forgive them…" Seems this research of the number 777 has to do with salvation, not just for my friend or my four and no more, but it seems it's a message for the whole entire, world. It's God's desire for all to be saved, He doesn't want anyone to die in their sins and go to a place He created for the devil and his demons. Gives a lot more meaning to the scriptures about in "trying to save your life, you will lose it." Read Matthew 10:39, Matthew 16:25, Luke 9:24 and Luke 17:33.

"To be a Christian means to forgive the inexcusable because God has forgiven the inexcusable in you." This is a famous C.S. Lewis quote. I'm not saying it's easy to forgive people, it's hard but this is where God comes in. We need to be like Paul. "Three different times I begged the Lord to take it away. Each time he said, "My grace is all you need. My power works best in weakness." So now I am glad to boast about my weaknesses, so that the power of Christ can work through me. That's why I take pleasure in my weaknesses, and in the insults, hardships, persecutions, and troubles that I suffer for Christ. For When I am weak, then I am strong." 2 Corinthians 12:8-10. It's better to take it to the Lord, than to harbor ill feelings and let them bubble over and cause you to do something that you will regret and suffer the consequences for later.

I've never been a person who holds a grudge, but there are many who do and can't seem to just let it go, when holding a grudge keeps the door open for the enemy to come in and wreak havoc in your mind, your life, your finances and in your relationships. Resentment is like poison. Unforgiveness is poison in your body. "Don't copy the behavior and customs of this world, but let God transform you into a new person by changing the way you think. Then you will learn to know God's will for you, which is good and pleasing and perfect." (Romans 12:2) I prayed this prayer: "Jehovah El Gemuwal forgive me for when I try to take my own revenge. Forgive me for when I fear that you won't. Forgive me for those times when I am angry and fearful because I am being bullied or wronged, and I forget to trust in your great name Jehovah El Gemuwal. You see all. You know all. You leave no stone unturned. I don't need to go and tell everyone else when I am wronged, rather I only need to look to you because you will repay. You will not be mocked. Forgive me for forgetting this far too often. In Christ's name, Amen." This is a prayer from a Bible study plan by Pastor Talmai (meaning Plowman), called the 30 Names of God and this prayer was right in the mist of everything – God's timing is perfect!

The Lord had already spoken to me through His word in Jeremiah letting me know that He would certainly carry out all His plans (Jeremiah 1), but now I understand the portion of scripture before that. "And don't be afraid of the people, for I will be with you and will protect you. I, the LORD, have spoken!" Then the LORD reached out and touched my mouth and said, "Look, I have put my words in your mouth! Today I appoint you to stand up against nations and kingdoms. Some you must uproot and tear down, destroy and overthrow. Others you must build up and plant." I'm beginning to understand why God told me to write the book. He's on the way to rule and reign. He's establishing His Kingdom on the earth. He's coming to set the captives free and He's going to be with His servants. It's time for the healing to begin. It's time for the wrongs to be corrected. It's time to leave the past behind us and move forward.

"Christ is the visible image of the invisible God. He existed before anything was created and supreme over all creation, for through him God created everything in the heavenly realms and on earth. He made the things we can see and the things we can't see – such as thrones, kingdoms, rulers, and authorities in the unseen world. Everything was created through him and for him. He existed before anything else, and he holds all creation together. Christ is also the head of the church, which is his body. ***He is the beginning, supreme over all who rise from the dead.*** So, he is first in everything. For God in all his fullness was pleased to live in Christ, and through him God reconciled everything to himself. He made peace with everything in heaven and on earth by means of Christ's blood on the cross. This includes you who were once far away from God. You were his enemies, separated from him by your evil thoughts and actions. Yet now he has reconciled you to himself through the death of Christ in his physical body. As a result, he has brought you into his own presence, and you are holy and blameless as you stand before him without a single fault. ***But you must continue to believe this truth and stand firmly in it.***

Don't drift away from the assurance you received when you heard the Good News. The Good News has been preached all over the world, and I, Paul, have been appointed as God's servant to proclaim it." Colossians 1:15-23 Paul took credit in this verse for preaching the Good News of Jesus all over the world. So, Jesus could come back anytime. The rapture could happen at any time. He gave us all these years to repent and get it right, but people think He's going to wait forever. Not so! Jehovah was giving us this time to repent. God is deep. God is loving. God is merciful and He's been extremely patient. Again, I see that He does things in threes – symbolically, metaphorically, and literally. In dreams and visions of the Apostles and prophets, they saw real things, but because it was centuries before these events would take place, they saw symbols – and I believe that's why it's called a mystery and the secret things of God.

I've even considered all the dreams He's given me and how they've come true – in an extraordinary fashion. They also came to fruition not in the order in which I had them. "When we tell you these things, we do not use words that come from human wisdom. Instead we speak words given to us by the Spirit, using the Spirit's words to explain spiritual truths. But people who aren't spiritual can't receive these truths from God's Spirit. It all sounds foolish to them and they can't understand it, for only those who are spiritual can understand what the Spirit means. Those who are spiritual can evaluate all things, but they themselves cannot be evaluated by others. For, who can know the LORD's thoughts? Who knows enough to teach him?" But we understand these things, for we have the mind of Christ." (1 Corinthians 2:14-16)

The spiritual meaning of God's laws and Commandments should be saved and kept in the heart of the believer, so we can be ready at all times to explain the reasons why we have the hope we have and why we believe. Paul, in the book of Corinthians told us that there are 16 things connected to love that God has and that should be achieved by people as well. Love is kind, patient, non-jealous, humble, durable, non-egotistic, is not easy to provoke and has no dark intentions. Love is joyful, forgiving, and positive about the future, and it will never disappear. The state of the world as it stands today is separated from the God who created it because things are out of order due to sin and immorality, making it a toxic place. The love of money and materialism, the lust of the eyes and flesh and the hardness of man's heart and his unforgiving ways have resulted in the people living in bondage and slavery.

Remember the number 18 represents, bondage and slavery and He came on the clouds to me and my family in 2018. The slavery I speak of is a spiritual bondage, and some in the world are in a physical bondage due to their spiritual state. I'm specifically speaking of slaves to sin and death and many are dying young and sick because they live outside of the will of God and they are not following Christ, and I can testify that living outside of Christ is a miserable life. Thank God for His saving grace. Jesus came as the light and life. Jesus died to all these things so that we could live free. Jesus came to show us the way and He was victorious! We can have that same victory! He was tempted and did not sin. He was offered the kingdoms of this world and He resisted the devil. He sent us the gift of the Holy Spirit as our helper after His ascension to Heaven so that we could have the same resurrection power! We must begin to change our minds and make Him a priority in every place in our life, starting with our hearts. When my thoughts and heart changed from the world and began to gravitate more towards the Lord, the things of Heaven - my blinders were removed. I was able to see things more clearly from a spiritual point of view. I had crystal clear vision. More importantly, God was able to see me, because He could see Jesus in me, and I had postured myself to receive with clarity the messages that He was communicating to me.

At the time I was reviewing the book in preparation for publishing, the world was thrust into the midst of a pandemic, senseless murders, wars and rumors of wars, riots, and people dying by the thousands. It was like the Lord was showing me, Revelations 9 was happening now, hell on earth in real time and people having a choice to make. Right before the Passover, I was having visions and dreaming a lot. But before I tell this dream, I was reminded of one I had almost 5 years ago to the date. I woke up from a dream on the morning of July 17, 2015. I had a dream two days prior where I was walking with lions on the beach. However, this dream was altogether different, and I was troubled by the dream. In the dream, the world was in chaos. There were tsunami's, earthquakes, tornadoes, hurricanes, and nuclear bombs. I saw a four headed dragon that was killed in a land I had never been to. People were running everywhere in a panic, but I was just walking through the land. Then I was headed towards Long Beach to pick up a Mexican baby and all of sudden there was a huge wave of water that came rushing towards us as we fled to a building for safety.

Then I was transported to a boat with my family and a there were a lot of other people on the boat that I didn't immediately recognize but they were with us sailing away from the land towards safety. That was 5 years ago. As we approached Passover, I had this dream on April 6, 2020. I was in my room writing the book and I was on my computer and also handwriting in my books. My brother David was in the room talking to me in the corner, but it was dark like he was hiding and I couldn't see his face, but I was talking to him about the plan the Lord had given me. I stopped in mid-sentence and I told him that we need to do a podcast and that it was going to be very important. Then all of a sudden, it was like I had an urge to lay down. Then my vision became blurred, but I could halfway see and it's like I was in deep thought and was overtaken by the Holy Spirit. At this time, as I was laying in the bed, I begin to tell my brother that he needs to pray to the Lord and ask for more boldness and confidence to speak the word of God as I drifted off to sleep. I dozed off in the dream and began having another dream. I had a dream within a dream.

When I dozed off, I woke up laying in my bed with my eyes still closed and I felt a huge shaking and I heard like a huge presence walking by, it's like with each huge step there was a jolt, like huge footsteps and I started praying more in the Holy Spirit, but I was scared and crying out as I heard the crying and screaming voices and heard the noises, I was saying "no God, please God! Have mercy!" It's like I heard God walking on the earth. I heard a terrible noise, and it was like all hell had broken loose. I woke up in the dream and looked out my window, but I couldn't see anything happening around me, and actually there was nothing happening. Then I opened my bedroom door walked down the hallway and my sons were flipping through the channels and looking out the windows to see if we could see what was going on outside. And then I said, "It has begun" and I woke up for real this time. That dream shook me but excited me at the same time because I heard God walking on the earth and what I believe to be passing judgement.

Fast forward to the present day, we are celebrating the life of Mr. John Lewis who passed away on July 17, 2020, at the age of 80 years old. Mr. Lewis was an American hero and legend, politician and civil-rights leader who served in the United States House of Representative for Georgia's 5th congressional district for 33 years, 1987 until his death in 2020 from pancreatic cancer. I was 17 when he began serving in a state that has the same name as my mother. This is not a coincidence. Especially considering the day that he would go to heaven would be the same day I would awake from a dream about the end of the world. Mr. Lewis served as a chairman of the Student Nonviolent Coordinating Committee (SNCC) from 1963 to 1966 (3 years). This morning was his homegoing service, it was broadcast for the world to see. He passed away 13 days ago. The celebration of his life was set to air on live television this morning, and I was awakened by a series of earthquakes in my city in the Grape State.

We had six earthquakes between the time of 4:29 am and 7:24 am. Six represents the creation of man. The first quake was a 4.5, which those numbers represent the physical creation and God's grace and it was exactly how I described in my dream, a very hard shaking and the quakes were in two sets of threes, it was odd. That's not happened here since I've lived here, and it's been 11 years. I was calling out Jesus' name during the earthquake and praying in tongues just like in the dream and asking for mercy because I could hear people crying in the distance. I believe that a portion of the dream came true this morning, and here's why. John Lewis was born on the same day that Billy Graham and my great-grandmother Uziel went to be with the Lord and seven days after God gave me the dream. They were both 99 years old and the Lord told me we've been here, in the last days since 1999, just how Prince sang about it.

As a matter of fact, the Lord gifted me a Georgia state quarter that was engraved with the years 1778-1999 which is 221 years, exactly five (5) days after George Floyd's murder. Five is the number representing God's grace. The quarter highlighted the dates of the Declaration of Independence. I'm thinking the United States has broken its covenant with the chosen people of God, the true descendants of Abraham – the slaves. Another thing I'd like to highlight is that he was also born in 1940 and remember the number 19 biblically represents the beginning or the closing of a season and the number 40 represents a "period of testing". When I looked up the name of the fault line that I'm on, the name means executioner, hangman, cruel master, tyrant, and tormentor. And there was a word of the day right underneath the definition. It read, "July 30th word of the day, 'Reclaiming My time. When people are on your time but wasting it!" That's a huge statement from God! He said, He is reclaiming His time!

Then when I text my sister and shared all of this with her, this was her response. "I understand. God is REALLY trying to get our attention!! He wants us to focus. The woman at the well. The Living Water…the ground is on a fault line and it looks like a river ran through it. His timing is PERFECT!" During Moses' life he lived forty years in Egypt and forty years in the desert before God selected him to lead his people out of slavery. It's been 40 years that we've been living in Reaganomics. Moses was also on Mount Sinai for 40 days and nights, on two separate occasions (Exodus 24:18, 34:1 - 28), receiving God's laws. I fasted two years in a row for 40 days and nights. The first fast was without food. The second fast was Daniel's fast. I was lead by the Holy Spirit to study the book of Revelation and the writings of the prophets, but specifically the Apostle Paul during that time. Moses also sent spies, for forty days, to investigate the land God promised the Israelites as an inheritance (Numbers 13:25, 14:34). I've been trying to get someone I trust to go and check out the Georgia Stones. I do believe that these stones were put there to help us, after all the Bible does say that what the devil means for evil, God works out for the good of those that love Him and that are called according to His purpose. I know people get all touchy about the number of people the stones suggest not to fall under, but I think it's there because they were trying to get people to stop murdering each other and killing the children by way of abortion. I believe that is a significance of the 40 days.

The prophet Jonah powerfully warned ancient Nineveh, for forty days, that its destruction would come because of its many sins. The prophet Ezekiel laid on His right side for 40 days to symbolize Judah's sins (Ezekiel 4:6). The Lord told me it's been 40 years since Reaganomics and since that particular president threw out the gauntlet by reading the scripture 2 Chronicles 7:14, at his inaugural, "If my people who are called by my name would humble themselves and pray…" you know the rest. Elijah went 40 days without food or water at Mount Horeb. Jesus was tempted by the devil not just three times, but many times during the 40 days and nights he fasted just before his ministry began. He also appeared to his disciples and others for 40 days after his resurrection from the dead. The number forty can also represent a generation of man. Because of their sins after leaving Egypt, God swore that the generation of Israelites who left Egypt in bondage would not enter their inheritance in Canaan (Deuteronomy 1).

The children of Israel were punished by wandering the wilderness for 40 years before "a new generation" was allowed to possess the promised land. Jesus, just days before his crucifixion, prophesied the total destruction of Jerusalem (Matthew 24:1-2, Mark 13:1-2). Forty years after his crucifixion in 30 A.D., the wicked Roman Empire destroyed the city and burned its beloved temple to the ground. The Lord has been telling me that we've been in the wilderness for far more than 40 years and that it is time to possess the land, the promised land. The promised land is one that is like Heaven, but here on earth, where the people of God, the true servants of the Highest God – rule and reign with His Son, Jesus Christ. I decided to include Mr. Lewis' speech he wrote and left with the New York Times to be published after his passing. I believe it is very relevant to the call of the day for God's chosen people. As you read his words, I pray they flow into your heart and inspire you to make a change, thee change! Salvation has come!

"While my time here has now come to an end, I want you to know that in the last days and hours of my life you inspired me. You filled me with hope about the next chapter of the great American story when you used your power to make a difference in our society. Millions of people motivated simply by human compassion laid down the burdens of division. Around the country and the world, you set aside race, class, age, language, and nationality to demand respect for human dignity. That is why I had to visit Black Lives Matter Plaza in Washington, though I was admitted to the hospital the following day. I just had to see and feel it for myself that, after many years of silent witness, the truth is still marching on. Emmett till was my George Floyd [my Tupac, Prince, Kobe, Michael Jackson and Nipsey Hussle – all slain). He was my Rayshard Brooks, Sandra Bland and Breonna Taylor and the list goes on. He was 14 when he was killed, and I was only 15 years old at the time.

I will never ever forget the moment when it became so clear that he could easily have been me. In those days, fear constrained us like an imaginary prison, and troubling thoughts of potential brutality committed for no understandable reason were the bars. Though I was surrounded by two loving parents, plenty of brothers, sisters and cousins, their love could not protect me from the unholy oppression waiting just outside that family circle. Unchecked, unrestrained violence and government-sanctioned terror had the power to turn a simple stroll to the store for some Skittles or an innocent morning jog down a lonesome country road into a nightmare. If we are to survive as one unified nation, we must discover what so readily takes root in our hearts that could rob Mother Emmanuel Church in South Carolina of her brightest and best, shoot unwitting concertgoers in Las Vegas and choke to death the hopes and dreams of a gifted violinist like Elijah McClain.

Like so many young people today, I was searching for a way out, or some might say a way in, and then I heard the voice of Dr. Martin Luther King Jr. on an old radio. He was talking about the philosophy and discipline of nonviolence. He said we are all complicit when we tolerate injustice. He said it is not enough to say it will get better by and by. He said each of us has a moral obligation to stand up, speak up and speak out. When you see something that is not right, you must say something. You must do something. Democracy is not a state. It is an act, and each generation must do its part to help build what we called the Beloved Community, a nation and world society at peace with itself. [Like a holy and righteous nation - like Heaven on Earth] Ordinary people with extraordinary vision can redeem the soul of America by getting in what I call good trouble, necessary trouble. Voting and participating [love one another] in the democratic process are key.

The vote is the most powerful nonviolent change agent you have in a democratic society. You must use it because it is not guaranteed. You can lose it. You must also study and learn the lessons of history because humanity has been involved in this soul-wrenching, existential struggle for a very long time. People on every continent have stood in your shoes, through decades and centuries before you. The truth does not change, and that is why the answers worked out long ago can help find solutions to the challenges of our time. Continue to build union between movements stretching across the globe because we must put away our willingness to profit from the exploitation of others. Though I may not be here with you, I urge you to answer the highest calling of your heart and stand up for what you truly believe.

In my life, I have done all I can to demonstrate that the way of peace, the way of love and nonviolence is the more excellent way. Now it is your turn to let freedom ring. When historians pick up their pens to write the story of the 21st century, let them say that it was your generation [X] who laid down the heavy burdens of the hate at last and that peace finally triumphed over violence, aggression and war. So, I say to you, walk with the wind, brothers, and sisters, and let the spirit of peace and the power of everlasting love be your guide."

The Speaker of the house spoke about how they saw a double Rainbow on the morning of Mr. Lewis' service over the place where his body lay, which was God's confirmation of His promise and those rainbows were seen shortly after 8 am she said. Double rainbows are symbolic of a double promise. The Holy Spirit lead me to Revelations 4 which we will cover in a later chapter. Mr. Lewis' letter confirms what the Lord has been speaking to me since 2014, that we have been wandering in the wilderness far, far too long because we've gotten too far away from God's laws, His principles and His word. We have the power to make a difference and we can make the changes America needs so desperately.

The reason the 13 days is significant is because the number 13 is symbolic of rebellion and lawlessness. This is the state of our union and our country at this very moment. It also represents Nimrod, the mighty hunter who was 'before the Lord' (meaning he tried to take the place of God -Genesis 10:9), who was the 13th in Ham's line (Ham was one of Noah's three sons who survived the flood). Thirteen (13) also represents all the governments created by men, and inspired by Satan, in outright rebellion against the Eternal.

I heard a prophet say that all the governments of this world are sacrificing their population on the alter of big billion dollar pharmaceutical industry. (YouTuber Computing Forever). Mr. Lewis spoke of injustice and protested against the lawlessness and spoke about how the government gave sin it's power.

The phrase 'valley of Hinnom' (or variation thereof) occurs in 13 places in Scripture. The valley was the scene of the evil-inspired rites of the pagan god Moloch (or Molech). The practices related to this false deity received some credibility when they were knowingly allowed by King Solomon, "On the Mount of Olives, east of Jerusalem, he even built a pagan shrine for Chemosh, the detestable god of Moab, and another for Molech, the detestable god of the Ammonites." 1Kings 11:7, in order to please his non-Israelite wives. One-way Molech was appeased and worshipped was through the sacrifice of children who were placed on the red-hot arms of the idol and burned alive. The valley's tie to fire made for an apt backdrop of the ultimate punishment, the unrepentant and rebellious sinners will receive in the lake of fire. "For the lawlessness is already at work secretly, and it will remain secret until the one who is holding it back steps out of the way. Then the man of lawlessness will be revealed, but the Lord Jesus will slay him with the breath of his mouth and destroy him by the splendor of his coming." – 2 Thessalonians 2:7-8"

Remember we covered this in an earlier chapter and also interestingly enough, Thessalonians is the longest chapter name in the book at 13 letters. 7 is God's perfect number and the number 8 represents Jesus' name, resurrection, regeneration and no lack. More on the number 13, it represents the dragon, a symbol for Satan and is found 13 times in the book of Revelations. Satan is behind all rebellion against God. "And the beast was captured, and with him the false prophet who did mighty miracles on behalf of the beast – miracles that deceived all who had accepted the mark of the beast and who worshipped his statue. Both the beast and his false prophet were thrown alive into the fiery lake of burning sulfur. – Revelation 19:20"

"And I saw them as they went up on the broad plain of the earth and surrounded God's people and the beloved city. But fire from heaven came down on the attacking armies and consumed them. Then the devil, who had deceived them, was thrown into the fiery lake of burning sulfur, joining the beast and the false prophet. There they will be tormented day and night forever and ever. Then death and the grave were thrown into the lake of fire. This lake of fire is the second death. And anyone whose name was not found recorded in the Book of Life was thrown into the lake of fire. Revelation 20:9-10, 14-15."

Now it completely makes sense why I had a dream within a dream, because John Robert Lewis was one of the original dreamers along with Rev. Dr. Martin Luther King, Jr. They both saw a better world for the future generations, and they tried standing, but a few men by themselves can't accomplish what a mighty army can do together. We don't have to listen to the lies of the devil or be enslaved to a master that is not the Lord Jesus Christ. We don't have to bow to a false god or tyrant! We have free will and it was God given! Man has no right to take this away from us, and when I say us, I mean children of the Most High God! We have a choice. There is power in unity, especially if we are united in Yeshua Messiah. We do not have any control over when we are born and we die, that is determined and allowed by the Creator, Yahweh.

"Then I saw four angels standing at the four corners of the earth, holding back the four winds so they did not blow on the earth or the sea, or even on any tree. And I saw another angel coming up from the east, carrying the seal of the living God. And he shouted to those four angels, who had been given power to harm land and sea, "Wait! Don't harm the land or the sea or the trees until we have placed the seal of God on the foreheads of his servants." And I heard how many were marked with the seal of God – 144,000 were sealed from all the tribes of Israel: from Judah 12,000, from Reuben 12,000, from Gad 12,000, from Asher 12,000, from Naphtali 12,000, from Manasseh 12,000, from Simeon 12,000, from Levi 12,000, from Issachar 12,000, from Zebulun 12,000, from Joseph 12,000, from Benjamin 12,000. After this I saw a vast crowd, too great to count, from every nation and tribe and people and language, standing in front of the throne and before the Lamb. They were clothed in white robes and held palm branches [victory, triumph, peace, and eternal life] in their hands.

And they were shouting with a great roar, "Salvation comes from our God who sits on the throne and from the Lamb! And all the angels were standing around the throne and around the elders and the four living beings. And they fell before the throne with their faces to the ground and worshipped God. They sang, "Amen! Blessing and glory and wisdom and thanksgiving and honor and power and strength belong to our God forever and ever! Amen." Then one of the twenty-four elders asked me, "Who are these who are clothed in white? Where have they come from? And I said to him, "Sir, you are the one who knows." Then he said to me, "These are the ones who died in [Greek says who came out of] the great tribulation [or the great suffering]. They have washed their robes in the blood of the Lamb and made them white. That is why they stand in front of God's throne and serve him day and night in his Temple. And he who sits on the throne will give them shelter. They will never again be hungry or thirsty; they will never be scorched by the heat of the sun. For the Lamb on the throne [Greek says on the center of the throne – Mesis] will be their Shepherd. He will lead them to springs of life-giving water. And God will wipe every tear from their eyes." Revelation 7:1-17 (17 symbolizes victory)

We were born for such a time as this! We are living in biblical times! We do not have control over other people's choices. We the people, do however, have control over minds, our thoughts, our bodies and our own choices as individuals, under God. We can make better decisions than our ancestors made in the past which is what Mr. Lewis was saying in his final speech to the world. Jesus said, we would do greater things than He did, and He died for us, giving us this great power of the Holy Spirit that is in each and every believer! We can make a difference if we pray and stand together for change. As it was first given to me on that faithful Wednesday night bible study, it's time to speak up because we have backup! It's time to wake up, stand up and rise up!

I'll end this chapter with a few of my notes and scriptures that were given to me on this day, exactly two years ago, just to show you how amazing Jesus is and how the Holy Spirit is divine. I couldn't write this if I tried, it's all God! It's all the Holy Spirit! It's all Jesus! Glory to God! The three godheads are ONE! They all function together, just as our soul, body and spirit are one. "Therefore, I tell you, whatever you ask for in prayer, believe that you have received it, and it will be yours. – Mark 11:24" Journal notes, Day 3 of 5,

"Wait and See" Bible plan. "Pasture experiences. Sometimes you have to wait for God to tell you where to walk after He's called you. We shouldn't run ahead of Him or lag behind. We should take steps in line with His word and be ready when He delivers our heart's desires.

When we step out in faith, He will show us the way either by opening the door or closing it. Sometimes that means doing a new thing or doing what we already know to do. Sometimes it's necessary to tend to our sheep as David did because it was preparing him to be king. Scripture reading: "Not only so, but we also glory in our sufferings, because we know that suffering produces perseverance; (Romans 5:3) "We wait in hope for the Lord; he is our help and our shield, for we trust in his holy name. May your unfailing love be with us, Lord, even as we put our hope in you. (Psalms 33:20-22) I'm standing on the solid rock of my Salvation, the Lord God Almighty.

Chapter 7: Wake Up Church

Jesus said, "How can I describe the Kingdom of God? What story should I use to illustrate it? It is like a mustard seed planted in the ground. It is the smallest of all seeds, but it becomes the largest of all garden plants; it grows long branches, and birds can make nests in its shade." – Mark 4:30-32

Rabbi taught recently that the Songs of Songs or the Songs of Solomon scriptures reveal the emotional side of God. I'm finding myself relating more and more to the Shulamite bride. In the scriptures, she's crying out to God to kiss her with the kisses of His mouth. She desires intimate time with Him. She, like myself understood that there was nothing on the earth that completely satisfies like the love of God. Material things cannot satisfy the soul because we were made for God and He is a Spirit. Fleshly desires cannot satisfy the soul because they are only pleasurable for a season, when God is forever. We were created to know God. She was longing to feel complete with the Father. Though the Holy Spirit helped me to see through Rabbi that in these scriptures, the Lord is using human language to convey something that can be seen with the human eye or understood by human intellect. There is nothing greater than knowing the Creator. Focusing on God and making Him my closest friend was becoming my number one priority.

The Lord called Abraham a friend of God, "And so it happened just as the Scriptures say: "Abraham believed God, and God counted him as righteous because of his faith (Genesis 15:6). He was even called the friend of God (Isaiah 41:8). – James 2:23" The Rabbi helped me understand that unlike virtually all women in the biblical narratives, the Shulamite woman is not presented as the "wife" of anyone. I too am not lawfully wed to any man. She is both independent and maternal, powerful, and pious. I am a mother, and I would say that I was more spiritual than religious, definitely dutiful, and loyal to God and I walk in my Resurrection power in the Holy Spirit, so we have some similarities. Paul said if you are going to boast, boast in Christ!

I heard a Pastor speak these words that very evening on TV: "Let go of the plow. Pick up your mantle. It is not what you push anymore, it's what you carry. Let go of your plow and pick up your Mantle. Get ready to run with it." This is the second time I heard those words to "pick up your mantle," but the first time I was being told to let go of the plow. I guess you can compare my service to God as plowing in the fields. A plough or plow is a tool or farm implement used for initial cultivation to loosen or turn the soil in preparation for sowing seed or planting. I am finding a constant with the farming metaphors and remember my grandfather and mother's name both meant farmers and tillers of the soil. I also love the country, the simple life and find myself longing to return to those summers with my greats in Louisiana and Texas.

Maybe I was the seed that was planted in the earth for such a time as this. Ploughs were traditionally drawn by working animals such as oxen and horses, but in modern farms are drawn by tractors (machines). He said, "The plow of perseverance will lead to a season of promotion." Perseverance is the persistence in doing something despite difficulty or delay in achieving success, almost like writing these books. God told me to write them, and the rest is up to Him. He said, "The prophet was never known for what he pushed but only what he (she) carried." Grace upon grace. I say yes to all Your promises Father God, in the name of Jesus. My way of putting down the plow as instructed by the angel of the Lord was to take a leave of absence from all the helps ministries that I was involved in, so that I could focus my attention solely on writing the book and continuing my growth in the Lord as I was being led by the Holy Spirit.

"Then he gave them this illustration: "Notice the fig tree, or any other tree. When the leaves come out, you know without being told that summer is near. In the same way, when you see all these things taking place, you can know that the Kingdom of God is near. I tell you the truth, this generation will not pass from the scene until all these things have taken place. Heaven and earth will disappear, but my words will never disappear. "Watch out! Do not let your hearts be dulled by carousing and drunkenness, and by the worries of this life. Do not let that day catch you unaware, like a trap. For that day will come upon everyone living on the earth. Keep alert at all times. And pray that you might be strong enough to escape these coming horrors and stand before the Son of Man." (Luke 21:29-36) "Search for the LORD and for his strength; continually seek him." 1 Chronicles 16:11 and that is my mission, to seek the Kingdom.

I woke up to an astounding 11,737 emails in my inbox, most of it junk mail and advertisements which is ridiculous but the significance for me was the number. The number eleven (11) with four sevens (7's). I don't disregard anything now, I see God speaking to me in every way, He uses all of His creations to speak to me. The number 7777 meaning is one of the most powerful spiritual numbers. This number is associated with my name in way I can't reveal right now, but it's pretty powerful. This is what I read about this number. "Seeing this number sequence signifies that great progress is being made for the new beginning you have always desired. With the added influence of number 1 which indicates that you are striving forward and progressing by self-discovery. Like number 777, its meaning is that you will progress through the path, however there are no wrong paths, whichever path you have chosen is the right one and you have chosen it by revealing your complete self."

I heard this message by the same brother who did the 30 names of God in the YouVersion Bible App. "God informs the Holy Spirit. The Spirit informs the soul. The soul informs the body. The Spirit is informed by the truth of God's word. God's word in the body transforms you. God gave Adam instruction in the Garden of Eden. The devil came along after said instruction and the first conversation he had in the garden was with Eve, and not

Adam; and it was about God's word. He comes to the garden to distort the word. He wants to get to the word before it gets into the soil (soul) because inside the seed is the life of whatever the seed is. The life of the human being is the seed God planted and remember in an earlier chapter Jesus told us in a parable that the seed is the Word of God. It is undeveloped life when it is born. It has to be developed, just like a baby doesn't stay an infant, it grows as it is fed and nurtured. If the egg can be stolen from the soil – you kill its potential for development. That is what the devil does with the hard hearts of men, before the word has time to settle into the soil of the heart. (I just said above, I am the seed God planted in the earth for a time such as this., but more importantly – His word is the seed that was planted into my heart.)

There is life in the seed." Jesus said, "Now listen to the explanation of the people about the farmer planting seeds: The seed that fell on the footpath represents those who hear the message about the Kingdom and don't understand it. Then the evil one comes and snatches away the seed that was planted in their hearts. The seed on the rocky soil represents those who hear the message and immediately receive it with joy. But since they do not have deep roots, they don't last long. They fall away as soon as they have problems or are persecuted for believing God's word. The seed that fell among the thorns represents those who hear God's word, but all too quickly the message is crowded out by the worries of this life and the lure of wealth, so no fruit is produced. The seed that fell on good soil represents those who truly hear and understand God's word and produce a harvest of thirty, sixty, or even a hundred times as much as had been planted! – Matthew 13:18-23" Which path of your heart did the seed fall on? The way it's looking for me, the seed fell on good soil because I both hear and understand God's word clearer than I ever have in my entire life.

"Don't settle for death. When the seed is stolen, the heart is rebellious however restoration is possible when you seek the Kingdom." Hearing this message took me back to my childhood and I now understand why I experienced the physical and mental abuse, the rejection, humble beginnings, attacks on my life, loneliness etc. because while the devil was trying to steal the seed because he did not want me to know who I was, God was allowing it because the Lord was preparing me for my purpose and destiny. He was always trying to keep me in a low place, and always second guessing myself and God's word. He wanted me to kill myself or feel so rejected that I would turn away from God. He wanted to destroy me and give me great pain, but God never left me alone. He always put someone on my path to help me, I will call them travelers because that's we are. "Hear my prayer, O Lord! Listen to my cries for help! Do not ignore my tears. For I am your guest – a traveler passing through, as my ancestors were before me. – Psalms 39:12"

God is growing me. I am going through a process of development and it's not just for me, but apparently to assist the people of God, the descendants of Abraham. I cannot skip the process to see the product of the blessing – the seeds must develop first. Saints need to be saved for earth and earth is symbolic for man. I am saved for heaven, but I needed to be delivered for His story or history. My spirit was saved but my soul needs saving on a daily basis and that could only happen when I receive and take into my heart on a consistent basis, God's holy word and in the appropriate soil (ground) which has to be holy and righteous, living a state of daily repentance – a life lived in full surrender to please the Father God. I had to leave the wilderness of sin. "They left the wilderness of sin and camped at Dophkah [meaning a knocking]." Numbers 33:12 It is funny that the name of the place in which they camped means "a knocking" because remember I was awakened in the summer of 2018, by knocking.

This is a word from the Lord of Heaven's Armies and from the One who is Faithful and True to the children still wandering in the wilderness of sin: "O Israel," says the LORD, "if you wanted to return to me, you could. You could throw away your detestable idols and stray away no more. Then when you swear by my name, saying, 'As surely as the Lord lives,' you could do so with truth, justice, and righteousness. Then you would be a blessing to the nations of the world, and all people would come and praise my name." This is what the LORD says to the people of Judah and Jerusalem: "Plow up the hard ground of your hearts! Do not waste your good seed among thorns. O' people of Judah and Jerusalem, surrender your pride and power. Change your hearts before the LORD [Hebrew Circumcise yourselves to the LORD and take away the foreskins of your heart] or my anger will burn like an unquenchable fire because of all your sins.

Shout to Judah, and broadcast to Jerusalem! Tell them to sound the alarm throughout the land: 'Run for your lives! Flee to the fortified cities! Raise a signal flag as a warning for Jerusalem [Hebrew Zion]. 'Flee now! Do not delay!" For I am bringing terrible destruction from the north." A lion stalks from its den, a "destroyer" [Revelation 9] of nations. It has left its lair and is headed your way. It is going to devastate your land! Your towns will lie in ruins, with no one living in them anymore. So, put on clothes of mourning and weep with broken hearts, for the fierce anger of the LORD is still upon us. "In that day," says the LORD, "the king and the officials will tremble in fear. The priests will be struck with horror, and the prophets will be appalled." Then I said, "O Sovereign LORD, the people have been deceived by what you said, for you promised peace for Jerusalem. But the sword is held at their throats!"

The time is coming when the LORD will say to the people of Jerusalem, "My dear people, a burning wind is blowing in from the desert, and it's not a gentle breeze useful for winnowing grain. It is a roaring blast sent by me! Now I will pronounce your destruction!" Our enemy rushes down on us like storm clouds! His chariots are like whirlwinds. His horses are swifter than eagles. How terrible it will be, for we are doomed! O Jerusalem cleanse your heart that you may be saved. How long will you harbor your evil thoughts? Your destruction has been announced from Dan and the hill country of Ephraim. Warn the surrounding nations and announce this to Jerusalem: The enemy is coming from a distant land, raising a battle cry against the towns of Judah. They surround Jerusalem like watchman around a field, for my people have rebelled against me," says the LORD. Your own actions have brought this upon you. This punishment is bitter, piercing you to the heart!" Jeremiah 4:1-18

Though the number 18 represents bondage and slavery, it also signifies being "alive" also. I was saying in a few paragraphs up above that the earth is symbolism for man and here is why, land or earth in the Word of God signifies the church. Christ is the head of the church and the "body". Christ is the head of the earth and the land. It also signifies and in some cases specifies, what is not the church because every such word has contrary or opposite meanings; as for example when it speaks of the various lands of the Gentiles; in general it's speaking of all lands outside the land of Canaan. So, all lands outside the land of Canaan, or the promised land are lands of the Gentiles or unbelievers. Remember, Canaan (meaning land of the immigrants or land of purple) is the land the Lord God Almighty promised to Abraham and his descendants. The name Canaan means land of purple, purple dye and to be brought into synchronicity and comes from the word Chenaanah which means International Trade. Lord have mercy! The Lord was giving me all this information in 2018.

Canaan was the name of the fourth son of Ham, the youngest son of Noah, the father of all humanity (Genesis 9:18). This Canaan would give his name to the much-coveted country of Canaan and the people who live there. What is sad is that people have not yet grasped that God cannot be put in a box, Jesus dying on the cross changed the game! Jesus sent the Holy Spirit which is both wisdom and knowledge. Also, God promised Abraham and his descendants "the land that he was a foreigner in." God's words are so important, they tell you everything you need to know. Real people, places, and history. The original Canaanites (meaning an ethnically diverse group of people) were displaced by Israel, "When the LORD your God brings you into the land you are about to enter and occupy, he will clear away many nations ahead of you: the Hittites, Girgashites, Amorites, Canaanites, Perizzites, Hivites, and Jebusites. These seven nations are greater and more numerous than you. - Deuteronomy 7:1."

The ethnonym Canaanite appears to have applied mostly to people who lived in urban environments and in complex economies and stratified societies. People who lived in the territory of Canaan but rejected urban living and lived in rural tribal chiefdoms (like Nomads, Aborigionists, Native Americans) were referred to as Perizzites (meaning rural or villagers). Canaan became the recipient of a curious curse that made him the perpetual servant of his two uncles Japheth and Shem. After having survived the flood and their 230 days stay in the Ark (40 days of rain, 150 days of floating, 40 days of drying) Noah planted a vineyard (a common symbol of general human culture), made wine and got drunk, and lay naked in his tent. Then not Canaan but Ham, the father of Canaan, saw Noah naked and quipped about it to Shem and Japheth. The two older brothers walked into their father's tent backwards and covered Noah without looking at him.

Seems that Canaan was paying for the sins of his father Ham almost like Esau losing his birthright. Eerily similar to the ancestors going through 400 years of slavery for the sin and rebellion of their ancestors. Canaan's (11) eleven sons as listed in 1 Chronicles 1:13 are also all known nations, among whom Sidon, Heth, Jebusites (who owned Jerusalem, read Joshua 10:1, 2 Samuel 5:6), Amorites and Hivites come from. In the Greek New Testament the name Canaan is spelled Χαναав in Acts of the Apostles 7:11 and 13:19 and Canaanite (female) is spelled Χαναναια (MATTHEW 15:22). The masculine form Χαναναιος does not occur in the New Testament but both Matthew and Mark make mention of a Simon the zealot as a Cananean, an Aramaic term for Jewish nationalists, listed as one of the first twelve disciples (Matthew 10:4, Mark 3:18). Not sure if that epithet has anything to do with the country or if they reference it just to distinguish between the two disciples, because both were named Simon.

Also very interesting, the word "land" is therefore taken for the people and for the man outside the church, and hence for the external man, for his will, his own, and so forth.

The term earth is rarely used in the Word of God to mean the whole world, except when the whole human race is meant and this regards their state of being, whether of the church or not of the church. The earth is the containment of the ground (dirt/soil/earth), which also signifies the church, because our bodies are considered the Temple of God or a house that contains or holds our spirits. The ground is also the containment of the field the word earth signifies because it involves many things. This should be a testament for the scientists that God made us to live on the earth, and not to try and live on the moon or any other planet for that matter. Why do they want to know if there is life on other planets so badly when they insist on killing the life that resides on earth?

From all this it is evident that by the whole earth that was overspread by the sons of Noah, is does not signify the whole world, or the whole human race, but all the doctrines both true and false that were of the churches. Remember the Lord said in the last days it would be like the days of Noah because Noah was preaching something that the people had not heard before, that it was going to rain. Furthermore, in the days of Noah, a lot of the wickedness was going on in the earth realm as well as the fallen angels were having sex with the daughters trying to pollute the bloodline and stop the coming of the pure offspring that was to crush his head, but I digress. I believe this is all symbolism for the Holy Spirit pouring out in the last days, the false prophets and doctrine being revealed and God revealing who His true children are, as well as the new creation. Just as the Lord God Almighty told Noah to build a boat, He told me to write a book.

"What sorrow awaits the leaders of my people – the shepherds of my sheep – for they have destroyed and scattered the very ones they were expected to care for," says the LORD. Therefore, this is what the LORD the God of Israel, says to these shepherds: "Instead of caring for my flock and leading them to safety, you have deserted them and driven them to destruction. Now I will pour out judgement on you for the evil you have done to them. But I will gather together the remnant of my flock from the countries where I have driven them. I will bring them back to their own sheepfold, and they will be fruitful and increase in number. Then I will appoint responsible shepherds who will care for them, and they will never be afraid again. Not a single one will be lost or missing. I, the LORD, have spoken! For the time is coming," says the LORD, "when I will raise up a righteous descendant [Hebrew a righteous branch] from King David's line. He will be a King who rules with wisdom. He will do what is just and right throughout the land.

And this will be his name: 'The LORD is Our Righteousness [Hebrew Yahweh Tsidqenu or Jehovah Tsidkenu]. In that day Judah will be saved, and Israel will live in safety. "In that day," says the LORD, "when people are taking an oath, they will no longer say, 'As surely as the LORD lives, who rescued the people of Israel from the land of Egypt.' Instead, they will say, 'As surely as the LORD lives, who brought the people of Israel back to their own land from the land of the north and from all the countries to which he had exiled them.' Then they will live in their own land. My heart is broken because of the false prophets, and my bones tremble. I stagger like a drunkard [like Noah], like someone overcome by wine, because of the holy words the LORD has spoken against them. For the land is full of adultery, and it lies under a curse. The land [the people] itself is in mourning – its wilderness pastures are dried up. For they all do evil and abuse what power they have.

"Even the priests and prophets are ungodly, wicked men. I have seen their despicable acts right here in my own Temple," says the LORD. Therefore, the paths they take will become slippery. They will be chased through the dark, and there they will fall. For I will bring disaster upon them at the time fixed for their punishment. I, the LORD, have spoken! I saw the prophets of Samaria were terribly evil, for they prophesied in the name of Baal and led my people of Israel into sin. But now I see that the prophets of Jerusalem are even worse! They commit adultery and love dishonesty. They encourage those who are doing evil so that no one turns away from their sins. These prophets are as wicked as the people of Sodom and Gomorrah once were." Therefore, this is what the LORD of Heaven's Armies says concerning the prophets:

"I will feed them with bitterness and give them poison to drink. For it is because of Jerusalem's prophets that wickedness has filled this land." This is what the Lord of Heaven's Armies says to his people: "Do not listen to these prophets when they prophesy to you, filling you with the futile hopes. They are making up everything they say. They do not speak for the LORD! They keep saying to those who despise my word, 'Don't worry! The LORD says you will have peace!' And to those who stubbornly follow their own desires, they say, 'No harm will come your way!" "Have any of these prophets been in the LORD's presence to hear what he is really saying? Has even one of them cared enough to listen? Look! The LORD's anger bursts out like a storm, a whirlwind that swirls down on the heads of the wicked. The anger of the LORD will not diminish until it has finished all he has planned.

In the days to come you will understand all this very clearly. "I have not sent these prophets, yet they run around claiming to speak for me. I have given them no message, yet they go on prophesying. If they had stood before me and listened to me, they would have turned my people from their evil ways and deeds. Am I a God who is only close at hand?" says the LORD. "No, I am far away at the same time. Can anyone hide from me in a secret place?" says the LORD. "I have heard these prophets say, 'Listen to the dream I had from God last night.' And then they proceed to tell lies in my name. How long will this go on? If they are prophets, they are prophets of deceit, inventing everything they say. By telling these false dreams, they are trying to get my people to forget me, just as their ancestors did by worshipping the idols of Baal.

Let these false prophets tell their dreams, but let my true messengers faithfully proclaim my every word. There is a difference between straw and grain! Does not my word burn like fire?" says the LORD. "Is it not like a mighty hammer that smashes a rock to pieces? Therefore," says the LORD, "I am against these prophets who steal messages from each other and claim they are from me. I am against these smooth-tongued prophets who say, 'This prophecy is from the LORD! I am against these false prophets. Their imaginary dreams are flagrant lies that lead my people into sin. I did not send or appoint them, and they have no message at all for my people. I, the LORD, have spoken! Suppose one of the people or one of the prophets or priests asks you, 'What prophecy has the LORD burdened you with now?' You must reply, 'You are the burden [Greek and Latin Vulgate – Roman Catholic Church]!" to be continued after the following scripture:

Jesus said to the people who believed in him, "You are truly my disciples if you remain faithful to my teachings. And you will know the truth, and the truth will set you free."

"But we are descendants of Abraham," they said. "We have never been slaves to anyone. What do you mean, 'You will be set free'?" Jesus replied, "I tell you the truth, everyone who sins is a slave of sin. A slave is not a permanent member of the family, but a son is part of the family forever. So, if the Son sets you free, you are truly free. Yes, I realize that you are descendants of Abraham. And yet some of you are trying to kill me because there's no room in your hearts for my message. I am telling you what I saw when I was with my Father. But you are following the advice of your father." "Our father is Abraham!" they declared. "No," Jesus replied, "for if you were really the children of Abraham, you would follow his example. Instead, you are trying to kill me because I told you the truth, which I heard from God. Abraham never did such a thing. No, you are imitating your real father."

Jesus told them, "If God were your Father, you would love me, because I have come to you from God. I am not here on my own, but he sent me. Why can't you understand what I am saying? It's because you can't even hear me! For you are the children of your father the devil, and you love to do the evil things he does. He was a murderer from the beginning. He has always hated the truth because there is no truth in him. When he lies, it is consistent with his character; for he is a liar and the father of lies. So, when I tell the truth, you just naturally don't believe me! Which of you can truthfully accuse me of sin? And since I am telling you the truth, why don't you believe me? Anyone who belongs to God listens gladly to the words of God. But you don't listen because you don't belong to God." – John 8:31-47

"If any prophet, priest, or anyone else says, 'I have a prophecy from the LORD,' I will punish that person along with his entire family. You should keep asking each other, 'What is the LORD's answer? Or 'What is the LORD saying?' But stop using this phrase, 'prophecy from the LORD.' For people are using it to give authority to their own ideas, turning upside down the words of our God, the living God, the LORD of Heaven's Armies. This is what you should say to the prophets: 'What is the LORD's answer?' or 'What is the LORD saying?' But suppose they respond, 'This is a prophecy from the Lord!' Then you should say, 'This is what the LORD says: Because you have used this phrase, "prophecy from the LORD," even though I warned you not to use it, I will forget you completely. I will expel you from my presence, along with this city that I gave to you and your ancestors. And I will make you an object of ridicule, and your name will be infamous throughout the ages.'" Jeremiah 23:1-40 And we covered all the meanings of the 40 in the previous chapter. The Lord is coming back to judge, soon.

Now, I'm understanding that there will be an attack coming from the left, which is the devil, because I was attacked on my left arm, and it was the back of my left hand that was inflamed, itching, and all scratched up when I woke up the morning of October 30. When I looked up the phrase "backhanded" the following synonyms and antonyms came up: artificial, counterfeit, double-dealing, fake, feigned, hypocritical, insincere, jive, left-handed, lip, mealymouthed, two-faced, pretended, phony and phony-baloney. Wow! So, this is why discernment is key and the reason I had the dreams about the wolves and the trash, because I had to be able to disseminate between the truth and the trash.

Just so happened to be the "eve" of a day when evil is celebrated and people, party parading around in costumes and masks – symbolic of a cover up. Also, I would like to note that this particular date is represented by a "scorpion" in the zodiac sign. It's also a representative of the season of fall and its element is water. Scorpions are predatory arachnids of the order Scorpiones. Scorpions have (8) eight legs and are easily recognized by the (two) pair of grasping pedipalps and the narrow, segmented tail, often carried in a characteristic forward curve over the back, ending with a venomous stinger. I saw a scorpion in the clouds as well and I believe this is symbolic of poison. Scorpions range in size from the 9–12 mm (0.35–0.47 in) Microtityus minimus to the 23 cm (9.1 in) Heterometrus swammerdami. This could symbolize the beast coming up out of the water during this time in the future between the months of September and December, but also Christ's second coming and Him coming to save the day. The wounds were similar to stings.

I knew I was attacked that night in my sleep, but I'm now understanding that it's some sort of sign of things to come. Afterall, there was nothing in my bed. I was attacked by an invisible enemy in my sleep. It was a spiritual attack that manifested in the natural. I could both see it and feel it, but I have no idea where it came from. I'm thinking because of the events that happened with the guy on that Friday before, maybe the enemy was trying to keep me in bondage and slavery. I thought at the time it could have been an attachment (or idol worship, same as adultery) to him, a stronghold or a foot still in the world, either way it seems I hadn't fully surrendered the situation to God and He was allowing the torment. I had to let it go and give it to God. I'm hearing the Lord telling me to come out of the world completely and separate myself from the pretenders because I know the truth and I must walk in it, even it's a road I walk alone. "Run from anything that stimulates youthful lusts. Instead, pursue righteous living, faithfulness, love, and peace. Enjoy the companionship of those who call on the Lord with pure hearts," 2 Timothy 2:22. "For if we are faithful to the end, trusting God just as firmly as when we first believed, we will share in all that belongs to Christ." Hebrews 3:14

The Lord is calling the church to wake up and come out of the world. A dark time is ahead and discernment will be needed to disseminate between the trash and the truth.

Chapter 8: The Time of the 4th Beast

"Then he said to me, "This fourth beast is the fourth world power that will rule the earth. It will be different from all the others. It will devour the whole world, trampling and crushing everything in its path." Daniel 7:23

I was out and about running errands with my son and as I sat in the car waiting for him to exit the store, the Bible Bus or 'Thru the Bible' was on the radio and I was listening to the great theologian Dr. J. Vernon McGee who just so happened to be talking about what, you may ask? The fourth beast and the end times, God's timing is perfect! My mother loved listening to the Bible Bus, and I have grown to love it as well – when I'm able to catch it, because it airs early in the morning and at 8pm in the evening in my time zone. I have learned so much from this program and this great servant of the Lord. On this evening though, he said something that caught my attention right away.

He said that we were living in the time of the fourth beast! Right then, alarms started going off in my head like that day in church. This awesome man of faith passed away December 1, 1988, which was 31 years ago, and I was 18 (there's that number again) and this originally was the 18th chapter but the book the original book had too many pages so in splitting it up it became chapter 8. Mind blowing, nevertheless. I thought about the scorpion sting again. Scorpions with their powerful sting appear in art, folklore, mythology, and numerous brands. Scorpion motifs are woven into kilim carpets for protection. Scorpio is the name of a constellation and the corresponding astrological sign; a classical myth tells how the giant scorpion and its enemy, Orion, became constellations on opposite sides of the sky. I just discovered that I can see Orion's belt in the night sky right from my patio.

The scorpion also lead me to the Scorpion weapon. The fourth century army officer and historian Ammianus Marcellinus witnessed the use of scorpiones during several engagements in the Persian wars of Constantius II, and described the one-armed version as synonymous with the onager, with the vertical upraised arm as the 'scorpion's sting'. This is eerily similar to the description of a syringe. The complexity of construction and in particular the torsion springs (which the Romans referred to as tormenta) led to great sensitivity to any variation in temperature or moisture, which limited their use. Wow. While this type of technology continued to be used in the Byzantine Empire, which was the continuation of the Roman Empire through the Middle Ages, it had disappeared in the Middle Ages in Western Europe. I believe this is symbolism for the Roman Empire coming back together because I believe they are the 4th beast rising up out of the sea.

I believe this is the four headed dragon I've dreamt about twice and seen in the clouds heading towards the Midwest in April 2020. "In my vision that night, I, Daniel, saw a great storm churning the surface of a great sea, with strong winds blowing from every direction. Then four huge beasts came up out of the water, each different from the others. The first beast was like a lion with eagles' wings. As I watched, its wings were pulled off, and it was left standing with its two hind feet on the ground, like a human being. And it was given a human mind. Then I saw a second beast, and it looked like a bear. It was rearing upon one side, and it had three ribs [women] in its mouth between its teeth. And I heard a voice saying to it, "Get up! Devour the flesh of many people!" Then the third of these strange beasts appeared, and it looked like a leopard. It had four bird's wings on its back, and it had four heads. Great authority was given to this beast.

Then in my vision that night, I saw a fourth beast – terrifying, dreadful, and very strong. It devoured and crushed its victims with huge iron teeth and trampled their remains beneath its feet. It was different from any of the other beasts, and it had ten horns, suddenly another small horn appeared among them. Three of the first horns were torn out by the roots to make room for it. This little horn had eyes like human eyes and a mouth that was boasting arrogantly. I watched as thrones were put in place and the Ancient One [Aramaic an Ancient of Days – Jesus Christ] sat down to judge. His clothing was as white as snow, his hair like purest wool. He sat on a fiery throne with wheels blazing fire, and a river of fire pouring out, flowing from his presence. Millions of angels ministered to him; many millions stood to attend to him. Then the court began its session, and the books were opened." (Daniel 7:2-10) (17) If you notice, the scripture says that while the fourth beast is coming together, the Ancient of Days takes his throne of judgement and opens the books. As we saw above, the scorpion name has been used for a Roman siege engine, several warships, a type of tank, and a yoga pose with the legs pointing forward over the head, like the animal's tail. It's like a blow to the head or the mind. God is warning me about a coming attack on the people of God.

Now, Brother McGee was saying that back in the 80's that we were in the time of the 4th beast, so then we must surely be closer than we've ever been before to the Second Coming of Christ. Could it be the church has missed it because they are so wrapped up in the world, and so busy stifling the Holy Spirit that they didn't recognize the signs of His coming? "Then he said to me, "This fourth beast is the fourth world power that will rule the earth. It will be different from all the others. It will devour the whole world, trampling and crushing everything in its path. (Daniel 7:23) God keeps saying in His word that He's going to send an army to do His bidding. The 23,000th verse of the Bible tells us that in the last days people will seek out the Jews because God is with them. It's incredible that I found every 1000th verse of the Bible has very special meaning associated with the number 23. Remember, March 23, 2018, was the day I heard the trumpet sound and I saw the Lord coming on the clouds.

"Ten men from all the nations will grasp the garment of a Jew saying, "Let us go with you, for we have heard that God is with you." Zechariah 8:23 "the Lord is our shepherd and I will fear no evil, for You are with me." Psalm 23 and "They shall call His name Immanuel," which translated means "God with Us. Matthew 1:23" The Holy Spirit is telling me that the Lord is with me and coming closer to reveal Himself and my purpose. Verses with like chapter and verse (23:23) Exodus 23:23 "For my angel will go before you." Jeremiah 23:23 "Am I a God who is near," declares the LORD, "And not a God far off?" 1 Samuel 23:23, says "Discover his hiding places, and come back when you are sure. Then I'll go with you. And if he is in the area at all, I'll track him down, even if I have to search every hiding place in Judah!" There are more but hopefully this will cause you to do your own Bible study and meditation of the scriptures. I believe this number 23 has the meaning of "God with us" when you run across the number in scriptures. On September 23, 2017, a great sign appeared in the sky and it was the date the perfect alignment happened and the star was born over Jerusalem.

On the morning of November 5, 2019, Eight horns blew at 12:59 am. I heard the Holy Spirit say, "We are in the 11th hour." I didn't know what it meant, but I had a dream on the previous night three years prior November 4, 2016, where a judge from up high told me, "Double for your trouble." I know it's not a coincidence that the young Pastor just prophesied over me those same words on the night of November 3rd. "Come back to the place of safety, all you prisoners who still have hope! I promise this very day that I will repay two blessings for each of your troubles." (Zechariah 9:12). If you reverse the numbers in this scripture, you will get 12:9 and December 9, 2019, was when the volcano erupted on White Island. Also, the 12th month on the Hebrew calendar is February and it was the evening of February 14-15 that the Lord gave me an extraordinary dream and told me all my dreams were going to come true, and it appears that it is happening just as He told me. I found something else interesting about that dates on which I had the dream, they are found in the scriptures.

"Mordecai recorded these events and sent letters to the Jews near and far, throughout all the provinces of King Xerxes, calling on them to celebrate an annual festival on these two days [Hebrew on the fourteenth and fifteenth days of Adar – February, of the ancient Hebrew lunar calendar]. He told them to celebrate these days with feasting and gladness and by giving gifts of food to each other and presents to the poor. This would commemorate a time when the Jews gained relief from their enemies, when their sorrow was turned into gladness and their mourning into joy. So the Jews accepted Mordecai's proposal and adopted this annual custom." (Esther 9:20-23) This scripture wrecked me and I sat with my face in my hands and wept because this day is also celebrated around the world as Valentines Day. I never liked Valentines Day because I never had a Valentine and yet I always wanted to be love. Its amazing to know that the God of the Universe loves me so much that He not only sent His Son, but He sent His love to not only save me and rescue me, but to completely give my life meaning and purpose. Something else I noticed about the scripture reference was the numbers of the scriptures coincide with the time and season of Rosh Hashanah. On Rosh Hashanah, Jews from all over the world celebrate God's creation of the world. Rosh Hashanah is two days long, and it usually occurs during the month of September. During Rosh Hashanah, Jewish people ask God for forgiveness for the things we've done wrong during the past year. I believe the scripture and the celebration are connected. Rosh Hashanah (Hebrew), literally meaning "head [of] the year", is the Jewish New Year. The biblical name for this holiday is Yom Teruah, literally "day of shouting or blasting". It is the first of the Jewish High Holy Days (Yamim Nora'im).

Now, it totally makes sense why on that beautiful day, February 14, 2018, I saw and heard the bellowing of the crane. The white crane actually flew ahead of me and stood in my path and turns it's head in my direction. This is so deep. Now, I also understand why on the morning of March 23, 2018, I heard the trumpet sound and why the clouds rolled over the land.

The timing of the horns represents faith, grace and God's movement and judgement. Again, I heard the LORD say that "we are in the 11th hour." I prayed this prayer: Jehovah Elohim Tsaba thank you that you are the Lord God of hosts. Thank you that you have made your strength available to me through my relationship with you. I'm grateful to you for each time in my past that you have shown up to right a wrong, or to defend me in a situation where I had been wronged. I have seen your powerful hand in history, and I trust I will continue to see it in the days ahead. Thank you for your presence as I face trials and troubles in my life. In Christ Jesus name I pray, Amen"

This is another prayer on the Bible study app 30 Days Closer to God in the YouVersion Bible app. God orchestrated the timing of all of this. I'm just beside myself. It's been extraordinary how He's leading and guiding and telling me the words I need to hear, read, write, and pray. "In those days, the people of Judah and Israel will return together from exile in the north. They will return to the land I gave your ancestors as an inheritance forever." Jeremiah 3:18 Then, I saw another hand in the clouds and the Holy Spirit lead me to the scripture of Daniel 12:5-7. "Then, I, Daniel, looked and saw two others standing on opposite banks of the river. One of them asked the man dressed in linen, who was now standing above the river, "How long will it be until these shocking events are over?" The man dressed in linen, who was standing above the river, raised both his hands toward heaven and took a solemn oath by the One who lives forever, saying, "It will go on for a time, times, and a half a time. When the shattering [shocking or upsetting time] of the holy people has finally come to an end, all these things will have happened."

I believe this verse has to do with the church as much as it has to do with the holy people or chosen children of the Highest God, because I believe they are one in the same. God has declared He has a "special" people as it is written, "For you are a holy people, who belong to the LORD your God. Of all the people on earth, the LORD your God has chosen you to be his own special treasure. The Lord did not set his heart on you and choose you because you were more numerous than other nations, for you were the smallest of all nations! Rather, it was simply that the LORD loves you, and he was keeping the oath he had sworn to your ancestors. - Deuteronomy 7:6-8" and He went on further to say, "You have been set apart as holy to the LORD your God, and he has chosen you from all the nations of the earth to be his own special treasure. – Deuteronomy 14:2" Thank you Lord! I don't deserve it, but I will honor you with all I have and all that you made me to be.

Israel's name meaning is "who prevails with God." It has more to do with what God has placed inside of you and your bloodline, and nothing at all to do with where you were born. When the Lord gives you dreams, visions, or speaks to you audibly instructing you to give messages to others or gives you a special assignment, like telling me to write this book – it means that God has chosen me and/or you or that person to be a messenger of His Good News! It means that God has chosen me as His special treasure! You, like I can say "I am the one He loves." And if this is coming in loud and clear and you have your spiritual glasses on, and walking in His love and following His commands, you are the one He loves. This would be true for any man or woman of God whom the Lord gives dreams and visions and special messages and assignments.

I believe in this time, the real Jews, not Jewish, but the true children of God and descendants of Abraham are going to be revealed. In the book of Revelations 2:9, Jesus is speaking, "I know about your suffering and your poverty – but you are rich! I know the blasphemy of those opposing you. They say they are Jews, but they are not, because their synagogue belongs to Satan." Also, in Revelations 3:7-9, he says, "Write this letter to the angel of the church of Philadelphia. This is the message from the one who is holy and true, the one who has the key of David. What he opens, no one can close; and what he closes, no one can open (Isaiah 22:22): "I know all the things you do, and I have opened a door for you that no one can close.

You have little strength, yet you obeyed my word and did not deny me. Look, I will force those who belong to Satan's synagogue – those liars who say they are Jews but are not – to come and bow down at your feet. They will acknowledge that you are the ones I love. Because you have obeyed my command to persevere, I will protect you from the great time of testing that will come upon the whole world to test those who belong to this world. I am coming soon [or suddenly or quickly]." The scripture says that He will save His children from the great testing that will come upon the whole world. See, it's God who does the choosing, not the other way around and maybe this is what they fear. People tend to fear things that they don't have any control over and things that they don't understand. But every human on this planet has access to God through His word, the Bible and that's the choice God has given you, free will. He created us for His good pleasure and to worship only Him.

The choice you are given is to believe or not to believe and in choosing, you choose your path. "Also, today the LORD has proclaimed you to be His special people, just as He promised you, that you should keep all His commandments, and that He will set you high above all nations which He has made, in praise, in name, and in honor, and that you may be a holy people to the LORD your God, just as He has spoken. (Deuteronomy 26:18-19) "I will give him the key to the house of David – the highest position in the royal court. When he opens doors, no one will be able to close them; when he closes doors, no one will be able to open them. He will bring honor to his family name, for I will drive him firmly in place like a nail in the wall.

They will give him great responsibility, and he will bring honor to even the lowliest members of the family [Hebrew says: They will hang on him all the glory of his father's house: its offspring and offshoots, all its lesser vessels, from the bowls to all the jars]. But the LORD of Heaven's Armies also says: "The time will come when I will pull out the nail that seemed so firm. It will come out and fall to the ground. Everything it supports will fall with it. I, the LORD, have spoken! (Isaiah 22:22-25) Israel was holy because God declared them to be so. They were holy in the sense of being set apart – not because of any inherent goodness, not because of a certain location, not because they held certain positions in the church or in society, not because they were wealthy, but because of the oath that God swore to their fathers (Deuteronomy 7:7-8). Because of the Word God gave to them. God keeps His promise. I am the living proof.

Therefore, while the Israelite nations at this end time are not holy in their conduct, they are still holy in that God has set them apart to fulfill a purpose and these people are scattered all over the world – not necessarily living in the state called Israel. Notice that Daniel 12:7 does not say that the people are shattered, but that their "power" is shattered. The church has no power in this world at this present time. The churches as a matter of fact, at the time I was reviewing this book for publishing – were closed by government order under the guise of a fake pandemic and have been for 5 months but I digress. If we interpret the holy people to be Israel in general, their power would be representative of their political clout, military ascendancy, financial control, and cultural influence. The church has no power over or clout in any of these areas at present day.

Seeing the hand in the clouds, lead me to a prophetic word about the "hand" which means strength, effectiveness, means, and capabilities of the nations of Israel being completely shattered before the end. The church's overriding focus in times past has been on preaching the gospel of Jesus Christ and the Good News to the entire world, and the power of the church is related to its effectiveness in preaching said gospel. But we read in scripture earlier that Paul claimed to preach the gospel all over the world. Time, specifically thousands of years, was given for us to accept and live by God's laws and statues, more specifically His Word and believe in His Son whom He sent, Jesus Christ, whom Himself was sent and who sent the Holy Spirit so that He could be with us and we would have power. Acts 1:8 says, "But you shall receive power when the Holy Spirit has come upon you; and you shall be witnesses to Me in Jerusalem, and in all Judea and Samaria, and to the end of the earth."

Paul also tells Timothy that Christians have not been given a Spirit of fear but of power, and of love, and of a sound mind in 2 Timothy 1:7. When these two verses are put together, they show that it is the Holy Spirit – the essence of God's mind, and the agency by which the Father and the Son live in the begotten Christian – that is the "power of the holy people" where the church is concerned. Furthermore, the church's power is God Himself, the source of that Spirit. Jesus even tells His disciples that "All power had been given to Him in heaven and on earth. - Matthew 28:18." This is why believing in Jesus Christ is important because it's the only way to receive the Holy Spirit, which is the power of the resurrection of Christ. It's Jesus' spirit in you literally. So, if a person does not believe in Jesus, and the power in His name, then said person will not have access to His Holy Spirit and no communion or relationship with the Lord or the Father God, because they are One; rendering said person hopeless and powerless.

God did empower His servants to preach the gospel in a way that had not been done for 1900 years. When Jesus was here with us in the flesh, He had to touch people in order to transfer His holy spirit to them or speak a word – so even though He could only be in one place at a time – His spoken word also had power when faith was present. When He ascended to Heaven to be with the Father, He sent down His Holy Spirit [Pentecost] and that allowed Him to go and be wherever He is called. "Listen to me, all who hope for deliverance – all who seek the LORD! Consider the rock from which you were cut, the quarry from which you were mined. Yes, think about Abraham, your ancestor, and Sarah, who gave birth to your nation. Abraham was only one man when I called him. But when I blessed him, he became a great nation. The LORD will comfort Israel [Hebrew Zion] again and have pity on her ruins. Her desert will blossom like Eden, her barren wilderness like the garden of the LORD. – Isaiah 51:1-3."

So, to limit the church's power to preach publicly is to limit God Himself, so it would seem to man – for He is involved in far more than merely making a witness to the world before the end. "And the Good News about the Kingdom will be preached throughout the whole world, so that all nations [all peoples] will hear it; and then the end will come." His work is centered on true belief, Jesus told them, "This is the only work God wants from you: Believe in the one he has sent." (John 6:29) Jesus said, one thing is needed – to believe in the One who He has sent! Believing begins with the prodding of the Holy Spirit and ends in the "regenerated" Christian inheriting the Kingdom of God. "I say to myself, "The Lord is my inheritance; therefore, I will hope in him!" (Lamentations 3:24) "What joy for the nation whose God is the Lord, whose people he has chosen as his inheritance." (Psalms 33:12)

This work requires much more than a public witness; it requires the transformation of individuals from sinful humans to spirit-composed members of God's Family. Remember the scripture we just read said to remember "the rock" from which you were cut and "the quarry" from which you were mined – I believe this reference is about our ancestors and to remember their plight. God is a Spirit! A quarry is a place, typically a large, deep pit, or mine from which stone or other materials are or have been extracted i.e. diamonds! I believe this is also a reference to our bloodline and DNA. The Lord is saying to remember that you are precious stones, you are where diamonds come from.

"But the time is coming – indeed it's here now – when true worshippers will worship the Father in spirit and in truth. The Father is looking for those who will worship him that way. For God is Spirit, so those who worship him must worship in spirit and in truth." The woman said, "I know the Messiah is coming – the one who is called Christ. When he comes, he will explain everything to us." Then Jesus told her, "I AM the Messiah! (or "The 'I AM' is here"; or "I am the LORD"; Greek reads "I am, the one speaking to you." See Exodus 3:14). The Lord is speaking to us through His word. The Lord is speaking to us through His creations. The Lord is speaking to us in the heavens! The power of transformation of the human heart can only happen through God and through the agency of the Holy Spirit. If the church's power – Jesus Christ, living in us by His Spirit – were ever "completely shattered," the gates of the grave would prevail against the church, and God's purpose would fail! But we know that cannot be so! Even though it is prophesied that the "holy" set apart peoples of Israel will fall. The Bible says, "For everyone has sinned; we all fall short of God's glorious standard." (Romans 3:23). There's the number 23 again. Jesus has already won the victory because the Holy Spirit is speaking, that means He accomplished what He set out to do on Calvary and that is to defeat death!

"Jesus replied, "You are blessed Simon son of John, because my Father in heaven has revealed this to you. You did not learn this from any human being. "Now I say to you that you are Peter [which means 'rock'], and upon this "rock" I will build my church, and all the powers of hell [Greek and the gates of Hades] will not conquer it. And I will give you the keys of the Kingdom of Heaven. Whatever you forbid [or bind or lock] on earth will be forbidden in heaven, and whatever you permit [loose or open] on earth will be permitted in heaven." Then he sternly warned the disciples not to tell anyone that he was the Messiah. – (Matthew 16:17-20) Notice the scriptures coincide with the years that the Lord has been speaking to me and I've been telling people ever since to get on the holy road. I believe I am the watcher, a prophetess and a messenger of some sort. "You can enter God's Kingdom only through the narrow gate. The highway to hell is broad, and its gate is wide for many who choose that way. But the gateway to life is very narrow and the road is difficult, and only a few ever find it.." (Matthew 7:13-14)

The church of God has not always had an open door to preach the gospel powerfully to the world but I have every confidence that the power of the church under the new covenant will never be shattered – for that power is God Himself! You cannot kill the Holy Spirit! The doors to the church building may close, but those buildings are what Jesus called "the synagogues of Satan." The Bible says, that your body is the Temple of God. You are the church because your body is the Temple of God. He's been showing me open doors and telling me He's opening doors, and I believe the time is drawing near for Him to come, reveal Himself to the world and fulfill His word. In general, the book of Daniel contains prophecies of the world-ruling empires that are mentioned only as they encounter Israel [the holy people].

The "holy people" spoken of in Daniel 12:7 could just as easily represent the scattered tribes and nation of Israel, after all Daniel himself was a slave in Babylonian captivity and Babylonian captivity was the subject of the day on March 23, 2018, and it was what the Lord brought me to in relation to my son, his dreams and our trials. The fact is their "power" being shattered strongly implies that God's power is not under discussion, just the people's power. Maybe, I'm being shown all these signs to communicate that Jesus Christ, through the power of the Holy Spirit, will lead and sustain His church, the chosen people of God through the rough time ahead.

We can, and must, trust God and all that He has spoken through His prophets in the Bible which is the Holy Spirit inspired Word of the Living God. The same God of Abraham, Isaac, and Jacob! This is the reason I chose to read the New Living Translation because God's word is alive! Remember that's also the meaning of the number 18, "Chai" meaning alive. "He gives power to the weak and strength to the powerless." Isaiah 40:29 "With Christ as my witness, I speak with utter truthfulness. My conscience and the Holy Spirit confirm it." Romans 9:1 "But when the Father sends the Advocate as my representative – that is, the Holy Spirit – he will teach you everything and will remind you of everything I have told you." John 14:26 "He is the Holy Spirit, who leads into all truth. The world cannot receive him because it isn't looking for him and doesn't recognize him. But you know him because he lives with you now and later will be in you." John 14:17 See, even this scripture says I know Him because he lives with me, but later will be in me.

I hear the Holy Spirit speaking to me loud and clear. He is telling me that those who belong to this world and are caught up in these government systems and cannot receive the Holy Spirit because they aren't looking for him. They are focused on man and what he is saying and doing which matters not to Yahweh. They are listening to the whispering god. God has been waiting on the church to be the church, but His patience is wearing thin. We have to follow Christ, not man. "But you have received the Holy Spirit [Greek the anointing from him], and he lives within you, so you don't need anyone to teach you what is true. For the Spirit [the anointing] teaches you everything you need to know, and what he teaches is true – it is not a lie. So, just as he taught you, remain in fellowship with Christ." (1 John 2:27)

My prayer: Lord Jesus Christ, today I thank You that the same God Who wrestled with Jacob is wrestling with me. Heavenly Father, today I surrender my will to Yours. Today I am giving You all the glory, all the honor and all the thanksgiving for every blessing, ever received because it all came from You and therefore You deserve the glory. Father today, I trust You that the problem I'm facing is not bigger than the promise you made, and I know that You will keep Your word and bring me victory. So today Father, in Jesus name, I'm not letting go until you bless me. God bless my family, my children, my children's children, my finances, and the works of my hands. Thank You Father God for Your Word, the teachers of your Word and all the blessings Your Word has brought into my life. Thank You for strengthening Your people in these last days and in these times of persecution and thank you for helping us to be bold, courageous, and victorious in this spiritual battle. Your will be done in my life, in the lives of those I pray for today and may we have it here on earth as it is in Heaven. And Father I pray for my enemies that Your will be done in their lives. In Jesus mighty name, Amen.

"So, we have stopped evaluating others from a human point of view. At one time we thought of Christ merely from a human point of view. How differently we know him now! This means that anyone who belongs to Christ has become a new person. The old life is gone; a new life has begun! And all of this is a gift from God, who brought us back to Himself through Christ. And God has given us this task of reconciling people to Him. For God was in Christ, reconciling the world to Himself, no longer counting people's sins against them. And he gave us this wonderful message of reconciliation. So, we are Christ's ambassadors; God is making his appeal through us. We speak for Christ when we plead, "Come back to God!" For God made Christ, who never sinned, to be the offering for our sin, so that we could be made right with God through Christ." (2 Corinthians 5:16-21) "The day is coming when you will see what Daniel the prophet spoke about – the sacrilegious object that causes desecration standing in the Holy Place." (Reader, pay attention!)

"Then those in Judea must flee to the hills. A person out on the deck of a roof must not go down into the house to pack. A person out in the field must not return even to get a coat. How terrible it will be for pregnant women and for nursing mothers in those days. And pray that your flight will not be in winter or on the Sabbath. For there will be greater anguish than at any other time since the world began. And it will never be so great again. In fact, unless that time of calamity is shortened, not a single person will survive. But it will be shortened for the sake of God's chosen ones." "Just as the gathering vultures shows there is a carcass nearby, so these signs indicate that the end is near." (Matthew 24:15-22, 28) It's time to come back to God. Another thing I've been noticing during my walks near the lake, the increase in the number of vultures hovering over the park. Vultures are symbolic of "terror, clothed in black."

On the morning of November 7, the Lord woke me up at 4:44 am. This isn't the first time I've been awakened at this time. Thinking back, I was 44 years old when the angel of the Lord touched me and told me to wake up. I'm beginning to think that it was either the spirit of Daniel or Jeremiah, I can't be sure. In looking at the clock, it seemed to have stopped on this time, I felt like I stared at it for way more than a minute, like time had stopped long enough for me to focus in on it. So I stayed up and did some research. According to Gematria, the number 444 means the Coming Messiah. This number also lead me to some interesting facts about the Messiah Jesus and that is that He started His ministry on September 10 or 11, 26 A.D. My dad was born on September 10. I then thought about the 9/11 attacks, seems they were indeed the start of a holy war and an attack against the faith. This is when I believe the shattering took place or as I called it earlier, the signs of his second coming and the fall of America.

Chapter 9: Roots the Next Generation

"The Spirit of the Lord is upon me, for he has anointed me to bring Good News to the poor. He has sent me to proclaim that captives will be released, that the blind will see, that the oppressed will be set free, and that the time of the Lord's favor has come (and to proclaim the acceptable year of the Lord)." Luke 4:16-21

I continued to wake up to the numbers 4:44 on the clock. I searched the scriptures and found the following. "This is the body of instruction that Moses presented to the Israelites." Deuteronomy 4:44 "So he continued to travel around, preaching in synagogues throughout Judea." Luke 4:44 "He himself said that a prophet is not honored in his own hometown." John 4:44 "You are my King and my God. You command victories for Israel." Psalms 44:4 "They will thrive like watered grass, like willows on a riverbank." Isaiah 44:4 "Then the man brought me through the north gateway to the front of the Temple. I looked and saw that the glory of the Lord filled the Temple of the Lord, and I fell face down on the ground." Ezekiel 44:4 "And when they gave it to the people, there was plenty for all and some left over, just as the Lord had promised." 2 Kings 4:44 "Again and again I sent my servants, the prophets, to plead with them, 'Don't do these horrible things that I hate so much.'" Jeremiah 44:4. It's important to keep in mind that the number (4) four represents the physical creation, because Jesus was the Messiah! So, three fours must represent the Father, the Son and the Holy Spirit being represented in the natural, and Jesus did that!

Something else I found interesting about the number 444, "according to the book 'The Appointed Times of Jesus the Messiah' (page 213), "there seems to exist an interesting relationship between the number 444 and Christ's ministry. Jesus' ministry began in the fall of 26 A.D." Oddly enough, my mother passed away on the 26th day of the month of June. "In Jesus' first public address, he links ministry and message to the start of the Jubilee year", and that too caught my eye and I thought it was funny because 2020 it is my Jubilee year. "When he came to the village of Nazareth, his boyhood home, he went as usual to the synagogue on the Sabbath and stood up to read the Scriptures. The scroll of Isaiah the prophet was handed to him. He unrolled the scroll and found the place where this was written:

Isaiah 61:1-2 and it says, "The Spirt of the Sovereign Lord is upon me, for the Lord has anointed me to bring good news to the poor. He has sent me to comfort the brokenhearted and to proclaim that captives will be released, and prisoners will be freed [the Greek version reads, and the blind will see]." The blind seeing is a reference to the word becoming crystal clear. This special period of liberty and freedom began every 50th year on the Day of Atonement, which is the 10th day of Tishrei, (September 10, August 21 on the Hebrew calendar) read Leviticus 25. Christ's linkage suggests that his ministry, like the Jubilee, also started on this holy day." I will be 50 years old in 2020, and this is my Jubilee year! It's also a leap year and the Year of the Lord! Additionally, the Day of Atonement in 26 A.D. My mother went to be with the Lord on June 26. On the Hebrew calculated calendar (used to determine God's annual Feast Days) it was Wednesday, Tishri 10 (September 10) in the Hebrew year 3787. That's God perfect number, three 7's and that year was 1752, by the way I was 17 years old in 87. I was 25 when my mother was taken and 28 when my father and grandfather were taken from me. I keep hearing that my father was like King David. My father was the first-born son with many brothers, and he shared his father's name making him the Second and he was born on September 10, 1947, year of the 4, 7's. However, it was the "black sheep" of the family. Though he was smart and kind and loving, He was treated as such. I know he experienced a lot, especially going to Vietnam twice. He was 50 when he passed away of unknown causes. I also heard from my uncle that the government gave him a lot of money right before, but I don't have all the details; however, I suspect it had something to do with his death.

The book went on to say, "If Christ's ministry began on this day, it means it lasted 44 months (Hebrew years 3787 and 3789 had 13 months in them) and 4 days (444) until his crucifixion on Passover in 3790 (30 A.D.)" So, the Lord kept giving me 1993. If these numbers are correct, that means that it has been 1993 years since Jesus' crucifixion and corresponds with the visions and dreams He's given to me and appear to be a preview of what is to come. The Second Coming of Jesus is surely closer than ever before; however I believe that the Lord was back the moment He sent His Holy Spirit. And we must remember that God's timing is not our timing. It seems we are now living within the last seven years of the Gentile (Unbelievers) Age and we were in the half time as of March 23, 2018. Let us however remember what the scriptures say, “But you must not forget this one thing, dear friends: A day is like a thousand years to the Lord, and a thousand years is like a day,” 2 Peter 3:8. It’s because Jesus steps in and out of time as Maya said in her beautiful poem. God’s timing is His timing. Time is nothing to God and everything to us.

So, it makes sense to me that we are drawing closer to this great time of testing and trouble that the scriptures speak about because it’s the great and terrible day of the Lord! I understand why it’s both great and terrible. It’s great because Jesus lives! It’s terrible because a lot of evil is going to be revealed, deep hurts as well as many will perish in their ignorance and wickedness. It will thrust us right into the Kingdom Age because its clear to me that the Church Age, the time of sin and rebellion, has ended. When I was telling my circle that we were living in the Book of Revelation, people were giving me crazy looks! At this point, I’m not even trying to convince anybody anymore. God has spoken and there have been times when He has flat out told me, have nothing to do with them! “Them” being people who practice evil. Listen, these are not just words, God is speaking! I’m determined to do what the Lord is instructing me to do and that is to write it down and tell of the Good News of His coming. “Write down what you have seen – both the things that are now happening and the things that will happen,” Revelation 1:19.

“At that time Michael, the archangel who stands guard over your nation, will arise. Then there will be a time of anguish greater than any since nations first came into existence. But at that time every one of your people whose name is written in the book will be rescued. Daniel 12:1” See, after I was attacked by the demon, the Lord gave me the scripture where he told me that Michael the arc angel is with me and that He had to go with Jesus and fight the King of Persia. He awoke me in the wee hours of the morning, it was dramatic but afterwards, I felt safe and I wasn’t afraid anymore. God told me through a female minister in the very beginning, after I had the dream with the octopus, not to be afraid because He was going to be with me. That afterall, was what I saw in the sky with the stars, I saw the Father, the Son and the Holy Spirit, as One in the second Heaven. Through this woman of God, He said he had something important for me to do and she said she saw me crossing oceans and seas, but she told me twice not to be afraid. I knew it was the Lord speaking through her.

After spending all morning praying and be engrossed in the scriptures, I decided to clean my room. I had the 700 Club playing in the background as I cleaned, and Pat Roberson and Terry Meeuwsen were praying for the audience when I heard Terry say, “Somebody watching is under a strong demonic attack, raise your hands above your head, we are going to pray for you.” I stopped what I was doing immediately, turned towards the television, lifted both my hands to the sky and I received and agreed with the prayer for my life. That was a confirmation for me because this was now the third time I was hearing about a demonic attack. All this time, I was the one under the demonic attack. I felt an instant calm in my home. Soon after the prayer and apparent breakthrough - spiders started coming out from their hiding places and we were killing them. We were being bitten and attacked by things we couldn’t see, invisible enemies so to speak just like I said when I awoke with the burns. So, when the spiders started coming out in the open – that was very telling. I believe these are the spiders I saw in another dream, because the spiders represent these kings of this world. This is all symbolic of what's to come in 2020.

I realized at this moment that the dream I had of the eagle came true on November 3, 2019, at the believer's night service. Remember I said the eagle in my dream was crying and flew to the top of a mansion, well that church had a steeple and looked like a castle and the Pastor was moving all around, sort of flapping his arms, opening his mouth wide and making facial expressions like a bird. "Then I looked, and I heard a single eagle crying loudly as it flew through the air, "Terror, terror, terror to all who belong to this world because of what will happen when the last three angels blow their trumpets. Revelation 8:13" The scripture says terror to all who belong to this world. Remember that the number 8 represents a new beginning, the Lord Jesus, resurrection, regeneration, and abundance with no lack. "Now, dear brothers and sister, let us clarify some things about the coming of our Lord Jesus Christ and how we will be gathered to meet him. Don't be easily shaken or alarmed by those who say that the day of the Lord has already begun. Don't believe them, even if they claim to have had a spiritual vision, a revelation, or a letter supposedly from us.

Don't be fooled by what they say. For that day will not come until there is a great rebellion against God and the man of lawlessness [man of sin] is revealed – the one who brings destruction. He will exalt himself and defy everything that people call god and every object of worship. He will even sit in the temple of God, claiming that he himself is God. Don't you remember that I told you about all of this when I was with you? And you know what is holding him back, for he can be revealed only when his time comes. For this lawlessness is already at work secretly, and it will remain secret until the one who is holding it back steps out of the way. Then the man of lawlessness will be revealed, but the Lord Jesus will slay him with the breath of his mouth and destroy him by the splendor of his coming. This man will come to do the work of Satan with counterfeit power and signs and miracles. He will use every kind of evil deception to fool those on their way to destruction, because they refuse to love and accept the truth that would save them. So God will cause them to be greatly deceived, and they will believe these lies. Then they will be condemned for enjoying evil rather than believing the truth." (2 Thessalonians 2:1-12) (6)

Regeneration keeps coming up and so I looked up the definition. Regeneration is the action of process of regenerating or being regenerated, the formation of new animal or plant tissue. In biology, regeneration is the process of renewal, restoration, and growth that makes genomes, cells, organisms, and ecosystems resilient to natural fluctuations or events that cause disturbance or damage. Wow, that's a lot. I see the positive and the negative, but here is the good news - ***Every species is capable of regeneration, from bacteria to humans.*** This means that you don't have to stay the way you are, there is hope for transformation. Wow! This is why we don't need people testing our cells and poking and prodding us like cattle trying to figure out how our bodies work because God is in control. He said he was doing a new thing and it had already begun. This took me back to 'Roots, the Next Generation' in earlier chapters and now regeneration has come up again with the number 8. It's all relevant. The Holy Spirit is the water that holds memory.

"He testifies about what he has seen and heard, but how few believe what he tells them? Anyone who accepts his testimony can affirm that God is true. For he is sent by God.

He speaks God's words, for God gives him the Spirit without limit. The Father loves his Son and has put everything into his hands. And anyone who believes in God's Son has eternal life. Anyone who doesn't obey the Son will never experience eternal life but remains under God's angry judgement." (John 3:27-30, 32-36) It seems to be some sort of attack coming that we won't be able to see with our natural eyes, an invisible enemy. "My heart, my heart – I writhe in pain! My heart pounds within me! I cannot be still. For I have heard the blast of enemy trumpets and the roar of their battle cries. Waves of destruction roll over the land, until it lies in complete desolation. Suddenly my tents are destroyed; in a moment, my shelters are crushed. How long must I see the battle flags and hear the trumpets of war?

"My people are foolish and do not know me," says the LORD. "They are stupid children who have no understanding. They are clever enough at doing wrong, but they have no idea how to do right! I looked at the earth, and it was empty and formless. I looked at the heavens, and there was no light. I looked at the mountains and hills, and they trembled and shook. I looked, and all the people were gone. All the birds of the sky had flown away. I looked, and the fertile fields had become a wilderness. The towns lay in ruins, crushed by the LORD's fierce anger. This is what the LORD says: "The whole land will be ruined, but I will not destroy it completely. The earth will mourn, and the heavens will be draped in black [symbolism for both darkness and skin color] because of my decree against my people. I have made up my mind and will not change it."

At the noise of charioteers and archers, the people flee in terror. They hide in the bushes and run for the mountains. All the towns have been abandoned – not a person remains! What are you doing, you who have been plundered? Why do you dress up in beautiful clothing and put on gold jewelry? Why do you brighten your eyes with mascara? Your primping will do you no good! The allies who were your lovers despise you and seek to kill you. I hear a cry, like that of a woman in labor, the groans of a woman giving birth to her first child. It is beautiful Jerusalem [Hebrew the daughter of Zion] gasping for breath and crying out, "Help! I'm being murdered!" Jeremiah 4:19-31

Chapter 10: The Year of the Supernatural

"You are worthy, O Lord our God, to receive glory and honor and power. For you created all things, and they exist because you created what you pleased." – Revelation 4:11

The year 2019 seemed to be the year of the supernatural for me. I on the Bible bus with my favorite prophet, Dr. J. Vernon McGee's and he was still teaching on the end times. Mind you, these recordings are from the mid to late 80's, he passed away in 1988. He said, "a great deal of prophecy has already been fulfilled in startling, striking and spectacular fashion." Three played their part in the lawlessness and godlessness and that's the Babylonian Empire, Persia and Macedonia under Alexander the Great. He said, "the fourth kingdom of Rome did not die, it just fell apart like a piece of bad fruit." That Rome was full of abnormal sexual sin, corruption, violence, and murder – sound familiar? In speaking of the end times, Brother McGee spoke of captains and kings departing and then a great Stone, cut out without human hands coming and putting down Satan's reign here on the earth. He was speaking of King Jesus and the resurrection power of the Holy Spirit, and Jesus was the Holy Spirit, the Holy One.

He had me thinking about what's going on in the world today. He was talking about a man being a political anti-Christ. He said the church exits the world (or comes out of the world), remember we talked about the shattering of the holy people as it speaks of in Daniel, this where they meet the Lord through the Holy Spirit [in the air] and then Jacob's trouble tribulation period is to come. He talked about a power overall, speaking great words against the Most High, changing customs and laws, bringing grief to the saints – a blasphemer, someone who doesn't believe in Jesus/Yeshua – coming against the tabernacle (and against Christ). He talked about 2 beasts (the government and antichrist) against Christ, a false prophet, and a wolf in sheep's clothing wearing out the saints. This brings about judgement (The Great White Throne Judgement) where the Ancient One shall sit and take away his dominion, and the judgement will be determined by the one on the central (middle) throne and the Lamb – the beast must be put down – followed by the return of Christ.

If you look at the world with your spiritual glasses on, you can clearly see we have arrived in the end times and the spirit of the antichrist all in the details and the spirit behind the beast which is the government. I believe when Mr. John Lewis was laid to rest as I mentioned in Chapter 6 and 7 of this book, the rainbows that were seen over his casket along with the earth shaking me out of my sleep and the dream of God walking on the earth, because it was a prophetic fulfillment of scripture. I knew when I saw that special star in the night sky next to the morning star, the Lord placed as a sign for me.

Worship in Heaven. "Then as I looked, I saw a door standing open in heaven, and the same voice I had heard before spoke to me like a trumpet blast. The voice said, "Come up here, and I will show you what must happen after this." And instantly I was in the Spirit, [on in spirit] and I saw a throne in heaven and someone sitting on it. The one sitting on the throne was as brilliant as gemstones [remember the quarry]– like jasper and carnelian [red, yellow, and brown stones]. And the glow of an emerald [precious jewel, daughter] circled his throne like a rainbow. Twenty-four thrones surrounded him, and twenty-four elders sat on them. They were all clothed in white [holiness and righteousness] and had gold crowns on their heads [grey hair from wisdom]. (4.5) From the throne came flashes of lightning and the rumble of thunder. And in front of the throne were seven torches with burning flames. This is the sevenfold Spirit [Greek They are the seven spirits] of God. (4.6) In front of the throne was a shiny sea of glass [pearls of love, life, and flow], sparkling like crystal [meaning, clarity, a protective stone, Abalone shell – one of solace, cycle of life]. (Six earthquakes on July 30, 2020, first at 4:29 a.m. – the physical creation, rise and shine).

In the center and around the throne were four living beings, each covered with eyes, front and back. The first of these living beings was like a lion [Zion]; the second was like an ox [The Father]; the third had a human face [The Son]; and the fourth was like an eagle (Holy Spirit) in flight. Each of these living begins had six wings, and their wings were covered all over with eyes, inside and out. Day after day and night after night they keep on saying, "Holy, holy, holy is the LORD God, the Almighty – the one who always was, who is, and who is still to come." Whenever the living beings give glory and honor and thanks to the one sitting on the throne [the one who lives forever and ever], the twenty-four elders fall down and worship the one sitting on the throne [the one who lives forever and ever – the LORD Yahweh]. And they lay their crowns before the throne and say, "You are worthy, O

Lord our God, to receive glory and honor and power. For you created all things, and they exist because you created what you pleased." Revelation 4:1-11 (The four living beings.) Mind blowing.

I am now for certain that God told me to write this book and it will play a key role in bringing Satan's rule to an end. And why am I so confident? Because the bible has a lot to say about what happens when you tell the truth. "An honest witness tells the truth; a false witness tells lies – Proverbs 12:17" "The Lord detests lying lips, but he delights in those who tell the truth. – Proverbs 12:22" "I tell you the truth, anyone who believes has eternal life. – John 6:47" "Jesus replied, "I tell you the truth, everyone who sins is a slave to sin. – John 8:34" "Jesus answered, "I tell you the truth, before Abraham was even born, I Am! – John 8:58" Jesus said, "I tell you the truth, I am the gate for the sheep. – John 10:7" Then in the book of Matthew Chapter 5, the Lord speaks about not swearing by heaven but letting your yes be yes, and your no be no. "Just say a simple, 'Yes, I will' or 'No, I won't.' Anything beyond this is from the evil one. – Verse 37.

Revelation 20 speaks of the time of the Gentiles (unbelievers) and isn't it something that the year 2020 is coming up and it has been proclaimed as the year of the Lord! It seems no one is thinking about eternity in this world, it's about the right here and right now. It's all about the money, seeking pleasure and being famous for nothing. However, the supernatural is taking place all around us and all over the world. C.S. Lewis believed that a vigorous supernaturalism was essential to understanding Christianity. Central to Lewis's supernaturalism was an unapologetic belief in heaven and hell. He believes, as do I, that without a supernatural world, especially heaven and hell, there is much about our lives, this human experience, and Christianity that just doesn't fit. It's like there are missing pieces, sort of like a puzzle of missing or scattered pieces or people.

C.S. was a scholar of medieval times, in which the entire culture lived and breathed the daily consequences of believing in the reality of heaven and hell. Lewis was equipped to see the far-ranging change and destructive consequences of the world moving into the modern era, just like Mr. Lewis who recently passed and its exactly what I've been seeing since 2011. Think about it. We begin our education at age five or six and attend school six hours a day, five days a week, nine months a year, until we are eighteen, twenty-two, or older and what are we learning? Certainly not about the things that truly matter like the Creator of the heavens and everything in it. God was taken out of everything. Sadly, some people have gone to school all of their lives and they are no closer to knowing the truth than when they first began.

We learn about physics, biology, math, chemistry; in short, we study the physical side of life. However, this is what actually aided America in its downfall because the current educational system has been polluted with science and false histories. For many sincere Christian believers, it is not that "matter is all there is"; it is "matter is all that matters." Seems our world is about to change drastically though. People think the world is coming to an end, but I already know that God said He would not destroy His creation for the wickedness of man, and He has already come in fire. "The Lord observed the extent of human wickedness on the earth, and he saw that everything they thought or imagined was consistently and totally evil. So, the Lord was sorry he had ever made them and put them on the earth. It broke his heart. And the Lord said, “I will wipe this human race I have created from the face of the earth. Yes, and I will destroy every living thing – all the people, the large animals, the small animals that scurry along the ground, and even the birds of the sky. I am sorry I ever made them.” But Noah found favor with the Lord. – Genesis 6:5-8” Hallelujah for Noah finding favor with the Lord!

You see that, it says, “BUT Noah found favor with the Lord.” This scripture allows us to see what it was like in the days of Noah and exactly what the Lord was warning us about in Matthew 24, and what the times would look like at the end of the Gentile age. It seems somehow, I have found favor with the Lord. Thank you, Jesus! Hallelujah! So, this means that God is not going to destroy His creations or flood the earth again like he did in Noah’s time. There is much symbolism in Jesus coming in fire. Fire burns but it also cleanses. Fire is the rapid oxidation of a material in the exothermic chemical process of combustion, releasing heat, light, and various reaction products. Fire is hot because the conversion of the weak double bond in molecular oxygen, O_2, to the stronger bonds in the combustion produces carbon dioxide and water releases energy, the bond energies of the fuel play only a minor role here.

At a certain point in the combustion reaction, called the ignition point, flames are produced. The flame is the visible portion of the fire. Flames consist primarily of carbon dioxide, water vapor, oxygen, and nitrogen. If hot enough, the gases may become ionized to produce plasma (blood). Depending on the substances alight, and any impurities outside, the color of the flame and the fire's intensity will be different (nations, tribes, and tongues). “To the Israelites at the foot of the mountain, the glory of the Lord appeared at the summit like a consuming fire.” (Exodus 24:17) “I, the Lord of Heaven’s Armies, will act for you with thunder and earthquake and great noise, with whirlwind and storm and consuming fire.” (Isaiah 29:6) “So now I will pour out my fury on them, consuming them with the fire of my anger. I will heap on their heads the full penalty for all their sins. I, the Sovereign Lord, have spoken!” “The Lord will consume Assyria’s (Arabs) like a fire consumes a forest in a fruitful land; it will waste away like sick people in a plague.” (Joel 1:19) Plague and poison and war seems to be the recurring theme of the messages. Also, repentance and living holy and righteous for the Lord.

“When the Son of Man returns, it will be like it was in Noah’s day. In those days before the flood [the outpouring – Holy Spirit] the people were enjoying banquets and parties and weddings right up to the time Noah entered his boat. People didn’t realize what was going to happen until the flood came and swept them all away. That is the way it will be when the Son of Man comes.” (Matthew 23:37-39) I kept saying in 2019 that it’s been 39 years that we’ve been in this forest, hard to see the trees. This will be a world as we’ve never seen it before, all things new. People aren’t thinking about eternity, heaven or hell, but truly it’s the most important thing, especially considering that the Lord said we could pray for it to be as it is in heaven, here on the earth – speaking of matter, it should matter a great deal. I was blind, but now I see! It’s time for the blinders to come off, and the great awakening to happen.

Jesus Heals a Blind Man “When they arrived at Bethsaida, some people brought a blind man to Jesus, and they begged him to touch the man and heal him. Jesus took the blind man by the hand and led him out of the village. Then, spitting on the man's eyes, he laid his hands on him and asked, "Can you see anything now?" The man looked around. "Yes," he said, "I see people, but I can't see them very clearly. They look like trees walking around." Then Jesus placed his hands on the man's eyes again, and his eyes were opened. His sigh was completely restored, and he could see everything clearly. Jesus sent him away, saying, "Don't go back into the village on your way home." (Mark 8:22-26) Jesus gave the man spiritual sight first, a glimpse into the future. He said he saw people, they looked like trees walking around. **A Lampstand and Two Olive Trees** "Then the angel who had been talking with me returned and woke me, as though I had been asleep. "What do you see now?" he asked. I answered, "I see a solid gold lampstand with a bowl of oil on top of it. Around the bowl are seven lamps, each having seven spouts with wicks. And I see two olive trees, one on each side of the bowl." Then I asked the angel, "What are these, my lord? What do they mean?" "Don't you know?" the angel asked. "No, my lord," I replied.

Then he said to me, "This is what the Lord says to Zerubbabel: It is not by force nor by strength, but my Spirit, says the Lord of Heaven's Armies. Nothing, not even a mighty mountain, will stand in Zerubbabel's way; it will become a level plain before him! And when Zerubbabel sets the final stone of the Temple in place, the people will shout: 'May God bless it! May God bless it!' ['Grace, grace to it.']" Then another message came to me from the Lord: "Zerubbabel is the one who laid the foundation of this Temple, and he will complete it. Then you will know that the Lord of Heaven's Armies has sent me. Do not despise these small beginnings, for the Lord rejoices to see the work begin, to see the plumb line in Zerubbabel's hand." (The seven lamps or the seven facets – Hebrew reads These seven.] represent the eyes of the Lord that search all around the world.) Then I asked the angel, "What are these two olive trees on each side of the lampstand, and what are the two olive branches that pour out golden oil through two gold tubes?" "Don't you know?" he asked. "No, my lord," I replied. Then he said to me, "They represent the two anointed ones [or two heavenly beings; Hebrew reads two sons of fresh oil] who stand in the court of the Lord of all the earth." Zechariah 4:1-14 Wow! I believe this is what the blind man saw when Jesus first touched his eyes. I also believe this whole story is symbolism for the time ahead because Jesus did something before He touched the blind man, He spit in the dirt. I believe when Jesus spit in the dirt, He removed the curse from the ground, because He was the Holy One. Think about it, how could the "holy" people be shattered if there not holy to begin with. What made them holy? The Holy Spirit! Think about that old song the saints used to sing, "What can wash you white as snow, nothing but the blood of Jesus." When Jesus came the first time, it was preparation for this time, the end times. Him spitting has a lot of to do with the importance of DNA and the bloodline, but I digress. There is more to this scripture, but it will be covered at a later time.

God kept telling me something was going to happen on 9/11 but I was looking at our calendar when I should have been looking at the Hebrew calendar because it's God's calendar. This month is 9/11, understand? I'll explain it this way, November is the 9th month on the Hebrew calendar which would make this 9/11. However, on said same calendar the actual date of 9/11 is October 29 on the 2020 calendar and October 29 is the date the Israelites were set free from Babylonian captivity in 539 B.C. The end could not come until the 70th Anniversary of Israel and as I mentioned in an earlier chapter, that took place on May 14, 2018. He came to me the week of March 17-25, 2018. I'm sure the time of testing is drawing near and actually, I feel it has already begun. We have been being tested since before Obama ran for office. We are about to enter the New Age, the Kingdom Age where the Lord will come and establish His Kingdom in the mist of the Tribulation and right here on the earth. I think the world is coming to an end as we known it to be.

I found out that Jesus Ministry lasted 44 months and it was also a leap year. I believe on August 9, 2019, the Father God said, "No more delay." "The Romans fill the world and the world has become a dreary prison and it's becoming fatal to resist and impossible to fly" as Gibeon said. The promise of Abraham to his many descendants and it must also happen before the end comes. The state of prophecy is supposed to change you and make you have an urgency to spread the gospel and spread God's word of hope to the world. The hope that salvation is available today. I've had this urgency from the moment God began speaking to me in 2018, but it's been a beast of a time getting people to listen and believe. Afterall, I'm very aware that my only responsibility is to write and that's planting the seed in the atmosphere and in the earth – and I'm for certain now the Holy Spirit will do the watering.

In studying the Hebrew calendar, it gave me a lot of insight about days, months, years and Jewish holiday, and their times and meanings. This is where I saw this language of "Second beginning" referenced for the first time. The Hebrew calendar has two first months, Nisan (March/April) and Tishrei (September/October). So, the calendar begins in March/April and begins again (second beginning) with a new year in September/October. Apparently, September is not only the 7th month on the Hebrew calendar but the beginning of something new. God told me more than once, He's doing a new thing. "This is what the LORD says – your Redeemer, the Holy One of Israel: "For your sakes I will send an army against Babylon, forcing the Babylonians to flee in those ships they are so proud of. I am the LORD, your Holy One, Israel's Creator and King. I am the LORD, who opened a way through the waters, making a dry path through the sea. I called forth the mighty army of Egypt with all its chariots and horses. I drew them beneath the waves, and they drowned, their lives snuffed out like a smoldering candlewick [symbolism of the latter rain, the Holy Spirit and the oil and fire for the Menorah].

"But forget all that – it is nothing compared to what I am going to do. For I am about to do something new. See, I have already begun! Do you not see it? I will make a pathway through the wilderness. I will create rivers in the dry wasteland. The wild animals in the fields will thank me, the jackals, and owls, too, for giving them water in the desert. Yes, I will make rivers in the dry wasteland so my chosen people can be refreshed. I have made Israel for myself, and they will someday honor me before the world." Isaiah 43:14-21" All while the Holy Spirit was showing me these visions and clues, there were lots of Jewish holidays going on. Jesus was a Hebrew and a Jew, and he honored the law and participated in the Jewish festivals and celebrations. He was not a blasphemer, unlike the religious leaders and the pharisees back then and today!

I was hearing God tell me to go back to the beginning and so I started spending my study time in Genesis. "In the beginning God created the heavens and the earth. The earth was formless and empty, and darkness covered the deep waters. And the Spirit of God was hovering over the surface of the waters. Then God said, "Let there be light," and there was light. And God saw that the light was good. Then he separated the light from the darkness. God called the light "day" and the darkness "night." And evening passed and morning came, marking the first day. Then God said, "Let there be a space between the waters, to separate the waters of the heavens from the waters of the earth." Genesis 1:1-6 (1-God 5-Grace 6-Creation of Man) God was bringing me out of the darkness into the light, and He was not only separating me, but he was setting me apart from the world so I can shine for Him and become His new creation. "Those who are wise will shine as bright as the sky, and those who lead many to righteousness will shine like the stars forever." Daniel 12:3

The Holy Spirit is the water, giving me life and speaking into my life and giving me guidance, wisdom, knowledge, and revelation because the water was there at the beginning. The scripture says that God was hovering over and then He separated the waters. He bent down from heaven and turned on my light. The Holy Spirit (water) spoke to me very clearly. He began calling me. "But if we are living in the light, as God is in the light, then we have fellowship with each other, and the blood of Jesus, his Son, cleanses us from all sin." (1 John 1:7) It's the blood of Jesus that cleanses you, it's a spiritual cleansing. This is going to be a spiritual awakening. I'm thinking, who will believe me? "After Jesus rose from the dead early on Sunday morning, the first person who saw him was Mary Magdalene, the woman from whom he had cast out seven demons. She went to the disciples, who were grieving and weeping, and told them what had happened. But when she told them that Jesus was alive and she had seen him, they didn't believe her.

Afterward he appeared in a different form to two of his followers who were walking from Jerusalem into the country. They rushed back to tell the others, but no one believed them. Still later he appeared to the eleven disciples as they were eating together. He rebuked them for their stubborn unbelief because they refused to believe those who had seen him after he had been raised from the dead [Some early manuscripts add: And they excused themselves, saying "This age of lawlessness and unbelief is under Satan, who does not permit God's truth and power to conquer the evil [unclean] spirits. Therefore, reveal your justice now." This is what they said to Christ. And Christ replied to them, "The period of years of Satan's power has been fulfilled, but other dreadful things will happen soon. And I was handed over to death for those who have sinned, so that they may return to the truth and sin no more, and so they may inherit the spiritual, incorruptible and righteous glory in heaven." And then he told them, "Go into all the world and preach the Good News to everyone. Anyone who believes and is baptized will be saved. But anyone who refuses to believe will be condemned. These miraculous signs will accompany those who believe: They will cast out demons in my name, and they will speak in new languages [or new tongues]. They will be able to handle snakes with safety, and if they drink anything poisonous, it won't hurt them. They will be able to place their hands on the sick, and they will be healed." When the Lord Jesus had finished talking with them, he was taken up into heaven and sat down in the place of honor at God's right hand. And the disciples went everywhere and preached, and the Lord worked through them, confirming what they said by many miraculous signs." (Mark 16:9-19) I believe this too is symbolism for what will take place in the end times because the Bible warns that it will be like the days of Noah, and something else that was happening at that the time when Jesus came was people were filled with demons and asking to be set free. Remember in Genesis 6, the Bible talks about the sons of God [fallen angels] having sex with the daughters because Satan was trying to pollute the bloodline and stop the birth of the pure One who was to come, but the Holy Spirit foiled that plan.

All of these things happened in the New Testament as described in the Acts of Apostles and so everything Jesus said came true. And that's how we know the Word of God as it is written in the Bible is true because it has already happened. The number 16 represents being perfected in God's love, 9 is God's movement and judgement and 19 is a new season or cycle of time. Pondering on the significant supernatural things that happened in the year 2018 and the number 18, I continued researching. "The LORD said to my Lord, "Sit in the place of honor at my right hand until I humble your enemies, making them a footstool under your feet." (Psalm 110:1) This scripture is the most quoted or referenced Old Testament passage found in the New Testament referenced "18" times and remember the number 18 represents bondage, slavery and also being alive. (Matthew 22:44, 26:64; Mark 12:36, 14:62, 16:19; Luke 20:42 – 43, 22:69; Acts 2:34 – 35; Romans 8:34; 1 Corinthians 15:25; Ephesians 1:20; Colossians 3:1 and Hebrews 1:3, 13, 8:1, 10:12 – 13, 12:2). I cannot take any credit for this work, I am grateful for to all the saints who came before me and all my sisters and brothers who did the work and were obedient in sharing the word that was given to them by the Holy Spirit.

All these scriptures talk about Jesus being both Messiah and Lord and sitting in the place of honor beside God's throne, not as the son of David – but the Son of Man, a title Jesus gave himself. I believe this title Jesus gave Himself had to do with the very beginning, parts of the bible that we do not have and that's the part when Adam and Eve were kicked out of the garden of Eden. It was in that place that the Lord gave Adam and Eve the plan for redemption, that He Himself would come back as the seed planted in the earth to redeem Adam and all humanity. That's why He is called the second Adam because Adam was the first man, and He is the Son of that first man because His conception was holy, a direct seed placed in Mary's womb by God Himself, the work of the Holy Spirit.

Lastly, in Gematria, the number 18 stands for "life," because the Hebrew letters that spell chai, meaning "living," add up to 18. Because 36 = 2x18, and it represents "two lives." Just like Jesus was the second and final Adam and He lives, He is with me and is the Holy Spirit dwelling among His people. That one life representing two and through the Holy Spirit, many, able to be anywhere and everywhere all at once! Now, that's genius! Go Jesus!

Chapter 11: The Barley Harvest

Here is another story Jesus told: "The Kingdom of Heaven is like a farmer who planted good seed in his field. But that night as the workers slept, his enemy came and planted weeds among the wheat, then slipped away. When the crop began to grow and produce grain, the weeds also grew. "The farmer's workers went to him and said, 'Sir, the field where you planted that good seed is full of weeds! Where did they come from?' "'An enemy has done this!' the farmer exclaimed. "Should we pull out the weeds?' they asked. "'No,' he replied, 'you'll uproot the wheat if you do. Let both grow together until the harvest. Then I will tell the harvesters to sort out the weeds, tie them into bundles, and burn them, and to put the wheat in the barn.'" Matthew 13:24-29

God is warning the believers to come out of the politically correct (extremely wrong) and corrupt government systems and start walking as children of the light so that the world can see your example of holy living and you can escape the coming horrors. When the Lord spoke to me last spring in the park, He had me to notice the weeds. They were growing just as healthy and strong as the wheat and they were nice to look at. As a matter of fact, I couldn't tell the difference between the flowers and the weeds because they looked the same, but weeds wreak havoc in the garden. We should be able to tell the difference between a weed and a flower, and the difference between weeds and wheat. The same goes with believers and non-believers, false prophets, and teachers, as well as wolves and sheep - you should be able to tell them apart – they should be altogether different in every way.

Remember Jesus said this, "So when the apostles were with Jesus, they kept asking him, "Lord, has the time come for you to free Israel and restore our kingdom?" He replied, "The Father alone has the authority to set those dates and times, and they are not for you to know. But you will receive power when the Holy Spirit comes upon you. And you will be my witnesses, telling people about me everywhere – in Jerusalem, throughout Judea, in Samaria, and to the ends of the earth." (Acts of the Apostles 1:7) This is why being on the holy road is important because when you have a relationship with the Lord, you will be able to discern the spirits. You will be able to identify the good fruit. The world has become so cosmetic, it's all about what feels good and what looks good, but God's word says, "Don't judge by his appearance or height, for I have rejected him. The Lord doesn't see things the way you see them. People judge by outward appearance, but the Lord looks at the heart. – 1 Samuel 16:7"

"Come, descendants of Jacob, let us walk in the light of the LORD! For the LORD has rejected his people, the descendants of Jacob, because they have filled their land with practices from the East and with sorcerers [witches, witchcraft, warlocks], as the Philistines do. They have made alliances with pagans. Israel is full of silver and gold, there is no end to its treasures. Their land is full of warhorses; there is no end to its chariots. Their land is full of idols; the people worship things they have made with their own hands. So now they will be humbled, and all will be brought low – do not forgive them. Crawl into caves in the rocks. Hide in the dust from the terror of the LORD and the glory of his majesty. Human pride will be brought down, and human arrogance will be humbled. Only the LORD will be exalted on that day of judgement. For the LORD of Heaven's Armies has a day of reckoning. He will punish the proud and mighty and bring down everything that is exalted. He will cut down the tall cedars of Lebanon and all the mighty oaks of Bashan.

He will destroy all the great trading ships [Hebrew every ship of Tarshish – meaning break or shatter] and every magnificent vessel. Human pride will be humbled, and human arrogance will be brought down. Only the LORD will be exalted on that day of judgement. Idols will completely disappear. When the LORD rises to shake the earth, his enemies will crawl into holes in the ground. They will hide in caves in rocks from the terror of the LORD and the glory of his majesty. On that day of judgment, they will abandon the gold and silver idols they made for themselves to worship. They will leave their gods to the rodents and bats, while they crawl away into caverns and hide among the jagged rocks in the cliffs. They will try to escape the terror of the LORD and the glory of his majesty as he rises to shake the earth. Don't put your trust in mere humans. They are as frail as breath. What good are they?" (Isaiah 2:5-22)

This year, 2019 God set me apart. He called me out of the world. I began to talk different and walk different. I received a lot of criticism, quite surprisingly from fellow believers who not only distanced themselves the more I talked about the Lord, but they complained that I was talking about the Word and the Lord far to much for them. Some even said I was acting "super spiritual" and "holier than thou". I was feeling like Joseph with his brothers, afterall I did decree over myself in 2017, that I was Joseph hidden in plain sight at the urging of the ministers who now know, did not know the season. I could tell that they didn't understand the times we were living in and they did know God saved me from death, hell, and the grave! People judge without knowing your struggle and that's why God said, judge not! I was living to please Him! I wasn't trying to be perfect – it's impossible and I wasn't passing judgement; however now that I had experienced a real saving grace, I was determined to walk in it and not let God down anymore. I just didn't want to abuse grace any longer and grieve my loving God. I saw Him, and I knew He was real. Now, I wasn't trying to get anyone else to do what I was doing, but I certainly didn't want to be a part of something or in a world that God called me out of. I felt compelled to share the Good News and with an urgency.

Those whom I served with in the choir would sometimes make fun of me during rehearsal because I was so deep into the worship. I wasn't concerned with why they came, for some it was "just rehearsal" – but I was always in worship mode. It became clear to me that they we were just there to practice and learn the song to sing on "stage", but that was not the only reason we were there. People had become so distant or "clickish." There was a certain group and if you weren't in it, you didn't get too many opportunities to use your gift and the gifts are for the body. For me it was a part of not forsaking the assembly, an opportunity for iron to sharpen iron and also a time of midweek fellowship with people of like precious faith.

I learned how very important worship is to God and I was serious about it. The church had the choir assessed by a Grammy award winning song writer and music producer. He told me that I could really sing, well he said "sang" and he also told me that he informed the church leadership that "whenever there was an opportunity for a mic to be in my hand – I should have one." He said I was able to be both a praise leader and on the frontline of the praise team. It seems like after that, the chill was real and I couldn't pay somebody to give me the mic and not that I tried or wanted to do something like that, but I did find myself begging to minister and use my gift. I felt alienated. I would be shushed in rehearsal or silenced by some in my group. Some of the members unfriended and blocked me on social media – I was shocked and disappointed.

It would continue, though it's not the first time a music ministry department has treated me indifferent and I never understood it. I would pray for them and leave the choir. Most times I would leave the church. However, this time I wasn't leaving, I decided to join other ministries in order to continue serving the Lord anyway I could. The Lord blessed me with many gifts. I joined cyber church and trained under a wonderful young sister who had worked in that department for many years. She would take the pictures and add captions for social media posts. She was happy I had joined her because she said I was able to capture more of the Word which gave her time to focus on the photography and recordings. When I signed up, it seems like I was only able to train with her for about six months and then the Lord gave her an assignment to move out of the state and she left the ministry under my care.

A year later, without warning or notice, and even though I had been told that I was being a blessing to the church in this area, a member from the main church campus came and sat quietly behind me and another worker to observe our ministry during serve one Sunday. After the service, she advised us that she was going to be taking over the media ministry. I tried not to be offended, but it was disconcerting that no one even considered me for the position, especially considering I had been doing it successfully for more than a year without complaint and blessings from the Pastor's wife. I politely answered all questions and went over all the procedures and continued under that person until the Lord released me from the ministry.

I was offended previously in the outreach ministry as well. I have been walking at the park by the lake for years and talking and praying with the homeless people, because the Lord gave me a heart for these people, after all I too was once homeless. Anyway, there was one Saturday I volunteered to help serve food with the street team for a youth group and because of the rain, the children didn't show up and we were stuck with food for about 50 people. When the director of the outreach ministry asked for suggestions of what to do with the food, I asked if I could take a few plates to my friends who lived in the middle of the park. I called the homeless people my friends. She expressed that she was not aware that there were homeless people living there. This prompted the leader to say that we should look for other homeless people in the area.

We found about three other encampments that day and fed as many people as we could until the food ran out. The coordinator was so excited about it that she decided to make this one of our street team ministries. I was so thankful to God that day because He again answered my prayers. Now, when we got to church that Sunday morning, the coordinator was called up by the Pastor to give a presentation and report to the church about our outreach and she took all the credit. It was about "her" mission and what "she's" always wanted to do, and she went so far as to ask certain members to stand up, but no mention of me. That day, my son could see I wanted to cry. She received all the accolades, and those whom she chose to call to stand up and be acknowledged. She went on and on about how it was "her" goal, and mission and dream and I'm not saying that it wasn't, but we are supposed to give honor to whom honor is due. My son reminded me that God is watching and He sees everything and that God had answered my prayer to help feed the people and I didn't need a "that-a-boy," or pat on the back from man. "But the earth helped her by opening its mouth and swallowing the river that gused out from the mouth of the dragon." (Revelation 12:16) My son was right. But my eyes were beginning to open up to what was happening in the church. I rejoiced that God had answered my prayer and that was the most important thing, that people were getting fed. It wasn't important to be called up to take credit for something God did. "The mouths of fools are their ruin; they trap themselves with their lips." (Proverbs 18:7)

It would have been nice to be included, afterall, we are all humans with feelings and being excluded doesn't feel good, especially when it was your idea and suggestion, but this is exactly why I can't live without Yah. It's exactly why my worship is different. We need the Holy Spirit and we need Jesus because we humans mess things up when we don't get the Creator involved and we try to take the credit for things that the Lord orchestrated. People have lost sight of why we do things. You can do the right thing for the wrong reason. And who is to say that just because something has been done a certain way it can't be improved? Why can't the conversation be had? We should serve so that God gets the glory and not do things to please man. It was beginning to look that way, that people were wanting to be called out and recognized and receive a special word and get the glory, not for God but for themselves. If you didn't get a word, you felt ignored. God has no favorites, although He does have a chosen people and a special treasure – there is a difference.

It's because everyone can't handle everything. Brother Ochieng (meaning born when the sun shines) said, "When we don't talk about it, we get devastated by it. Where people have revelation the gates of hell cannot prevail against it but where we are ignorant, we are vulnerable," and I agree. Just because you choose not to talk about the elephant in the room, doesn't change the fact that the elephant is in the room and it doesn't make the elephant go away – it's still sitting there needing to be dealt with. I was moving different and living by my convictions because I was determined to follow God and I desperately wanted to understand what it was that He was calling me to do. It's something about waking up and everyone else around you is sleeping. People were just going through the motions; they had no connection to the Holy Spirit.

I was never one to take pictures or post when I go out and serve the homeless because if I were homeless, I wouldn't want to be on anyone's camera. As a matter of fact, I've been homeless after my mother died and my son was a young boy, and I was fortunate enough to have people in my life who allowed me to sleep on their couches and in their kid's bunkbeds and not on the street – so I understand and sympathize. I had a dream that there was a blackhole in the back of the church where the choir rehearsed, and choir members were falling in it, one by one. This is significant, because there were so few people serving in the church that most of the members were serving on multiple help's ministries. For example, you were discouraged from serving in more than three ministries at a time, but most people were serving on 4 and 5 because the turnout was so low from people being so "busy" and the people serving, who had a heart for the people, didn't want to disappoint the people or the organizations they committed to serve. People were just inundated with their busy lives and too busy to serve the Lord, and if they did, it was all about them. Not all, but most at that time.

I served in outreach missions, street team, prison ministry, cyber church, convalescent ministry, choir, praise team and from time to time supported their bereavement program. I also attended almost every class and conference, bible study and church service, even the supernatural services on Sunday evenings. I was hungry for the Word of God. Anyway, in the dream I also fell in the black hole trying to pull them out, but one of the elder members, the father of one of the choir members (see the symbolism), reached down his hand and pulled me up and the hole closed behind me. When it was all said and done, the Holy Spirit told me after the last time I ministered on October 20, 2019, that I was going to start the ministry the Lord had planned for me. I didn't know then, but I'm beginning to see now that those things were preparing me for what's to come.

I didn't go and complain to the leadership about what was going on because they seem to be disconnected from their ministry. Sure, they had the quarterly meetings with the help's ministry, but it was all organized and the time was limited so it wasn't a place for you to air your grievances or even suggest things. Also, the Pastors were guarded. Yes, sure I could get in a few minutes here and there but there was no relationship. I tried talking with my brothers and sisters in Christ who were over the ministries I served instead but to no avail. I prayed and asked the Lord what I should do, if I should leave or stay and I received a message telling me that I was released. The man of God's exact words was, "You are on your way to the top! Can't nobody stop you now! You are released!" "Then God said, "Let there be a space between the waters, to separate the waters of the heavens from the waters of the earth." And that is what happened. God made this space to separate the waters of the earth from the waters of the heavens. God called the space "sky." And evening passed and morning came, marking the second day."

The second day is the only day that God didn't label what he had done as being good. On Day 2, God separated the heavens [pure body of water] from the earth [dirty water muddied by the world]. This is symbolism for being born again, living holy and being set apart, and chosen by God. "Don't team up with those who are unbelievers. How can righteousness be a partner with wickedness? How can light live with darkness? (2 Corinthians 6:14) 'A Prophecy from Jesus to All' "Jesus said, "These things are now beginning in the earth, are yet to be, and are soon coming upon all the earth. The fiery serpent is part of the beast. These prophecies you are about to read are true. The revelations are true. Watch and pray. Love one another. Keep yourselves holy. Keep your hands clean. "Husbands love your wives as Christ loved the church. Husbands and wives love each other as I have loved you. I ordained marriage and blessed it with MY Word. Keep the marriage bed holy. Cleanse yourself from all unrighteousness and be pure, even as I am pure. "The holy people of God have been led away by flatterers. Do not be deceived; God is not mocked. Understanding will come to you if you will open your ears and listen to Me. This is the Lord's message to the churches:

Beware of false prophets who stand in My holy place and deceive with flatteries. O earth, my holy people have fallen asleep to the sound of false doctrine. Awake, Awake! I tell you that all unrighteousness is sin. Cleanse yourself from all sin of the flesh and the spirit. My holy prophets lived holy lives, but you have rebelled against Me and My holiness. You have brought evil upon yourself. You have sinned and brought yourself into bondage to sickness and death. You have committed iniquity and have done wickedly and have rebelled against Me. You have departed from My precepts and My judgements. You have not hearkened to the words of My servants, the prophet, and the prophetess. Curses instead of blessings have come upon you, and still you refuse to return to me and repent of your sins."

"If you will return and repent and if you will honor Me with the fruit of righteousness, I will bless your homes and honor your marriage beds. If you will humble yourselves and call upon Me, I will hear you and bless you. "Listen, you ministers of My Holy Word. Do not teach My people to sin against their God. Remember that judgment begins at the House of God; unless you repent, I will remove you for the sins you have taught my people. Do you think that I am blind that I cannot see and deaf that I cannot hear? "You who hold the truth and unrighteousness and line your pockets with silver and gold at the expense of the poor - repent, I say, before it is too late. On the day of judgment, you will stand alone before me to give an account of what you did with My Holy Word. If you call upon Me in repentance, I will remove the curse from your lands and bless you with a mighty blessing. If you will repent and be ashamed of your sins, I will have mercy and compassion on you, and I will not remember your sins anymore. Pray that you may be an overcomer."

"Awake to life and live. Repent to the people you have led astray and taught false doctrine tell them you have sinned and that you have scattered My sheep. Repent to them. Behold, I am preparing a holy army. They will do mighty exploits for me and destroy your high places. They are an army of holy men and women, boys, and girls. They have been anointed to preach the true gospel, to lay hands on the sick and to call the sinner to repentance. This is an army of working men, housewives, single men, single women, and school children. They are common people, for not many noble have responded to my call. In the past they have been misunderstood and abused and rejected. But I have blessed them with boldness and holiness and in Spirit. They will begin to fulfill my prophecy and to do my will. I will walk in them, talk in them and work in them. These are they who have turned to me with all their heart, soul, mind, and strength.

My Army will awaken to righteousness and purity of Spirit. I will soon begin to move upon them, to choose for My army those I desire. I will search for them in the cities and in the towns. Many will be surprised at those I have chosen. You will see them begin to move across the land and do exploits for my namesake. Watch and see my power at work. Again, I tell you do not defile the marriage bed. Do not defile the body in which the Holy Ghost dwells. Sins of the body lead to sins of the spirit. Keep the marriage bed holy. I made man for woman and woman for man and decreed that the two should be united in holy matrimony. Again, I say awake." 'A Divine Revelation of Hell', Chapter 14, pages 137-141. The origin of the word matrimony is a bit more intriguing.

The word matrimony comes from Latin word matrimonium. The root *matr-* means the Latin "mother" and *-mony* means 'the act of becoming". In other words, the act of a woman becoming a mother is the literal definition of matrimony. Another definition is found in the old French term, matrimoignie, which means to lock together or be obligated. This is where we get the phrase "wedlock." In other words, holy matrimony is not just the act of agreeing to be together. Holy matrimony is a sacred act of togetherness, honored by God, and created as a lifelong obligation to one another. In the garden, God did not ask Adam if he would take Eve, God gave Eve to Adam and that was that. Just like God gave messengers and prophets and appointed watchman, He didn't ask for man's permission or help. Religion is man-made just like the government. Like I said in an earlier chapter, the only true religion is no religion. God gave His commandments to Moses and Jesus Christ, thus we have the Ten Commandments and the Bible, our two witnesses. We should follow these instructions.

Kathryn went on to say, "This army," said the Lord, which was spoken of by the Prophet Joel, will arise from the land and do great works for God. The son of righteousness shall arise with healing in his wings. He shall tread down the wicked, and they shall be ashes under the soles of His feet. They shall be called the army of the Lord. I will give gifts unto them, and they will accomplish My mighty works. They shall do exploits for the Lord of glory. I will pour out My Spirit upon all flesh, and your sons and daughters shall prophesy. This army shall fight against the forces of evil and destroy much of Satan's work. They shall win many to Jesus Christ before the day the evil beast arises," said the Lord.

"I ask that your minds may be opened to see his light, so that you will know what is the hope to which He has called you, how rich are the wonderful blessings He promises His people, and how very great is His power at work in us who believe. This power working in us is the same as the mighty strength which He used when He raised Christ from death and seated Him at His right side in the heavenly realms. Christ rules there above all heavenly rulers, authorities, powers, and lords; he has a title superior to all titles of authority in this world and in the next. God put all things under Christ's feet and gave him to the church as supreme Lord over all things. The church is Christ's body, the completion of him who himself completes all things everywhere." Ephesians 1:18-23 GNB

Could it be that the LORD has made His covenant with me? It's beginning to look this way. When the Lord resurrected, He ascended or went up and later at Pentecost, His Holy Spirit descended coming back down. This means that the Lord came back the moment His Spirit was back in the earth. The whole thing with David being able to pick up the Arc of the Covenant was symbolic of the Holy Spirit coming out of a building and being transferred into the body. The Holy Spirit is not contained inside of a building, but inside the body of those that believe because God is a Spirit! "Then God said, "Let the waters beneath the sky flow together into one place, so dry ground may appear." And that is what happened. God called the dry ground "land" [the soil, our hearts] and the waters "seas" [the Holy Spirit]. And God saw that it was good. [This is symbolic of the Holy Spirit and the body becoming one and the dry bones coming alive.]

Then God said, "Let the land sprout vegetation – every sort of seed-bearing plant, and trees that grow seed-bearing fruit. These seeds will then produce the kinds of plants and trees from which they came." And that is what happened. The land produced vegetation – all sorts of seed-bearing plants, and trees with seed-bearing fruit. Their seeds produced plants and trees of the same kind. And God saw that it was good. And evening passed and morning came, marking the third day." (Genesis 1:9-13) These are the trees the blind man saw in the Spirit. Remember how I mentioned earlier the land and sea are symbolism or generalization for a certain or specific group of people.

I believe we are about to be the 3rd Day Saints. I keep seeing trees in the clouds, huge trees with many branches. I believe in August he was telling me that He's calling for the dry bones and dry hearts to wake up because the Holy Spirit was about to pour out! He started me on this journey with an ancient figure from the past touching me on the forehead and telling me to "wake up!" I'm beginning to think it was Jeremiah. He's calling for the prodigal sons and daughters to come home to Him because the year 2020 is His year, it is the year of the Lord and every day of that year is the day of the Lord. "People from many nations will come and say, "Come let us go up to the mountain of the Lord, to the house of Jacob's

God. There he will teach us his ways, and we will walk in his paths." For the LORD's teaching will go out from Zion; his word will go out from Jerusalem." Micah 4:2

I see Him pointing me in the direction of Jerusalem, but how Lord? He told me to write the book first, so that's the plan. He also told me that the people would come to me and seek me out. The bible says the exiles would come from the north. I'm in the west. I think once the book is done, then He will place me on the path and lead me to where I am to go. This scripture tells me that the Kingdom is to be here upon this earth – the new earth is coming down from Heaven. "But in the end, the holy people of the Most High God will be given the kingdom, and they will rule forever and ever." Daniel 7:18 (7 -God's perfect number 18 – Alive and 9 God's judgment and movement)

Journal Notes – November 7 – Obama justifies same sex marriage using the Bible, saying "love is the Golden Rule." This took place in 2015, and on the same day my mother passed away, June 26. This was sacrilegious and against the word of God. I explained in an earlier chapter how the promise of the rainbow was that He (God) would never again flood the earth, which has everything to do with God's love for us and Him keeping His promises. Could this be one of the graven images that was raised up? After all same sex relationships and marriages are forced on the believer through magazines, movies, television, cable channels, in music and huge billboard signs and now in the church! That's apostacy, embracing an opinion that is contrary to one's previous religious beliefs. At the time of this writing, there was a law that they were trying to get passed that would jail anyone who tried to counsel or speak to an individual about the Bible with regards to being attracted to the same sex. "Then he said to the disciples, "Anyone who accepts your message is also accepting me. And anyone who rejects you is rejecting me. And anyone who rejects me is rejecting God, who sent me."

The Lord said to Ms. Baxter on Page 189 of her book, "This vision is for the future, and it will come to pass. But I shall return to redeem My bride, My church, and they shall not see it. Awaken, O My people! Sound the alarm to the corners of the earth, for I shall return as My Word has spoken." I beheld the fiery serpent that was in the right arm of hell. Jesus said, "Come, see what the Spirit is saying to the world." I saw the horns of the fiery serpent as they entered the bodies of people on earth. Many were completely possessed by the serpent. As I watched, I saw a huge beast arise in a large place and turn into a man. The inhabitants of the earth ran from him, some into the wilderness, some into caves, and some into subway stations and bomb shelters. They sought any shelter to hide from the eyes of the beast. No one was praising God or talking about Jesus. A voice said to me "Where are My people?"

I looked closer and saw people like dead men walking. There was a desperate sadness in the air, and no one turned to the right or left. I saw that people were being led about by some unseen force. Now and then a voice spoke to them out of the air and they obeyed the voice. They did not talk to one another. I saw too that the number "666" was written on each one's forehead and on his hands. I saw soldiers on horses herding the people about as though they were cattle. The American flag, tattered and torn, lay forlornly on the ground. There was no joy, no laughter, no happiness. I saw death and evil everywhere. The people walked one behind another into a large department store they kept in step like discouraged soldiers and were dressed identically in a type of prison garb. A fence surrounded the store, and guards were stationed here and there. Everywhere I looked, I saw soldiers in battle-dress uniforms. I saw the zombie like people herded into the store, where they were able to buy only the bare necessities. As each completed his purchases, he was placed aboard a large green army truck. The truck, well-guarded, was then driven to another.

Here, in a type of clinic, these people were examined for communicable diseases or crippling handicaps. A small number of them were shuffled to the side as rejects. Soon, those who failed the examination were taken to another room. In that room, an impressive array of switches, buttons and gauges lined an entire wall. A door opened, and several technicians came in. One of them began to call the names of the people in the room. Without a struggle they arose when their names were called and marched into a large box. When they were inside, another technician closed the door and pull the switch in a panel on the wall. A few minutes later he opened the door, took down a broom and dustpan, and swept what remained of them off the floor. Nothing but a bit of dust was left of what had once been a room full of people! I saw those people who passed the medical exam being put back into the same truck and driven to a train. No one spoke or even turned to look at anyone else. At another building each person was assigned a job. They all went to work without a single dispute. I watched as they worked very hard at their assigned task, and then at the end of the day they were taken to an apartment building with a high fence around it. Each undressed and went to bed. Tomorrow they would work hard again.

Skipping to page 167. "The beast took the angry man into a large room and motioned for him to lie down on a table. The room in the table reminded me of a hospital emergency room. The man was given an anesthesia and wheeled beneath a vast machine. The beast attached wires to the man's head and turned on the machine. On top of the machine were the words "This mind eraser belongs to the beast number, "666." When the man was removed from the table, his eyes had a vacant stare, and his movements reminded one of a zombie in a movie. I saw a large blank spot on the top of his head, and I knew his mind had been surgically altered so he could be controlled by the beast. The beast said, "Now, sir, don't you feel better? Didn't I say I could take care of all your problems? I have given you a new mind. You will have no worries or troubles now. The man did not speak." She goes on to describe the beast downloading audibly his instructions into the man to do evil works.

"This is what the Sovereign Lord says: "Long ago my people chose to live in Egypt. Now they are oppressed by Assyria. What is this?" asks the LORD. "Why are my people enslaved again? Those who rule them shout in exultation. My name is blasphemed all day long. But I will reveal my name to my people, and they will come to know its power. Then at last they will recognize that I am the one who speaks to them." How beautiful on the mountains are the feet of the messenger who brings goods news, the good news of peace and salvation, the news that the God of Israel [Hebrew of Zion] reigns! The watchmen shout and sing with joy, for before their very eyes they see the LORD returning to Jerusalem [Hebrew Zion]. – Isaiah 52:4-8"

"When the seventy-two disciples returned, they joyfully reported to him. "Lord, even the demons obey us when we use your name!" "Yes," he told them, "I saw Satan fall from heaven like lightning! Look, I have given you authority over all the power of the enemy, and you can walk among the snakes and scorpions and crush them. Nothing will injure you. But don't rejoice because evil spirits obey you; rejoice because your names are registered in heaven." (Luke 10:16-20) Remember, they took the Bible and it's teachings out of school, the 10 Commandments off of government buildings and people are frowned upon for saying the name of Jesus or even praying in His name, but they can use His name as a curse word all day long. As a matter of fact, if you speak about sin, let's say the sin of engaging in homosexuality, they say the message is rooted is "harmful homophobic" and dangerous to the people who engage in the sin and their families – basically they call it hate speech.

However, it's actually the other way around. They are committing detestable and sinful acts against God's law and His Word, bringing judgement not only upon themselves but upon an entire nation. It's gotten so out of order that now there's the possibility you could face persecution, prosecution, or jail time for sharing the Word of God and trying to help someone who may be confused about life. I would say that the Holy people's power has been shattered and these laws are the culprit. After all the bible says, "For sin is the sting that results in death, and the law gives sin its power. But thank God! He gives us victory over sin and death through our Lord Jesus Christ. So, dear brothers and sisters, be strong and immovable. Always work enthusiastically for the Lord, for you know that nothing you do for the Lord is ever useless." (1 Corinthians 15:56-58)

I believe that the Lord did indeed visit my sister in Christ because I see her prophecies coming true, playing out live and in living color. I too experienced hell and I believe it was to confirm her story. I've also had dreams and visions of a similar nature. Exodus 19:3-6 says, "Then Moses climbed the mountain to appear before God. The LORD called to him from the mountain and said, "Give these instructions to the family of Jacob; announce it to the descendants of Israel: 'You have seen what I did to the Egyptians. You know how I carried you on eagles' wings and brought you to myself. Now if you will obey me and keep my covenant, you will be my own special treasure from among all the peoples on earth; for all the earth belongs to me. And you will be my kingdom of priests, my holy nation.' This is the message you must give the people of Israel."

This scripture talks about the saints, the Christians - being the nation of Israel (kingdom of priests – holy nation) and the word saints appears 92 times in the Holy Bible. Romans 1:3-7 declares, "the Good News is about his Son. In his earthly life he was born into King David's family line, and he was shown to be [and was designated] the Son of God when he was raised from the dead by the power of the Holy Spirit [or by the Spirit of holiness; or in the new realm of the Spirit]. He is Jesus Christ our Lord. Through Christ, God has given us the privilege [or the grace] and authority as apostles to tell Gentiles [unbelievers] everywhere what God has done for them, so that they will believe and obey him, bringing glory to his name. And you are included among those Gentiles who have been called to belong to Jesus Christ. I am writing to all of you in Rome who are loved by God and are called to be his own holy people." Rome will come alive under the anti-Christ; this is the little horn, blasphemy.

I believe that King #44 played a huge role in end time prophecy by doing several things – some good and some bad. I know a lot of people will not be happy about me saying this, but I'm only speaking the truth about his actions and measuring them under the word of

God. In 2012, when he was elected, he made it his immediate goal to negotiate peace in the Middle East, saying he would not wait until the last year of his presidency like President #43 did. He then appointed a man from Northern Ireland to this assignment and after two years, the guy resigned saying the people didn't want peace. Afterwards, he chose another politician who picked up the task to no avail. Then President #45 was elected in 2016, seeming to be the "hero". However, on December 23, 2016, President #44 pushed through the United Nations, Resolution 2334 which was passed and states "that Israel's settlement activity constitutes a "flagrant violation" of international law and has "no legal validity".

Knowing what I know now, that was a correct move because those are the fake Jews claiming sovereignty when they don't even believe in the One whom God sent and that is Jesus Christ of Nazareth. They still recite the teachings of Moses and they don't even acknowledge the New Testament. They still go to a wall to weep and wail, but God is not there. These are the "fake Jews" the Lord speaks about in both Revelation 2:9 and Revelation 3:9, and their buildings which Jesus calls the synagogue of Satan and so that move was a correct move. While at the same time, he was once again blaspheming against God because he said that Israel, had "no legal validity." The problem is because we didn't have this revelation, a lot of the saints were fooled, and this made President #45 look like he was making all the correct moves.

President #44's resolution demanded that Israel stop such activity and fulfill its obligations as an occupying power under the Fourth Geneva Convention. The Geneva Convention relative to the Protection of Civilian Persons in Time of War, more commonly referred to as the Fourth Geneva Convention and abbreviated as GCIV, is one of the four treaties of the Geneva Conventions. It was adopted in August of 1950 . While the first three conventions dealt with combatants, the Fourth Geneva Convention was the first to deal with humanitarian protections for civilians in a war zone. There are currently 196 countries party to the 1949 Geneva Conventions, including this and the other three treaties.

In 1993, the United Nations Security Council adopted a report from the Secretary-General and a Commission of Experts which concluded that the Geneva Conventions had passed into the body of customary international law, thus making them binding on non-signatories to the Conventions whenever they engage in armed conflicts. It was the first UNSC resolution to pass regarding Israel and the Palestine territories since Resolution 1860 in 2009, and the first to address the issue of Israeli settlements with such specificity since Resolution 465 in 1980. While the resolution did not include any sanction or coercive measure and was adopted under the non-binding Chapter VI (6- remember 6 is the number of man and imperfect) of the United Nations Charter, Israeli newspaper *Haaretz* stated it "may have serious ramifications for Israel in general and specifically for the settlement enterprise" in the medium-to-long term. In response, the government of Israel retaliated with a series of diplomatic actions against some members of the Security Council and accused the administration of U.S. President #44 of having secretly orchestrated the passage of the resolution.

Palestine's representatives stated this was an opportunity to end the occupation and establish a Palestinian state to live side by side with the state of Israel on the 1967 line. Due to this resolution, now it was encoded in international law that Israel should be out of there and with the full backing of the United States, even though they abstained from the vote, it passed 14-0. The number 14 keeps coming up because it represents "salvation." This action was certainly not in favor of the Messianic Jews living in the state of Israel. Interesting facts regarding religion in the whole of the Middle East – 93% of the population is Muslim, so the facts show #44 supported the Muslim nation by releasing funds and orchestrating change in their favor. ""The Lord said to my Lord, Sit in the place of honor at my right hand until I humble your enemies beneath your feet.'" Matthew 22:44

"At mealtime Boaz called to her, "Come over here, and help yourself to some food. You can dip your bread in the sour wine." So, she sat with his harvesters, and Boaz gave her some roasted grain to eat. She ate all she wanted and still had some left over. When Ruth went back to work again, Boaz ordered his young men, "Let her gather grain right among the sheaves without stopping her. And pull out some heads of barley from the bundles and drop them on purpose for her. Let her pick them up, and don't give her a hard time! So, Ruth gathered barley there all day, and when she beat out the grain that evening, it filled an entire basket. She carried it back into town and showed it to her mother-in-law. Ruth also gave her the roasted grain that was left over from her meal. "Where did you gather all this grain today?" Naomi asked. "Where did you work? May the Lord bless the one who helped you!" So, Ruth told her mother-in-law about the man in whose field she had worked. She said, "The man I worked with today is named Boaz." "May the Lord bless him!" Naomi told her daughter-in-law.

"He is showing his kindness to us as well as to your dead husband. That man is one of our closest relatives, one of our family redeemers." Then Ruth said, "What's more, Boaz even told me to come back and stay with his harvesters until the entire harvest is completed." "Good!" Naomi exclaimed. "Do as he said, my daughter. Stay with his young women right through the whole harvest. You might be harassed in other fields, but you'll be safe with him." So, Ruth worked alongside the women in Boaz's fields and gathered grain with them until the end of the barley harvest. Then she continued working with them through the wheat harvest in early summer. And all the while she lived with her mother-in-law." (Ruth 2:14-23 2:5:5) I believe Jesus is to me as Boaz was to Ruth and He continues to drop bundles of revelation and continues to love on me by revealing Himself to me. I also believe this is symbolism for women working in the field right alongside the men, and God showing us favor.

The barley harvest is, in fact, God's reset button to the final end-time countdown. Remember I keep saying it's a "second beginning." Seems it's going to be about the Daughters of Zion, it's their turn this go around. The barley ripens first around the time of Passover; the wheat ripens next around the time of Pentecost; and the grapes ripen last in the fall around the time of Tabernacles. Biblically, zero is a firm number since it represents God and His divine nature. It also symbolizes the relationship between God and all creatures of the earth. It cannot be interpreted without the mention of God and His love for all His creation. Number 16 is doubled from number 8 which is a symbol of spiritual purity and kindness.

Moses' prayer that all would have the gift of the Holy Spirit came true on Pentecost and I believe it will happen again. I believe there is going to be an extraordinary move of the

Holy Spirit during Passover and Pentecost. I believe the Holy Ghost fire is with me, considering my name in Hebrew, Euodia, means Jehovah's Fire. The angels are with me, protecting and shielding me because the Lord is with me. There were two major harvests each year in ancient Israel. The first harvest came from winter crops which were harvested in the spring. First fruits from the winter crops were presented to the Lord at the Feast of Weeks (also called the Feast of Pentecost) The second harvest came from summer crops which were harvested in the fall. First fruits from the fall harvest were presented to the Lord at the Feast of Ingathering (the Feast of Tabernacles, Tishrei or September/October). (Exodus 23:16; 34:22)

Given Israel's latitude in the northern hemisphere, the fall harvest was the largest and most abundant. There were two cycles of rain per crop. They were called "the early rain" and "the latter rain." (Joel 2:23) It is important to note that the names of the two rains were relative to their harvest, not the time of the year. This topic is important because the Holy Spirit is represented as Two Trees in Revelation 11. The work of the Holy Spirit can be described as two rains. (James 5:7) The first "rain" or "reign" of the Holy Spirit is to engage us spiritually. The Holy Spirit "rains down" on everyone at birth and this gift from God demonstrates His great compassion for fallen man – long before we could even know or want to know Him. That's why earlier I said that God wants us to know Him and this confirms that statement.

Chapter 12: The One Who is Faithful and True

Jesus said in Matthew 6:22-24, "Your eye is like a lamp that provides light for your body. When your eye is healthy, your whole body is filled with light. But when your eye is unhealthy, your whole body is filled with darkness. And if the light you think you have is actually darkness, how deep that darkness is! No one can serve two masters. For you hate one and love the other; you will be devoted to one and despise the other. You cannot serve God and be enslaved to money."

As I mentioned in the last chapter, the 44th President was saying a lot of good things, "intriguing talk" but he was orchestrating things behind the scenes that we weren't paying attention to that clearly were against Yahweh's chosen people or so it seemed. He was also speaking things that were against the word of God. People always ask me, when did he do such things. He said a lot of interesting things in his acceptance speech for the Nobel Peace Prize. He said, "For most of history, this concept of just war was rarely observed. The capacity of human beings to think up new ways to kill one another proved inexhaustible, as did our capacity to exempt from mercy those who look different or pray to a different God. Wars between armies gave way to wars between nations - total wars in which the distinction between combatant and civilian became blurred. In the span of thirty years, such carnage would twice engulf this continent. And while it is hard to conceive of a cause more just than the defeat of the Third Reich and the Axis powers, World War II was a conflict in which the total number of civilians who died exceeded the number of soldiers who perished.

In the wake of such destruction, and with the advent of the nuclear age, it became clear to victor and vanquished alike that the world needed institutions to prevent another World War. And so, a quarter century after the United States Senate rejected the League of Nations - an idea for which Woodrow Wilson received this Prize - America led the world in constructing an architecture to keep the peace: a Marshall Plan and a United Nations, mechanisms to govern the waging of war, treaties to protect human rights, prevent genocide, and restrict the most dangerous weapons." The funny thing, and it isn't funny, the very thing they were created to do, they have not done, but it man created these plans. What he didn't mention is something that I touched on in my first book. See, The Marshall Plan (officially the European Recovery Program, ERP) was an American initiative passed in 1948 for foreign aid to Western Europe. The United States transferred over $12 billion (equivalent to $130 billion in 2019) in economic recovery programs to Western European economies after the end of World War II. Replacing an earlier proposal for a Morgenthau Plan, it operated for four years beginning on April 3, 1948.

The Morgenthau Plan was a proposal to eliminate Germany's ability to wage war following World War II by eliminating its arms industry and removing or destroying other key industries basic to military strength. This included the removal or destruction of all industrial plants and equipment in the Ruhr. It was first proposed by United States Secretary of the Treasury Henry Morgenthau Jr. in a 1944 memorandum entitled Suggested Post-Surrender Program for Germany While the Morgenthau Plan had some influence until July 10, 1947 (adoption of JCS 1779) on Allied planning for the occupation of Germany, it was not adopted. US occupation policies aimed at "industrial disarmament", but contained a number of deliberate "loopholes", limiting any action to short-term military measures and preventing large-scale destruction of mines and industrial plants, giving wide-ranging discretion to the military governor and Morgenthau's opponents at the War Department.

An investigation by Herbert Hoover concluded the plan would result in up to 25 million Germans starving to death. From 1947, US policies aimed at restoring a "stable and productive Germany" and were soon followed by the Marshall Plan. When the Morgenthau Plan was published by the US press in September 1944, it was immediately seized upon by the Nazi Germany government, and used as part of propaganda efforts in the final seven months of the war in Europe which aimed to convince Germans to fight on. Seems to be the Marshall Plan and the United Nations took the form of the two beasts. Just the fact that in his speech he gives so much homage to the fake royals and all this talk of serving another God. It was a very long speech with a lot of fillers but he ended the speech by saying, "But we do not have to think that human nature is perfect for us to still believe that the human condition can be perfected. We do not have to live in an idealized world to still reach for those ideals that will make it a better place. The non-violence practiced by men like Gandhi and King may not have been practical or possible in every circumstance, but the love that they preached - their faith in human progress [their faith was not in humans though]- must always be the North Star that guides us on our journey. For if we lose that faith [what faith is this?] - if we dismiss it as silly or naïve; if we divorce it from the decisions that we make on issues of war and peace - then we lose what is best about humanity. We lose our sense of possibility. We lose our moral compass. [He got that part correct].

"Like generations have before us, we must reject that future. As Dr. King said at this occasion so many years ago, "I refuse to accept despair as the final response to the ambiguities of history. I refuse to accept the idea that the 'isness' of man's present nature makes him morally incapable of reaching up for the eternal 'oughtness' that forever confronts him." [Notice Dr. King said "reaching up for the eternal" – He was talking about the Lord God Almighty, the Most High God] So let us reach for the world [not the word?] that ought to be - that spark of the divine that still stirs within each of our souls. Somewhere today, in the here and now, a soldier sees he's outgunned but stands firm to keep the peace. Somewhere today, in this world, a young protestor awaits the brutality of her government, but has the courage to march on. Somewhere today, a mother facing punishing poverty still takes the time to teach her child, who believes that a cruel world still has a place for his dreams. Let us live by their example. We can acknowledge that oppression will always be with us, and still strive for justice. We can admit the intractability of depravation, and still strive for dignity. We can understand that there will be war, and still strive for peace. We can do that - for that is the story of human progress; that is the hope of all the world; and at this moment of challenge, that must be our work here on Earth." See, he was wrong, none of that is the hope of all the world. Jesus is the hope, the only hope! The word of God says, "We are merely moving shadows, and all our busy rushing ends in nothing. We heap up wealth, not knowing who will spend it. And so, Lord, where do I put my hope? My only hope is in you…Hear my prayer, O Lord! Listen to my cries for help! Don't ignore my tears. For I am your guest – a traveler passing through, as my ancestors were before me." (Psalms 39:6-7;12)

President #44 had it all wrong and once again, he showed that while he was saying he was a Christian to get the votes, everything he said and did represented Muslims. He only used Dr. King because of the color of his skin. The God of the Bible is the same God of Israel and while He has many names, He has identified Himself unto Moses as Yahweh, and unto me as Yehovah, Yeshua and Jesus Christ, the Messiah. "Be still and know that I am God! I will be honored by every nation. I will be honored throughout the world." The Lord of Heaven's Armies is here among us; the God of Israel is our fortress," Psalm 46:10-11. Exodus 3:11-16 says, "But Moses protested to God, "Who am I to appear before Pharaoh? Who am I to lead the people of Israel out of Egypt?" God answered, "I will be with you. And this is your sign that I am the one who has sent you: When you have brought the people out of Egypt, you will worship God at this very mountain [Mt. Sinai not a physical mountain].

But Moses protested, "If I go to the people of Israel and tell them, 'The God of your ancestors has sent me to you,' they will ask me, 'What is his name?' Then what should I tell them?" God replied to Moses, "I AM WHO I AM. Say this to the people of Israel: I AM has sent me to you." God also said to Moses, "Say this to the people of Israel: Yahweh, the God of your ancestors – the God of Abraham, the God of Isaac, and the God of Jacob has sent me to you. This is my eternal name, my name to remember for all generations." So, we see that Israel is very important to God, and the nation itself Israel – not any specific place but His chosen people Israel, those who are called by His name.

This scripture took me back to that faithful weekend in April 2016. It was Saturday April 9, that I kneeled down and prayed to hear from God and Sunday, April 10 that I went to church and heard the message. It was the cry of the mourning dove that appeared above my door, sending me to church and giving me this exact scripture! And now, four years later it's the exact same dates as Passover. The message: God is the great I AM! I'm for certain now that it was an angel of the Lord who awakened me in 2014, because I needed to repent, get on the holy road, get the Word in my heart and live holy because God chose me for such a time as this! It's no coincidence that it was the 2nd month, well now we know it to be the 12th month on the Hebrew calendar, and the 14th day of the month that God would tell me all my dreams would come true.

You know, I was all for President #44, and it made me proud as a person of color to see something so historical take place, and to experience and see something manifest that my parents and grandparents imagined and could now only see from heaven. Now, it was only my brother's and I, along with my sons would be alive to see this historic event take place. I cried during the inauguration and I think it was because many had given up hope that it was possible. Something they long waited to see, it was both beautiful and overwhelming, however it was just cosmetics. No real change happened for my people, not even in the man's own hometown of Chicago. He said all the right stuff, spoke very eloquently and gave us hope that "yes we can" but we didn't. One thing we seem to have is peace in other countries, but it was a façade and a set up for something later to come.

Thinking back to that crazy political time in history, there was so much hatred going on. Hate crimes rose above 80 percent. His election season was possibly the ugliest time I can remember in politics, though our present time seems to exceed it! The worst I've ever experienced since I've been participating in the election process, and I started voting at 18 years old. While my defense of the first family held up in the first four years, I worked in local government during that time, things start going downhill after the same sex marriage approval and then other things began to come to light. It was like dark portals opened up after that and all hell start breaking loose. New "laws and customs" were being made to accommodate a sinful lifestyle and people were now being forced by the law to conform to the world's systems or suffer the consequences.

He set up a graven image and committed a sacrilegious offence by allowing this detestable abomination, that's what God calls relationships of the same sex. Then he left a note in the wall during his visit to Jerusalem; the people over there were so offended by it that they removed the note from the wall, they opened and read it and published its contents in the local paper which is something that is uncommon since the wall is considered sacred and holy. Sacrilege is putting ecclesiastical vestments to secular use and the violation or injurious treatment of a sacred object or person. The Bible is sacred because it's God's living word. It's being fulfilled daily. As a matter of fact, every single word of Daniel's prophecies has come true over time and exactly as he said they would happen. Sacrilege can take the form of irreverence to sacred persons, places, and things. When the sacrilegious offence is verbal, it is called blasphemy, and when physical, it is often called desecration.

So, he committed both the verbal offence and the physical offence and a foreshadow of what was to come. "His army will take over the Temple fortress, pollute the sanctuary, put a stop to the daily sacrifices, and set up the sacrilegious object that causes desecration. He will flatter and win over those who have violated the covenant. But the people who know their God will be strong and will resist him." (Daniel 11:31-32) I believe the approval of same sex marriage and the changing of the constitution to accommodate it, was just a test. If the "Christians" let this one go through, then what's to stop the next big thing, say doing away with "religious freedom." Let's also remember that the number of the proposition for same-sex marriage was the No. 8. The number 8 is representative of Jesus' name. This act of making same sex marriage legal, I believe ushered in the last days and this is not hate speech, I'm quoting scriptures from the Bible, these are God's words – not my words. I also found out that #44 only went to church 16 times in the 8 years he was in office and that was extremely low compared to the other Presidents in their perspective terms, but why? Did he know something we didn't know? Or is it because he is not a Christian, but a Muslim? He actually slipped and said he was Muslim and the reporter corrected him and had to "remind him" that he was a Christian.

This confirmed for me that we are in the half time for sure. Speaking of the number 16, it was in 2016 that I saw my mother in a dream saying, "I saw you" and the same year that Yahweh told me to write this book. Some of the longest words in the King James Bible are sixteen letters long, they include "covenant breakers" (Romans 1:31), "evilfavouredness" (Deuteronomy 17:1) and "unprofitableness" (Hebrews 7:18). These scriptures speak about doing things that are against God and against God's covenant. I believe that making same sex marriage legal was breaking the covenant between America and God. "Happy are those who wash their robes clean and so have the right to eat the fruit from the tree of life and to go through the gates into the city. But outside the city are the perverts and those who practice magic, the immoral and the murderers, those who worship idols and those who are liars both in words and deeds." (Revelation 22:14-15 GNB) It's pretty clear to me.

Again, I know that people think that #44 was the greatest president since the creation of slice bread, but the proof is in the yeast and dough. I don't worship any man; I only worship the Lord and I had to write it how the Holy Spirit revealed it to me. Leviticus kept coming up repeatedly during my studies, so I decided to include the scriptures that are relevant. "It is the glory of God to conceal a thing: but the honour of kings is to search out the matter."(Proverbs 25:2) Leviticus contains "the law for her that hath born a male or female" this is a precept for being born again and connected to Revelation 12 and the book. "If it's going to be birthed in the earth, it's going to come from a woman." I don't remember who said this, but it's a very true statement. Remember Eve was the Mother of all the living. It says the law for her because women give birth, not men.

"The LORD said to Moses, "Give the following instructions to the people of Israel. If a woman becomes pregnant and gives birth to a son, she will be ceremonially unclean for seven days, just as she is unclean during her menstrual period. On the eighth (8) day the boy's foreskin must be circumcised. After waiting thirty-three (33) days, she will be purified from the bleeding of childbirth. During this time of purification, she must not touch anything that is set apart as holy. And she must not enter the sanctuary until her time of purification is over. If a woman gives birth to a daughter, she will be ceremonially unclean for two weeks (14 days), just as she is unclean during her menstrual period. After waiting sixty-six (66) days, she will be purified from the bleeding of childbirth." Lev 12:5 Translation: For a boy it was 33 (Jesus was 33 when He started His ministry), but for a girl (Holy Spirit/Wisdom) it was 66 (there are 66 books in the Bible and the whole book of Isaiah, contains 66 chapters, which is the most prophetic book in the Bible and has had the most prophecies fulfilled in the new testament thus far.

What does this mean you may ask? Why all these references to blood purification? We need purifying to go to heaven, and belief in the blood sacrifice made by Jesus Christ is that required ticket to enter. "The Jew first, and then the Gentile" is from Romans 1:16 and Romans 2:9-10. The Jews were a schoolmaster to bring us to Christ, and a Jew is someone that is chosen by the Lord God Almighty. "Let me put it another way. The law was our guardian until Christ came; it protected us until we could be made right with God through faith. And now that the way of faith has come, we no longer need the law as our guardian. – Galatians 3:24-25" I'm learning that this was the importance of the teachings of Rabbi – I needed to learn these things, the foundation of Judaism and the meaning behind the celebrations, and I still don't have a complete understanding of the lunar calendar the way I would like to, but I get the gist and I'm learning more daily about Judaism because it is the foundation of Christianity.

Judaism is defined as an "ethnic" religion comprising the collective religious, cultural, and legal tradition and civilization of the Jewish people. Judaism is considered by religious Jews to be the expression of the covenant that God established with the Children of Israel. I'm finding this to be absolutely true and correct. "For whatsoever things were written aforetime were written for our learning, that we through patience and comfort of the scriptures might have hope." (Romans 15:4) King David lived about 1,000 B.C., smack in the middle of the Old Covenant, and was the 33rd generation from Adam. Jesus was the 66th generation, like the number of books in the Bible and the same number of chapters in the book of Isaiah. That's extraordinary! Man could not think of this! David was considered "God's Ruler," the King of Jews. **David was anointed, but God was kept "hidden," especially because of David's many sins.** This go around, I've been His hidden treasure. I don't know what generation I would be from Adam, I know that's funny because I'm nobody. What I do know is that being born in 1970, I am considered Generation X and that's 10 in Roman numerals and December is the 10th month on the Hebrew calendar.

Jesus Christ came 66 generations after Adam. He was "God's Ruler," the Messiah, the King of the Jews. Except, Jesus was God incarnate, God "Revealed," the "Light of the world." He did not sin. Jesus is the only human to walk the earth and not sin. So, the meaning of 33 and 66, which by the way add up to 99, has to do with both being born again and Jesus being God's Ruler and the Messiah and also the root from the line of King David! Jesus is God's Ruler! He's on the way to rule and reign and establish His Kingdom. Also, 33 x 2 = 66. The Second Adam – Jesus. The Second coming of Jesus to marry or unite (2) with His bride and church. Also, the new creation and I believe that may be me. Two is union and division, like 66 divided by 33 is 2, Adam and Eve – the LORD made THEM.

The context of the numbers 33 and 66 is in Leviticus Chapter 12. Leviticus is the 3rd book and the text is the 12th chapter. This represents the Trinity or the three Godheads in One. 3 means "God," and 12 represents faith and a "Faith Ruler." So, the theme of the chapter is "God's Ruler." The number 33 is 3 x 11. 3 means "God" and 11 means "Hidden." The number 66 is 3 x 22. 3 means "God" and 22 means "Revealed" or "Light." Jesus is coming to rule and reign through the Holy Spirit and He judged me first. He started with the church first. "Because you have obeyed my command to persevere, I will protect you from the great time of testing that will come upon the whole world to test those who belong to this world." (Revelation 3:10) The scripture says, "to test those who belong to this world." Jesus said that He was in the world, but not of it. "The nation of Israel is the vineyard of the LORD of Heaven's Armies. The people of Judah are his pleasant garden. He expected a crop of justice, but instead he found oppression. He expected to find righteousness, but instead he heard cries of violence. What sorrow for you who buy up house after house and field after field, until everyone is evicted, and you live alone in the land.

But I have heard the Lord of Heaven's Armies swear a solemn oath: "Many houses will stand deserted; even beautiful mansions will be empty. Ten acres [Hebrew a ten yoke, that is, the area of land plowed by ten teams of oxen in one day] of vineyard will not produce even six gallons [Hebrew a bath – 21 liters] of wine. Ten baskets of seed will yield only one basket [Hebrew a homer [5 bushels or 220 liters] of seed will yield only an ephah [20 quarts or 22 liters] of grain. What sorrow for those who get up early in the morning looking for a drink of alcohol and spend long evenings drinking wine to make themselves flaming drunk. They furnish wine and lovely music at their grand parties – lyre and harp, tambourine, and flute – but they never think about the LORD or notice what he is doing. So, my people will go into exile far away because they do not know me. Those who are great and honored will starve, and the common people will die of thirst. The grave [Hebrew Sheol] is licking its lips in anticipation, opening its mouth wide.

The great and lowly and all the drunken mob will be swallowed up. Humanity will be destroyed, and people brought down; even the arrogant will lower their eyes in humiliation. But the Lord of Heaven's Armies will be exalted by his justice. The holiness of God will be displayed by his righteousness. In that day lambs will find good pastures, and fattened sheep and young goats [Hebrew reads and strangers] will feed among the ruins. What sorrow for those who drag their sins behind them with ropes made of lies, who drag wickedness behind them like a cart! They even mock God and say, "Hurry up and do something! We want to see what you can do. Let the Holy One of Israel carry out his plan, for we want to know what it is." What sorrow for those who say that evil is good and good is evil, the dark is light, and light is dark, that bitter is sweet and sweet is bitter.

What sorrow for those who are wise in their own eyes and think themselves so clever. What sorrow for those who are heroes at drinking wine and boast about all the alcohol they can hold. They take bribes to let the wicked go free, and they punish the innocent. Therefore, just as fire licks up stubble and dry grass shrivels in the flame, so their roots will rot and their flowers wither. For they have rejected the law of the LORD of Heaven's Armies; they have despised the word of the Holy One of Israel. That is why the LORD's anger burns against his people, and why he has raised his fist to crush them. The mountains tremble, and the corpses of his people litter the streets like garbage. But even then, the LORD's anger is not satisfied. His fist is still poised to strike!

"He will send a signal to distant nations far away and whistle to those at the ends of the earth. They will come racing toward Jerusalem. They will not get tired or stumble. They will not stop for rest or sleep. Not a belt will be loose, not a sandal strap broken. Their arrows will be sharp and their bows ready for battle. Sparks will fly from their horses' hooves, and the wheels of their chariots will spin like a whirlwind. They will roar like lions, like the strongest of lions. Growling, they will pounce on their victims and carry them off, and no one will be there to rescue them. They will roar over their victims that day of destruction like the roaring of the sea. If someone looks across the land, only darkness and distress will be seen; even the light will be darkened by clouds." (Isaiah 5:7-30) I believe that the Lord is going to take his hand off of Jerusalem, and when I say Jerusalem, I mean the Jewish claiming to be Jews but are not, because they have not said, "Blessed is He [Jesus Christ] and She [Holy Spirit] that comes in the name of the Lord."

The Holy Spirit lead me to look up months with five weeks in them as it relates to the years 2019/2020. 2019: March, May, August, and November (the Lord spoke to me in all these months) 2020: January, May, July, and October. I believe prophetic things and Bible prophecy will take place in these months. The Lord gives me the scriptures and He continues to confirm His word. So, it was Michael the Arc angel that rose up over our nation on December 22, 2017, and that makes sense if I'm carrying the covenant. The night I prayed for my son to be saved was letting God know that not only did I believe, but I was finally ready to seek the Lord and my purpose. So, it must have been Gabriel who showed me myself laying in the bed and then Lazarus touched me in 2014. It was prophesied over me that God was going to break off the yokes and I was going to rise in power and double for my trouble. It's quite possible that #45 is Darius the Mede. So, my dream of the eagle was more than a warning dream but was also letting me know that the Lord was going to attach Himself to me. I would be carrying Him on my shoulders, as well as the government. I was chosen by God for this major task. He told me in August 2019, that he was creating a holy road, tell the church to wake up and that Yahweh was separating the weeds from the wheat. I believe He rescued me once again from the devil's grip and that 2020 is going to be perfect vision and a great awakening and a wondrous time of revival for the church because 2020 is the year of the Lord and the end of the Gentile age!

I believe Brother Aaron's prophecy about me, when he said he saw numbers, management, accounting, organization, and the like had to do with this book. He said he didn't' know what it meant and honestly, I didn't either. The fact that God speaks to me in nature, numbers, times, and dates, in the clouds, in dreams and visions is extraordinary. A woman once told me I had the mind of Adam and it's starting to make sense. Every time I'm in church and a Pastor prophesies, even if they are talking to other people, the message always pertained to me. It's like I was the only one on the planet, but I know I'm not. God has many, many children and I'm just a part of the remnant. In the 25th Chapter of 'A Divine Revelation of Hell', the writer speaks about her visions of heaven and on page 208 and 209, she said the following. Title: Gates of Heaven. "At another time when I was in prayer, I saw this heavenly vision. I was in the spirit and an angel came to me and took me into the heavens. Again, there were magnificent scenes of billowing light and dazzling glory such as I had seen behind the solid gold mountains. It was awe inspiring to behold the power of God displayed. As the angel and I approached two giant gates in a huge wall, we saw two exceptionally large angels with swords. They were about 50 feet tall, and they're hair was spun gold. The gates were so high I could not see the tops of them. They were the most beautiful works of art I have ever seen. They were hand carved, with intricate folds, drapes, layers in carvings, and were studded with pearls, diamonds, rubies, sapphires, and everything on the gates was in perfect balance, and the gates opened outward. An Angel with a book in his hand came out from behind the gates. After checking the book, the angel nodded, confirming that I could enter. Reader, you cannot get into heaven if your name is not in the Lambs book of Life."

Title: The File Room. In a vision, an Angel took me to heaven and showed me a very large room with walls of solid gold. Alphabetical letters were engraved here and there on the walls. The scene was much like a huge library, but the books were embedded into the wall instead of being shelved. (This is like a computer mainframe, hall of records, also like the books I saw being opened on that show about tracing your roots). Angels in long robes were taking books out of the walls and studying them closely. There seemed to be a rigid order and what they did. I noticed that the books had big gold covers and some of the pages were read. The books were very beautiful. The Angel with me said these books were a record of the lives of every person who has ever been on earth. I was told there were more rooms elsewhere with even more records. From time to time the archangels brought the records before God for his approval or disapproval. The books contained prayer requests, prophecies, attitudes, growth in the Lord, souls won to Christ, the fruit of the Spirit and much more. Everything we do on earth is recorded in one of the books by angels." I was blown away to read these words. I don't even remember where this book came from and I don't remember reading it until 2020, but it seems to be coming to life as well like the book I'm writing and like the Bible.

I too was scared when I first started having the dreams and visions. I was extremely frightened that day in the park with the clouds, but now I understand why the animals communicate with me, especially the squirrels and birds. I have been overwhelmed. I have felt alone and scared for years, but the Lord has continued to tell me that I am not alone and not to be afraid. I tried to go to people in the ministry to help me figure this out, but it was meant for me to stay close to the Lord and the Holy Spirit so that they could reveal these things to me and no one could say that they pointed me in this or that direction. No Pastor would give me the time of day, but the Lord gave me all the time in the world. Even the so-called prophets wanted something and not that I didn't or wouldn't have blessed them, but if God gave you something to do – He will add what and who you need to accomplish it. I couldn't get a phone call, text or emailed returned. Some were even calling me a witch, but I don't know of any witch pointing people towards the Bible and the Messiah, Yeshua, though Melchizedek was from Salem and he was a high priest and not a warlock. Though they wore cloaks but as a covering, but they were not wizards, they were priests of God. The great thing during all of this is that as much time as I had for God, He had it right back for me.

I also understand the raining of the tiny Pebbles and why it was so important for me to study Peter and Paul's writings. I was weeping and very sorrowful once again for the times that I had wasted but He highlighted Peter's journey for me to understand how much Peter loved the Lord. It's our heart God wants. He knows in our own human strength; we cannot please God. Peter delighted and was excited to be in the Lord's presence and He would give his life to defend Him, so he said; but when the time came, and things happened just as the Lord said they would, Peter had to fall back. Though Peter denied the Lord 3 times, he still followed close behind because deep in his heart, He knew the truth and that is that the Lord was indeed the Messiah and that was only revealed to him through the Holy Spirit. The Holy Spirit cannot reveal things to an unclean and unholy spirit, and perfect and holy are two different things. Seems Peter didn't get as far away from the Lord as he thought because the Lord still called to him on the water. Once Peter confirmed with his mouth and actions (Peter jumped in the water and didn't look back) that he loved the Lord and he was going to feed His sheep, that's what he committed to and he carried it out and these writing's bear witness to that. His writings were Holy Spirit inspired which is why they continue speaking to us today.

King David was also known for his passion for God, his touching psalms and musical abilities, his inspiring courage and expertise in warfare, his good looks and illicit relationship with Bathsheba, and his ancestral connections to Jesus of Nazareth in the New Testament. God chooses people by the heart they have for Him. Now I'm beginning to understand why He chose me. I love the Lord. I have always wanted to live for the Lord since I was a little girl, but the abuse, the loneliness, my fleshly desires, and my insecurities led me on a search for love down many of the wrong roads. Thank the Lord, He always allowed me to return to Him and I'm realizing now it's because He didn't let ***me*** get too far. So now here I am, but what is my role exactly in the whole scheme of things? Do I publish the book or sit and wait on instruction? I trust the Lord will tell me and, in the meantime, I'll just keep following the Holy Spirit. That's something that I learned from the movie the 'Shack' – to listen to God, walk with Jesus and let the Holy Spirit guide you. Remember I said God is time. At present, things are still unfolding and I'm enjoying the spiritual journey. I'm enjoying knowing that God loves me.

At 4:40 am, I heard eleven horns blow and I heard the Lord say, "We are in the 11th hour," I heard the Lord say and He seems to have moved closer to us than He's ever been before. "The Lord says, "I will rescue those who love me. I will protect those who trust in my name. When they call on me, I will answer; I will be with them in trouble. I will rescue and honor them. I will reward them with a long life and give them my salvation." (Psalm 91:14-16) The biblical expression 40 days and 40 nights just means a long time. The number forty to the Jews is a number that, when used in terms of time, represents a period of probation, trial, and chastisement (not to be confused with judgement which is represented by the number 9). Remember I said in an earlier chapter it's been 39 years since Reaganomics, and I felt my generation had been in slavery since then. I also moved to the valley when I was 39 years old. Martin Luther King Jr. was killed when he was 39 years old. He gave his last speech on March 31, and was killed on April 4.

Dr. King said in his last speech, 'I've Been to the Mountaintop' the following: "Well, I don't know what will happen now. We've got some difficult days ahead. But it really doesn't matter with me now, because I've been to the mountaintop. And I don't mind. Like anybody, I would like to live – a long life; longevity has its place. But I'm not concerned about that now. I just want to do God's will. And He's allowed me to go up to the mountain. And I've looked over. And I've seen the Promised Land. I may not get there with you. But I want you to know tonight, that we, as a people, will get to the Promised Land. So I'm happy, tonight. I'm not worried about anything. I'm not fearing any man. *Mine eyes have seen the glory of the coming of the Lord*." The Number 40 generally symbolizes a period of testing. I'm thinking now since this will be the 40th year, 2020 is going to be a significant year in the prophetic. Dr. King was like our Moses and like Moses, he died before the Israelites made it to the promised land.

Remember, Moses' life he lived forty years in Egypt and forty years in the desert before God selected him to lead his people out of slavery. Moses was also on Mount Sinai for 40 days and nights, on two separate occasions (Exodus 24:18, 34:1-28), receiving God's laws. He also sent spies, for forty days, to investigate the land God promised the Israelites as an inheritance (Numbers 13:25, 14:34). The prophet Jonah powerfully warned ancient Nineveh, for forty days, that its destruction would come because of its many sins. The prophet Ezekiel laid on His right side for 40 days to symbolize Judah's sin (Ezekiel 4:6). Let me just note right here that I have not been able to sleep on my left side for at least the last two months. I fasted for 40 days and nights in 2018 and 2019.

Elijah went 40 days without food or water at Mount Horeb [meaning Glowing and Heat]. Jesus was tempted by the devil not just three times, but many times during the 40 days and nights he fasted just before his ministry began. He also appeared to his disciples and others for 40 days after his resurrection from the dead. I believe something prophetic is going to happen on November 29. I wrote this in my notes because it is the 333rd day of the year (334th in leap years) in the Gregorian calendar; 32 days remain until the end of the year. It makes sense to me why the butterfly was a sign of Jesus' coming. To grow into an adult they go through 4 stages; egg (seed planted/sign of what's to come), larva (baby), pupa (growth and transformation) and adult (the physical creation emerges, flies and looks for a mate.) Each stage has a different goal. A butterfly starts life as a very small, round, oval or cylindrical egg. The coolest thing about butterfly eggs, especially monarch butterfly eggs, is that if you look close enough you can see the tiny caterpillar growing inside of it. Some butterfly eggs may be round, some oval and some may be ribbed while others may have other features. The egg shape depends on the type of butterfly that laid the egg. When the egg finally hatches, most of you would expect for a butterfly to emerge, right? Well, not exactly. In the butterfly's life cycle, there are four stages, and this is only the second stage.

Butterfly larvae are what we call caterpillars. Caterpillars do not stay in this stage for very long and mostly, in this stage all they do is eat. It's like when the baby Christian first gets saved, they are excited about the word and so they feast on it. The pupa stage is one of the coolest stages of a butterfly's life. As soon as a caterpillar is done growing and they have reached their full length/weight, they form themselves into a pupa, also known as a chrysalis. From the outside of the pupa, it looks as if the caterpillar may just be resting, but the inside is where all the action is. It's actually hidden inside, but it's not just sitting there. Inside of the pupa, the caterpillar is rapidly changing. Now, as most people know, caterpillars are short, stubby and have no wings at all. Within the chrysalis the old body parts of the caterpillar are undergoing a remarkable transformation, called 'metamorphosis,' to become the beautiful parts that make up the butterfly that will emerge. It's true transformation, from the inside out. Tissue, limbs, and organs of a caterpillar have all been changed by the time the pupa is finished and is now ready for the final stage of a butterfly's life cycle.

Finally, when the caterpillar has done all its forming and changing inside the pupa, if it makes it through, you will get to see an adult butterfly emerge. When the butterfly first emerges from the chrysalis, both wings are going to be soft and folded against its body. This is because the butterfly had to fit all its new parts inside of the pupa. As soon as the butterfly has rested after coming out of the chrysalis, it will pump blood into the wings to get them working and flapping – then they get to fly. Usually within a three or four-hour period, the butterfly will master flying and will search for a mate to reproduce. I'm blown away! God created everything! So, to recap, the butterfly starts off as an egg or seed in a shell. It then turns into the larva or the baby is birthed and planted in the earth and then it has to feed or be nourished so that it can make it through the pupa which is the transformation period and then it emerges as a butterfly and begins looking for its mate to make more butterflies!

One of the ladies at the church prophesied over me one Sunday and she shared with me the processing of the seed in the dark. She told me that I was hidden, and she was excited to see what I would be when I emerged. She told me that same day that I was in a dark season and was being processed and the good thing about seasons is that they don't last forever, they change and come to an end. She said she was excited for my future and couldn't wait to see what I will be when the bud breaks through the soil.

One more thing about the significance of the year and number 19, other than it being the beginning of a new season or cycle, 2020 will be the 100-year anniversary of the 19th Amendment. The Nineteenth Amendment to the United States Constitution prohibits the states and the federal government from denying the right to vote to citizens of the United States based on sex. This law gave women the right to vote. Initially introduced to Congress in 1878, several attempts to pass a women's suffrage amendment failed until passing the House of Representatives on May 21, 1919, followed by the Senate on June 4, 1919. It was then submitted to the states for ratification. On August 18, 1920, Tennessee was the last of the necessary 36 ratifying states to secure adoption. The Nineteenth Amendment's adoption was certified on August 26, 1920: the culmination of a decades-long movement for women's suffrage at both state and national levels. Susan B. Anthony said, "The day will come when man will recognize woman as his peer, not only at the fireside, but in councils of the nation. Then, and not until then, will there be the perfect comradeship, the ideal union between the sexes that shall result in the highest development of the race." It's almost harvest time!

Chapter 13: The Devil's Time is Short

"For a child is born to us, a son is given to us. The government will rest on his shoulders. And he will be called: Wonderful Counselor, Mighty God, Everlasting Father, Prince of Peace. He will rule with fairness and justice from the throne of his "ancestor" David for all eternity. The passionate commitment of the LORD of Heaven's Armies will make this happen!" Isaiah 9:6-7

The scripture says that He will rule from the throne of his ancestor David, it doesn't say male or female because Jesus is the ruler! Jesus is the King! Jesus is the Holy Spirit. "The message of the Lord to a lost world is this: "I do not desire that you go to hell. I made you for My own joy and for everlasting fellowship. You are My creation, and I love you. Call upon Me while I am near, and I will hear and answer you. I want to forgive you and bless you." To those who are born again, the Lord says: Forget not the assembling of yourselves. Come together and pray and study My Word. Worship Me in the spirit of holiness." The Lord says to the churches and the nations: "My angels fight always for the heirs of salvation and for those who will become heirs. I do not change. I am the same yesterday, today and forever. Seek Me, and I will pour out My Spirit upon you. Your sons and your daughters will prophesy. I will do great things among you." If you are unsaved, please take the time right now to kneel before the Lord and ask Him to forgive you of your sins and make you His child. Whatever the cost, you should determine now to make heaven your eternal home. Hell is awful and hell is real." 'A Divine Revelation of Hell' Chapter 26, Pages 211-212. Hell is also eternal.

The last days (also referred to as the End Time or the Great Tribulation) is more than just a period of roughly 3-1/2 years or 42 months. "But do not measure the outer courtyard, for it has been turned over to the nations. They will trample the holy city for 42 months. And I will give power to my two witnesses, and they will be clothed in burlap and will prophesy during those 1260 days." (Revelation 11:2-3) This trouble is said to come upon the entire earth, but it's a time of trouble, double trouble and a time that God will cut short to save the elect as I spoke about in earlier chapters. It will be a time just before Jesus' Second Coming, when the Beast and the False Prophet will rule the world through their counterfeit version of God's kingdom which is politics and the government system.

The 42 months (Revelation 11:3, 12:6) of the last or final period before Jesus' return, can further be divided into two distinct pieces. The first piece is about two years (24 months 2018-2020) in length. It's been two years since He showed me, we were in the halftime. He seems to be doing everything in 2-year cycles and every two to four months like the seasons. The second or last piece, biblically called "the day of the Lord" (Isaiah 2:12, Joel 2:11, 2 Peter 3:10), is about 18 months in duration and remember 18 means slavery and spiritual bondage so that would put us smack dab in the middle of 2021. This second part of the great tribulation represents God's direct punishment of unrepentant humanity. The Apostle Paul warned his friend Timothy, which I've referenced more than three times now where He speaks about the time before the return of Christ when he wrote, "Know this also, that in the last days perilous times shall come" (2 Timothy 3:1). Peter also warned the church regarding the state of the world near its end when he said, "Knowing this first, that in the last days there will come mockers, walking according to their own personal lusts." (2 Peter 3:3).

Humanity, in the last days, will increasingly adopt a negative attitude towards God's laws and reject keeping them (sound familiar?), opting instead to doing whatever they decide or "feel" is right, sounding like a politically correct way of doing things to me. This is the current state of the world. Changing the law to allow same sex marriage or anything that goes against God's laws is not right but politically correct which is wrong. This lawlessness, which at its core is selfish and self-centered, will cause people to greatly lack mercy, forgiveness, and love. Jesus told us, "And many false prophets will appear and will deceive many people. Sin will be rampant everywhere, and the love of many will grow cold. But the one who endures to the end will be saved. And the Good News about the Kingdom will be preached throughout the whole world so that all nations [all peoples] will hear it; and then the end will come." The world will experience an increased frequency of wars, rumors of wars, earthquakes, famines and still more calamities. Many false prophets will appear and deceive the masses with false hopes. Deception, in general, will be rampant. Wow!

The Lord is giving me a preview of what is to come in 2020. Many who considered themselves Christians and believers in the One and only true God will also abandon their beliefs in the last days (2 Thessalonians 2:1-3). I remember recently hearing about a popular Christian singing artist who abandoned his faith and ministry to support the lesbian and gay community. Why are the last days of man the worst time humanity will ever experience? One reason is that it will force ALL humans to choose one of two options – both of which bring pain and suffering. No one will be allowed to go "undecided" for exceptionally long! Should you choose to obey the Eternal, He will spare people from His wrath. "They were told not to harm the grass or plants or trees, but only the people who did not have the seal of God on their foreheads." (Revelation 9:4) and "Then I heard another voice calling from heaven, "Come away from her, my people. Do not take part in her sins, or you will be punished with her." (Revelation 18:4)

Understand however, people for God will be considered enemies of the world, rebels, anarchists, hunted down and martyred as it says in Revelation 6:11, 7:14, 13:7-10, and 15. This has been happening for centuries but specifically since the 40's and is continuing to happen. People have been murdered, heads cut off, blown up, bombed and abducted while they chant hate slurs for America and sayings like "death to America" and "death to Jews" flow through the airwaves. Satan the devil will launch his second but last offensive in heaven in the hope he can wrestle control of the universe away from God. He and his evil army, however, WILL be defeated by righteous angels. We have covered many scriptures from the book of Daniel as it offers a rare glimpse into the events that occur with angels in the unseen spirit-based realm. The battles between righteous spirits who obey God and demonic and evil angels have, and will, affect world history and the destiny of nations. We will see it play out with our natural eyes, but people won't understand what's going on unless they have their spiritual glasses on.

We see in Daniel 10:1-3, that Daniel had been fasting and mourning for three full weeks when he sees a vision of one of God's angels. The angelic being states that God sent him the moment he began to humble himself and pray (verse 12), which we read earlier. Why did it take one of the most powerful angels ever created a few weeks to spiritually travel to Daniel? What caused such a great delay? Gabriel, who normally would have delivered God's message the moment after he got it, was unable, of himself, to get past the "prince of the kingdom of Persia" (Daniel 10:13)! It took another of God's powerful angels, whose name is Michael, to come and help him fight his way through to deliver his message. Whoever hindered Gabriel was almost certainly an enemy of righteousness who could not have been a human being because human beings have no power, of themselves, to fight even the weakest of spirit beings.

"Long ago God spoke many times and in many ways to our ancestors through the prophets. And now in these final days, he has spoken to us through his Son. God promised everything to the Son as an inheritance, and through the Son he created the universe. The Son radiates God's own glory and expresses the very character of God, and he sustains everything by the mighty power of his command. When he had cleansed us from our sins, he sat down in the place of honor at the right hand of the majestic God in heaven. This shows that the Son is far greater than the angels, just as the name God gave him is greater than their names and that name is Yeshua Messiah or Jesus Christ. For God never said to any angel what he said to Jesus: "You are my Son. Today I have become your Father. [Today I reveal you as my Son.] God also said, "I will be his Father, and he will be my Son." (2 Samuel 7:14) And when he brought his supreme [firstborn] Son into the world, God said, [or when he again brings his supreme Son [or firstborn Son] into the world, God will say] "Let all of God's angels worship him." (Deuteronomy 32:43) Regarding the angels, he says, "He sends his angels like the winds, his servants like flames of fire." But to the Son he says, "Your throne, O God, endures forever and ever. You rule with a scepter of justice. You love justice and hate evil. Therefore, O God, your God has anointed you, pouring out the oil of joy on you more than anyone else."

He also says to the Son, "In the beginning, Lord, you laid the foundation of the earth and made the heavens with your hands. They will perish, but you remain forever. They will wear out like old clothing. You will fold them up like a cloak and discard them like old clothing. But you are always the same; you will live forever. And God never said to any of the angels, "Sit in the place of honor at my right hand until I humble your enemies, making them a footstool under your feet." Therefore, angels are only servants – spirits sent to care for people who will inherit salvation." (Hebrews 1:1-14) (7). Remember the angel of the Lord touched me on the forehead in 2014. So, the angels are the wind and servants are the flames of fire. This means that while a human prince could not have resisted a holy angel, it must have been a spirit who was evil and willing to fight a righteous and powerful being making his way to Daniel.

In Revelations 12:7-10, the scripture says that the evil army will be cast back down to earth, which I believed happened on September 17, 2019. It says that they will be permanently banned from heaven and this complete rejection causes the full force of Satan's wrath to come upon the earth for a short period of time. Therefore, I believe this is why the visions came from the angel of the Lord revealing to me that he was creating a Holy road that no evil-minded people could walk on, nor any ferocious beasts. (It's been two years exactly since the 9/23/17 alignment in year 5777, and it will be three years in 2020). A unique paradox will exist during the time of Satan's visible rule on earth. On the one hand, Christians will be persecuted and killed in great numbers (happened and happening) while others will be made to serve the devil's agenda. For some it will be a physical death. For others it will be a spiritual resurrection and awakening.

It will be the greatest period of trial, testing, and temptation the world has ever or will ever see as it says in Matthew 24:21. Yet, on the other hand, in the last days many people will grow rich and prosperous. In fact, the merchants and businesses who got incredibly wealthy through the new one world system will mourn when it is finally destroyed and this is in Revelation 18:9-19! I've mentioned before that the one world system has already been set up through the United Nations, but actually it goes further back than that. The one world government was set up in 1776. I believe therefore the Lord had me to find the $2 bill and lead me to the Declaration of Independence. Wake up America! It's time to Repent! God is watching.

Chapter 14: The Two Witnesses

"My old self has been crucified with Christ. It is no longer I who live, but Christ lives in me. So, I live in this earthly body by trusting in the Son of God, who loved me and gave himself for me. I do not treat the grace of God as meaningless. For if keeping the law could make us right with God, then there was no need for Christ to die." Galatians 2:20-21

It's important to live holy and righteous right now. All the signs of His coming have taken place. Scripture is being daily fulfilled. This is what Paul was talking about in Galatians, living a crucified or a surrendered life for and to Christ. The time is quickly approaching where God's Two Witnesses will soon begin their ministry of confronting the powers that be while at the same time calling upon all those on the earth to repent of their sins before Christ is revealed to the whole world. "These two prophets are the two olive trees and the two lampstands that stand before the Lord of all the earth. If anyone tries to harm them, fire flashes from their mouths and consumes their enemies. This is how anyone who tries to harm them must die. They have power to shut the sky so that no rain will fall for as long as they prophesy. And they have the power to turn the rivers and oceans into blood, and to strike the earth with every kind of plague as often as they wish." (Revelation 11:4-8)

This is so exciting to me. It's truly been a wonderful experience to know that the God I have pledged my allegiance to and tried to serve all these years is real! It's been awesome, terrifying, and sad all at the same time. I'm sad for the believers who are asleep and blinded. I'm sad for those who will turn away. I'm sad for those that don't know God. I am sad for those who reject God because they don't know who they reject and the consequences they will suffer for making the wrong choice. I find myself praying constantly for them. I think that's where this book comes in. God's law insisted it was necessary to have more than one witness to make good an accusation against a person (read Deuteronomy 17:6, 19:15). This principle is reiterated by the apostle Paul to his friend Timothy (1 Timothy 5:19). The opinion of one person was not enough to convict someone of a sin or crime, although all throughout the history of the United States and especially during the Jim Crow south, many were executed, beaten and mistreated due to the testimony of one witness – who most times was not telling the truth. The testimony of at least two witnesses were needed to condemn a person to death (Hebrews 10:28).

One of the primary purposes of these two individuals is to witness against the end time Beast and False Prophet, (see Revelation 19:20). The two witnesses will be "called or commissioned" to prophesy for 3-1/2 years (42 months). The word "prophesy" in biblical terms means to foretell divine events or to speak under the inspiration of God. Part of the two witnesses' message during their ministry will include preaching, holding up, and maintaining the truth of God before the world. They will give warnings and utter judgements against those who are not following God. For believer's in Christ, choosing to be disobedient will only bring you pain. Anytime you know God's instruction for your life, but you choose to do your own thing, it means you don't trust that God really knows what's best for you. God has promised you that if you take "a step" in His direction, it will always work out for your good! Trust Yahweh. Ask the Lord to open your heart and mind to the things that are being said in this book because they are all the Lord God Almighty's words. God so loved the world!

The Bible says, "These two prophets are the two olive trees and the two lampstands that stand before the Lord of all the earth." (Revelation 11:4) God's Two Witnesses have existed throughout eternity. They are omniscient and omnipresent, and their testimony is infallible. The Two Witnesses are two observers! They testify about God to His subjects and they report back with their observations. During the great tribulation period, God's Two

Witnesses will be given greater power than at any previous time in Earth's history. They will boldly declare the truth about God. Their testimony will be confirmed with powerful signs and wonders and they will measure and observe man's response. They will faithfully report their observations to God. In fact, Jesus will hear from the Two Witnesses before He passes judgement on any person.

God's Two Witnesses work in both directions. They come from God, they witness our response, and report back to God. Their testimony is unimpeachable. The Two Witnesses are the Ten Commandments/The Torah (represented by two lampstands- two tablets 4/6) and the Holy Spirit/The Bible (represented by two olive trees). One Witness is a member of the Godhead and the other Witness comes from the mouth of God. Additionally, Romans 11:17 says, "And you Gentiles (unbelievers), who were branches from a wild "olive tree," have been grafted in. So now you also receive the blessing God has promised Abraham and his children, sharing in the rich nourishment from the root of God's special "olive tree." Because they are divine, these Two Witnesses have no conflict. They operate in perfect harmony. The Ten Commandments were written on two tablets of enduring and changeless stone. (Read Exodus 34:1). One tablet contains the first (4) four commandments (defining man's duty to God). The other tablet contains the remaining (6) six commandments (defining man's duty to man). The Ten Commandments are based on principle of love – total devotion to God and selfless service for others.

King David understood the perfection of God's law. He wrote, "The law of the Lord is perfect, reviving the soul. The statues of the Lord are trustworthy, making wise the simple. The precepts of the Lord are right, giving joy to the heart. The commands of the Lord are right, giving joy to the heart. The commands of the Lord are radiant, giving light to the eyes. The fear of the Lord is pure, enduring forever. The ordinances of the Lord are sure and altogether righteous. They are more precious than gold, than much pure gold; they are sweeter than honey, than honey from the comb." (Psalm 19:7-10) The Two Witnesses are personified in Revelations 11 as two prophets because they will work through God's prophets during the great tribulation.

The Holy Spirit will empower each of the 144,000 plus to present God's law to the world and the results will be spectacular. Honest hearted people will be "cut to the heart" with guilt when they hear about the demands of God's law. This is what was taking place before the politically correct movement came into place. The word of God affects the heart. Jesus predicted, "When he (the Holy Spirit) comes, he will convict the world of guilt in regard to sin and righteousness and judgement." (John 16:8) Of course, human beings can reject the law of God and the demands of the Holy Spirit because nothing trumps free will in God's universe. This is how we know that we can trust God, because He will never violate your will. He gives you the choice, but just remember you can't choose your consequence should you decide not to obey.

That embarrassing moment of Peter rejecting Christ and seeing what Jesus said come to pass was a turning point in Peter's life. Peter realized that Friday morning that there was a huge difference between knowing Jesus and surrendering to Jesus. A few weeks later, Peter was chosen as the primary speaker at Pentecost because he had openly betrayed Christ and repented. Jesus gave this converted disciple a chance to let his countrymen clearly know where he now stood. I mention this because Peter knew first-hand the internal struggle between loyalty and cowardice. He wrote "For it is time for judgement to begin with the family of God; and if it begins with us, what will the outcome be for those who do not obey the gospel of God? And 'if it is hard for the righteous to be saved, what will become of the ungodly and the sinner?" (1 Peter 4:17,18) Peter is proof that man can be saved. Paul is proof that man can be saved. I am proof that the Word works, the Holy Spirit is real, and Jesus really does love us and He alone saves.

The numbers of the scriptures correlate with the years of the supernatural experiences I've been having over the years. This takes me back to that faithful night I heard the woman of God say, "Somebody's got to do it! Somebody's got to live right!" I was born into a sinful world to live a righteous life through the power of the blood of Christ Jesus. History has shown that I cannot live righteous on my own, but I needed saving, something that could only be done through the blood of Jesus, with the aid of the Holy Spirit and taking in the full word of God. I had to learn what the word of God said and put into action. I had to become the thing I was talking about. I had to live it. The time seems to be swiftly approaching or we may be in the mist of it. The Bible predicts that mankind has a divine appointment. We are about to be caught (caught up) in a great valley between two kings, the one in the south and the other in the north. The laws of one king will stand in direct opposition to the law of God, the Ten Commandments. These two kingdoms will sharply compete for citizens and distinct lines will be drawn in the sand. (Political arenas all over the world.)

Everyone will be forced into making a choice. The consequence for taking sides – either way – will be dramatic. God's Two Witnesses will make this contest embarrassingly simple. They will cut through religious diversity, languages, confusion, and cultures with a simple declaration. It will be a Mt. Carmel type of experience. "Elijah went before the people and said, "How long will you waver between two opinions? If the Lord is God, follow him; but if Baal is god, follow him…" 1 Kings 18:21. As I was doing some research on the Two Witnesses mentioned in Revelations 10 & 11, I found another interesting view which I've now adopted as my view as well. During the judgement of the living (notice the word "living"), three forces will be working together. The Word of God will be heard by everyone. Then, the Holy Spirit will apply great pressure within every heart to obey God's law, and last, persecution will force everyone into deciding.

At first, you might think that the Two Witnesses are pulling people toward the shores of salvation and persecution is driving them away, but it is not what you think! Those who love God and His law will receive the testimony of the Holy Spirit. They will be willing to accept persecution because they are committed to pleasing God at any cost. On the other hand, those who love their lives and their possessions more than God will not be able to take the heat and accept the suffering that comes with their decision. Jesus said, "The man who loves his life will lose it, while the man who hates his life in this world will keep it for eternal life." (John 12:25) "And everyone who has left houses or brothers or sisters or father or mother or children or fields for my sake will receive a hundred times as much and will inherit eternal life." (Matthew 19:29) Again, 19 is the beginning or ending of a cycle or season and 29 is rise and shine!

There are always some people who will waver back and forth for a time, however increasing pressures from persecution will eventually force everyone into their final decision. Everyone living on Earth will either receive the mark of the beast or the seal of God. There is a simple reason for the persecution of the saints: Salvation comes through faith in Christ. Therefore, the Great Tribulation will be a test of faith. Faith in God quickly separates people. Remember the twelve spies that Moses sent into the Promised Land? (Numbers 14) Faith is a scary thing to those who do not know God and the power of His Word. Faith in God separates sheep from goats. Our actions declare our faith as spoken by James, "…I will show you (and God) my faith by what I do," chapter 2, verse 18.

Jesus, in one of his letters to the angels of the seven churches (specifically Philadelphia) assured them in his letters that after they suffered persecution for some years, "Because you have obeyed my command to persevere, I will protect you from the great time of testing that will come upon the whole world to test those who belong to this world. I am coming soon [or suddenly or quickly]. Hold on to what you have, so that no one will take away your crown. All who are victorious will become pillars in the Temple of my God, and they will never have to leave it. And I will write on them the name of God, and they will be citizens in the city of my God – the new Jerusalem [Hebrew Zion] that comes down from heaven from my God. And I will also write on them my new name. Anyone with ears to hear must listen to the Spirit and understand what he is saying to the churches." (Revelation 3:10-13) Jesus' new name is 'The Lord is Our Righteousness'. With Abraham, it was his faith that made him righteous before Yahweh because his covenant was with the Lord God Almighty directly; however, with us, it is the Lord Jesus Christ who makes us righteous before God. It makes sense that this is chapter 14, because that number represents salvation.

"Then I fell down at his feet to worship him, but he said, "No, don't worship me. I am a servant of God, just like you and your brothers and sisters who testify about their faith in Jesus. Worship only God. For the essence of prophecy is to give a clear witness for Jesus." (Revelation 19:10) We cannot worship angels. We cannot worship the messengers. We cannot worship man. We must worship the Lord God Almighty only. The Seal and the Tattoo: Every person who surrenders to the law of God and the Holy Spirit will fall in line with the testimony of Jesus. After choosing to obey Jesus without regard for the consequences, each person will be given the strength and faith to pass any test which persecution might impose. The fires of persecution will refine and purify the faith of the saints. "I will refine them like silver and test them like gold. They will call on my name and I will answer them; I will say, 'They are my people,' and they will say, 'The Lord is our God." (Zechariah 13:9) After passing some fiery [my burns, job loss, friend abandonment etc.] tests of faith, a dramatic miracle will happen. It is ironic that after losing everything he owns; each faithful person will then lose his carnal nature which is the same as picking up your cross and denying yourself daily, it's dying to the flesh. The sealing of the saints requires the testimony of Two Witnesses. The law of God will serve as the plumb line. It will measure the actions of the person. Jesus will see to it that the believer, in fact, submits to God's law.

The believer will then demonstrate his or her love for Jesus and his or her neighbor. The Holy Spirit will testify that the believer's faith was thoroughly tested and that they love God with all their heart, mind, and soul, and his neighbor as himself. The believer will give everything he or her owns for the sake of the gospel! The believer will be persecuted for worshipping Jesus on His Sabbath day. The believer's actions will clearly show his or her love for God and man. The testimony of God's Two Witnesses will establish the fact that the believer loves God and man. Jesus will announce His judgement: "Seal [Euodia]! Set her free from sin's curse. Give her the wedding dress!" At that moment, [her] carnal nature will be removed, and [she] will no longer have a propensity for sinning! [Euodia] will be like Adam before he fell. She will feel a joyful difference and if she is in prison, she just might start singing at midnight. (Read Acts 16:25) Notice, I put my name in the scriptures because that is exactly what has taken place in my life, though I am not perfect, I don't have a propensity (or readiness) for sinning. I cry out to God in weakness. I live in constant repentance and He always strengthens me, provides a way of escape, and sends an encouraging word. We are supposed to see ourselves in the word, the way God sees us – new creations in Christ Jesus.

Wake Up America Seminars shares my views and I quote: "Consider this: If you hear a thunderous voice from Heaven and you understand the words that were spoken, your own ears will confirm that you have been sealed! The voice of the seven thunders are for the benefit of the people who have been thoroughly tested and proven faith full. (Remember the two thunders I heard after I revealed my purpose to my son? I heard God confirming my words.) As, the Great Tribulation progresses, more and more people will be sealed, and more and more people will hear and understand. I believe almost everyone who receives the seal of God will hear and understand at least one thunder! Regardless of when the seven thunders occur, I believe those who have received the seal of God will hear and understand the seven thunders simultaneously all over the world and their courage will be renewed."

"Then the angel I saw standing on the sea and on the land raised his right hand to heaven. And he swore [made a solemn promise] by him who lives for ever and ever, who created the heavens and all that is in them, the earth and all that is in it, and the sea and all that is in it, and said, 'There will be no more delay.' But in the days when the seventh angel is about to sound his trumpet, the mystery of God [the sealing] will be accomplished, just as he announced to his servants the prophets." Revelation 10:5-7. When the perfect time arrives for the administration of God's wrath, Jesus will make a solemn promise to the Father to faithfully and completely carry out all the objectives which the Father embedded into the plan of salvation. For example, Jesus will have to administer the Father's wrath (seven redemptive judgments and seven destructive judgments).

Jesus must ensure that the gospel will be presented to every person, and that every soul will be tested. Jesus will have to release the devil from the abyss and execute vengeance on the wicked – all this without any deviation from the plan which the Father gave Jesus. Most of all, Jesus promises to seal every person who is willing to obey the gospel. In other words, when Jesus declares there will be no more delay, Jesus promises the Father that His plan for salvation will be carried out as planned. Therefore, one God (Jesus the Son) swears to fully carry out the will of God (the Father). Jesus loves each person (saints and sinners alike) beyond human comprehension, to the point that He would gladly give up His eternal life to save each person. Consequently, this assignment will be more difficult for Jesus in some ways than going to the cross! It will crush Jesus' heart, full of love and grace, to do what He must do. Despite this heavy burden, He promises to faithfully discharge His duties.

After His resurrection, Jesus was given authority as the Head of His Church. (Ephesians 1:22, Colossians 1:18) On the basis of this authority, Jesus gave the gospel commission to His disciples just before He left Earth (Matthew 28:19,20), and the gospel of Jesus has been proclaimed for almost 2,000 years as I mentioned in an earlier chapter. Over the past twenty centuries, the gospel has become contaminated with the traditions and opinions of men. There is One gospel that perfectly aligns with the plumb line of God's law and it will be delivered to the world and it will be free of traditions or opinions of men. The written Word (the Bible) and the spoken Word (the testimony of Jesus) will work together. The Bible will be studied, and Jesus will be heard! The Holy Spirit will be pounding on every heart – demanding that every sinner submit to the law of God!

The Babylonian Empire fell to the Medes and Persians in 539 B.C. About two years later, Darius I [the king of the Medes who ruled over the province of Babylon] died. The death of Darius enabled Cyrus (who had been king of the Persians for several years) to become sovereign over the province of Babylon. When Cyrus learned [through Daniel] that the Highest God of the Jews had called him by name 150 years before he was born and appointed him to rebuild His temple, Cyrus was deeply impressed with the God of the Jews. [It's been 157 years since the Declaration of Independence was signed. Just wanted to throw that in there.] The timing of Darius' death could not have been more perfect because Cyrus inherited the province of Babylon. In other words, a Persian king was put in a position where he could set the Jews free from a province that was formerly governed by a Mede and restore them to Judea. Because Cyrus ruled over Judea and Babylon during the seventieth year of Israel's captivity, the restoration of the Jews became possible through one man.

With God, timing is everything. The 70th Anniversary of Israel has happened on May 14, 2018. * Note: Prior to the Babylonian captivity, the Lord had spoken through Jeremiah: "'This whole country [of Judea] will become a desolate wasteland, and these [tribal] nations [of Israel] will serve the king of Babylon seventy years. But when the seventy years are fulfilled, I will punish the king of Babylon and his nation, the land of the Babylonians, for their guilt,' declares the Lord, 'and will make it desolate forever.'" (Jeremiah 25:11,12) Babylon is the most famous city from ancient Mesopotamia whose ruins lie in modern-day Iraq. Babylon is also false religion and doctrine (you will read Revelation 19 a whole new way understanding this information.)

Songs of Victory in Heaven "After this, I heard what sounded like a vast crowd in heaven shouting, "Praise the Lord! [Greek Hallelujah – Hebrew term "Praise the Lord"] Salvation and glory and power belong to our God. His judgements are true and just. He has punished the great prostitute who corrupted the earth with her immorality. He has avenged the murder of his servants." And again, their voice rang out "Parise the Lord!" The smoke from that city ascends forever and ever!" Then the twenty-four elders and the four living beings fell down and worshipped God, who was sitting on the throne. They cried out, "Amen! Praise the Lord!" And from the throne came a voice that said, "Praise our God, all his servants, all who fear him, from the least to the greatest." Then I heard again what sounded like the shout of a vast crowd or the roar of mighty ocean waves or the crash of loud thunder: "Praise the Lord! For the Lord, our God [the Lord God], the Almighty, reigns. Let us be glad and rejoice and let us give honor to him. For the time has come for the wedding feast of the Lamb, and his bride has prepared herself. She has been given the finest of pure white linen to wear." For the fine linen represents the good deeds of God's holy people. And the angel said to me, "Write this: Blessed are those who are invited to the wedding feast of the Lamb." And he added, "These are true words that come from God." Then I fell down at his feet to worship him, but he said, "No don't worship me. I am a servant of God, just like you and your brothers and sisters who testify about their faith in Jesus. Worship only God. For the essence of prophecy is to give a clear witness for Jesus [the message confirmed by Jesus].

The Rider on the White Horse "Then I saw heaven opened, and a white horse was standing there. Its rider was named Faithful and True, for he judges fairly and wages a righteous war. His eyes were like flames of fire and on his head were many crowns. A name was written on him that no one understood except himself. He wore a robe dipped in blood, and his title was the Word of God. The armies of heaven, dressed in the finest of pure white linen, followed him on white horses. From his mouth came a sharp sword to strike down the nations. He will rule them with an iron rod. He will release the fierce wrath of God, the Almighty, like juice flowing from a winepress. On his robe at his thigh was written this title: King of all kings and Lord of all lords. Then I saw an angel standing in the sun, shouting to the vultures [black and tan birds] flying high in the sky: "Come! gather together for the great banquet God has prepared. Come and eat the flesh of kings, generals, and strong warriors; of horses and their riders; and of all humanity, both free and slave, small and great."

Then I saw the beast and the kings of the world and their armies gathered together to fight against the one sitting on the horse and his army. And the beast was captured, and with him the false prophet who did mighty miracles on behalf of the beast – miracles that deceived all who had accepted the mark of the beast and who worshipped his statue. Both the beast and his false prophet were thrown alive into the fiery lake of burning sulfur. Their entire army was killed by the sharp sword that came from the mouth of the one riding the white horse. And the vultures all gorged themselves on the dead bodies." (Revelation 19: 1-21) I believe this is going to happen both physically and spiritually. We are going to see the dark hidden things come to light and it will happen in the years of the verses, 19-21.

At the Second Coming, Jesus will "spiritually" awaken Abraham and all his faith-full heirs to live in the New Jerusalem! Paul understood God's abandonment of biological Israel, that means those physically born in that place. He also understood the redefinition of Israel, that is, the Christian church was the new Israel. "Then Paul and Barnabas answered them [a group of abusive Jews] boldly: 'We had to speak the word of God to you first [because you are close to the truth, but so far away from Christ. However,] Since you reject it and do not consider yourselves worthy of eternal life, we now turn to the Gentiles (unbelievers or non-Jews). For this is what the Lord has commanded us [Christians]: "I have made you a light for the Gentiles, that you may bring salvation to the ends of the earth."'

When the Gentiles heard this, they were glad and honored the word of the Lord; and all who were appointed for eternal life believed. The word of the Lord spread through the whole region." (Acts 13:47-49) Remember above I said the bells rang in church for two minutes between 12:47 – 12:49. I think this again has something to do with 2-3 years of prophesying because the first lights in the sky were seen in 2017 and I was 47, 2018 I was 48 and I'm currently, in 2019, I'm 49. I was chosen for such a time as this. Also, notice how Paul and Barnabas redirected to Isaiah 42:6,7 pointing towards the Gentiles and Christian faith. "I, the LORD, have called you to demonstrate my righteousness. I will take you by the hand and guard you, and I will give you to my people, Israel, as a symbol of my covenant with them. And you will be a light to guide the nations. You will open the eyes of the blind. You will free the captives from prison, releasing those who sit in dark dungeons. "I am the LORD; that is my name! I will not give my glory to anyone else, nor share my praise with carved idols. Everything I prophesied has come true, and now I will prophesy again. I will tell you the future before it happens. (Isaiah 42:6-9) The Word of God is alive and active and my tongue is a sword.

Chapter 15: Abraham's Seed

"If you belong to Christ, then you are Abraham's seed, and heirs according to the promise." (Galatians 3:29)

People are confused today as it relates to the identity of Israel. The new covenant redefines the seed (the sperm) of Abraham. God redefined Israel because God's covenant with Abraham was not conditional. The covenant God gave to Abraham was unilateral – one sided. Jesus made three promises to Abraham which He will keep. First, He promised that Abraham would become the father of many nations. (Genesis 17:4) Second, God told Abraham that all nations would be blessed through his offspring. (Genesis 18:18) Last but not least and the most important of them all, God promised to give the land where Abraham lived as a foreigner to his descendants. (Genesis 15:18) Notice how these three promises will be fulfilled when God's people are preserved as it says in Revelation 7:9-10, "After this I saw a vast crowd, too great to count, from every nation and tribe and people and language, standing in front of the throne and before the Lamb. They were clothed in white robes and held palm branches in their hands." Remember the scripture we read above said that the fine linen represented "the good deeds of God's holy people." Also, remember it was the week of Palm Sunday, specifically March 23, 2018, that the Lord showed me we were in the halftime and when I saw Him coming on the clouds.

Finally, because Jesus came through Abraham's lineage, people from every nation will be saved and this fulfills the promise that all nations would be blessed through Abraham's offspring. (Acts 4:12; and Ephesians 2) Galatians 3 says, "Dear brothers and sisters, here's an example from everyday life. Just as no one can set aside or amend an irrevocable agreement, so it is in this case. God gave the promises to Abraham and his child. And notice that the Scripture doesn't say "to his children, "as if it meant many descendants. Rather, it says, "to his child" – and that, of course means Christ. This is what I am trying to say: The agreement God made with Abraham could not be canceled 430 years later when God gave the law to Moses. God would be breaking His promise He originally made to Abraham and God has shown Himself trustworthy keeping His word time and time again. For if the inheritance could be received by keeping the law, then it would not be the result of accepting God's promise. But God graciously gave it to Abraham as a promise.

Why, then, was the law given? It was given alongside the promise to show people their sins. But the law was designed to last only until the coming of the child who was promised. God gave his law through angels to Moses, who was the mediator between God and the people. Now a mediator is helpful if more than one party must reach an agreement. But God, who is One, did not use a mediator when he gave his promise to Abraham. Is there a conflict, then, between God's law and God's promises? Absolutely not! If the law could give us new life, we could be made right with God by obeying it. But the Scriptures declare that we are all prisoners of sin, so we receive God's promise of freedom only by believing in Jesus Christ.

Basically, the law was our guardian until Christ came; it protected us until we could be made right with God through faith. And now that the way of faith has come, we no longer need the law as our guardian. For you are all children of God through faith in Christ Jesus. And all who have been united with Christ in baptism have put on Christ, like putting on new clothes. There is no longer Jew or Gentile, slave or free, male, and female. For you are all one in Christ Jesus. And now that you belong to Christ, you are the true children of Abraham. You are his heirs, and God's promise to Abraham belongs to you." Paul leaves no wiggle room on the redefinition of Israel: "A man is not a Jew if he is only one outwardly, nor is circumcision merely outward and physical. No, a man is a Jew if he is one inwardly; and circumcision is circumcision of the heart, by the (Holy) Spirit, not by the written code. Such a man's praise is not from men, but from God." (Romans 2:28,29) "If you belong to Christ, then you are Abraham's seed [the Greek word for seed is sperma], and [as a descendant of Abraham you are] heirs according to the promise [which God gave to Abraham]." (Galatians 3:29).

The abandonment of Israel and the establishment of Christianity is being discussed so that you can understand why seven lampstands replaced the lampstand that once stood before the Lord in Heaven's temple. This is when they entered the holy of holies, the building or place was holy. The seven lampstands represent a new covenant – a new trusteeship for the gospel of Christ. "It is not as though God's word had failed. For not all who are descended from Israel [Jacob] are Israel [God's children]. In other words, it is not the natural children [of Jacob] who are God's children, but it is the children of the promise [people who live by faith as did Abraham] who are regarded as Abraham's offspring." (Romans 9:6,8)

Unlike the old covenant, which was based on bloodline, the new covenant is an open covenant. It is based on the blood of Jesus. Anyone can become a believer in Christ, and through Jesus, receive all that was promised to Abraham! When I hear New Jerusalem, my heart wants it to be here in the United States, the Grape State even. I want to remain within the states where I was born, especially now that I know that my ancestors were from Africa, Europe, France, Scotland, Ireland and Germany which makes me the orphan of immigrants. I have grown to love The Grape State so much, it truly is the land of milk and honey, even though I am not rich and don't enjoy the materialism of it – the beauty of the land is the real treasure. Though I will go where my Father tells me to go and He hasn't told me I'm going anywhere. It may be that people will come looking for me or come to see me instead; I don't know as of yet. I'm going to look to God for direction as always because the United States, has stood with and for Israel as have the evangelical Christians; but again according to what we just read above, being Jewish has nothing to do with your bloodline or your birthplace but everything to do with your relationship with the Lord Jesus Christ and the Holy Spirit. I believe when they were praying for Jerusalem and Israel, it was receiving the blessing and that is of God's revelation knowledge and understanding of the true Word of God. So those claiming to be Jews in Israel have a lot of explaining to do. Although, there are some Messianic Jews in Israel who believe in Jesus Christ and have a real understanding of the word, like Rabbi.

Furthermore, there have been changes on paper when it comes to the abolishment of slavery, but I found out that the 13th Amendment was never ratified. So declarations of freedom have been made, but that freedom was only on paper for the African Americans and people of color in the United States. John writes, "On the Lord's Day I was in the Spirit, and I heard behind me a loud voice like a trumpet, which said: 'Write on a scroll what you see and send it to the seven churches: to Ephesus, Smyrna, Pergamum, Thyatira, Sardis, Philadelphia and Laodicea.' I turned around to see the voice that was speaking to me. And when I turned, I saw seven golden lampstands, and among the lampstands was someone 'like a son of man,' dressed in a robe reaching down to his feet and with a golden sash around his chest. His head and hair were white like wool, as white as snow, and his eyes were like blazing fire. His feet were like bronze glowing in a furnace, and his voice was like the sound of rushing waters [peaceful streams]." (Revelation 1:10-15) Remember this scripture, we are going to come back to it later.

Even though there were more than seven churches in Asia Minor in A.D. 95 when God gave John this vision, Jesus chose these specific seven churches to represent the whole of Christianity. Together, the seven churches had all the strengths and problems that every Christian church faces today. Jesus foreknew that some Christians would fall into the Ephesus experience and they would lose their first love. Jesus also foreknew that some Christians would have the Laodicean experience and that they would become lukewarm – distracted from the rigor of living by faith through the comforts of pleasure and wealth. Sound familiar? Other Christians would be corrupted by sexual immorality like Thyatira and Pergamum. In A.D. 95, Jesus selected seven churches (seven is God's perfect number) – six churches having serious problems and one church hanging on under very difficult circumstances – so that He could praise the good and identify the bad in each case. I love the Pastor with the three heavenly names, the Holy Spirit is with Him. He didn't know it, but He was spot on almost every time he spoke about prophecy. I also like that he acknowledged, as did Dr. J. Vernon McGee when he didn't know something.

Unfortunately, the testimony of Jesus to the seven churches did not keep the seven churches from falling into apostasy. I think I've been a member at one time or another of each of these churches, physically and spiritually. Remember, our body is the Temple of God and so we are the church. Notice that Jesus threatened the church at Ephesus with abandonment. "To the angel of the church in Ephesus write: These are the words of him who holds the seven stars in his right hand and walks among the seven golden lampstands: I know your deeds, your hard work and your perseverance. I know that you cannot tolerate wicked men, that you have tested those who claim to be apostles but are not and have found them false. You have persevered and have endured hardships for my name and have not grown weary. Yet I hold this against you: You have forsaken your first love. Remember the height from which you have fallen! Repent and do the things you did at first. If you do not repent, I will come to you and remove your lampstand from its place." Revelation 2:1-5

Given that Israel's lampstand had been removed at the end of the seventy weeks, the words of Jesus must be treated seriously. His threat, even though directed at Ephesus, also holds true for the other six churches because Ephesus was a part of the whole – one of the seven. I am highlighting this threat because the seven churches did not last long. One Sunday after service, I told the Pastor and his wife that I considered his church to be the church of Ephesus and now I know I was right. He was like the modern day King Saul in my story. They turned their backs on the Lord during the next seventy weeks (490 years). By A.D. 538, Christianity was in total apostasy. Dr. J. Vernon McGee said that the apostasy would be a sign that we were in the end times and he was correct.

If any of the seven churches escaped the Roman purges, they either gave in to the demands of Constantine (A.D. 306-337) and the heresies taught by the Church at Rome, or they simply disappeared and went underground. These seems symbolic of what is ahead. Finally, Islamic conquests in Asia Minor during the seventh and eighth centuries A.D. terminated the existence of all Christian churches in a region that is modern day Turkey. (This is happening again today and made headline news in 2019). Even though the seven churches disappeared, God's Word was not totally extinguished. "The "woman" [symbolizing faithful believers] fled into the desert to a place prepared for her by God, where she might be taken care of for 1,260 days." (Revelation 12:6) I've been telling those that have ears to hear that God is going to use the woman in this dispensation of time because of what it says in 2 Timothy about the men. God has also used women at pivotal times during His ministry and great stories are told about these women's historic and faithful acts whether they were identified by name in the Bible or not, most were not, but the Lord recognized them as faithful. The Lord recognized them and that was the problem the religious leaders really had with Jesus. He gave the woman worth. It's possible that first lampstand was God's law which was given by Moses.

We have seen how lampstands are used in prophecy. In Zechariah's day, there was one lampstand with seven lamps on it that stood before the Lord. That lampstand represented the nation of Israel, the chosen agent or trustee of God's Word. In John's day, there were seven lampstands, each lampstand representing a church – the chosen agent or trustee of God's Word. Then, the seven lampstands disappeared. We talked about Revelation 11 above and the Two Witnesses. God's law is His chosen agent at the end of the Ages. That law is written in the Bible. God has proven with Jews and Christians alike that human beings cannot be trusted as agents of His law. One lampstand represents the first tablet of stone and the other represents the second tablet of stone. There are 4 laws written on one and 6 laws written on the other as we stated above. I just want to note that my mother was 46 when she passed away, or should I say when her life was taken because I believe that she was taken from this world.

The law of the Lord is changeless, a perfect light displacing darkness. The law of God is the plumb line of Truth. The law is found and explained in the Word of God and it testifies about the actions of the living. Our actions during the Great Tribulation will be measured by the law's definition of true vertical (the Truth). I think this may be the reason I saw the vertical lions in the clouds – I saw horizontal and vertical positions as the lions rose up in the clouds. The testimony of Jesus will be heard, and this will cause people to give God's law due consideration. Make no mistake about this, the gospel of Jesus will be preached, as a witness to all nations, and then the end shall come. (Matthew 24:14) Not the end of the earth, the Bible doesn't preach the end of the earth, but the end of the world and the government systems as they have been.

Most Bible scholars believe the end of the old earth as we know it today will be at the end of the millennium or after the thousand year reign of Christ and His saints on earth. Then the New Jerusalem or actually heaven itself descends out of the sky and rests where Jerusalem is during the present time (Rev 21). Revelation 20:5 says, "This is the first resurrection. (The rest of the dead did not come back to life until the thousand years had ended.) The Lord is telling me that He was the first to resurrect from the dead, but when He returns it will be the bride who resurrects first, and then the rest of His church and it's a spiritual awakening. Then for those who are spiritually dead, after the Holy Spirit pours out, they will be given one last chance to choose Jesus. This is what it speaks about in Revelation 9. Please believe, we are living in the time John spoke about in Revelation.

The Holy Spirit is anxious that we hear the gospel of Jesus because the truth about Jesus and our need of the Savior comes from hearing the Word of God. The reason we will need to be closer to Jesus is because He sits on the right side of the Father in heaven as our advocate and He and the Father communicate with the Holy Spirit who communicates with us. If you don't have a relationship with Jesus Christ, you cannot hear from the Holy Spirit. If you don't hear from the Holy Spirit, how will you know what is going on? (Romans 10:17; 1 Corinthians 1:18-21) After hearing the terms and conditions of the gospel, the Holy Spirit can bring a person to repentance. The Spirit enabled me to see myself as God saw me and this view was shocking. Suddenly, my need for a Savior became a matter of life or death. You can see that once I totally surrendered my will to Jesus and His teachings, the Holy Spirit caused me to have the "born again experience." Almost identical to what I just talked about above, the born-again experience can be likened to the early rain in ancient Israel. Just before the early rain came, seeds were planted, and of course, the early rain and the sunshine [the light] that followed caused the seeds to germinate and grow. In a few days, the bare ground produced new life! Once the seed of truth is planted in good soil, the Holy Spirit will "rain down" on a thirsty soul and overnight, signs of new life will appear. This is the "early rain" experience.

Whether it is a summer crop [representing early in life] or a winter crop [representing the latter], which seems to be in my case - the rain that produces the harvest is the latter rain. I seem to be experiencing the summer crop and the winter crop is coming. The world has never experienced the latter rain of the Holy Spirit, but it will only occur during the Great Tribulation. For 1,260 days, the law of God will be presented with power and clarity, and the Holy Spirit will pound on every heart. The contest will be difficult and painful. Those who submit to the law of God will suffer the penalties of Babylon. Those who submit to the laws of Babylon will receive the seven bowls and lose eternal life. Each person's decision will be thoroughly tested. Babylon the Greek form of BABEL; Semitic form Babilu, meaning "The

Gate of God." In the Assyrian tablets it means "The city of the dispersion of the tribes." The monumental list of its kings reaches back to B.C. 2300, and includes Khammurabi, or Amraphel (q.v.), the contemporary of Abraham. I keep saying we've been transported back to Babylonian times in the spirit realm and they have been trying to get Christians to bow to the golden image and it's not just one image, there are many, just like there are many idols.

"Therefore, this is what the Sovereign LORD says: "Look! I am placing a foundation stone in Jerusalem, [Hebrew in Zion] a firm and tested stone. It is a precious cornerstone that is safe to build on. Whoever believes need never be shaken [Greek version reads Look! I am placing a stone in the foundation of Jerusalem [literally Zion], / a precious cornerstone for its foundation, chosen for great honor. /Anyone who trusts in him will never be disgraced]. I will test you with the measuring line of justice and the plumb line of righteousness. Since your refuge is made of lies, a hailstorm will knock it down. Since it is made of deception, a flood will sweep it away. I will cancel the bargain you made to cheat death, and I will overturn your deal to dodge the grave. When the terrible enemy sweeps through, you will be trampled into the ground. Again, and again that flood will come, morning after morning, day, and night, until you are carried away."

"This message will bring terror to your people. The bed you have made is too short to lie on. The blankets are too narrow to cover you. The LORD will come as he did against the Philistines at Mount Perazim and against the Amorites at Gibeon. He will come to do a strange thing; he will come to do an unusual deed: For the Lord, the Lord of Heaven's Armies, has plainly said that he is determined to crush the whole land. So, scoff no more, or your punishment will even be greater. Listen to me; listen and pay close attention. Does a farmer always plow and never sow? Is he forever cultivating the soil and never planting? Does he not finally plant his seeds – black cumin, cumin, wheat, barley, and emmer wheat [all of these are brown and tanned by the way] – each in its proper way, and each in its proper place? The farmer knows just what to do, for God has given him understanding. A heavy sledge is never used to thresh black cumin; rather, it is beaten with a light stick. A threshing wheel is never rolled on cumin; instead, it is beaten lightly with a flail. Grain for bread is easily crushed, so he doesn't keep on pounding it. He threshes it under the wheels of a cart, but he doesn't pulverize it. The Lord of Heaven's Armies is a wonderful teacher, and he gives the farmer great wisdom. – Isaiah 28:16-29" Isaiah was letting us know that God had a chosen people and they were going to experience slavery and rough times because of their sin and rebellion but they were not going to be slaves forever and through repentance they would receive wisdom and knowledge.

The Holy Spirit [Jesus] and the Word of God [Bible/10 Commandments] are the Two Witnesses and they will come together in an extraordinary way at the end of the Gentile Age [2019]. I know this to be true because the word Apocalypse is a Greek word meaning "revelation" and it means "an unveiling or unfolding of things not previously known and which could not be known apart from the unveiling." "If the old way, which brings condemnation, was glorious, how much more glorious is the new way, which makes us right with God!" (2 Corinthians 3:9) I went to Lake Balboa today to look for a stone that I could bless because the Lord had spoken to me many times in this place. As I walked around the lake, I found a huge stone right near the water and it was underneath a small tree. There were white ducks around it and so I bent over, and I blessed the rock and intend to return with the wine and olive oil, today I just wanted to find the place. My mother loved being by the lake and feeding the ducks. I always feel close to her when I'm at this park as well, though I don't believe she ever visited this place in the natural, but I know she is here with me in spirit.

As I stood up and looked across the lake to the other side, I heard the Lord say, "We are about to cross over to the other side." I didn't know what it meant but it made me happy. "Joshua recorded these things in the Book of God's instructions. As a reminder of their agreement, he took a huge stone and rolled it beneath the terebinth tree beside the Tabernacle of the Lord. Joshua said to all the people, "This stone has heard everything the Lord said to us. It will be a witness to testify against you if you go back on your word to God." (Joshua 24:26-27) "Jacob set up a stone pillar to mark the place where God had spoken to him. Then he poured wine over it as an offering to God and anointed the pillar with olive oil. And Jacob name the place Bethel [which means "house of God"], because God had spoken to him there." (Genesis 35:14-15) "O Jerusalem, Jerusalem, the city that kills the prophets and stones God's messengers! How often I have wanted to gather your children together as a hen protects her chicks beneath her wings, but you wouldn't let me. And now, look, your house is abandoned. For I tell you this, you will never see me again until you say, 'Blessings on the one who comes in the name of the LORD!'" Matthew 23:37-39

Chapter 16: He's Making Everything New

"When Jesus spoke again to the people, he said, "I am the light of the world. Whoever follows me will never walk in darkness but will have the light of life." John 8:12

Friday, December 22, 2017, was the day I saw the light and the night I prayed to God about saving my son. That night I prayed that God would help me to teach my son about Him and that He would come to know Him the way that I did. I didn't know at the time that my dream for my son, would actually increase my faith. The Lord answered my prayer 39 days later by giving my sons dreams that would set me and my family on a collision course with destiny. I also didn't know at the time that the 39 was going to be so significant. I've covered it in earlier chapters how it has to do with hatred, punishment, slavery and dictatorship. Though I didn't understand the significance of numbers at the time, I've come to learn that God is very intentional with everything.

The number 22 is the Number of Revelation. In the 22nd chapter of the gospel of John, he identifies himself as the Alpha and Omega which would be the first and last letters of the Greek Alphabet, Aleph and Tav. The aleph () is the first letter of the Hebrew alephbet (alphabet), and the tav () is the last letter of the alephbet. It is in the placement of these two incredibly significant letters at strategic locations within many verses of Hebrew scripture that express the understanding of a total completeness. Unequivocally the greatest symbol in biblical history since it was revealed by the Apostle John is the Aleph/Tav את Character Symbol. John talks about the New Jerusalem in Revelation 21.

"Then I saw a new heaven and a new earth, for the old heaven and the old earth had disappeared. And the sea [the people] was also gone. And I saw the holy city, the new Jerusalem (Zion), coming down from God out of heaven like a bride beautifully [female spirit] dressed for her husband [male spirit]. I heard a loud shout from the throne, saying, "Look God's home is now among his people! He will live with them, and they will be his people. God himself will be with them [their God]. He will wipe every tear from their eyes, and there be no more death or sorrow or crying or pain. All these things are gone forever. And the one on the throne said, "Look, I am making everything new!" And then he said to me, "Write this down, for what I tell you is trustworthy and true." And he also said, "It is finished! I am the Alpha and the Omega – the Beginning and the End. To all who are thirsty I will give freely from the springs of the water of life. All who are victorious will inherit all these blessings, and I will be their God, and they will be my children.

"But cowards, unbelievers, the corrupt, murderers, the immoral, those who practice witchcraft, idol worshippers, and all liars – their fate is in the fiery lake of burning sulfur. This is the second death." Then one of the seven angels who held the seven bowls containing the seven last plagues came and said to me, "come with me! I will show you the bride, the wife of the Lamb." So, he took me in the Spirit [or in spirit] to a great, high [Holy] mountain, and he showed me the holy city [Zion], Jerusalem descending out of heaven from God. It shone with the glory of God and sparkled like a precious stone – like jasper [a brown stone] as clear as crystal [the Holy Spirit and clarity]. (Revelation 21:1-11) "The wall was made of jasper, and the city was pure gold [luminous, bright, translucid, expressed clearly and easy to understand], as clear as glass [2020 vision]. – Revelation 21:19" (On December 9, 2019, the Lord told me He was pleased with me, the change happened on March 11, 2020 and June 1, 2020 I saw a vision in the daytime of a beautiful Holy mountain and a lion floating right above my house and I was blinded a little by the light as I looked up. I will include all of these visions and dreams in a Dream Book.)

Jesus also told them other parables. "He said, "The Kingdom of Heaven can be illustrated by the story of a king who prepared a great wedding feast for his son. When the banquet was ready, he sent his servants to notify those who were invited. But they all refused to come! "So, he sent other servants to tell them, 'The feast has been prepared. The bulls [sacrifice] and fattened cattle [sacrifice] have been killed, and everything is ready. Come to the banquet!' But the guests he had invited ignored them and went their own way, one to his farm, another to his business. Others seized his messengers [prophets] and insulted them and killed them. The king was furious, and he sent out his army to destroy the murderers and burn their town. And he said to his servants, 'The wedding feast is ready, and the guests I invited aren't worthy of the honor. Now go out to the street corners and invite everyone you see.'

So, the servants brought in everyone they could find, good and bad alike, and the banquet hall was filled with guests. But when the king came in to meet the guests, he noticed a man who wasn't wearing the proper clothes for a wedding. 'Friend,' he asked, 'how is it that you are here without wedding clothes?' But the man had no reply. Then the king said to his aides, 'Bind his hands and feet and throw him into the outer darkness, where there will be weeping and gnashing of teeth.' For many are called, but few are chosen." (Matthew 22:1-14) The Number 22 unites the entire body of Scripture and is also the numerical value for the Hebrew word Yachad, meaning Unite. The number 22 has long been known to represent a Cipher or key from God. Number 22 is the number of Light, sons and daughters of Light, spiritual illumination, and Revelation. The Egyptian priesthood showed great reverence for the number 22, with many sacred writings being centered around this number. Wow, that's amazing because December 22 thrust us right into Babylonian times.

There are (22) twenty-two books in the Aaronic (Levitical) Old Testament, which is the light of God for Israel. There are twenty-two generations from Adam to Jacob. When Moses raised up the tabernacle of God there were exactly 22,000 Levites consecrated to serve. Light is used (22) twenty-two times in the Gospel of John. The 22nd time John uses the word, he quotes Jesus. December 22, 2017, was a signal to me that the beginning of the end has begun. On December 22, the Falcon X flew across the sky, and then on December 22, 2019, it was Hanukkah which is when Jesus passed through the Temple and lit the candle that burned for 8 days and nights, which was representative of the holy oil and it's been on fire ever since. Jesus claimed to be the Alpha and Omega, the beginning and the end and it's interesting that "Mesis" is the word for "in the middle of" because history or His story is everything. He was there in the beginning. He's been with us all in between and He will be at the very end. I'm the elect lady, the seed, and the wild olive branch. He chose me to write the ending and the second beginning. I bear witness of both the Father God and Christ Jesus because my visions and dreams and the experiences I've had – my testimony confirm the Word of God as written in the Bible is true. Though, there are more who have been awakened and it's happening all over the world.

Jesus shouted to the crowds: "If you trust me, you are trusting not only me, but also God who sent me. For when you see me, you are seeing the one who sent me. I have come as a light to shine in this dark world, so that all who put their trust in me will no longer remain in the dark. I will not judge those who hear me, but don't obey me, for I have come to save the world and not to judge it. But all who reject me, and my message will be judged on the day of judgement by the truth I have spoken. I don't speak on my own authority. The Father who sent me has commanded me what to say and how to say it. And I know his commands lead to eternal life; so, I say whatever the Father tells me to say." - John 12:44-50.

Christians are to walk in the light of Christ as it is written in the Bible in John 3:20-21, "All who do evil hate the light and refuse to go near it for fear their sins will be exposed. But those who do what is right come to the light so others can see that they are doing what God wants [or can see God at work in what he is doing]. It is also written, "You are the light of the world – like a city on a hilltop that cannot be hidden. No one lights a lamp and then puts it under a basket. Instead, a lamp is placed on a stand, where it gives light to everyone in the house. In the same way, let your good deeds shine out for all to see, so that everyone will praise your heavenly Father." Matthew 5:14-16. What's so awesome about all of this is that I was hearing the messages correctly, the Lord was telling me in my dreams that He was returning, and it would be soon. So, the FalconX was a signal that he was coming on December 22, 2017, and He ignited the fire (the candlestick) on December 22, 2019, and the flame in my heart that burns for Yah! It was also a signal of what was ahead, a very serious threat.

"Therefore, just as fire licks up stubble and dry grass shrivels in the flame, so their roots will rot and their flowers wither. For they have rejected the law of the LORD of Heaven's Armies; they have despised the word of the Holy One of Israel. That is why the LORD's anger burns against his people, and why he has raised his fist to crush them. The mountains tremble, and the corpses of his people litter the streets like garbage. But even the LORD's anger is not satisfied. His fist is still poised to strike! He will send a signal to distant nations far away and whistle to those at the ends of the earth. They will come racing toward Jerusalem. They will not get tired or stumble. They will not stop for rest or sleep. Not a belt will be loose, not a sandal strap broken. Their arrows will be sharp and their bows ready for battle. Sparks will fly from their horses' hooves, and the wheels of their chariots will spin like a whirlwind. They will roar like lions, like the strongest of lions. Growling, they will pounce on their victims and carry them off, and no one will be there to rescue them." (Isaiah 5:24-29) The Lord God Almighty has been very patient with Jerusalem, but God's patience is growing thin and He is being tested and we should not test God!

"Then the devil took him to the holy city, Jerusalem, to the highest point of the Temple, and said, "If you are the Son of God, jump off! For the Scriptures say, 'He will order his angels to protect you. And they will hold you up with their hands, so you won't even hurt your foot on a stone (Psalms 91).' Jesus responded, "The Scriptures also say, 'You must not test the LORD your God (Deuteronomy 6)." Next the devil took him to the peak of a very high mountain of the world and their glory [the haftorah]. "I will give it all to you," he said, "if you will kneel down and worship me." "Get out of here Satan," Jesus told him. "For the Scriptures say, 'You must worship the LORD your God and serve him.' Then the devil went away, and angels came and took care of Jesus." (Matthew 4:5-11) Jesus would not bow to Satan. Jesus spoke the Word of God in defense, there was no fighting here. This was no physical fight over the Word. I keep saying, this is a spiritual battle over the word of God. Therefore, they want to do away with the Bible because it's the truth!

"Those who live in the shelter of the Most High will find rest in the shadow of the Almighty. This I declare about the LORD: He alone is my refuge, my place of safety; he is my God, and I trust him. For he will rescue me from every trap and protect me from deadly disease. He will cover me with his feathers. He will shelter me with his wings. His faithful promises are my armor and protection. I will not be afraid of the terrors by night, nor the arrow that flies in the day. I will not dread the disease that stalks in darkness, nor the disaster that strikes at midday. Though a thousand fall at my side, though ten thousand are dying around me, these evils will not touch me. I will open my eyes and see how the wicked are punished.

I will make the LORD my refuge, I will make the Most High my shelter, no evil will conquer me; no plague will come near my home. For He will order His angels to protect me wherever I go. They will hold me up with hands, so I won't even hurt my foot on a stone. I will trample upon lions and cobras [beasts of the field]; I will crush fierce lions and serpents under my feet! The LORD says, "I will rescue those who love me. I will protect those who trust in my name. When they call on me, I will answer; I will be with them in trouble. I will rescue and honor them. I will reward them with a long life and give them my salvation." (Psalms 91:1-16) I didn't change the scripture, I just made it personal.

"This is the message from the LORD against the land of Aram [Hebrew the land of Hadrach – Syria] and the city of Damascas [Hill Country], for the eyes of humanity, including all the tribes of Israel, are on the LORD. Doom is certain for Hamath [Gaza], near Damascus, and for the cities of Tyre [Lebanon] and Sidon [Galilee] though they are so clever. Tyre has built a strong fortress and has made silver and gold as plentiful as dust in the streets! But now the Lord will strip away Tyre's possessions and hurl its fortifications into the sea, and it will be burned to the ground. The city of Ashkelon [Israel] will see Tyre fall and will be filled with fear. Gaza will shake with terror, as will Ekron, for their hopes will be dashed. Gaza's king will be killed, and Ashkelon will be deserted. Foreigners will occupy the city of Ashdod. I will destroy the pride of the Philistines [Palestine]. I will grab the bloody meat from their mouths and snatch the detestable sacrifices from their teeth. Then the surviving Philistines will worship our God and become like a clan in Judah [Hebrew like a leader in Judah]. The Philistines of Ekron will join my people, as the ancient Jebusites once did. I will guard my Temple and protect it from invading armies. I am watching closely to ensure that no more foreign oppressors overrun my people's land.

Rejoice, O people of Zion [Hebrew O daughter of Zion]! Shout in triumph, O people of Jerusalem! Look, your king is coming to you. He is righteous and victorious [Hebrew is being vindicated] yet he is humble, riding on a donkey – riding on a donkey's colt. I will remove the battle chariots from Israel [Hebrew Ephraim, referring to the northern kingdom of Israel] and the warhorses from Jerusalem. I will destroy all the weapons used in battle, and your king will bring peace to the nations. His realm will stretch from sea to sea and from the Euphrates River [Hebrew the river] to the ends of the earth [or the end of the land]. Because of the covenant I made with you, sealed with blood, I will free your prisoners from death in a waterless dungeon. Come back to the place of safety, all you prisoners who still have hope! I promise this very day that I will repay two blessings for each of your troubles [double for your trouble].

Judah is my bow, and Israel is my arrow. Jerusalem [Hebrew Zion] is my sword, and like a warrior, I will brandish it against the Greeks [Hebrew the sons of Javan – Noah's descendants]. The Lord will appear above his people; his arrows will fly like lightning! The Sovereign LORD will sound the ram's horn [me] and attack like a whirlwind from the southern desert. The LORD of Heaven's Armies will protect his people, and they will defeat their enemies by hurling great stones. They will shout in battle as though drunk with wine. They will be filled with blood like a bowl, drenched with blood like the corners of the altar. On that day, the LORD their God will rescue his people, just as a shepherd rescues his sheep. They will sparkle in his hand like jewels in a crown. How wonderful and beautiful they will be! The young men will thrive on abundant grain, and the young women will flourish on new wine. – Zechariah 9:1-17" The number 9 represents God's movement and judgement, 2 the union between Christ and the church, 8 represents Jesus, resurrection, regeneration and no lack and the number 18 represents slavery and bondage and double blessing. Psalms 22:6 says, "But I am a worm and not a man. I am scorned and despised by all!" A butterfly starts as a worm and a woman is scorned and King David said many times he was despised, but we also see in this day and age, Jesus is despised because people don't want to do what's right and pure, but they want to go on sinning.

I believe this number 22 relates to me in more ways than one. We saw Isaiah 22:22 which talks about the key to the house of David – the highest position in the royal court. Now, the 22nd book written and included in the New Testament, in chronological order, is the book of 3 John. John wrote this book to his friend and fellow elder Gaius. Gaius means "of the Land or earth". Remember we talked about the earth being symbolism for soil, and the soil as the land or our hearts. The name Gaius is old enough to be the product of an obscure etymology, but obscure as the formal etymology might be, this name, then and now, most reminds of the familiar Greek noun γαια (gaia), meaning earth or land. Gaius seems to reflect the considerations of an agricultural society, which would make sense seeing the bible uses lots of symbolism and mainly vegetation, trees, and farming analogies to represent people and places in the Bible and also representative of the name Adam in Hebrew, and Gaius primarily means made of earthly material. I guess I do have the mind of Adam.

This letter is from John, the elder. "I am writing to Gaius, my dear friend, whom I love in the truth. Dear friend, I hope all is well with you and that you are as healthy in body as you are strong in spirit. Some of the traveling teachers recently returned and made me very happy by telling me about your faithfulness and that you are living according to the truth. I could have no greater joy than to hear that my children are following the truth. Dear friend, you are being faithful to God when you care for the traveling teachers who pass through, even though they are strangers to you. They have told the church here of your loving friendship. Please continue providing for such teachers in a manner that pleases God. For they are traveling for the Lord [Greek They went out on behalf of the Name] and they accept nothing from people who are not believers [Greek from Gentiles].

So, we ourselves should support them so that we can be their partners as they teach the truth. I wrote to the church about this, but Diotrephes [meaning nourished by Jupiter – false light appearing real, antichrist, government], who loves to be the leader, refuses to have anything to do with us [the people]. When I come, I will report some of the things he is doing and the evil accusations he is making against us. Not only does he refuse to welcome the traveling teachers, he also tells others not to help them. And when they do help, he puts them out of the church. Dear friend, don't let this bad example influence you. Follow only what is good. Remember that those who do good prove that they are God's children, and those who do evil prove that they do not know God [Greek they have not seen God]. 3 John 1:1-11 (7)

God is all about liberty, justice and freedom through His word, and freedom both in heaven eternally and on the earth. Notice heavens is plural, because while there is only one earth, there are three heavens. A heaven to be established on earth, a second heaven and a third heaven where God sits on the throne. I said in the first book God told me to write that it's not right to cry out for justice for things that are against God! In all these instances things go terribly wrong and judgements come against that situation or people. It makes sense that the Ten Commandments would cause such a ruckus because people are rebellious and have sinful natures and they want to follow their fleshly desires instead of fighting against flesh and sin they choose evil, because God gave us free will, instead choosing Jesus and being led by the Word of God, which is the Spirit of God.

America seems to prefer living by their emotions and what "feels" good instead of doing what is "right" in the eyes of God, thus choosing the ways of the evil one verses choosing to live by the Lord's righteous statues. However, if people would live this way, the righteous way and by God's rules, it would bring about the change this world so desperately needs and desires – unity, peace, love, no more war or weapons and true harmony. Just maybe we could be in pursuit of the plans our Creator had in mind when He created us if we took the correct path. "Because God's children are human beings – made of flesh and blood – the Son also became flesh and blood. For only as a human being could he die, and only by dying could he break the power of the devil, who had the power of death. Only in this way could he set free all who have lived their lives as slaves to the fear of dying. We also know that the Son did not come to help angels; he came to help the descendants of Abraham. Therefore, it was necessary for him to be made in every respect like us, his brothers, and sisters, so that he could be our merciful and faithful High Priest before God. Then he could offer a sacrifice that would take away the sins of the people. Since he himself has gone through suffering and testing, he is able to help us when we are being tested." Hebrews 2:14-18 Wow, did you read that, "slaves to the fear of dying?" This is what America has done, they have created fear in the people so that they will trust man, over God.

Therefore, Jesus and His word are the answer. Furthermore, now we understand that the enemy began with the attack on the word in the garden and he's always attacked from the darkness – it's plain to see that he is not of the light but is himself the darkness. Satan is the invisible enemy working through those who deny Christ Jesus as their Savior and Lord. I found this to be true when reading the Book of Adam and Eve and the Conflict in the Garden. While Adam and Eve were in the darkness, specifically in the Cave of Treasurers, the devil cast a shifting shadow and made the false lights appear real so that he could trick Adam and Eve into coming out of the cave [their safe place, the holy road] or off the chosen path so he could kill them.

Jesus is the true light and it makes sense that the days are getting shorter, and the nights longer. The sun has been setting at 4:44 p.m. and I explained that the 444 means the coming Messiah, meaning its almost night. God wanted me to notice the time because there is a dark time coming ahead and night is symbolic of dark and evil times. He will be the light or the righteousness. As for now, the followers of Christ are the light until He returns. "You are the light of the world – like a city on a hilltop that cannot be hidden. No one lights a lamp and then puts it under a basket. Instead, a lamp is placed on a stand, where it gives light to everyone in the house. In the same way, let your good deeds shine out for all to see, so that everyone will praise your heavenly Father. Don't misunderstand why I have come. I did not come to abolish the law of Moses or the writings of the prophets. No, I came to accomplish their purpose. I tell you the truth, until heaven and earth disappear, not even the smallest detail of God's law will disappear until its purpose is achieved. So, if you ignore the least commandment and teach others to do the same, you will be called the least in the Kingdom of Heaven. But anyone who obeys God's laws and teaches them will be called great in the Kingdom of Heaven." Matthew 5:14-19

How can you be a light in a dark world if there is no light in you? Jesus lights the lamp and God's word is the illumination, the instructions and the lamp that guides your path. That path to that light can be found in His word, the Holy Bible. "And the city has no need of sun or moon, for the glory of God illuminates the city, and the Lamb is its light." (Revelation 21:23) My prayer is that everyone, all over the world will read this book and understand that first and foremost, God said all He made was "good" and He proved that He loved us when He sent Jesus as a gift to the world. I hope and pray that instead of people being afraid of what's to come that they will bury themselves in the Word of God and do all within themselves to get close to Him so that He can reveal His goodness to them and they won't be afraid but instead surrender and obey. Because it's only in the surrender and obedience that the peace comes.

I also pray they do this so that they can escape the terror coming on the world as it is written in the Good Book and that's the Bible. I pray that anyone who's ever had an encounter with God would remember Him and that special day you met Him. If you met Him one time, you know He is real. Remember that moment. I pray you would seek His face and His righteousness and His Kingdom so that you can be freed from your prison and enjoy the rich benefits of knowing the Creator and be rescued from certain death and judgement when He returns. I've learned, the more you give to God, the more He will give to you and I'm not talking about the tangible things that are important to this world, but hidden treasures, the riches of His glory in Christ Jesus, the real gems that are important to God and in heaven. I'm telling you; He can transform your entire life, improve your relationships, and make your life a whole lot better. I found the true love of my life in Jesus; He is the gift and I would not advise anyone to chance living without Him.

All of this made me think about the prophets and those used by God, like Abraham, Noah, Jeremiah, Ezekiel, Isaiah, Elijah, Jonah and many, many others, and how the people didn't believe them or accept their messages from the LORD. They didn't believe the Lord at first either and that's the issue today, and it's not that they didn't believe, they were afraid of the unknown. However, once they saw that God kept His promises and His word, they believed! How can you believe in something or someone you don't know, you don't read about and you don't listen to? This is where the Holy Spirit comes in and why communication from and with the Holy Spirit is so important because it's the same as being in communication with the Father and the Son.

"Look! I stand at the door and knock, if you hear my voice and open the door, I will come in, and we will share a meal together as friends. Those who are victorious will sit with me on my throne, just as I was victorious and sat with my Father on his throne. Anyone with ears to hear must listen to the Spirit and understand what he is saying to the churches."' (Revelation 3:2-5, 20-22) He knocked, I answered. He pursued me and I pursued Him right back. He was faithful to His word, and He spoke to me. I said, "Yes".

Chapter 17: He left the 99

"If a man has a hundred sheep and one of them wanders away, what will he do? Won't he leave the ninety-nine others on the hills and go out to search for the one that is lost?" Matthew 18:12

The shepherd left the ninety-nine safely on the hill to go after the one sheep that was lost. Seems like we've been in the wilderness in America for much longer than 39 years, surely much longer than that and I am only ten (10) years older than the time we've been beholden to the government and it's systems under Reaganomics, but I refuse to bow! Remember I talked about the number 39 in an earlier chapter and how it was significant in more ways than I could have imagined. I've always had a fighting spirit especially when it comes to injustice, hatred, and cruelty! One common form of corporal punishment, recorded in both the Old and New Testaments, is the receiving of stripes (also called scourging, Leviticus 19:20). The practice is based on Deuteronomy 25:1-3 where up to forty stripes could be administered. Such correction was labeled "forty stripes save one" (2 Corinthians

11:24) as Jews limited themselves to carrying out, at most, only 39 stripes. This is symbolic and connected to the parable about the prodigal son, where Jesus speaks about the Father leaving the 99 to go after the one. I was 39 when I moved to the valley and it was the Lord that moved me here. The Old Testament consist of 39 books.

Jewish religious leaders, especially in the first century, set the maximum number of stripes to 39 because they feared making a mistake and going beyond the prescribed limit. The Romans, however, had no such limit in their law. Therefore, the Word of God tells us that it is the law that gives sin it's power. The law is not good if its intention is to protect those who hurt others. Christ was scourged by the Romans so many times that it rendered him too weak to carry his crucifixion stake to Golgotha (Read Matthew 27:26, 32, Mark 15:21, Luke 23:26). The 1906 Jewish Encyclopedia states that stripes would be administered using a fourfold thong of leather. Sounds very much like the whips used in the south during slavery time, which sadly a lot of people want to erase from the history books, but it happened.

Commentaries like Gill's, Matthew Henry's, and others, however, believe that a three-fold lash or cord was used and thirteen strokes (at most) were carried out to achieve 39 blows because 13 times 3 is 39. Jesus warned Christians they could be beaten by religious authorities, who think they are doing God a service, for the truth they taught (Matthew 10:17, 23:34, John 16:2). This is what's happening in today's society and all over the world. People really believe that the people of color were meant to be slaves for life and that is a lie from Satan! Such unrighteous abuse happened to the apostles a short time after Christ's ascension. Such unrighteous abuse also happened during slavery in the United States. The Apostles were arrested and beaten as foretold by Jesus by the Sanhedrin and, were beaten (likely with thirty-nine stripes, see Acts 5:17 - 41). God's law allowed, and Jewish tradition upheld, the role of judgment in determining the number of stripes a criminal would receive, but Jesus was no criminal and had committed no crime, yet he took these stripes for us, His chosen people. He did it for me. It's the nation of Israel, Zion the one nation he left the other 99 for.

"Blessings on the King who comes in the name of the Lord! Peace in heaven, and glory in highest heaven (Psalms 118:26; 148;1)! Peace in heaven, and glory in highest heaven!" But some of the Pharisees among the crowd said, "Teacher, rebuke your followers for saying things like that! He [Jesus] replied, "If they kept quiet, the stones [the living stones – 10 Commandments and the Bible] along the road would burst into cheers!" But as he came closer to Jerusalem and saw the city ahead, he began to weep. "How I wish today that you of all people would understand the way to peace. But now it is too late, and peace is hidden from your eyes. Before long, your enemies will build ramparts against your walls and encircle you and close in on you from every side. They will crush you into the ground, and your children with you. Your enemies will not leave a single stone in place, because you did not recognize it when God visited you [Greek says - did not recognize the time of your visitation, a reference to the Messiah's coming]." (Luke 19:38-44) Praise God! I recognize my time of visitation, and I responded. I am the righteousness of God in Christ Jesus. An angel in linen cloths, seemingly inching into this world from an ancient time, touched me in 2014 and said, "Wake up."

Something else interesting about 39, divided by 2 is 19.5, and it was midway through 2019, in August that the Lord began to show me heaven on earth. This is also when I began to find out the significance of the number 39. Aries is the 39th largest constellation in the sky, occupying 441 square degrees. It lies in the first quadrant of the northern hemisphere and can be seen at latitudes between +90 degrees and minus 60 degrees. The neighboring constellations are Cetus, Perseus (flying horse), Pisces (Fish), Taurus (Bull) and Triangulum (triangle). Aries constellation is located in the northern hemisphere. Its name means "the ram" in Latin. The symbol for the constellation is and it represents a ram's horns. So many scriptures, where it says, "blow the ram's horns." The constellation Aries is usually associated with the story of the Golden Fleece in Greek mythology.

Like other zodiac constellations, Aries was first catalogued by the Greek astronomer Ptolemy in his Almagest in the 2nd century. In Greek mythology, the Golden Fleece (Greek: Χρυσόμαλλο δέρας, *Chrysómallo déras*) is the fleece of the golden-woolled, winged ram, Chrysomallos, which was held in Colchis. Colchis is known in Greek mythology as the destination of the Argonauts, as well as the home to Medea and the Golden Fleece. "In those days, and for some time after, giant Nephilites lived on the earth, for whenever the sons of God had intercourse with women, they gave birth to children who became the heroes and famous warriors of ancient times." (Genesis 6:4) It was also described as a land rich with gold, iron, timber and honey that would export its resources mostly to ancient Hellenic city-states.

The fleece is a symbol of authority and kingship. It figures in the tale of the hero Jason and his crew of Argonauts, who set out on a quest for the fleece by order of King Pelias, in order to place Jason rightfully on the throne of Iolcus in Thessaly. Through the help of Medea, they acquire the Golden Fleece. The story is of great antiquity and was current in the time of Homer (eighth century BC). It survives in various forms, among which the details vary. The Argonauts were a band of heroes in Greek mythology, who in the years before the Trojan War (around 1300 BC) accompanied Jason to Colchis in his quest to find the Golden Fleece. Their name comes from their ship, *Argo*, named after its builder, Argus. They were sometimes called Minyans, after a prehistoric tribe in the area. Now, I'm understanding why the movie of the same name affected me so.

The Aries constellation is also associated with "The Age of War, Fire, and the Ram," and Moses represents the age of Aries. Bull worshipping cults began to form in Assyria, Egypt, and Crete during this mythological age. When Moses was said to have descended from the mountain with the ten commandments (c. 17th – 13th century BC, the end of the Age of Taurus), some of his people or followers were found by him to be worshipping a golden bull calf. He instructed these worshippers to be killed. This represents Moses "killing" the bull and ending the Age of Taurus, and ushering in the Ages of Aries, which he represented. Interestingly enough, my mother's name was Georgia and she was a Taurus and I believe, because of who she was and the blood she carried, she too was killed.

Aries represents a Fire symbol as well as bold actions, a lot of these behaviors can be seen during any age. However, the themes emphasized during this age relate to courage, initiative, war and adventure. Nations during this age such as the expanding empires of China, Persia, Greece, and Rome, are often cited as examples of the archetypes of Aries in action. Also, the Aries constellation shows a ram running. This could correspond with the sacrifice of Abraham's Ram, the Binding of Isaac. Genesis 22 gives the narrative of when

God tells Abraham to sacrifice his son, Isaac, on Moriah. Abraham begins to comply, when a messenger from God interrupts him. Abraham then sees a ram (the ram in the bush) and sacrifices it instead. "It was by faith that Abraham offered Isaac as a sacrifice when God was testing him. Abraham, who had received God's promises, was ready to sacrifice his only son, Isaac, even though God had told him, "Isaac is the son through whom your descendants will be counted [Genesis 21:12]." Abraham reasoned that if Isaac died, God was able to bring him back to life again. And in a sense, Abraham did receive his son back from the dead. It was by faith that Isaac promised blessings for the future to his sons, Jacob and Esau." (Hebrews 11:17-20) Wow!

Abraham's faith in God is such that he felt God would be able to resurrect the slain Isaac, in order that his prophecy might be fulfilled. This great story of faith was symbolic of the Word of God, who prefigured Christ. This interpretation can be supported by symbolism and context such as Abraham sacrificing his son on the third day of the journey (Genesis 22:4), or Abraham taking the wood and putting it on his son Isaac's shoulder (Genesis 22:6). Another thing to note is how God reemphasizes Isaac being Abraham's one and only son whom he loves (Genesis 22:2, 12, 16). As further support that the binding of Isaac foretells the Gospel of Jesus Christ, when the two went up there, Isaac asked Abraham, "where is the lamb for the burnt offering" to which Abraham responded "God himself will provide the lamb for the burnt offering, my son." (Genesis 22:7-8). However, it was a Ram (not a Lamb) that was ultimately sacrificed in Isaac's place, and the Ram was caught in a thicket (i.e. thornbush).

In the New Testament, John the Baptist saw Jesus coming toward him and said, "Lo, the Lamb of God, who takes away the sins of the world!" (John 1:29) Thus, the binding is compared to the Crucifixion and the last-minute stay of sacrifice is a type of Resurrection. However, this time around, I'm the ram in the bush, the one who has been hidden for such a time as this. When researching Moses and his representation of the Age of Aries, I found a well written article to support my findings, entitled 'The Biblical Astronomy of Moses Birth.' Here is what it said: Why did the Heavenly Father, our All-Powerful, All-Knowing and Loving God, order and arrange the heavens as He did? One major reason was He wanted His people, the human family of His own Creation, to understand Him and some of the wondrous aspects of His glory and majesty.

He also wants us to be aware of the adversary, our spiritual enemy & destroyer. Perhaps most importantly, He wants to show us the panoramic view in His celestial narrative, of the deliverance made available in His only begotten Son, Jesus Christ, the purpose of the ages. We have seen how the celestial record of the stars and planets in their courses contains a special oracle which supports and agrees with the truths of God's Written Word. Read Psalms 19. This celestial showcase and epistle of the Creator's Natural Law works according to keys and principles which will open its secrets unto us, even as Scripture does when it is rightly divided. "Work hard so you can present yourself to God and receive his approval. Be a good worker, one who does not need to be ashamed and who correctly explains the word of truth." (2 Timothy 2:15) The Lord said that he was going to shake the heavens.

A central theme in God's plan of the ages becomes evident in the triple conjunctions of Jupiter-Saturn in celestial history. As we have seen in the signs surrounding the birth of Christ, the Celestial Prelude involving the triple Conjunction of Jupiter-Saturn in 7-6 BC, was a key that unlocked the understanding of the Magi in recognizing the actual signs of Jesus' birth in 3-2 BC. As we focus on the celestial signs surrounding the birth of Moses, a forerunner of Jesus Christ, we can witness a recurring theme involving the retrograde motion of the King planet-Jupiter, in relation to Saturn. The central theme regarding these Jupiter-Saturn unions delineates along four major interrelated Biblical lines, the first of which is spiritual warfare between the celestial powers of light vs. darkness. As we have seen regarding the signs surrounding the birth of Christ, Jupiter was "his star," and proven to be the star of the Messiah, the one which the *Magi* followed as it led them to Jerusalem, and finally Bethlehem.

As the King planet, in reference to the spiritual dominion associated with God's second in command, it is significant to remember that Jupiter, was identified with Jesus as "King of the Judeans," [Matt. 2:2]. Another aspect of Jesus' celestial identity is the Morning Star, [Rev. 2:28, 22:16]. This relates to the planet Venus, significant for its morning and evening star appearances. This title of the Morning Star only occurs one other place in God's Word, [Isa. 14:12], in reference to Lucifer, while still in his first estate, prior to his fall. As the initial bright and Morning Star, Lucifer was second only to God in authority, in the First Heavens and Earth, but his dominion over the angelic realms was stripped from him when iniquity was found in him, at his attempted coup' in heaven.

Christ has superseded him as the Morning Star, and Lucifer's former authority over the archangels Mars-Michael and Mercury-Gabriel was transferred to Christ, who is ascended and seated at the right hand of the Heavenly Father. Venus embodies the original ministry of the Bright and Morning Star, which was delivered to Christ Jesus after Lucifer lost it, because he was unworthy to retain it. Yet Jesus as the King of Kings, and the ascendant Morning Star, embodies much more authority than Lucifer did in the **First Heavens and Earth**, since man was as yet uncreated. One facet of the symbolism of the planet Venus signifies this angelic spiritual dominion as the "covenant angel named wonderful," [**Judges 13:18**].

This reveals a second Biblical element of the theme of Jupiter-Saturn conjunctions-Lucifer/Satan as the fallen Morning star. God has chosen to relate the narrative of this theme of the fallen Lucifer to us, with multiple celestial figures.

Another major aspect of these Jupiter-Saturn unions, is how they ultimately recognize, and point towards the birth of the Promised Seed, Jesus Christ, the purpose of the ages. As we will see in even greater detail regarding the signs surrounding the birth of Moses, God set the celestial orbs in their coordinated paths to witness to His glory, and the arrival of Jesus, His only begotten Son. All Nature stands, to honor and recognize this long awaited and sought for, Day of the Promised Seed. All human kind will ultimately bow to the majestic authority of Jesus Christ our Promised Seed. All Creation will soon worship the glory of the King of Kings, or come to nought. There will be a Jupiter-Saturn union on December 21, 2020 and I don't think it's a coincidence. The Jupiter-Saturn triple union marking the birth of Moses took place over a two-year period from **1536-1535 BC**. The Holy Spirit seems to be working in seasons and cycles of two, afterall I was born at 8:02.

The Israelites traditionally recognized the importance of Jupiter-Saturn celestial unions, and even as they believed these signs would precede the birth of Jesus, so they held the same belief regarding the birth of Moses. The first of three Jupiter-Saturn conjunctions during this period took place on June 25th, 1536 BC. Wow! On June 25, 1776, the Continental Congress authorized the issue of two-dollar bills of credit for the defense of the America. I found a $2 bill on April 13, 2018, which happen to be Thomas Jefferson's birthday and I know it was an angel who left me this clue. Only 49,000 bills were issued at that time. The meaning of the number 49 is derived from the fact that it is **7 times 7**. I believe the Lord was confirming that the 70 years had passed. The two-dollar bill was first commissioned in March,1862. I was born in March. The second Conjunction occurred on July 11th of 1536 BC, followed by the third union on January 4th of 1535 BC. Not only did all three of these Jupiter-Saturn unions take place in the Constellation Taurus the Bull, but Jupiter and Saturn remain for the most part, stationed in Taurus for nearly this entire two-year period.

The general meaning of Taurus in its Biblical significance is the coming Judge and Ruler. This meaning is preserved in ancient Egyptian Astronomy and their pagan star religion, as the Apis Bull. Apis referred to the head or chief savior, who was associated with Isis in the ancient Egyptian cult of the Bull, and was also another name for Saturn. Let's take a moment to inspect some of the root structure of the Apis Bull cult, seen also as the "golden calf" idol adopted by the Israelites in the wilderness, as they tired awaiting Moses' return from the mountaintop, and take note of its cultural influence exerted in the pages of history. The following paraphrase from Oakes & Gahlin, reveals the connection between Isis and the Apis Bull in Egyptian star mythology, which unveils the back-drop that influenced the pagan concept of a Trinitarian Godhead throughout the ancient world.

"Isis tended to be represented as a woman with a throne or solar disc between Cow's horns… She was also frequently depicted with huge sheltering wings, and as part of the Ennead of Heliopolis, was consort to Osiris and mother of Horus, she appeared in the triad {trinity} of deities worshipped at Abydos. As the Isis-cow which gave birth to the sacred Apis Bull of Memphis, her following eventually spread beyond Egypt, to Syria, Palestine, Greece, and throughout the whole Roman Empire, where she was worshipped until well into Christian times." Contributing to the spread of Isis' influence around the Greco-Roman world, we find this "Egyptian cult of Osiris-Apis transferred from Memphis to Alexandria, where the god was called Serapis. He was given the form of a Greek god, but embodied both Greek and Egyptian deities: he was not only Osiris-Apis, but also Zeus, Dionysus, Hades, and Askelpios. Serapis was the god of the underworld, a healing god, a god of fertility, and also the protector of sailors."

This quote provides strong support, pointing out the powerful influence that the Astrology and heathen star religions of Egypt and the ancient world, had on the worldview of ancient, & even modern religions. The ancient Greek Trinity consisted of Zeus, Athena and Apollo, while the Roman version was composed of Jupiter, Mercury and Venus. The ancient Babylonian Trinity consisted of the Morning Star-Venus, the Moon and the Sun.

The heathen astrological traditions seen here, influenced the early Christian Church as many ancient pagans converted to Christianity, but did not fully alter their old heathen practices. Also sects like the Gnostics, for example, set the stage for modern Christian adaptations of Trinitarian dogma, that hold Jesus' physical body was only borrowed temporarily, like the body of Horus-Osiris.

Added to this pagan Trinitarian concept of god, we should also notice that the structure and role-relationship of the mother-goddess Isis, as the consort of Osiris and mother of Horus, is the typical pattern adopted into Roman Catholic traditions of Mary, as the "mother of God," seen also in Hathor, the Egyptian "queen of heaven," as Jeremiah called her namesake [Jer. 7:18, 44:17-19, 25]. Hislop confirms this background in the following statement: "Osiris, in Egypt, is represented at different times, not only as the son and husband of Isis, but also as her father and brother (Bunsen vol. 1, p. 438); then secondly, whatever the deified mortals might be before deification, on being deified they came into a new relationship. On the apotheosis of husband and wife, it was necessary for the dignity of both, that both alike should be represented as of the same celestial origin…"

Hislop documents how this concept was assimilated in ancient Nineveh, in a "horned man-bull," worshipped as an Assyrian divinity. This is also revealed in Hebrew word origins because the Hebrew word for "bull," or "ruler" is *Shur*, which in the Chaldee, becomes *Tur*. From this word Tur, in the sense of a ruler, we get Turannus, giving us a "tyrannical" ruler. But from Tur, in the sense of a Bull, we get the Latin, Taurus. This brief discourse gives us a case in point of the corrupting influence of Astrology from ancient to modern times. It also illustrates the central position of the Jupiter-Saturn conjunctions in this process. However, as we strip away these false astrological veneers and ancient heathen idols, we can restore to a great degree, the original beauty of the starry witness as God intended it to be.

Those who endeavor to study the heavens with the idea of revealing the corrupt practices of the ancient heathen star religions, will never plumb the depths of the Creator's Omniscient Wisdom contained in His order of the Heavens. But as we allow the heavens to speak in unison with God's Written Word, the glorious and matchless majesty unveiled will be truly breathtaking. The celestial oracles not only set the context of events leading to Moses' birth, but they also pointed out key aspects of his ministry, which undeniably identifies Moses in the unique things he accomplished as the Lawgiver, & Forerunner of Jesus Christ. And it seems that a time is fast approaching where this conjunction will appear in the heavens once more, but like the aligning of the planets in 2017, which was a sign of his return over Jerusalem in the heavens – the conjunction will be a sign of His return to His people.

I'm only going to mention ten (10) of the 37 astrological signs leading up to Moses birth during that two year period as I feel they are more significant to my story. The first sign, which occurred on January 11, 1536 B.C., Venus the Morning Star is partially occulted by the Moon in Sagittarius. Here the approaching victorious Morning Star is partially covered by the Crescent Moon, in an attempt by the enemy to obscure its immanent defeat to the forces of light. This lunar occultation also directs our attention to a series of lunar signs that permeate the celestial showcase marking Moses' birth. Mercury-Gabriel is in Capricorn, relating the sufferings of Christ, foreshadowing the Passover Lamb sacrifice, which Moses would install as a holy feast in the Old Testament Law. Thus in the first two aspects of these initial signs marking the birth of Moses, we are shown the sufferings and glory of the Lord, but not the mystery of the Age of Grace between these events, only prophesied of indirectly, both in the Old Testament Scriptures, and the Stars.

We never see the sufferings mentioned apart from the glory of Christ in the Scriptures, and we expect the same in the Stars. Mars-Michael is in Libra, exhibiting the conflict endured by the Passover lamb, as he paid the ultimate price to cover for man's sin. This also relates to the sufferings of the promised seed, and implies Moses' struggle to lead the stiff-necked nation of Israel out of bondage, to institute their Holy Law, The second sign, March 17, 1536 B.C. was the massing of the Planets Jupiter, Saturn and Mercury in Aries. Mercury-Gabriel announces the appearance of Jupiter-Saturn in Aries, the Lamb. This in effect, serves as a prelude to the first Jupiter-Saturn union in Taurus, three months later. This union of the King planet-Jupiter in Aries on the positive side, illuminates the King planet in association with the Passover Lamb of God, coming to supplant what is negatively emphasized with Jupiter-Saturn here, the adversary's emnity as god of this world, to the Lawgiver and forerunner of the Passover Lamb. As the Deliverer of Israel, Moses was a forerunner of the Lord Jesus Christ, and a type of Savior.

As the Lawgiver, He instituted the feast of the Passover lamb in Israel, as part of the 10th plague pronounced on Egypt, immediately after which Israel was released from bondage by Pharaoh. Mars-Michael remains in Libra (scales of justice), during this second sign marking Moses' birth, complementing the redemptive truths that we find here in the sign Aries, relating to the Passover lamb. The archangel Mars-Michael symbolizes the conflict between the Lamb of God and the god of this world as we see them juxtaposed, throughout these signs of 1536 BC, pointing out Michael's allegiance with the forces of light, against the forces of darkness. The Sun/daystar is found in Aries/Pisces while Venus the Morning Star is in Pisces/ Sagittarius. With the Sun in Aries, close to the spring equinox, we see a potential processional marker for the Age of Aries, during which the birth of Moses took place, looking toward the coming Piscean Age, marking the birth of Jesus Christ the ascendant Morning Star.

We also find during this sign, the first in a series of lunar occultations of the red star of the Bull's eye-Aldebaran, in Taurus. Here the lesser light ruling the night attempts to obscure the vision and coming judgment of the true and righteous Man-Bull, Jesus Christ. It also carries more immediate implications for the birth of the Lawgiver Moses. This dual theme depicting the participants in the war in heaven, will run as a consistent thread through many of these signs surrounding the birth of Moses, which will be pointed out in various ways as they arise. This is what is spoken of in Revelations 12, this very things. The 7th sign took place on July 4, 1536 B.C., when Jupiter- Saturn remain in Taurus, as the third lunar occultation of Aldebaran-the eye of the Bull, by the Crescent Moon, in this series occurs. Here once again, we see the enemy attempting to obscure the view of the coming righteous judge, doing every-thing in his power to oppose the forces of light. In the study of the Hebrew calendar, the Moon many times is an indicator of the movements of the serpent's seed behind the scenes, opposed to the Creator's plans. During the time of Moses' birth, a new Pharaoh, had come to power in Egypt, who was not sympathetic to the welfare of Israel, as the previous Pharaoh had been to Joseph and his family.

He began a systematic effort to "control" the male population amongst the Hebrews, by killing the baby Hebrew boys at birth. This was one manifestation of the serpent's efforts to blot out the genetic line which would bear the seed promised by God in Genesis 3:15, going a long way towards the explanation of the "persecution of the Judeans" in history. We also witnessed a similar effort during the birth of Christ in Israel, carried out by the serpent's seed Herod. Venus the bright & Morning Star, remains in Gemini, as does the Sun in Cancer, continuing the theme of the Lord's sufferings and glory, beginning in Moses. Here we can see the protection of the Heavenly Father over those who carry out His plans and purposes, even before they themselves are aware of them. God worked in Pharaoh's own royal house, to protect Moses as a young child, so that he would have the proper upbringing, not to mention the best education that was available at the time, to equip Moses for his important ministry work.

The 8th sign which took place on July 11, 1536 B.C., was the second of three Jupiter-Saturn conjunctions in Taurus, in 1536-1535 BC. This is marked by an Annular solar eclipse at sunrise in Leo, approaching Regulus-the king star. This continues the theme of the enmity symbolized in the lunar activity, to the coming victorious reign of the Lion of the tribe of Judah. Venus the bright and Morning Star is approaching the occultation of the Southern Ass in Cancer. With this Sunrise lunar eclipse taking place concurrent with the second Jupiter-Saturn Conjunction, we can see a dual emphasis on the forces of darkness exerting their dominion to oppose the forces of light. It is worthy to note that the second Jupiter-Regulus Conjunction in Leo, in 3-2 BC, also had a decidedly negative theme, with a strong emphasis on the workings of the serpent's seed. This is all telling of times to come. "For I will shake the heavens. The earth will move from it's place when the Lord of Heaven's Armies displays his wrath in the day of his fierce anger." (Isaiah 13:13)

The 11th sign took place on September 11, 1536 B.C. The triangular union of Venus, Spica/Al Zemach, and the Sun in Virgo. Mercury-Gabriel is also in Virgo, close to the star Porrima, and the Moon is in Scorpius. With the Morning Star/daystar clothing Virgo in unity with the Star Spica, representing the 4-D ministry of the promised seed Jesus Christ as King, Servant, Son of Man and Son of God, on the day of the birth of Christ, 1533 years prior, we have a significant indicator of Moses, a fore-runner of Christ in these four significant aspects of his ministry. As the Lawgiver, Moses embodies the Old Testament Law as Jesus did the Word of God for Israel. Moses instituted the Passover sacrifice, which was fulfilled in the ministry of Christ. Moses was also the Deliverer of Israel, leading them out of bondage, as Christ delivered them from the bondage and letter of the O.T. Law, which only he could fulfill. As I stated in my writings, Jesus also started His ministry on September 10-11.

Moses was an Apostle for Israel shedding new spiritual light for his nation, even as Christ was the Apostle, bringing the new light of the Kingdom of Heaven to Israel. Mars-Michael is in Sagittarius at the star Nunki, indicating the glorified nature of the conqueror, as Prince of the Earth. The Moon is also in Scorpius, unified with the Scorpion, stinging the heel of the Man of God-Ophiuchus, in his struggle against the serpent-Serpens. The archangel-Michael is allied in the coming victory over the minions of darkness, embodied in the ministry of Christ. The 4-D ministry of Moses/ Christ, here is reflected in the Cardinal Directions of the heavens, and opposed by the four celestial serpents set against these aspects of the ministry of the promised seed. The activity of this sign focused around the star Spica is also intriguing, in that Spica/ AlZemach is what is known as a “spectroscopic binary," or one of those stars which the spectroscope shows to be attended by an invisible companion of enormous Mass. Remember I talked about how Satan is the “invisible enemy.” Spica’s dark companion revolves about it in a close orbit, making a complete revolution in the remarkably short period of 4-days.”

These physical characteristics of this important star of the Messiah illustrate a truth which agrees with a major theme of the witness of the stars. The light of the world is ever-shadowed by his nemesis, the spirit of antichrist, who is constantly at work through the ages Jupiter & Saturn remain in Taurus as they do for the majority of these signs surrounding the birth of Moses. “Don’t be fooled by what they say. For that day will not come until there is a great rebellion against God and the man of lawlessness is revealed – the one who brings destruction. He will exalt himself and defy everything that people call god and every object of worship. He will even sit in the temple of God, claiming that he himself is God. Don’t you remember that I told you about all this when I was with you? And you know what is holding him back, for he can be revealed only when his time comes. For this lawlessness is already at work secretly, and it will remain secret until the one who is holding it back steps out of the way. Then the man of lawlessness will be revealed, but the Lord Jesus will slay him with the breath of his mouth and destroy him by the splendor of his coming.” (2 Thessalonians 2)

The 13th sign of Moses birth happened on November 7, 1536 B.C., Venus, Mercury and the Moon are in Sagittarius. Here the Morning Star and Gabriel remain unified in the promised victory over the enemy and his dark minions. Mars-Michael remains in Capricorn at the star Deneb Al Gedi, referring to the coming sacrifice. As the forerunner of Christ, Moses set the standard as the Lawgiver who instituted the sacrifice of the Passover lamb. This was embodied in the ministry of the Lord Jesus Christ, as he fulfilled every jot and tittle of the O.T. Law. Mars-Michael in Capricorn indicates the conflict that Moses would first endure to lead the nation of Israel out of bondage with the institution of the Law, setting the stage for the ultimate conflict that Jesus would endure to fulfill it. The Sun/ daystar is in Ophiuchus putting emphasis on the victory of the man over the serpent, in their struggle for the Crown of Creation-Corona. Jupiter and Saturn remain in Taurus.

The 14th sign took place on November 11, 1536 B.C., Mercury and Venus remain in Sagittarius, with the Moon in occulting both Mars and the star Deneb Al Gedi in Capricorn, showing the enmity of the dark forces opposing their coming demise, with all their efforts. These efforts were clearly seen in the attempt on the life of the infant Moses by Pharaoh, even as Herod’s attempt on the life of Jesus came 1533 years later. These Mass murderers who got into a position of political leadership, and worldly prestige are only minor actors leading up to the embodiment of evil-the antichrist, who will take power in the not too distant future. In spite of the efforts of the serpent’s seed to resist his doom, nothing can stop his inexorable destruction, which is indicated again in the position of Sun/daystar in Ophiuchus, showing Christ’s ultimate victory, which is already in the books. Jupiter and Saturn remain in Taurus. This is chapter 17 and 17 represents victory! Remember, I kept seeing the number 11:11 which has a lot of meaning, one of which "The Israelites completely destroyed [11:12,20,21] every living thing in the city, leaving no survivors. Not a single person was spared. And then Joshua burned the city." (Joshua 11:11) I believe all idols and false doctrine are going down in flames.

The 16th sign which happened on December 6, 1536 B.C., A Total lunar eclipse occurs in Sagittarius, heralded by Mercury-Gabriel. This seems to be a direct response by the forces of darkness, attempting to cover and obscure the light of the Daystar, shed forth in Sagittarius in the previous sign. Venus the bright and Morning Star is found in Capricorn here, signifying the sufferings of the sacrifice that the Passover lamb would have to endure to redeem Israel, and all Mankind. Thus we see both the sufferings and glory of the Lord represented here, as we do throughout the signs leading to the birth of Christ. As in the previous sign, Mars is still in Aquarius with Jupiter-Saturn remaining in Taurus. Since Jupiter and Saturn maintain their position in Taurus throughout these signs of 1536-1535BC, we should note that as a consistent celestial backdrop and common element to all these signs, they also form a dual symbolism of one of the major themes we pointed out in our introduction: the theme of light vs. darkness. This is a theme that continues unto this day, and even beyond the victorious return of the Lord. Remember that it was December 6, 2017, that President #45 moved the United States embassy from Tel Aviv to Jerusalem.

The 17th sign, which took place on January 4, 1535 B.C., This marks the Third Conjunction of Jupiter-Saturn in Taurus marking the birth of Moses, completing the triple Conjunction of Jupiter-Saturn in Taurus in 1536-1535 BC. This sign is highlighted by a total lunar eclipse in Capricorn, along with the lunar occultation of both the stars Nashira, and Deneb Al Geidi, denoting the coming sacrifice in Capricorn. Again, we can see this as an attempt to obscure the light of the coming lamb of God, by the forces of darkness. We should notice that, it was Moses the Lawgiver who instituted the precedent of the Passover Lamb in Israel, as part of their deliverance from bondage in Egypt, which was fulfilled in Christ, who embodied every aspect of the Passover Lamb, as he fulfilled the entire OT Law. This imagery is supported here with Mars in Pisces, showing Michael fighting for, and protecting Israel against the Egyptians.

Pisces two fish represent the two houses of Israel and Judah, as they are fastened to the neck of Cetus the adversarial sea monster, in the sky pictures of the ecliptic and the Celestial Equator. The enemy is always opposing the will of God in any and every way he can. We also find Venus the bright and Morning Star in Aquarius during this sign, showing the spiritual light of Israel's deliverer embodied in the birth of Moses. Aquarius the water bearer represents the pouring out of holy spirit upon Gods people, which during the Patriarchal Age was largely done with individual men of God. This changed however with Moses, as he ministered to Israel. Here we have the first instance where God's spirit was poured out among the group of the 70 elders of Israel. This foreshadows the Church in the Age of Grace, where God is able to abundantly minister His spirit via the new birth to all who believe. Hallelujah! This is what is described in Joel 2, which I believe to be the latter rain. I believe this will happen in 2020.

And lastly, the 34th sign which took place on August 6, 1535 B.C. Mars and Regulus are in Conjunction in Leo, showing Michael in unity with the King Star, the heart of the Lion of the tribe of Judah. Mercury, & the Sun are also in Leo, showing the unity of the archangels with the Daystar & the King Star in Leo. With Venus in Cancer and Jupiter in Gemini, we have a complete departure from Saturn, which is isolated and alone between the Bull's Horns in judgment, in Taurus. This isolation is a direct response not only to the enemy's false claims of kingship throughout these signs, but also the recent Regulus occultations which mirror the Regulus occultation series in 3-2 BC. I knew that the Lord was with me in August of 2019, because I began to have day visions. And the word that came on August 7, 2019, was as follows: "Salvation is not a reward for the good things we have done, so none of us can boast about it. For we are God's masterpiece. He has created us anew in Christ Jesus, so we can do the good things he planned for us long ago." (Ephesians 2:9-10) Part of the meaning of the number 34 may be related to the naming of a son. The 34th time Abraham's name is recorded in Scripture is when he named his first and only son, through Sarah, Isaac (Genesis 21:3). Remember how I talked about the number 22 uniting the scripture and it seems to be unfolding as I write this book and my life experiences. The supernatural experiences and the visions and dreams seem to coincide with the things going on in both the heavens and on the earth.

The Bible is a book to be studied. The bible brings us to our knees where we need to be. It's a searchlight into our hearts. It saves us from stupid nativity and the tendencies to sit on a throne that is God's alone. Thank you for forgiving us Lord. Thank you for the steadfast love that never ends and for your mercies that are new every morning. The importance of me speaking about the Age of Aries, besides the fact that I am a Aries who was born on Resurrection Sunday, is the fact that the ages put on Earth the main characteristics related to that current sign and also express the values of the opposite sign. Aries and Libra were the two signs ruling the planet that time, which happened 2,300 Bc up to 150 Bc. Humanity underwent major changes when it passed from the Age of Taurus to Aries. During the taurine regency, the societies organized themselves having farming as the main pillar. The great empires prospered from what land and water (polarity with Scorpio) gave. The Age of Aries, having the fire as its main element, represented a new beginning, purer and stronger. Also, somewhat aggressive, but the impulsivity of this sign caused a wave of wars and conquests, but also brought a sense of independence.

"One day Moses was tending the flock of his father-in-law, Jethro [Reuel], the priest of Midian. He led the flock far into the wilderness and came to Sinai, the mountain of god. There the angel of the Lord appeared to him in a blazing fire from the middle of a bush. Moses stared in amazement. Though the bush was engulfed in flames, it didn't burn up. "This is amazing," Moses said to himself. "Why isn't that bush burning up? I must go see it." When the Lord saw Moses coming to take a closer look, God called to him from the middle [Mesis] of the bush, "Moses! Moses!" "Here I am!" Moses replied. "Do not come any closer," the Lord warned. "Take off your sandals, for you are standing on holy ground. I am the God of our father [Greek version reads your fathers] – the God of Abraham, the God of Isaac, and the God of Jacob."

When Moses heard this, he covered his face because he was afraid to look at God. Then the Lord told him, "I have certainly seen the oppression of my people in Egypt. I have heard their cries of distress because of their harsh slaves drivers. Yes, I am aware of their suffering. So I have come down to rescue them from the power of the Egyptians and lead them out of Egypt into their own fertile and spacious land. It is a land flowing with milk and honey – the land where the Canaanites, Hittites, Amorites, Perizzites, Hivites, and Jebusites now live. Look! The cry of the people of Israel has reached me, and I have seen how harshly the Egyptians abuse them. Now go, for I am sending you to Pharaoh. You must lead my people Israel out of Egypt." But Moses protested to God, "Who am I to appear before Pharaoh? Who am I to lead the people of Israel out of Egypt?"

God answered, "I will be with you. And this is your sign that I am the one who has sent you: When you have brought the people out of Egypt, you will worship God at this very mountain." But Moses protested, "If I go to the people of Israel and tell them, 'The God of your ancestors has sent me to you,' they will ask me, 'What is his name?' Then what should I tell them?" God replied to Moses, "I AM WHO I AM. Say this to the people of Israel: I AM has sent me to you." God also said to Moses, "Say this to the people of Israel: Yahweh, the God of your ancestors – the God of Abraham, the God of Isaac, and the God of Jacob – has sent me to you. This is my eternal name, my name to remember for all generations. "Now go and call together all the elders of Israel. Tell them, 'Yahweh, the God of your ancestors – the God of Abraham, Isaac, and Jacob – has appeared to me. He told me, "I have been watching closely, and I see how the Egyptians are treating you. I have promised to rescue you from your oppression in Egypt. I will lead you to a land flowing with milk and honey – the land where the Canaanites, Hittites, Amorites, Perizzites, Hivites, and Jebusites now live." "The elders of Israel will accept your message. Then you and the elders must go the king of Egypt and tell him, 'The Lord, the God of the Hebrews, has met with us. So please let us take a three-day journey into the wilderness to offer sacrifices to the Lord our God.'

"But I know that the king of Egypt will not let you go unless a mighty hand forces him. So I will raise my hand and strike the Egyptians, performing all kinds of miracles among them. Then at last he will let you go. And I will cause the Egyptians to look favorably on you. They will give you gifts when you go so you will not leave empty-handed. Every Israelite woman will ask for articles of silver and gold and fine clothing from her Egyptian neighbors and from the foreign women in their houses. You will dress your sons and daughters with these, stripping the Egyptians of their wealth." (Exodus 3:1-22) The victory belongs to Jesus! He is the only One who defeated death and conquered the grave! Every word of the Bible is coming true in spectacular fashion, just as the prophet said.

"When you go through deep waters, I will be with you. When you go through rivers of difficulty, you will not drown. When you walk through the fire of oppression, you will not be burned up; the flames will not consume you." Isaiah 43:2

Chapter 18: Touched by an Angel

"And we know that God causes everything to work together for the good of those who love God and are called according to his purpose for them." Romans 8:28

I was born in the wilderness. I was born into a war, an invisible war. I was walking around on a battlefield unarmed and ill equipped, but I've always had what I needed in reach. Thank you, Lord! The above scripture speaks about God causing everything to work out for my good because I love Him, because He called me for a purpose. It's been a lonely road, but I haven't been alone. Just as He promised in His word, He never left me. I've discovered that the descendants of Abraham have been in the wilderness for 79 years as of 2019. It's been me and the Holy Spirit and the angels. It takes me back to the day I was floating above myself, outside of my body and it's the best way I can describe it. It's kind of like what Paul speaks about in 2 Corinthians 12:1-10, "I was caught up to the third heaven fourteen (2014) years ago. Whether I was in my body or out of my body, I don't know – only God knows.

Yes, only God knows whether I was in my body or outside my body. But I do know that I was caught up to paradise and heard things so astounding that they cannot be expressed in words, things no human is allowed to tell." I can relate to this because I remember crying as I was up there and feeling so afraid as I saw myself in a deep sleep, lying on that bed. I was feeling as though I had let my mother down. I was feeling worthless and God let me see myself. Then I saw, coming in the distance a man wrapped in linen cloth, like a mummy coming out of a tomb and he touched me on the forehead and a man's voice spoke these words "wake up." Somehow I found myself back on the bed, laying on my back, wide awake and shakened. I will never forget this experience. It changed my life. I was caught up that day.

I don't think it's a coincidence that he says it was fourteen (14) years ago considering it was 2014 when I had this experience, and the number 14 represents deliverance and salvation. Being a multiple of 7, 14 partakes of its importance and, being double that number, implies a double measure of spiritual perfection. The number two (2) with which it is combined (2x7) may, however, bring its own significance into its meaning, as it does in Matthew 1, where the genealogy of Jesus Christ is divided up and given in sets of 14 (2x7) generations, two being associated with incarnation. There are three sets of 14 generations between (and including) Abraham to Joseph (husband of Mary). "So all the generations from Abraham to David are fourteen generations, from David until the captivity in Babylon are fourteen generations, and from the captivity in Babylon until the Christ are fourteen generations." I'm just blown away right now! That's why 14 is so important in my story. Could it be that I am a direct descendant of Abraham in the literal sense? Is that even possible? This is why it's so important for people to know their family history and where they come from. We shouldn't have to pay thousands of dollars or be a celebrity and it be privileged information, it's our birthright!

The number 14 is used 22 (revelation) times in the Bible. The term "14th" is found 24 (priesthood) times in scriptures. The fourteenth day of the first month is the Passover, when God delivered the firstborn of Israel from death. I was 24 years old when my mother gave me the gift of Jesus. Since the number 24 is composed of a multiple of 12, it takes on some of 12's meaning (which is God's power and authority, as well as perfect foundation) except in a higher form. Twenty-four, therefore, is also connected with the worship of God, especially at the temple. It was King David who divided those responsible for the music in temple services, those who served as priests, and the Levites who aided the priests, into 24 courses (1Chronicles 23 - 24). When a particular course of priests served, they usually divided their work amongst themselves by lot. Numbers have a lot of meaning. The New Testament makes reference to one of the priestly courses when it states that the father of John the Baptist was a priest who served in Abia's (Abijah's) course (Luke 1:5). Abijah's course was the eighth one that rotated responsibilities with other priests. Although the book of Luke only has 24 chapters, it has more words than Acts, which has 28 chapters. Therefore, in a real sense, it is correct to say that Luke is the longest New Testament book. Of the top five New Testament writings that contain the most material from the Old Testament, the book of Mark has content from a total number of 24 books. Baasha, the third king of Israel to reign after the kingdom split in 930 B.C., ruled for 24 years.

The number 24 is also related to Christ's rule and reign on the earth when He returns. Psalm 72 lists 24 things that Jesus Christ, as High Priest after the order of Melchizedek, will do when He sits upon His throne and rules as King and Priest during the Millennium. 1. He will righteously judge the people. 2. He will judge, with justice, the poor and needy. 3.Peace will be brought by the mountains. 4. Small hills shall also experience peace. 5. He shall judge the poor. 6. He shall save the children of the needy. 7. Those who oppress will be crushed. 8. He shall rule like rain upon grass. 9. He shall rule like the water that showers the globe. 10. He will cause the righteous to flourish.

11. He will bring the righteous an abundance of peace. 12. He shall rule from sea to sea. 13. He shall rule from the river unto the ends of the earth. 14. When he hears the needy cry out he will deliver him. 15. The poor and those who have no help will also be delivered. 16. Those who are needy and weak will receive compassion. 17. The lives of those in need will be saved. 18. The needy who are oppressed and experience violence will be redeemed. 19. The blood of those in need will be precious in His sight. 20. He will cause an abundance of grain on the earth. 21. He will bring an abundance of fruit. 22. He will make those of the city flourish like grass. 23. He will make His name to be continued. 24. He will bless all men. Wow! Around God's heavenly throne are 24 elders, each wearing crowns sitting on thrones, who assist him in the governing of the universe (Revelation 4:1-4) (9 – God's movement and judgement).

Some 430 years earlier, on the night of the 14th day of the first month, God made two covenant promises to Abraham - one of the physical seed, Isaac, and his descendants, and one of the spiritual seed, Jesus Christ, and the sons of God who would come through Him, who would shine like the stars of heaven (Matthew 13:43). On the day portion of the 14th, God confirmed the promises with a special covenant sacrifice. "After these things the word of the Lord came to Abram in a vision, saying, 'Do not be afraid, Abram. I am your shield, your exceedingly great reward.' But Abram said, 'Lord GOD, what will You give me, seeing I go childless [I am an orphan], and the heir of my house is Eliezer of Damascus?' . . ."And behold, the word of the Lord came to him, saying, 'This one shall not be your heir, but one who will come from your own body shall be your heir.' Then He brought him outside and said, 'Look now toward heaven, and count the stars if you are able to number them.' And He said to him, 'So shall your descendants be'" (Genesis 15:1-2, 4-5, NKJV).

On the 14th day of the first month in 30 A.D. Jesus Christ, God manifested in the flesh, the only begotten Son of God the Father, and the Lamb of God to take away the sin of the world, was crucified as the perfect sacrifice to save mankind from sin. Jesus' death on Passover completed His ministry in the flesh. I heard a Rabbi teach recently that the same time that Jesus was born is the same time that he was crucified. Jesus was born in the spring equinox. Could it be the same period of time that He returns to His bride and to help the descendants of Abraham? Seven represents completion - thus 7 + 7 = 14, indicating a double completion. I am forty-nine currently which is the double sevens.

Jesus ministry in the flesh was completed at Passover. Jesus sacrifice ended and fulfilled the need for animal sacrifices. Wow! That was deep. Thank you Jesus! I don't deserve it, but I am so comforted knowing that my family was chosen for such an honor. They were very special and it was so sad to lose them. I'm sure this is the same way that the saints of old felt, the disciples that were there when Jesus died and the ones that followed. They were good and descent and loving human beings. God is amazing! I was 44 years old when the angel of the Lord touched me on the forehead. I knew at that moment He was giving me time to get my life together. I knew it was God and I immediately began pursuing Him because I wanted to know why He touched me.

When I started going to church and sitting up under the word, it was the equivalent of being fed and I was hearing God's voice at first. I knew that Jesus was the Son of God. I knew it was the angel of the Lord who touched me. My life has not been the same. "Elijah was afraid and fled for his life. He went to Beersheba, a town in Judah, and he left his servant there. Then he went on alone into the wilderness, traveling all day. He sat down under a solitary broom tree and prayed that he might die. "I have had enough, LORD," he said. "Take my life, for I am no better than my ancestors who have already died." Then he lay down and slept under the broom tree. But as he was sleeping, an angel touched him and told him, "Get up and eat!" He looked around and there beside his head was some bread baked on hot stones and a jar of water! So he ate and drank and lay down again." (1 Kings 19:3-6) This scripture talks about baked bread on hot stones and a jar of water which is symbolism for the Word of God, a consuming fire, living stones which are people and the jar of water which is the Holy Spirit.

The broom tree is a desert shrub that grows across Arabia and throughout the Judean wilderness. Its deep roots draw in the moisture of land that is otherwise barren. In the Bible, desert shrubs such as the broom tree appear in moments of despair as well as times of divine encounter. "But if you pray to God and seek the favor of the Almighty, and if you are pure and live with integrity, he will surely rise up and restore your happy home. And though you started with little, you will end with much. Just ask the previous generation. Pay attention to the experience of our ancestors. For we were born but yesterday and know nothing. Our days on earth are as fleeting as a shadow. But those who came before us will teach you. They will teach you the wisdom of old. Can a papyrus reeds grow tall without a marsh? Can marsh grass flourish without water? While they are still flowering, not ready to be cut, they begin to wither more quickly than grass.

The same happens to all who forget God. The hopes of the godless evaporate. Their confidence hangs by a thread. They are leaning on a spider's web. They cling to their home for security, but it won't last. They try to hold it tight, but it will not endure. The godless seem like a lush plant growing in the sunshine, its branches spreading across the garden. It's roots grow down through a pile of stones; it takes hold on a bed of rocks. But when it is uprooted, it's as though it never existed! That's the end of its life, and others spring up from earth to replace it. But look, God will not reject a person of integrity, nor will he lend a hand to the wicked. He will once again fill your mouth with laughter and your lips with shouts of joy. Those who hate you will be clothed with shame, and the home of the wicked will be destroyed." (Proverbs 8:5-22)

"Then Christ will make his home in your hearts as you trust in him. Your roots will grow down into God's love and keep you strong." (Ephesians 3:17) "Let your roots grow down into him, and let your lives be built on him. Then your faith will grow strong in the truth you were taught, and you will overflow with thankfulness." (Colossians 2:7) "And you who are left in Judah, who have escaped the ravages of the siege, will put roots down in your own soil and grow up and flourish." (Isaiah 37:31) "This is what the Sovereign Lord says: When Assyria went down to the grave, I made the deep springs mourn. I stopped it's rivers and dried up its abundant water. I clothed Lebanon in black and caused the trees of the field to wilt. I made the nations shake with fear at the sound of its fall, for I sent it down to the grave with all the other proud trees of Eden, the most beautiful and the best of Lebanon, the ones whose roots went deep into the water, took comfort to find it there with them in the depths of the earth. Its allies, too, were all destroyed and had passed away. They had gone down to the grave – all those nations that had lived in its shade. O Egypt, to which of the trees of Eden will you compare your strength and glory? You, too, will be brought down to the depths with all these other nations. You will lie there among the outcasts [Hebrew uncircumcised] who have died by the sword. This will be the fate of Pharaoh and all his hordes. I, the Sovereign Lord, have spoken!" (Ezekiel 31:15-18)

A broom is defined as a long-handled brush of bristles or twigs, used for sweeping, it's also a cleaning tool, used for sweeping up a mess in lieu of using your own hands. "Who is this sweeping in from the wilderness like a cloud of smoke? Who is it, fragrant with myrrh and frankincense and every kind of spice? Look it is Solomon's carriage, surrounded by sixty (60) heroic men, the best of Israel's soldiers. They are all skilled swordsmen, experienced warriors. Each wears a sword on his thigh, ready to defend the king against an attack in the night. King Solomon's carriage is built of wood imported from Lebanon. Its posts are silver, its canopy gold, its cushions are purple. It was decorated with love by the young women of Jerusalem." (Song of Songs 3:6-11) Words like carriage have many different meanings and I've listed them in the next paragraph in detail.

The word carriage brought forth these words: Armour(-bearer), artillery, bag, carriage, + furnish, furniture, instrument, jewel, that is made of, one from another, that which pertaineth, pot, psaltery, sack, stuff, thing, tool, vessel, ware, weapon, and whatsoever. Definition: Something prepared, i.e., any apparatus (as an implement, utensil, dress, vessel or weapon). Detailed definition: 1. Article, vessel, implement, utensil. 2. Article, object (generally). 3. Utensil, implement, apparatus, vessel. 4. Implement (of hunting or war).. 5. Implement (of music). 6. Implement, tool (of labor). 7. Equipment, yoke (of oxen). 8. Utensils, furniture. 9. Vessel, receptacle (generally). 10. Vessels (boats) of paper-reed. I referenced Strong's Concordance Hebrew version (H3627). In Judges 18:21 it **means** valuables, wealth, or booty. In Isaiah 46:1 (RSV, "the things that ye carried about") the word **means** a load for a beast of burden. In 1 Samuel 17:22 and Isaiah 10:28 it is the rendering of a word ("stuff" in 1 Samuel 10:22) meaning implements, equipment, baggage. The phrase in Acts 21:15 , "We took up our carriages," means properly, "We packed up our baggage," as in the Revised Version.

In my first book I talk a lot about how the Lord loves using symbolism, which is why our dreams come the way they do. Sometimes, most times, they aren't literal. It's like God leaving us a trail of breadcrumbs to lead us back to Him. He wants us to ask Him what the dream means. 'Peter's Declaration about Jesus'. "When Jesus came to the region of Caesarea Philippi, he asked his disciples, "Who do people say that the Son of Man is?" "Well", they replied, "some say John the Baptist, some say Elijah, and others say Jeremiah or one of the other prophets." Then he asked them, "But who do you say I am?" Simon Peter answered, "You are the Messiah, [or the Christ Messiah [a Hebrew term] and Christ [a Greek term] both meaning "Anointed One] the Son of the living God."

Jesus replied, "You are blessed, Simon son of John, [daughter of Melech and Karmel] because my Father in heaven has revealed this to you. You did not learn this from any human being. Now I say to you that you are Peter [which means 'rock'] [Greek that you are Peter] and upon this rock I will build my church, and all the powers of hell [Greek and the gates of Hades] will not conquer it. And I will give you the keys of the Kingdom of Heaven. Whatever you forbid [or bind, or lock] on earth will be forbidden in heaven, and whatever you permit [or loose, or open] on earth will be permitted in heaven." (Matthew 16:13-19) This seems to be the order in which God is going to move in this next season. I have to be very careful with the words that come out of my mouth. Maybe this is why I awoke to the call of "mercy, mercy, mercy!" The star was born over Jerusalem during the perfect alignment on September 23, 5777/78.

He told me all my dreams were going to come true on February 14-15, 5778/79. The trumpet blew and He came on the clouds on March 23, 5778/79, and He told me we were in the halftime. He showed me things were out of order and that He was coming to separate the weeds from the wheat on April 13, 5778/79. He showed me the kings rising in the south and north, as I was being tempted in the wilderness – I saw the goat scattering the sheep. He showed me heaven on earth and the Holy Spirit told me to get some oil in my lamp. This happened over a period of 40 days and nights and the same period of time that I fasted the previous year, from July 3 through to August 14, 5779/80.

I saw a bright light in the daytime, the same day of the volcano eruption on White Island on December 9, 5780/81 and he returned to the temple to ignite my fire on December 22, 5780/81. Wow! "Who is this sweeping in from the desert, leaning on her lover? I aroused you under the apple [Sodom] tree, where your mother gave you birth where in great pain she delivered you. Place me like a seal over your heart, like a seal on your arm. For love is as strong as death, its jealousy [or its passion] as enduring as the grave [Hebrew as Sheol]. Love flashes like fire, the brightest kind of flame. Many waters cannot quench love, nor can rivers drown it. If a man tried to buy love with all his wealth, his offer would be utterly scorned." (Song of Songs 8:5-7) (20)

"This letter is from John, the elder. I am writing to the chosen lady and to her children [or the church God has chosen and its members] whom I love in the truth – as does everyone else who knows the truth because the truth lives in us and will be with us forever. Grace, mercy, and peace, which come from God the Father and from Jesus Christ – the Son of the Father will continue to be with us who live in truth and love. "Then Jesus entered the Temple and began to drive out the people selling animals for sacrifices. He said to them, "The

Scriptures declare, 'My Temple will be a house of prayer,' but you have turned it into a den of thieves." (Luke 19:45-46) Notice these scriptures have the numbers of the Presidents that are currently in office and running for office in November 2020, but I keep telling people, it doesn't matter who becomes President if we keep the same government systems in place. And it's bothering me that people are acting so scared, especially the men. I mean, I understand it, but if you believe the Word of God, you can stand on Matthew 49:26, "With God all things are possible!"

No matter what's going on in the world, the believer must keep their eyes on Jesus and keep the word in the forefront of their minds and hearts. I believe it will be the only way to make it through what's ahead. This book is being filled with water from the Rock, and the rocks are crying out. The rocks crying out are in reference to the scriptures, they are alive. Also with the Lord shaking the heavens, the planets (the other rocks) are crying out as well. Read Psalms 19. The prophets are speaking and I'm beginning think they are my ancestors. I am a daughter, by spirit and blood, somehow and someway.

"He turned the rock into a pool of water; yes, a spring of water flowed from solid rock. (Psalms 114:8) I am a living stone! "The Lord lives! Praise to my Rock! May God, the Rock of my salvation, be exalted! (2 Samuel 22:47) Jesus is alive, in me! His Spirit lives! "Then he and Aaron summoned the people to come and gather at the rock. "Listen, you rebels!" he shouted. "Must we bring you water from this rock?" Then Moses raised his hand and struck the rock twice with the staff, and water gushed out. So, the entire community and their livestock drank their fill." (Numbers 20:10) The stones live! The Lord is coming back to help the descendants of Abraham!

I was listening to Max Lucado talk about the night the angels visited the shepherds in the field to tell them about the birth of Jesus. This was also symbolic of Christ second return, representing how and when He would return to His bride, church. He was saying the night Jesus was born was an ordinary night, with ordinary sheep and ordinary shepherds. The angel came in the night because that is when the lights can be most seen and that's when they are most needed. All this talk of constellations and stars and heaven, wow! Meaning, the angel came during a dark time, almost like he did back in 2014. Remember, the Magi were astronomers following the star, but the king was looking for the Messiah or child to miracle child to kill it because he didn't want to share his kingdom with the real King.

After the appearance of the angel, the night became extraordinary. The angel made me curious to learn about my Creator. God comes into the common for the same reason. He spoke about how the most powerful tools are the simplest. God went to the shepherds – meek men who didn't know enough to tell God that angels don't sing to sheep and Messiah's aren't found wrapped in rags. I also found out that the shepherds watch over their sheep in anticipation of birth because they are only born one time a year and that's during the spring equinox. To see the world, you must stand tall but to see the Savior you must stoop down and get on your knees and look up. Back on August 3, 2018, in that service where I surrendered, and the Minister was talking about "blessing" and/or "bowing?" This is what his message reminded me of, that I had to bow down and look up to Jesus; and He responded and that's the blessing! The Lord answering my prayers is the blessing! Being able to recognize the voice of God, is the blessing! Knowing that there is a God, is the blessing! I will only bow to God.

I will continue to be grateful for those the Lord has placed on my path and those who have encouraged me since I've been on this journey, I'll call them travelers. Even though some became jealous and hateful and spiteful, I forgive them and still love them. I believe I will see the miracles come to pass because my heart is in the right place with the Lord and I believe He is the Messiah – He has surely always saved me and He won't fail me now. I finally came to myself. I know the Lord has spoken over me; I believe. I'm seeing my dreams come true now, just as the Lord told me they would. God gives the dreams because the dream is not dead! You can't kill a Spirit!

I must keep following Him so that He can tell me what they mean, and I can do what He called me to do. I had to let go to be free. When I turned my heart towards Christ, it took the veil away and allowed the Holy Spirit to move into my life and made everything real. It seems I'm growing, and my knowledge is increasing, just what I prayed for. God is extraordinary. I wish I had other words to express His greatness. It's as if God trusts me more and more as I get closer and closer to Him. I needed Him to trust me too! Brother Tadesse (meaning revived) said, "God knows where you need to be to release what He gave you to carry."

When I woke up on the morning of December 7, 2019, God brought to my remembrance a dream I had in October where I saw mountains collapsing behind me as I ran out of the forest towards safety. I was able to take cover in a car [vehicle] as the dust flew over my head as I ran away from the crumbling mountains. When I arose, and the dust cleared, I looked over and saw what appeared to be an animal Kingdom in the near distance. I saw white lions and tigers in royal purple and white garments standing on a stage and they were cheering and celebrating. I was clutching a book in my hand and began to walk towards the Kingdom and I woke up. That same morning, I saw memories on my social media account from (7) seven years prior, on the morning of December 7, 2012, when I was visited by 16 red Rose-ringed parakeets. I'll never forget that morning because I was walking my dog and I heard this very loud noise and when I looked up, there was the source – 16 of the most beautiful birds I have ever seen and yes, I counted them. It was such a special moment. It's like they were singing me a song and talking to me. In the Old Testament, 16 of the various names and titles for God signify His constant, never-ending love for the children of Israel.

Turns out this bird is from New Zealand. When I put the name of the bird in the Bible search engine, it took me to Ezekiel 11 which is the Judgement of Israel's Leaders, but specifically to this verse: "Then the cherubim lifted their wings and rose into the air with their wheels beside them, and the glory of the God of Israel hovered above them. Then the glory of the Lord went up from the city and stopped above the mountain to the east. Afterward the Spirit of God carried me back again to Babylonia, to the people in exile there. And so, ended the vision of my visit to Jerusalem. And I told the exiles everything the Lord had shown me." (Ezekiel 11:22-24)

I believe this scripture is symbolic for the star that was born over Israel on September 23, 2017, and the beginning of the end as I've been telling people. The Lord is near. I believe we are in modern day Babylonia, quite possibly Mystery Babylon, about to go through the fire, but God is going to save us from the great time of testing that seems to be fast approaching. "Because you have obeyed my command to persevere, I will protect you from the great time of testing that will come upon the whole world to test those who belong to this world." (Revelation 3:10) (13)

Then the Holy Spirit lead me to this scripture: "The coming of the Son of Man can be illustrated by the story of a man going on a long trip, when he left home, he gave each of his slaves instructions about the work they were to do, and he told the gatekeeper to watch for his return. You, too, must keep watch! For you don't know when the master of the household will return – in the evening, at midnight, before dawn, or at daybreak. Don't let him find you sleeping when he arrives without warning. I say to you what I say to everyone: Watch for him."' (Mark 13:34-37) He gave the slaves, the disciples, His followers instructions about the work they were to do, heal the sick, speak the word etc. And then he told the gatekeeper, the watchman on the wall, to watch for his return.

I think that most of the world is guilty of not watching, but it seems that in 2014, I took the helm as watcher. So much Bible prophecy has happened but because people didn't have an understanding of the Word, the prophetic word, the wisdom knowledge or an authentic relationship with the Holy Spirit, they couldn't receive the revelation and therefore have been looking for the prophetic signs to happen in a literal sense, the way they were written, but this is not the case. These are those who were trying to sneak over the wall and the weeds that came in wreaked havoc in the garden, spoken about in Matthew 13.

""Then I heard again what sounded like the shout of a vast crowd or the roar of mighty ocean waves or the crash of loud thunder: "Praise the Lord! For the Lord our God, the Almighty, reigns. Let us be glad and rejoice and let us give honor to him. For the time has come for the wedding feast of the Lamb, and his bride has prepared herself. She has been given the finest of pure white linen to wear. For the fine linen represents the good deeds of God's holy people [prophets]. And the angel said to me, "Write this: Blessed are those who are invited to the wedding feast of the Lamb." And he added, "These are the true words that came from God." Then I fell down at his feet to worship him, but he said, "No, don't worship me. I am a servant of God, just like you and your brothers and sisters who testify about their faith in Jesus. Worship only God. For the essence of prophecy is to give a clear witness for Jesus."" (Revelation 19:6-10) I don't understand how the Bible can make so many references to daughters, and "she" and "bride" and "sisters" and men still want to silence women from speaking in the church. It's disgusting at this point.

Reinhard Bonnke, the man who is credited with changing the face of Christianity in Africa, died this morning at the age of 79 years old. Remember earlier I said we have been in the wilderness for 79 years and I'll explain why I say that. The ancient Greeks and Romans recognized people from different parts of the world tend to look different, but they did not describe these differences in physical appearance using racial terms that we would be familiar with today. For them, a person with dark skin was not a member of the so-called "black race," but rather simply a person with dark skin. The color of a person's skin was ascribed no more significance than the color of a person's eyes or hair color. Consequently, the Greeks and Romans paid very little attention to skin color. Indeed, ancient text written in

Greek or Latin rarely even mention the subject. There were no concepts of a “white race” or a “black race.” These are peculiarly modern notions that first developed during the Early Modern Period (c. 1450 – c. 1750) to justify the enslavement of people of African ancestry. So, this means that the time of sin and rebellion had passed, and we were truly free according to God’s word in 1940! Also, no one is black or white, both are devoid of color. We are bronze, brown, caramel, peach and so many other colors of the rainbow, and black is not a color in the rainbow.

Reinhard Bonnke’s message of redemptive hope became important, particularly in African nations affected by drought, civil strife, and other tragedies. He founded ‘Christ For All Nations’ (CFAN) mission organization in 1974. (I was 4 years old at the time). He oversaw more than 79 million conversions to Christianity. Mr. Bonnke’s focus on evangelism inspired millions of Christians in Africa to have a personal relationship with Jesus Christ. He was born on April 19, 1940. What does the number 19 mean in relation to Israel? Isaiah prophesied in Chapter 9, verses 1 and 2 that the land of Naphtali and Zebulon would someday see a shining beacon in their lands, “Nevertheless, that time of darkness and despair will not go on forever. The land of Zebulun and Naphtali will be humbled, but there will be a time in the future when Galilee [meaning rolling and region – land of earthquakes] of the Gentiles [meaning unbelievers], which lies along the road [leading to the promised land] that runs between the Jordan and the sea, will be filled with glory.” Reinhard Bonnke’s many trips to Africa, as well as Dr. Billy Graham’s travel’s all over the world fulfilled this scripture. God raised them up a prophet like them to help them turn from their wicked ways and repent and turn to God. Just like He raised up Martin Luther King, Jr. and Malcolm X, both encouraged the reading of the Bible and fought for equality, liberty and justice. Both prophets killed, whereas the other men died in their beds surrounded by their families.

This scripture was also fulfilled in my mother’s lifetime through Dr. Billy Graham tent revivals and in my lifetime through Reinhard Bonnke and the vision he had at 9 years old to save Africa and he too was inspired by Billy Graham. This makes me think about when God told me to write the book back on December 28, 2016, the scripture that was given was John 6:1 which is about Jesus crossing over to the far side of the Sea of Tiberias [meaning in the center of the land of Israel (Mesis) and her sight is goodly]. Hebrew Teverya, city, northeastern Israel, is on the western shore of the Sea of Galilee; one of the four holy cities of Judaism (Jerusalem, Hebron, Tiberias, Ẕefat [Safed]). Zefat is the city of Upper Galilee. Ẕefat, Israel - Matic18 is first mentioned at the time of the Jewish revolt against Rome.

Strategically situated in scenic hill country, Ẕefat passed from hand to hand during the Crusades until captured by Baybars I, who razed its citadel (1266). Ẕefat achieved renown in the 16th century as the principal centre of the Kabbala, the occult theosophy and interpretation of the Scriptures forming the principal mystical system of Judaism. Important Kabbalists such as Isaac ben Solomon Luria and Joseph Karo lived in the city, and the doctrines expounded there spread throughout the Jewish world. The Hebrew printing press established in Ẕefat in 1577 was the first in all Asia to use movable type. In the 18th and 19th centuries the city suffered from wars and insurrections on the part of the Druzes and local Bedouin tribes, as well as from the destructive earthquake of 1837. Looking at the picture, it reminded me of Beverly Hills and the Hollywood Hills.

Just before the proclamation of the State of Israel (May 1948), the population of Ẕefat was predominantly Arab. The British, evacuating the area, gave the Arabs the fortified police post on nearby Mount Canaan (Har Kenaʿan), 3,149 feet (960 m) above sea level and 500 feet (150 m) above the old Jewish section. The city was nevertheless taken on May 12, 1948, by the Haganah, the Jewish defense forces, and the Arab population fled. Subsequently, mountainous Upper Galilee attracted painters and other artists, many of whom now live in Ẕefat. Four ancient synagogues, associated with past masters of the Kabbala, survive. The city's economy is based on light industry and tourism. Pop. (2006 est.) 28,000. Looks like the mean, dirty pirates were at it again. Staking claim to property and then ordering the people around. Tiberias was founded by Herod Antipas (ruled 4 bc – ad 39), tetrarch of Galilee under the Romans, in ad 18, and named for the reigning emperor Tiberius.

I'm thinking this is why I had the dream of the tree with the black leaves falling from it and my breasts swelling up with milk because God is preparing me to minister His true word. Mr. John Lewis was also born in 1940 on February 21 and he was 79 years old in 2019. February 21 is also the same day of Billy Graham's passing in 2018 – 7 days after my dream and my great-grandmother Kerry's passing in 2005 – both born in November). I would also like to note that my dream was on the pagan holiday Valentines, but I didn't know at that time, that it was also a Jewish holiday called Purim (Esther 8 and 9). I had the dream, exactly seven (7) days before Dr. Billy Graham passed away in 2018 and he was born on November 7, 1918, twenty-two (22) years before 1940.

I believe the Lord marked me and the Holy Spirit gave me the gift of numbers. Since ancient times it has been believed that number 22 is the number of God, as well as the number of Revelation. The number 22 also represents love and loving. "For this is how God loved the world: He gave his one and only Son, so that everyone who believes in him will not perish but have eternal life." (John 3:16) Considering that the number 19 is prophetic and has to do with the love God has for the children of Israel, this is all becoming very clear. Another notable passing on February 21, 1965, was that of former Nation of Islam leader and Organization of Afro-American Unity founder Malcolm X who was assassinated at a rally. Then three years later, On April 4, 1968, (4/4) civil rights leader and Nobel Peace Prize recipient Martin Luther King, Jr. was assassinated on his hotel room's balcony.

Afterwards, emotionally charged looting and riots broke out, putting even more pressure on then President Johnson's administration to push through additional civil rights laws, but sadly history has proven that they were just words written on paper. President Johnson also started up the FBI at this time to "Stop the rise of the black Messiah." Facts. I had an opportunity to research the history of America, and since the inception of the Declaration of Independence in 1776, it's been the same old song and dance tune – and it's an awful tune. From 1776-1999 was 211 years and currently 222 years. "Then Lord God made a woman from the rib, and he brought her to the man." (Genesis 2:22)

I believe I could be the regenerated Eve. According to the Bible, number 22 is usually considered to be the symbol of disorganization. "Run from anything that stimulates youthful lusts. Instead, pursue righteous living, faithfulness, love and peace. Enjoy the companionship of those who call on the Lord with pure hearts." (2 Timothy 2:22) This number is made up of numbers 2 x 11 and it is known that the number 11 is a symbol of chaos and disorder. The world is in chaos and things are very much in disarray. So, it appears that I was correct when I said that the light we all saw in the sky on December 22, 2017, the Falcon X rocket that flew over the skies of Southern California from Vandenberg Air Force base, was indeed a signal of the beginning of the end and a sign that the Kingdom was near.

Very befitting, considering my dad was in the Air Force and served two terms in Vietnam and his name means king and dark horse. We were sitting on the patio in the dark that evening and we saw a great light. "The people who walk in darkness will see a great light. For those who live in a land of deep darkness, a light will shine." (Isaiah 9:2) My son was living in darkness before I said the prayer to God that night and the Lord answered the prayer exactly 39 days later. That's no coincidence, that's on purpose. I was 39 when I moved to the valley and it's been 39 years since Reaganomics.

Matthew (Levi) states, "The people who were sitting in darkness have seen a great light; and to those who were sitting in the realm and shadow of death, light has sprung up." (Matthew 4:16) The fulfillment of this prophecy related to 19 occurred when Christ, who had lived in Nazareth all his life, moved at the age of 30 to the Galilean city of Capernaum. Once in the city he started his ministry and began to preach the gospel (Matthew 4:14-17). Reinhard Bonnke said he had a vision of the African continent "washed in the blood of Jesus," when he was nine (9) years old which lead to his mass evangelism ministry. He labeled himself as a "salvation evangelist who also prays for the sick." "Billy Graham has inspired me personally," brother Bonnke wrote on Facebook after Graham's passing in 2018, "when he preached in a tent in Hamburg, Germany, I always felt connected to him."

Here we see the effects of Billy Graham's worldwide ministry, but sadly He didn't seem to have the same affect in his own hometown, the United States. He actually had the same effect as the Apostle Paul's ministry crossing international waters, reaching far and wide. It reached to a man who would lead a continent to the Lord and bring forth both relevant and timely messages for the ages. That's amazing and now they have both entered into God's rest and their words are still changing the hearts of men and affecting the lives of future generations because they live! Billy Graham said it! The Apostle Paul said, "Now if the Gentiles were enriched because the people of Israel turned down God's offer of salvation, think how much greater a blessing the world will share when they finally accept it.

I am saying all this especially for you Gentiles [unbelievers]. God has appointed me as the apostle to the Gentiles. I stress this, for I want somehow to make the people of Israel jealous of what you Gentiles have, so I might save some of them." (Romans 11:13-14) They were the Gentile nation. It seems it's time now for the promises of Abraham to take center stage. It's time to possess the land, the promised land of peace, liberty, and justice for all under God. I wrote this in my journal 3 years ago on August 28, 2016: 'Worship God in Spirit, and in truth. God seeks for the true worshipper (John 4:20-24). It's more than just about music, it's a lifestyle. Have you studied yourself? What are you practicing? Practice makes permanent – not perfect. Know what you are practicing. Most of the time we need adjusting. Don't be afraid of being corrected – adjustments help you do things correctly.

In the Kingdom, correction is different. God only adjusts the people He loves. You don't have to go to a building or church service to worship, you can worship outside of the four walls of the church. Worship is in exchange – it's you in relationship with your Father God. Worship is in an intimate word. It's not a ritual. It's a lifestyle and a "liftstyle", lifting Jesus higher, lifts your spirit higher. I know this to be true because before I started this reading and writing session, I worshipped God for an hour and the Holy Spirit poured out greatly. I was caught up in praising Him for His goodness, not anything that He had done, but just because He is and when I sat down to write, all of the revelation poured out because God speaks through His Holy Spirit and His Word, and through worship.' America must repent or it will get worse before it gets better, but regardless as we see in this book, God's word is moving forward regardless. "For the Lord had made a covenant with the descendants of Jacob and commanded them: "Do not worship any other gods or bow before them or serve them or offer sacrifices to them." (2 Kings 17:35)

Chapter 19: The Tree of Life

"Then God turned away from them and abandoned them to serve the stars of heaven as their gods! In the book of the prophets it is written, 'Was it to me you were bringing sacrifices and offerings during those forty years [80] in the wilderness, Israel? No, you carried your pagan gods – the shrine of Molech, the star of your god Rephan, and the images you made to worship them. So, I will send you into exile as far away as Babylon'." Acts of the Apostles 7:42-43

The people were put in slavery for worshipping the stars instead of acknowledging them as signs. The bible also says in Zephaniah 1:6, "And I will destroy those who used to worship me but now no longer do. They no longer ask for the Lord's guidance or seek my blessings." The people of Israel, meaning God's chosen people, were put into slavery by the Lord for worshipping false gods, and they continue in their unbelief today. In 2018, the angel of the Lord made the parable of the Wheat and Weeds (Matthew 13:24-30) come to life right in front of my eyes, the Rhema word, through signs he showed me in nature and that's the time I found the two-dollar (2) bill folded up on a pile of grass and leaves.

I know I sound like a broken record, but that was the significance of the parrot, it's a talking bird and it repeats itself. The spring visits happened in March 17-25, April 13, and May 13-14. He showed me we were in the halftime in the stars, sun, and the moon. All the signs were pointing to Him coming to separate the weeds from the wheat. He was also showing me the end of the world as we know it. He was doing something new and a great time of testing and trouble was ahead; as well as a new season/cycle, a second beginning and the second coming of my Lord and Savior Jesus Christ. Before anyone accuses me of worshipping the sun or the moon or the stars, or the zodiac - think again.

And the Bible says, "When you begin living in the towns the Lord your God is giving you, a man or woman among you might do evil in the sight of the Lord your God and violate the covenant. For instance, they might serve other gods or worship the sun, the moon, or any of the stars – the forces of heaven – which I have strictly forbidden." It was around 2018 that I learned to make the Bible my reference and guide and the final word on everything. If I can't find it in the Bible, I pray for the Holy Spirit to lead me to the truth and confirm it in His word, doing this increased my wisdom and knowledge.

"I will crush Judah and Jerusalem with my fist and destroy every trace of their Baal worship. I will put an end to all the idolatrous priests, so that even the memory of them will disappear. For they go up to their roofs and bow down to the sun, moon, and stars. They claim to follow the LORD, but then they worship Molech (Hebrew Malcam or their king), too." (Zephaniah 1:4-5) Remember, Molech sacrificed and murdered children i.e. abortion, pedophilia, child molestation etc. ""When I wrote to you before, I told you not to associate with people who indulge in sexual sin. But I wasn't talking about unbelievers who indulge in sexual sin, or are greedy, or cheat people, or worship idols. You would have to leave this world to avoid people like that.

I meant that you are not to associate with anyone who claims to be a believer yet indulges in sexual sin, or is greedy, or worships idols, or is abusive, or is a drunkard, or cheats people. Don't even eat with such people. It isn't my responsibility to judge outsiders, but it certainly is your responsibility to judge those inside the church who are sinning. God will judge those on the outside; but as the Scriptures say, "You must remove the evil person from among you." (1 Corinthians 5:9-13) This is why the Jews, children of the Most High God, request Sovereignty and need to live separated from Gentiles or unbelievers. It has nothing to do with race, and more to do with nationality, being a citizen of the nation of Israel by birthright and that birthright is being born again.

A Warning against Idolatry "But be very careful! You did not see the Lord's form on the day he spoke to you from the heart of the fire at Mount Sinai. So do not corrupt yourselves by making an idol in any form – whether of a man or a woman, an animal on the ground, a bird in the sky, a small animal that scurries along the ground, or a fish in the deepest sea. And when you look up into the sky and see the sun, moon, and stars – all the forces of heaven – don't be seduced into worshipping them. The Lord your God gave them to all the peoples of the earth." (Deuteronomy 4:15-19) So, why did God make the sun, moon and stars? "God made two great lights – the larger one to govern the day, and the smaller one to govern the night. He also made the stars. God set these lights in the sky to light the earth, to govern the day and the night, and to separate the light from darkness. And God saw that it was good. – Genesis 1:16-18" So these objects in heaven were put there to "govern" the day and the night, that's light and darkness and to separate the light (good) from the darkness (wicked). A set apart people means just that, set apart – to live separate from wickedness and evil doers.

The Hebrew calendar is the Biblical method for determining when God's seven (7) annual Feast days should be kept. It was the calendar that Jesus, the apostles, and the early church considered authoritative concerning when to keep such celebrations as Passover, Pentecost, and the Feast of Trumpets. Remember when Jesus walked the earth, He celebrated these feasts. This is right in line with everything the Holy Spirit has been showing me, from the calendar to the celebrations. It's not a form of worship of the sun, stars and moon but simply a guide to mark the seasons so you'll really know what "time" it is. This is covered in Genesis 1:14, and the seasons were to be marked so that you would recognize the signs of His coming and be ready for Kingdom and the work of the Messiah (Anointed One, Messenger sent by God).

The Scriptures tell us, "The first man, Adam, became a living person." But the last Adam – that is, Christ – is a life-giving Spirit. What comes first is the natural body, then the spiritual body comes later." (1 Corinthians 15:45-46) You are born of the flesh first, a natural body, birthed from a woman and then when you believe in your heart and confess with your mouth that Jesus is the Son of God and you accept Him as your Savior and Lord, you become born again by the Holy Spirit. This answers Nicodemus' question when he asked Jesus how to be born again.

Lastly, in Deuteronomy 6:14, it says "You must not worship any of the gods of neighboring nations." This puts a fork in a universal god and the myth that there are many roads to Him. It's also another reason I oppose this all-inclusive, fight for "all" religions because is in direct opposition of the Bible, which is confirmed the Word of God. "Do not worship the Lord your God in the way these pagan peoples worship their gods. Rather, you must seek the Lord your God at the place of worship he himself will choose from among all the tribes – the place where his name will be honored." (Deuteronomy 12:4-5) "Jesus replied, Believe me, dear woman, the time is coming when it will no longer matter whether you worship the Father on this mountain or in Jerusalem. You Samaritans know very little about the one you worship, while we Jews know all about him, for salvation comes through the Jews. But the time is coming – indeed it's here now – when true worshipers will worship the Father in spirit and in truth. The Father is looking for those who will worship him that way. For God is Spirit, so those who worship him must worship in spirit and in truth." (John 4:21-24)

I believe this is why King David was able to carry the Ark of the Covenant and not die was a foreshadow of what was to come. After all that David did, the Lord still allowed him to be in His presence, and He didn't take back His word from the King. I would have danced until my clothes fell off too! Remember he danced naked in the public square! He was rejoicing! He was chosen and from the looks of it, He chose me too! "For God knew his people in advance, and he chose them to become like his Son, so that his Son would be the firstborn among many brothers and sisters. And having chosen them, he called them to come to him. And having called them, he gave them right standing with himself. And having given them right standing, he gave them his glory." (Romans 8:29-30)

The first thing I notice in the scripture, is that Paul says the word "them" seven (7) times, and we know that seven (7) is God's perfect number with regard to both men and women being chosen and called by God, proof that God chooses both men and women AND the woman is included in God's plan. Remember, Eve didn't have a name before Adam named her, so she too was like Adam; both were made in the image of God and both with the same "bright" natures. You can read about this in the 'Conflict of Adam and Eve with Satan', a book of the early Eastern Church translated from the Ethiopic. "On the holy mountain stands the city founded by the Lord. He loves the city of Jerusalem more than any other city in Israel [He loves the gates of Zion more than all the dwellings of Jacob 44:4].

O city of God, what glorious things are said of you! I will count Egypt [Hebrew Rahab, Leviathan, used here as poetic name for Egypt] and Babylon among those who know me – also Philistia and Tyre, and even distant Ethiopia [Hebrew Cush]. They have all become citizens of Jerusalem! Regarding Jerusalem [Hebrew Zion] it will be said, "Everyone enjoys the rights of citizenship there." And the Most High will personally bless this city. When the Lord registers the nations, he will say, "They have all become citizens of Jerusalem." Interlude. The people will play flutes [or will dance] and sing, "The source of my life springs from Jerusalem!" (Psalms 87:1-7) (23) This proves that the prodigal son can come back home. "They will thrive like watered grass, like willows on a riverbank." (Isaiah 44:4) "Then the man brought me through the north gateway to the front of the Temple. I looked and saw that the glory of the Lord filled the Temple of the Lord, and I fell face down on the ground." (Ezekiel 44:4)

On page 7 in Book One, we find Eve was praying to God after Adam took his life because he was so distraught over falling from grace. Eve said, "For I alone caused Thy servant to fall from the garden into this lost estate; from light into this darkness; and from the abode of joy into this prison [The Cave of Treasures]. O God look upon Thy servant thus fallen, and raise him from his death, that he may weep and repent of his transgression which he committed through me. Take not away his soul this once; but let him [live] that he may stand after the measure of his repentance, and do Thy will, as before his death. But if Thou do not raise him up, then, O God, take away my own soul [that I be] like him; and leave me not in this dungeon, one and alone; for I could not stand alone in this world, but with him [only]."

"For Thou, O God, didst cause a slumber to come upon him, and didst take a bone from his side, and didst restore the flesh in the place of it, by Thy divine power. And Thou didst take me, the bone, and make me a woman, "bright" like him, with heart, reason, and speech; and in flesh, like unto his own; and Thou didst make me after the likeness of his countenance, by Thy mercy and power. O Lord, I and he are one, and Thou, O God, art our Creator, Thou art [He] who made us both in one day. Therefore, O God, give him life, that he may be with me in this strange land, while we dwell in it on account of our transgression. But if Thou will not give him life, then take me, even me, like him; that we both may die the same day."

And Eve wept bitterly and fell upon our father Adam; from her great sorrow." I believe the details of Adam and Eve's time outside of the garden in the darkness was left out of the bible intentionally. One reason, the enemy didn't want the child of God to see how immeasurable God's grace is. He wanted people to feel shame and confusion and cause doubt. Another reason was to keep man in a position of dominance and power because Adam and Eve did everything together from pray to fast, to work in the field to placing their sacrifices on the altar before God; they did it together. Yes, the Lord would take Adam to the side and they did have times where they fasted separately but for the most part, they were as Eve said above, "one."

And the last reason, I believe was to seal up the prophecy until the time for it to be revealed which seems to be now. See, the devil was doing it to be deceitful and kill people, destroy the world, have people take themselves out. The devil doesn't want us to have what God created for us. He is a thief, a liar and a murderer. Right now, he's attempting to keep the power, the title deed to the earth and money he stole from my/your ancestors, which rightfully belong to King Jesus and His heir. Remember in the earlier chapter, I make mention of the scripture that speaks about what the devil meant for evil, God works out for the good of those that love Him. Furthermore, in noticing the numbers in the verses of the scripture above, the number 8 represents Jesus, resurrection, regeneration and no lack; the number 29 means rise and shine and part of the meaning of the number 30 comes from it symbolizing dedication to a particular task or calling, like God giving me direction to write this book.

Now, Aaronic priests were initially dedicated to serving at the age of thirty (30) years (Numbers 4:3) and we just read in Matthew 4 about how Jesus started His ministry at 30 years old. Jesus also started His ministry in a Jubilee and leap year. 2020 is my Jubilee and a leap year! God likely chose this age because it was when a person reached both physical and mental maturity and could therefore handle major responsibilities. Seems Jesus starting his ministry in a Jubilee year was symbolic of His Holy Spirit coming back to His bride in a Jubilee year and leap year. Afterall, 50 is considered middle aged and remember Mesis means 'in the middle of'. What's also interesting is that I was born exactly 30 years after both Reinhard Bonnke and Mr. John Lewis, 41 years after Martin Luther King and 52 years after Billy Graham was born. All these numbers have significant and specific meaning as it relates to my personal journey and my Christian walk.

We covered the biblical meaning of the number 30 as well as it's symbolic meaning as it relates to Christ second coming. As for the number 41, although the precise meaning of the number in the Bible is not clear, it has to do with some relationship with the kings of ancient Israel and Judah. The phrase "His mercy endureth forever" occurs forty-one times (41) in the King James Bible. Hallelujah! God's mercy does endure, I'm living proof. Out of the large number of prophecies found in the Old Testament, forty-one (41) of them concern individuals and not nations or other groups of people. In 41 B.C., Marc Antony (of Antony and Cleopatra [who was the first to find an emerald when she ruled Ancient Egypt] fame) promotes Herod the Great to the position of Roman Tetrarch over Jerusalem and Galilee.

This is kind of like the Pope, the Queen, and the rich and famous, they have a lot of goings on with the politicians, but none of these were chosen by God. Herod Agrippa I, grandson of Herod the Great, is elevated by Caligula in 39 A.D. to Roman Tetrarch over Galilee and Perea. In 41, after Emperor Caligula is assassinated, he is made king over Judea and Samaria by Claudius. This Herod is notorious for murdering the Apostle James, thus becoming the first person to kill one of the original apostles (see Acts 12:1-5, 19-23). I consider Martin Luther King, Jr. a king, a prophet and royal priest, a type of shadow of the coming Messiah which is probably why the FBI was hot on his trail. He was the true Jew and royalty, and they knew it.

The meaning of the number 52 also has significant meaning. Oddly enough the Holy Spirit lead me to a page that was created by a married couple called 'The Bible Wheel'. The gentleman who created the page has since debunked it, and both he and his wife left the faith because they could never receive answers to the questions they had about the inconsistencies, mysteries and missing parts of the bible which we've been discussing in this book. I had questions too, especially about my dreams and visions and so I understand. The wife's reasons for leaving were specifically because women weren't being respected or acknowledged in the church and she is correct. But more than that, women to this date are not loved as the Lord said they should be, and He loved us unto death. Men just won't listen to women and this is why the world is how it is today. God sent the woman to be a help mate, but I digress.

This is a prime example of the tactics of the enemy discouraging people of faith and planting seeds of doubt and furthermore causing people to turn away. I have decided to include some of his earlier writings that directly relate to my journey. I knew it was the Holy Spirit when I read, "the number 52: Son, Messiah, Word and Light," and the scripture it gave was "The king proclaims the Lord's decree: "The Lord said to me, 'You are my son [daughter]. Today I have become your Father [or today I reveal you as my son [daughter] (remember son was also used to mean relative or descendant)." Psalm 2:7 God was literally revealing His mysteries to this guy, but he clearly wasn't receiving what the Holy Spirit was trying to communicate to him.

The Holy Spirit was not being included in his study time, even though he had access to the Tree of Life. This is what he said, "I was particularly impressed by the Kabbalistic Tree of Life because it provided a framework, or matrix, upon which to organize elements derived from highly diverse esoteric studies. The tree consists of 10 sephiroth (numerical categories) corresponding to the numbers from 1 (Crown) to 10 (Shekhinah/Kingdom) and twenty-two paths between the sephiroth corresponding to the letters of the Hebrew alphabet. It correlates the 22 Major Arcana [?] of the Tarot [not of God] with the 22 letters of the Hebrew alphabet, the 12 signs of the Zodiac, the 7 traditional astrological planets, the 7 colors of the rainbow, the patterns of sacred geometry, gematria (numerology), and pretty much everything under the sun [I say everything God created].

This fit perfectly with my intent as an "analytic mystic" to correlate all esoteric knowledge upon one diagram and so reveal the underlying unity of reality. It quickly captured my attention and became the fundamental matrix upon which I would base my analysis of dreams, synchronicities, and esoteric knowledge." Remember my research on Canaan brought to the light the word, synchronicities because again God is gathering His people. This is my everyday life since the angel of the Lord touched me back in 2014. The only difference is I ran to the Father, the Son and the Holy Spirit and the Bible for the answers to my dreams and visions and not a chart or zodiac or tarot cards, that's divination and a no-no for me. Though I thought the table in itself was interesting because 22 means unity and revelation and bringing all things under God together into one place, so the tree is appealing but if it is God, then there can be no evil.

He based his diagram on the raven's book 777 [September 23, 2017, Year 5777] which describes itself as "a complete dictionary of correspondences of all magical elements" designed to "systemize" alike the data of mysticism and the results of comparative religion." It contains table after table listing the correspondence of "everything under the sun" with the 32 paths of wisdom. This was a primary text I was using in the fall of 1990 [When I was 20 years old] when I had a very short enigmatic dream that launched me "out into the deep" of esoteric studies. On the morning of November 24, 1990 [29 years ago, also December 8 on the Hebrew Calendar], I found myself floating in a blank space half aware that I was dreaming when a woman with black hair in a red sweater suddenly appeared and said: **Are you looking for Dumbo? 12 x 44 (528) [Also on his website]** The Number 528 – THE KEY

"And the key of the house of David will I lay upon his shoulder; so he shall open, and none shall shut; and he shall shut, and none shall open." (Isaiah 22:22)

He then said, "That's it. I awoke, wrote down the dream, and consulted the raven's book 777 to find insight as to what the numbers might mean. My first discovery was that 44 was the value of the Hebrew word דם (DM, dawm) meaning blood. I immediately noticed that this correlated with the first two consonants in DuMbo. This gave me the feeling that I had "received information" in the dream, since I had only begun to study Hebrew gematria a few weeks earlier and did not know that word or it's numerical value. I then looked up the product 12 x 44 = 528 and found that it was the sum of all the natural numbers from 1 to 32. Mathematicians call such numbers "triangular" because they count the number of dots in a triangular array. Kabbalists call them "Mystic Numbers" because they are supposed to "sum up" the mystical meaning of that number." There are triangular star patterns. Tetragrammaton in a triangle was a common Christian symbol in Europe. It is said to represent the holy trinity. Tetragrammaton is a biblical proper name of God that also means YHWH or JHVH (four Hebrew letters). When I put in the numbers 528 in the Bible, this is what it gave me: "The Lord heard the request you made to me. And he said, 'I have heard what the people said to you, and they are right. Oh, that they would always have hearts like this, that they might fear me and obey all my commands! If they did, they and their descendants would prosper forever. Go and tell them, "Return to your tents." But you stand here with me so I can give you all my commands, decrees, and regulations. You must teach them to the people so they can obey them in the land I am giving them as their possession." (Deuteronomy 5:28-31) (19)

He continued "I was stunned to find my dream number was the Mystic Number of the 32nd Path on the Tree of Life that leads from Shehkinah (the Kingdom) to Yesod, the foundation of spiritual consciousness. Furthermore, the 32nd Path corresponds to the Universe Card of the Major Arcana in the Tarot and the final letter of the Hebrew alphabet Tav. Thus, I interpreted this information from my dream to be something like the "Mystic Number of the Universe" or more simply, the "Key to the Universe" which is what I wrote in my journal though I had no understanding of what that really meant as yet. (The Lord told me He gave me the Key in my dream).

My studies expanded to include gematria, by which I discovered many "meaningful coincidences" that helped convince me of the truth of Christianity as explained in my article Looking for Dumbo." Malkuth Hebrew MLKVTh, "kingdom," is the (9th) ninth Sephirah of the Kabbalah Tree of Life, representing the world of ordinary life. (Remember 9 represents God's movement and God's judgement.) (Additionally, the Lord showed me in two dreams He was giving me the keys and He was going to use ordinary men and women) Universal symbolism: Name of God: ADNI, Adonai [Lord] Archangel: MThThRVN, Metatron which is Enoch's name he received after his transformation into an angel (Matthew 22), Prince of Countenances; SNDLPVN, Sandalphon [Twin Brothers] Angelic Host: AIShIM, Ishim [Humanity]."

The numbers in his simple dream, had huge meaning. The number 12 represents faith in God. Part of the meaning of the number 44 comes from the final part of Jesus' earthly ministry. This last part begins on the day he was crucified, which is Wednesday, April 5 in 30 A.D. (Nisan 14 in the Hebrew year 3790). The sign happened in the sky on September 23,

2017 (Hebrew year 5777) which makes 1987 years. It ends on the day he gives final instructions and ascends to God's right hand from the Mount of Olives (Acts 1:4 - 12). This momentous day is Thursday, May 18 (Iyar 27). The period between his crucifixion and his ascension is 44 days. Again, I was 44 in 2014 and it was in December of 2017 that we witnessed the bright light night up the skies of the Grape State. December is the 12th month on the Gregorian calendar, but the 10th month on the Hebrew calendar and 10 signifies testimony, law, responsibility, and the completeness of order.

The scriptures that came up for the 1244 were amazing. "But any slave who has been purchased may eat if he has been circumcised." (Exodus 12:44) This is symbolic of being able to know the mysteries of God when you've fully surrendered your heart to Jesus. Only when you do this, are you able to clearly understand the Word of God. "On that day men were appointed to be in charge of the storerooms for the offerings, the first part of the harvest, and the tithes. They were responsible to collect from the fields outside the towns the portions required by the Law for the priests and Levites. For all the people of Judah took joy in the priests and Levites and their work." (Nehemiah 12:44) The Lord keeps telling me I'm a royal priestess and a Levite. "Then it says, 'I will return to the person I came from.' So, it returns and finds its former home empty, swept, and in order." (Matthew 12:44) Yes, I washed my robe and prepared myself for the Lord's return.

"For they gave a tiny part of their surplus, but she, poor as she is, have given everything she had to live on." (Mark 12:44) "I tell you the truth, the master will put that servant in charge of all he owns." (Luke 12:44) "Jesus shouted to the crowds, "If you trust me, you are trusting not only me, but also God who sent me." (John 12:44) Lastly, it was interesting that the person speaking to him in the dream was a woman and she was asking him a question about looking for a flying elephant and the revelation he received was about blood. Something else that was funny is that they remade the movie in 2019, and it premiered in Los Angeles on March 11, 2019 (the day my stepfather passed away in 2009) and officially in theaters on March 29, 2019.

I do not believe this has anything to do with brainwashing, only God could orchestrate all these things – all of the things happening in the universe surrounding life and death and nature and astronomy and the calendar. It's just too much and besides I'm a nobody! Why would all these things be connected to me and yet no one knows me, but God. My life seems to be the proof. I now understand, I've been hidden like David because of my sin and because I am a woman – it's the mystery! God was really talking to the guy, but He was searching for the answers from creation and not the Creator, even though he confirmed Christianity, he had no roots to stay connected.

This Hebrew calendar is a biblical method used to track time based on a repeating 19-year time cycle. We can't seem to get away from the number 19, the Holy Spirit is speaking loud and clear. Heaven seems to have come down, one more again. It's also interesting because here we are in the year 2019, and all God's words are coming true and being revealed to me. God's timing is His timing! That's why the word encouraged us to celebrate the feasts and to look up, so we would recognize His coming. The Hebrew civil calendar adds an additional month (making 13 months total) and I understand it now because the months collide, it's a continuation. I don't have all of it and I'm sure I won't, but I what I do understand is that it's possible the extra days in some of the years are due to leap years and that's what causes this duality in the months. I'm still learning. I'll be forever learning.

I'm certain the Holy Spirit will make it clearer as time goes on. He seems to be dealing with me in cycles of 2, i.e. (2) months, (2) years, (20) years. In the year 2014, the angel told me to wake up. In 2015, the dreams started coming faster and becoming more vivid. In 2016, my mother spoke to me for the first time in my dreams since her passing in 1995, and that Christmas my dream came true. In 2017, I received the signal that the angel was rising over my nation and the Revelation 12 sign appeared in the sky as a sign on September 23 as well as the bright light on December 22, 2017. In 2018, heaven came down and invaded earth and I was caught up in the supernatural. Now here we are in 2019, and He showed me all the disobedience and desolation and urged me to get on the Highway of Holiness (Isaiah 35). I was encouraged to live holy and righteous and encourage others to do the same.

Furthermore, leap years are powerful and supernatural, and such leap periods are necessary to help the lunar and solar years stay in sync. Remember Canaan, the foreign land the Lord promised Abraham, well Canaan is also representative of synchronicity as well. Synchronicity is another term for synchrony. Synchrony is a simultaneous action, development, or occurrence or the state of operating or developing according to the same time scale as something else. Wow! It's like the things that are happening in the earth are directly correlated to what is happening in the heavens and somehow connected to me and my ancestors. It's as if the world has been put on God's time scale when He said, "No more delay." Then he said in July 2020, He was reclaiming His time!

A synchronicity for someone on the spiritual path is that moment in the fabric of time when we suddenly and briefly become consciously aware that we have made a deeper connection with the Creator. When you notice the same coincidence happening more than once and it begins to take on meaning, then it becomes a Synchronicity. Synchronicities can also show us how there is a connection between your Spirit or inner man and the Holy Spirit and Creator of life, the one who created the heavens and the earth. They are not separate realities but one in the same, and consciousness itself is the bridge between these two dimensions. It's a state of being awake, having spiritual sight, like the blind man who saw men like trees walking.

The external and physical world that we can observe with our natural eyes is our 'reality', and the mirror reflection of the internal or spiritual being that we cannot see with our natural eyes. Synchronicities give us a glimpse into the inner workings of our own mind and how it relates to the very fabric of nature and reality itself. It's like putting on spiritual glasses, to make the invisible become visible. Many people who constantly seem to notice a certain pattern of number like 11:11 and other repeating number sequences, like 222, 333, 444 or 555 appearing over and over again when they least expect it, often consider the experience to be more than chance or coincidence and they are correct.

This belief is related to the concept of synchronicity. I see 11:11 quite often at first I related it to Veteran's Day being on the same day of the year no matter what day it falls on – which was metaphoric for Jesus because the Bible says, "Jesus Christ is the same yesterday, today, and forever." (Hebrews 13:8) I know this is a lot of information, but it's all relevant because God is the Creator of the numbers, and the calendar was Holy Spirit inspired because God marked the seasons with the moon and stars and it's apparent that He appears to move and the prophetic happens according to His calendar. The heavens governed our planet long before man tried taking it all over.

Lastly, Psalms number 19:1-4, written by King David, declares that the heavens and everything else humans see is a living testament to the existence, glory, and power of God. "The heavens proclaim the glory of God. The skies display his craftsmanship. Day after day they continue to speak; night after night they make him known. They speak without a sound or word; their voice is never heard. Yet their message has gone throughout the earth and their words to all the world." The Apostle Paul reiterates this fact in verse 19 of Romans 1, when he writes, "Because that which may be known of God is manifest among them, for God has manifested it to them." (HBFV).

I believe when I saw the three owls, they were not only signals to me of the spiritual climate of our world of disobedience and desolation, but they were foretelling of the upcoming deaths of great men of faith who would soon pass on. Billy Graham 2/21/18, Rabbi 2/6/19 and now Reinhard Bonnke on 12/7/19. These men made a huge impact on the world through their teaching and preaching of the Good News with conviction, boldness, passion, truth, love, confidence and pretty much influenced many generations around the world, both young and old including my ancestors as well as myself. [By the way, I learned that Rabbi is still alive, and another passed recently, Dr. Fred Price of CCC].

I also believe seeing the owls was metaphoric of the increase of wisdom, faith and knowledge as well as the prophetic clarity. They were preparing us for the Second Coming of Jesus Christ, the Messiah. Respectively, each one displayed honorable service to my Lord and did an awesome job carrying their mantles. I believe this is what I saw in my dream with the leveling of the mountains and hills and seeing the Kingdom near and it's also connected to the visions that day in the park when the Lord gave me Isaiah 35:8 and talked to me about the Holy Road. Making straight a highway for the Lord seems to consist of people coming out of the world (repentance) and living holy, communing with the Lord daily, and making themselves available for the Holy Spirit to use them for Kingdom Assignments. The time is coming where holy living will be the requirement for survival. "And the Good News about the Kingdom will be preached throughout the whole world, so that all nations will hear it; and then the end will come." (Matthew 24:14)

"Listen! It's the voice of someone shouting, "Clear the way through the wilderness for the Lord! Make a straight highway through the wasteland for our God! Fill in the valleys, and level the mountains and hills. Straighten the curves, and smooth out the rough places. Then the glory of the Lord will be revealed, and all people will see it together. The Lord has spoken!" A voice said, "Shout!" I asked, "What should I shout?" "Shout that people are like the grass. Their beauty fades as quickly as the flowers in a field. The grass withers and the flowers fade beneath the breath of the Lord. And so, it is with people. The grass withers and the flowers fade, but the word of our God stands forever."" Isaiah 40:3-8 Suggested Scripture Readings: Matthew 3:3, Mark 1:3 and Luke 3:4-6

The Apostle John warned about people removing words from the Bible and apparently many pages and words have been removed. "And if anyone removes any of the words from this book of prophecy, God will remove that person's share in the tree of life and in the holy city that are described in this book." (Revelations 22:19) It's time for people to get more acquainted with their Bible than anything else. "Blessed are those who wash their robes. They will be permitted to enter through the gates of the city and eat the fruit from the tree of life." (Revelations 22:14) How do you wash your robe? By feasting on the flesh of Jesus, which is the Word of God as it is written in the good book – the Bible. I like the New Living Translation because He lives!

Chapter 20: The Good News is Christ Lives

"How beautiful on the mountains are the feet of the messenger who brings good news, the good news of peace and salvation, the news that the God of Israel reigns!" (Isaiah 52:7)

We talked about in the last chapter how the number 52 represents the Messiah, the promised deliverer of the Jewish nation prophesied in the Hebrew Bible. This Good News tells us how God makes us right in his sight. This is accomplished from start to finish by faith. As the Scriptures say, "It is through faith that a righteous person has life [or the righteous will live by faith]." (Romans 1:16-17) When a person passes his or her test of faith, the righteousness of Christ will be imparted to that person. The Holy Spirit will remove the carnal nature and seal that "faith-full" person with a sinless nature like that of Adam and Eve before they fell. They both had bright natures, they were like the angels. This is the restoration of Eden, bringing heaven down to earth so that the Lord's righteousness will fill the earth. Before Adam and Eve sinned, they didn't need a mediator between them and God, they had free access to God. However, once they sinned, they felt shamed and hid from God. "At That moment, their eyes were opened, and they suddenly felt shame at their nakedness. So, they sewed fig leaves together to cover themselves." (Genesis 3:7)

When Adam and Eve fell, God cast them out of the garden into the darkness. It was not only pitch-black darkness with no light, but ferocious beasts would attack them. They had to hide in a cave, because Adam no longer had dominion over the animals and the wild beast. The place was called the Cave of Treasures and at night was so dark, pitch black, they couldn't even see each other because they were separated from God. I will cover more of their story later, but God sent His Word to them because the devil tried to kill them repeatedly while they were in this dark time period. The devil would do this by casting shifting shadows, or making a false light appear real to get them to come out of the cave to harm them. He was angry because God kept forgiving them no matter what they did. The devil hates you and he will make things look wonderful, but once you get on that sinful path, on his devious playground - you will see the real demon. Like Kato often says, the devil is in the details and he knows all about it.

The devil wants to kill your soul, steal from you, and destroy your dream. When I say, Adam and Eve killed themselves in the darkness, but the angels reported it to Yah and He kept giving them second chances, believe me. It was because of this situation in the very beginning that the redemption plan of Christ was written in the books. His death on the cross, would be the last time anyone had to die because they sinned. Yes, God gave Adam a promise in the darkness, after he told him to stop killing himself when he messed up. This is where this spirit of suicide comes from. The devil wants you to harm yourself because he wants you to lose out on the promise, not that he would get it; he just doesn't want you to have the good because he can't ever have it. The good is God's love and forgiveness. The treasures are understanding His word and communing with the Holy Spirit. That's the richness of the inheritance of Christ. He is the blessing!

He came to taunt them, and he was hurling threats at them because he hated seeing them get the love he could not and would never receive, sound familiar? He had the love the Father, but he wanted to be the Father God and there can only be one God. But God in His compassion and great love for His creation, sent His only begotten Son Jesus (John 3:16). He told us in Jeremiah that He had a plan to prosper us and give us a hope and a future and not to harm us, and God has been faithful to His word even up to this very day. All the evil acts that happen in this world, are done by men under the influence of the antichrist. This was the reason for The Book of Romans, Chapter 8 where the great Apostle Paul talks about living your life according to the Spirit.

"So now there is no condemnation for those who belong to Christ Jesus. And because you belong to him, the power of the life-giving Spirit has freed you [me] from the power of sin that leads to death. The law of Moses was unable to save us because of the weakness of our sinful nature [flesh]. So, God did what the law could not do. He sent his own Son in a body like the bodies we sinners have. And in that body God declared an end to sin's control over us by giving his Son as a sacrifice for our sins. He did this so that the just requirement of the law would be fully satisfied for us, who no longer follow our sinful nature but instead follow the Spirit." (Romans 8:1-4) Christian's are not under the law! We are under the blood covenant and walk in the Spirit of Christ.

"Then I saw four angels standing at the four corners of the earth, holding back the four winds so they did not blow on the earth or the sea, or even on any tree. And I saw another angel coming up from the east, carrying the seal of the living God. And he shouted to those four angels, who had been given power to harm land and sea, "Wait! Don't harm the land or the sea or the trees until we have placed the seal of God on the foreheads of his servants. And I heard how many were marked with the seal of God – 144,000 were sealed from all the tribes of Israel." (Revelations 7:1-4) God is about to seal and gather His children from all over the earth and this is not the time to be playing around with Him. His word seems to be unfolding before my very eyes and He's given me warning after warning to give the people.

"For God wanted them to know that the riches and glory of Christ are for you Gentiles, too. And this is the secret: Christ lives in you. This gives you assurance of sharing his glory." (Colossians 1:27) "When the seventh angel blows his trumpet, God's mysterious plan will be fulfilled. It will happen just as he announced it to his servants the prophets." The sealing will be caused by the latter rain experience. This experience is also called "receiving the seal of the living God." (Revelation 7:2) The latter rain is a second Pentecost, the Holy Spirit empowering the chosen people of God. Remember earlier I said that I felt as though God was stamping me.

When Jesus concludes the sealing of His people, the saints will no longer need an intercessor or mediator in Heaven. Remember we just talked about Abraham not having a mediator between Him and the Father God. "Then the angel showed me a river with a water (Holy Spirit) of life, clear as crystal (knowledge, wisdom and understanding), flowing from the throne of God and of the Lamb. It flowed down the center (Mesis) of the main street. On each side of the river grew a tree [books] of life, bearing twelve crops of fruits [nations, tribes, tongues] with a fresh crop each month [harvest]. The leaves [the pages] were used for medicine to heal the nations.

No longer will there be a curse upon anything. For the throne of God and the Lamb will be there, and his servants will worship him. And they will see his face…" (Revelation 22:1-4) When this happens, the latter rain will have fallen. The latter rain is the Holy Spirit and the reign of Jesus Christ [the Holy Spirit] dwelling on the earth with His people. We start out as baby Christians and hearing the word and trying to understand it. When we first receive the word and start hearing it or digesting it for the first time and in small doses, it's the same as a parent giving their newborn a bottle of milk. Therefore, I had the dream about being under that oak/peach/fig tree, haven't yet determined what kind of tree it was, but what I do know is that my breasts were filling up with milk.

As our faith increases, so does our intake of the word and we spend more time listening, helping us grow and transform, like the monarch butterfly [painted lady] when it is inside of the cocoon, it's eating and growing.

When transformation is complete, we finally emerge to shine adding color and beauty to our environments. We can't do life without the Word of the Lord because that's where the beauty and the life is. There is no life outside of Christ, after all He is the Creator. Only the Creator can fix, supply the correct parts, and maintain the upkeep on what He created. Like a Carpenter, he constructs and builds and maintains. God wants every sinner to become a spiritual being. Remember the word says, the Father is looking for those who worship Him in spirit and in truth. He wants us to overcome sin and live in the bright natures he first gave to our Father Adam and thus live victorious lives.

He is not willing that any person should be lost. "The Lord isn't really being slow about his promise, as some people think. No, he is being patient for your sake. He does not want anyone to be destroyed but wants everyone to repent." (2 Peter 3:9) The problem is that fallen man does not naturally feel any need for a Savior, but our need of a Savior is far greater than that of any emotion. We need a Savior to give us power to do what is right when the price for righteousness is high. We need a Savior who empowers us to forgive our debtors and love the unlovely. We need a Savior who will comfort us for doing right – even though the heavens may fall. Most of all, we need a Savior who has died in our place and paid the penalty for our sins. There is great peace and joy in having a Savior.

"And I will give power to my two witnesses and they will prophesy for 1,260 days, clothed in sackcloth [meaning rough fabric/distress/repentance and morning]. These are the two olive trees [Jesus, [The Bible]] and the two lampstands [the Ten Commandments, The Holy Spirit] that stand before [that is, these vessels are positioned before] the LORD of the earth [who rules from His temple in Heaven]. If anyone tries to harm them, fire comes from their mouths and devours their enemies. [At the appointed time, God will destroy those who reject the testimony of His Witnesses with fire]. This is how anyone who wants to harm them must die." (Revelation 11:3-5; 20:15) Let me just mention that missiles are a form of fire raining down and also fire does fall from heaven. The Holy Ghost is also considered a fire.

The Bible and the Holy Spirit [the Two Witnesses] will be supernaturally empowered for 1,260 days. God's wrath will tear down the foolishness that preoccupies people, and overnight, the Bible will become the most important book on Earth. For 1,260 days, the chosen servants of God will be "gifted" with the empowerment of God's Two Witnesses and a great contest for souls will unfold. There will be intense hatred for those who choose to obey God, but there will be genuine love among those who receive the gospel of Jesus. Was it not for the special protection which the Holy Spirit will give the chosen, they would be easy prey.

In fact, wicked men would kill them long before they could accomplish their task. The Bible says, "If anyone tries to harm them, fire comes from their mouths and devours their enemies" which means the chosen will remain invincible until they have completed their God-given work. "Therefore, this is what the Lord God of Heaven's Armies says: "Because the people are talking like this, my messages will flame out of your mouth and burn the people like kindling wood." (Jeremiah 5:14) God does not allow anything to stop them from their mission until their job is done and the caricature of a fire breathing monster [burning books] indicates their invincibility.

I believe we are getting closer and closer to this time; this is why it is important for the word of God to be in our hearts because they are going to try and do away with the Bible. I believe those people in China are experiencing this very thing. I decided to go to an evening service and I'm glad I did. Here I was again hearing a sermon on Joseph. I've been saying since 2017, that I am Joseph hidden in plain sight because of my dreams and it was prophesied over me – though they didn't understand how accurate they were when they said it to me. The reason I say that I am Joseph hidden in plain sight is because the sun, moon and stars in Revelation 12 have everything to do with Joseph's dream of his mother, father, and brother's bowing to him. It also says, the woman hid her face from the serpent. I believe I am the woman clothed with the sun, moon, and stars and hidden from the serpent. In Revelation 12, the woman is Israel and I am Israel. Joseph has been my role model as I've navigated into my kingdom assignment. I'm hearing the Lord say, "It's time for me to move into my purpose and position."

I'm beginning to understand that it's not a microwave or overnight success story, it's been unfolding for 13 years. I've had some challenges with getting my first writings back from the original publishing company. See, God told me to write the book, but I didn't understand why. I really didn't think there was anything interesting about my life that other people hadn't been through. I didn't understand that it wasn't time for me to publish the writings because it was the same as me telling my dreams to people who didn't have good intentions. However, once I started writing my eyes were opened. It was like pulling back a curtain and seeing things for the first time. I was excited to know God was really speaking to me. Though reliving some things was very painful but I was able to see that God was there all along.

In fact, as He promised in His word, He didn't leave or forsake me. It seems like God has pressed fast forward on our time though, like a "quantum leap," as was prophesied. He is a God of process. Going through this process is enabling me to stand more confidently and boldly in His word. He's constantly giving me new strategies and I'm inching closer to fulfilling this assignment He has given to me, though like the movie, I think it's a neverending story. You may ask what assignment? To tell the world that Christ lives, the Ark of the Covenant is with me, He's dwelling among His people and He's returning very soon to take back the title deed of the earth and rule and reign on the earth in His established Kingdom. The Holy Spirit is gathering His children.

It's my assignment to awaken hearts and let people know that there is life beyond themselves and beyond this world. To confirm to others that the dreams you have been given, come from your Creator and He is communicating with you and He has something for you to do, that only you can do. It's a life that can only be attained by surrendering to Jesus Christ. He wanted me to set the record straight that being politically correct is wrong. Being caught up in material things and being cold and not showing compassion is wrong. Not honoring your marriage vows is wrong. Worshipping idols or other gods is wrong! Joseph's identity was his resource. His ability and the grace he had on his life to manage resources correctly, found him in every season. Genesis 41 details Pharaoh's Dream and Joseph's interpretation. Now we understand God gave Pharaoh the dream to display His glory.

A gifted young lady said, "I'm finding it takes a unique set of circumstances to qualify the make-up of a person who has kingdom assignments. People who are called to greatness have lives of persecution, struggle, and opposition – history, stories and key indicators that set them apart from others. Joseph labeled himself an instrument that God can work through." I have learned that I cannot do things in and of my own strength, I must live holy so that I continue to be a vessel that God can use. Joseph was simply being used by God as an instrument. Mary was an instrument. King David was an instrument and the list goes on. Joseph became a resource. In Genesis 42 we see him offer a strategy after he gave an interpretation for the dream. There was no time to be afraid or to be insecure. My life as a resource is going to bring a solution. Hallelujah! It was prophesied that my life history and story combining will make me a resource in an area I am needed most – I receive that! Lord have mercy! I feel as though all that I have gone through in my life is about to make sense, and somehow my preparation is making me a resource. My brother Marcus prophesied that the works of my hands in this season will be blessed. If I build it, He will bless it.

After the service I went up for prayer and the woman of God, laid hands on me and prayed for God to give me the "new," and "the Joseph mantle to my generation." Then her husband started prophesying to different people in the room, though as I said in an earlier chapter, God speaks directly to me whenever a man or woman of God prophesies and he said, "You are a voice, the voice of the King – He's preparing you for your destiny and divine seat at the table, a place where women could have never walked, to speak for those that have been rejected or where words have been spoken against them. Joseph in spirit, a mantle to walk in the supernatural and to counsel. Giving you the ability to possess the land. You will walk in grace with multiple gifts and abilities because you are called to be your own leader – grace in this season to walk in boldness – there is more – you shall see, it will come to pass – you shall build your wealth. God said you are my gift and I send you out like an arrow. I will make a way for you and your future is in my hands. I give you entrance, and access" says the Father. "The walls are coming down. When they walked into their promise in Jericho, they had to walk around and shout! The walls are coming down!"

I believe the Bible is a great resource for people enslaved or in bondage because a lot of people chosen by the Lord were either slaves, in bondage or slave type situations or experiencing spiritual bondage. But you can be free. I'll never forget something I heard

Tupac say during his jail interview, he said "your body can be in the cell, but your mind doesn't have to be." He was so wise, yet so young. He was saying everything back then, even mentioned Trump, the homeless, how people live in huge mansions and step over homeless people and don't help and that was in the 90's.The people who succeeded in pleasing God are the ones who followed, obeyed, surrendered, served, listened, acknowledged, and prayed to Jesus. And though he prayed to black Jesus, he didn't know that we are not black, but that the Lord darkened our skin so we would be protected from the sun. We are brown, tanned or bronze. We are dark skinned because it's the only way that we could stand in the sun and not be burned by it. This is information from books that we have not had access to because we don't have all the books, because the bible could not contain all the works of Jesus, but I digress.

People who loved the Lord, were not perfect people – they didn't have to be, but they were delivered and deliverers, set free and they set others free, and they lived well in bad times and most times had a peace that people just couldn't understand like me. People don't understand why I'm at peace, why I smile, why I forgive and forget so quickly. They don't understand why I laugh and why I have joy. I am blessed to know God, and that's the big and small of it. Billy Graham said, "The cross is offensive because it causes people to choose." When I chose Jesus, it changed my whole world. Like the prophets of old, though the world was falling apart around them, they were cool as a breeze because the Lord was with them. They believed God and they took Him at His word. That's where I am. That's where my family is and the few that has allowed to be on this road with me. We have peace no matter what we see with our natural eyes.

That's what my dream was on the night of July 16, 2017. In the dream, the world was falling to pieces but me and my family were sailing away to safety on a huge boat. Funny thing is, that morning an angel of the Lord told me, "In order to hold on to something new, you have to let go of something old. You can't be more committed to a familiar discomfort than you are to an unfamiliar new possibility. Some of the best gifts of your life come out of being tested." Let's look at the life of Moses for example. The Israelites had settled in the Land of Goshen in the time of Joseph and Jacob, but a new Pharaoh arose who oppressed the children of Israel. At this time Moses was born to his father Amram [meaning People of Exaltation], son [meaning descendant or relative] of Kehath the Levite, who entered Egypt with Jacob's household; his mother was Jochebed [also Yocheved – meaning God is glory], who was kin to Kehath [Levite Patriarch].

Moses had one older [by seven years] sister, Miriam, and one older [by three years] brother, Aaron. The Pharaoh had commanded that all male Hebrew children born would be drowned in the river Nile, but Moses' mother placed him in an ark and concealed the ark in the bulrushes by the riverbank, where the baby was discovered and adopted by Pharaoh's daughter, and raised as an Egyptian. Now think about that, if Moses could be passed off as an Egyptian as a Hebrew baby, then he had to look like them. This had to be a very distressing time for the Hebrew mothers, much like it was for the mother's in the 80's and 90's with sons, they had to worry about gangs, drugs, violence and guns on the street as well as racism and social injustice in America. Again, I say no one has had it as bad as the people of color.

One day, after Moses had reached adulthood, he killed an Egyptian who was beating a Hebrew. Moses, in order to escape the Pharaoh's death penalty, fled to Midian [a desert country south of Judah], where he married Zipporah [meaning Bird, Goat, Crown, and Doom]. There, on Mount Horeb, God appeared to Moses as a burning bush, revealed to Moses his name YHWH [pronounced Yahweh] and commanded him to return to Egypt and bring his chosen people [Israel] out of bondage and into the Promised Land [Canaan]. During the journey, God tried to kill Moses. God was going to kill Moses for his sin, but Zipporah saved his life. Moses returned to carry out God's command, but God caused the Pharaoh to refuse, and only after God had subjected Egypt to ten plagues did the Pharaoh relent.

Moses led the Israelites to the border of Egypt, but there God hardened the Pharaoh's heart once more, so that he could destroy the Pharaoh and his army at the Red Sea Crossing as a sign of his power to Israel and the nations. After defeating the Amalekites in Rephidim, Moses led the Israelites to biblical Mount Sinai, where he was given the Ten Commandments from God, written on stone tablets. However, since Moses remained a long time on the mountain, some of the people feared that he might be dead, so they made a statue of a golden calf and worshipped it, thus disobeying and angering God and Moses. Moses, out of anger, broke the tablets, and later ordered the elimination of those who had worshiped the golden statue, which was melted down and fed to the idolaters. He also wrote the ten commandments on a new set of tablets.

Later at Mount Sinai, Moses and the elders entered a covenant, by which Israel would become the people of YHWH, obeying his laws, and YHWH would be their god. Moses delivered the laws of God to Israel, instituted the priesthood under the sons of Moses' brother Aaron, and destroyed those Israelites who fell away from worshipping God. In his final act at Sinai, God gave Moses instructions for the Tabernacle, the mobile [moving] shrine by which he would travel with Israel to the Promised Land. From Sinai, Moses led the Israelites to the Desert of Paran (meaning to glorify, beautify and adorn) on the border of Canaan. From there he sent twelve spies into the land. The spies returned with samples of the land's fertility, but warned that its inhabitants were giants [fallen angel hybrid children]. The people were afraid and wanted to return to Egypt [Africa], and some rebelled against Moses and against God.

Moses told the Israelites that they were not worthy to inherit the land, and would wander the wilderness for forty years until the generation who had refused to enter Canaan had died, so that it would be their children who would possess the land. When the forty years had passed, Moses led the Israelites east around the Dead Sea to the territories of Edom [Southern Israel] and Moab [meaning from father]. There they escaped the temptation of idolatry, conquered the lands of Og [meaning baked bread, round bread baked on hot stones] and Sihon [meaning wiping out, uprooting, eradicating, as a warrior sweeping all before him; with great extreme boldness] in Transjordan, received God's blessing through Balaam [meaning people or kinsmen and swallowing up and destroying the people] the prophet, and massacred the Midianites [meaning Seed of Abraham to the time of the Judges], who by the end of the Exodus journey had become the enemies of the Israelites due to their notorious role in enticing the Israelites to sin against God. Wow!

Moses was twice given notice that he would die before entry to the Promised Land, which makes me think of Dr. King, remember he said he saw the promised land but he wouldn't make it there with us and also the fact that I had the dream seven days before Billy Graham passed away, including the visitation from the birds from New Zealand on the 7th day of December, which just so happened to be the same day Reinhard Bonnke went to be with the Lord. He too would not see the Promised land manifest in His lifetime, but I believe they all will see it together with God's chosen. Seems like the Joshua mantle dropped on me. "One day the LORD said to Moses, "Climb one of the mountains east of the river [the mountains of Abarim] and look out over the land I have given the people of Israel.

After you have seen it, you will die like your brother Aaron [symbolic for dying to the flesh], for you both rebelled against my instructions in the wilderness of Zin [meaning in the dry place, thorn, barb, tradition]. When the people of Israel rebelled, you failed to demonstrate my holiness to them at the waters. [These are the waters of Meribah (meaning place of strife where Moses brought forth the water from the rock at Kadesh in the wilderness of Zin)." Then Moses said to the LORD, "O LORD, you are the God who gives breath to all creatures. Please appoint a new man as leader for the community. Give them someone who will guide them wherever they go and will lead them into battle, so the community of the LORD will not be like sheep without a shepherd." Numbers 27:13-17.

Once he had seen the Promised Land from a viewpoint on Mount Abarim, the Lord told him again, "Then the LORD said to Moses, "On behalf of the people of Israel, take revenge on the Midianites for leading them into idolatry. After that, you will die and join your ancestors." (Numbers 31:1) After the battle with the Midianites had been won, on the banks of the Jordan River, in sight of the land, Moses assembled the tribes. After recalling their wanderings he delivered God's laws by which they must live in the land, sang a song of praise and pronounced a blessing on the people, and passed his authority to Joshua, under whom they would possess the land.

Moses then went up Mount Nebo [meaning those on the other side of the Jordan] to the top of Pisgah [meaning split and cut off], looked over the promised land of Israel [meaning He retains God and God is Upright] spread out before him, and died, at the age of one hundred and twenty (120). Moses was also born in the Age of Aries or the Age of Law. I am an Aries by birth, making my spirit animal a ram. The *Age of Aries*, or the Ram, spans approximately the period between 2200 and 100 BC. It is the age defined by the Sun being in the constellation of Aries on the *spring equinox.* Additional influences during this age are of Cancer (June 26) in the *summer solstice*, Libra (September) in the *autumnal equinox (September 23)*, and Capricorn (December 22) in the *winter solstice.* The Libra (the Scales) influence is an especially important secondary influence, since during this period the first codes of justice in known history were recorded.

The more pure Aries influence, outside the influence of the *cusps* of the earlier Taurus and the later Pisces, was experienced between about 1700 and 600 BC. In this narrower period we see the regeneration of the Egyptian civilization as the New Kingdom, bringing Egypt to one of its most prosperous periods; At the same time the Hebrew people break away from their Egyptian benefactors turned enslavers and establish a line of prophets that lasts for centuries; Babylonia reaches its peak as a major regional power and its most well-known ruler, *Hammurabi*, presents one of the first codes of law; During this time the ancient sacred hymns of the Vedas were compiled and the *Vedic religion* thrived in India and this makes sense because the Lord threw the serpent into India but that's in another book we don't have.

"(Now Moses was very humble – more humble than any other person on earth.) So immediately the LORD called to Moses, Aaron, and Miriam and said, "Go out to the Tabernacle [Hebrew Tent of Meeting] all three of you!" (Numbers 12:3-4) I believe this is representative of the prophet, the High Priest and the Holy Spirit because this story involves the Word of the Most High God, the thirst for the Holy Spirit, the wayward son, God's name and one woman, a sister, a daughter, a prince servant and slave all wrapped up in one. There has not been another prophet like Moses since in Israel, whom YHWH knew face to face" as it states in Deuteronomy 34:10, "There has never been another prophet in Israel like Moses, whom the LORD knew face to face." The New Testament states that after Moses' death, Michael the Archangel and the devil disputed over his body. "Dear friends, I had been eagerly planning to write to you about the salvation we all share. But now I find that I must write about something else, urging you to defend the faith that God has entrusted once for all time to his holy people.

I say this because some ungodly people have wormed their way into your churches, saying that God's marvelous grace allows us to live immoral lives. The condemnation of such people was recorded long ago, for they have denied our only Master and Lord, Jesus Christ. So I want to remind you, though you already know these things, that Jesus [Lord God, or God Christ) first rescued the nation of Israel from Egypt, but later he destroyed those who did not remain faithful. And I remind you of the angels who did not stay within the limits of authority God gave them (read Genesis 6) but left the place where they belonged. God has kept them securely chained in prisons of darkness, waiting for the great day of judgement.

And don't forget Sodom and Gomorrah and their neighboring towns, which were filled with immorality and every kind of sexual perversion. Those cities were destroyed by fire and serve as a warning of eternal fire of God's judgement. In the same way, these people who claim authority from their dreams – live immoral lives, defy authority, and scoff at supernatural beings [at illuminated ones, evil angels]. But even Michael, one of the mightiest of the angels, [Greek Michael, the archangel] did not dare accuse the devil of blasphemy, but simply said, "The Lord rebuke you!" [This took place when Michael was arguing with the devil about Moses' body]." (Jude 1:9) I believe Moses' story is symbolic of the "seed" or "root" being born as it speaks about in Revelation 12, where the child was snatched away from the dragon and was caught up to God and to his throne; this all takes place in the constellations, i.e. the heavens.

Then she was hidden for growth and preparation for the time to come. Just as Moses was put in a basket and sent down the river so that he would not perish. His mother was a high priestess, and she conceived him in secret, he was delivered in secret and she then put him in a basket of rushes (means move with urgent haste); with bitumen (used for waterproofing and road construction) she sealed the lid and cast him into the river which rose up over him. So, she put the baby in a basket with a secured cover to protect it from the winds and waves and set it afloat in the water, all symbolic of a spirit man inside of a protected vessel with the holy spirit acting as a covering and moving pathway being represented by the river.

"Then I witness in heaven an event of great significance. I saw a woman clothed with the sun, with the moon beneath her feet, and a crown of twelve stars on her head. She was pregnant, and she cried out because of her labor pains and the agony of giving birth. Then I witnessed in heaven another significant event. I saw a large red dragon [God's judgement] with seven heads and ten horns [powerful], with seven crowns on his heads. His tail swept away one-third of the stars in the sky, and he threw them to the earth. He stood in front of the woman as she was about to give birth, ready to devour her baby as soon as it was born.

She gave birth to a son who was to rule all nations with an iron rod. And her child was snatched away from the dragon and was caught up to God and to his throne. And the woman fled into the wilderness, where God has prepared a place to care for her for 1260 days. – Revelations 12:1-6" I received my book and money back from the thieves on February 14, 2020, same day I had the dream exactly two years prior where the Lord told me all my dreams would come true and 1260 days from that date would be Thursday, July 28, 2022. "What sorrow awaits you teachers of religious law and you Pharisees. Hypocrites! For you are like whitewashed tombs – beautiful on the outside but filled on the inside with dead people's bones and all sorts of impurity." Matthew 23:27 "But anyone who eats my flesh and drinks my blood has eternal life, and I will raise that person at the last day." (John 6:54)

Moses is honored among Jews today as the "lawgiver of Israel", and he delivers several sets of laws in the course of the four books. The first is the Covenant Code (Exodus 20:19–23:33), the terms of the covenant which God offers to the Israelites at "biblical" Mount Sinai. Embedded in the covenant are the Decalogue (the Ten Commandments, Exodus 20:1–17) and the Book of the Covenant (Exodus 20:22–23:19). The entire Book of Leviticus constitutes a second body of law, the Book of Numbers begins with yet another set, and the Book of Deuteronomy another. Moses has traditionally been regarded as the author of those four books and the Book of Genesis, which together comprise the Torah, the first section of the Hebrew Bible. That's amazing! I'm pretty certain now that night I was attacked, it was my body they were fighting over. I told my children it felt like I had been in a fight in my sleep and then when I went to the eye doctor on February 3, 2020, they asked if I had been in a fight during my eye exam because I had a white scar and slash on my left cornea like I had an infection, but it had been healed. That blew my mind! God continues to blow my mind. Moses and Elijah being on the mount of transfiguration makes them the Two Witnesses, the two men walking like trees.

The Bible is a continuation of the Torah, but I recently found out that it too was the continuation of another book which I have shared bits and pieces here and there and will share more later; but all books that were written and inspired by the Holy Spirit are intended for the believers to use as a tool to break free from the slavery and captivity of sin and bondage, and to recognize the tricks of the enemy. Therefore, there is so much confusion today, because we do not have all the books or know all the stories about all that were chosen children of God. The bible gives us bits and pieces, and really the most important parts because it says it was written for those at the end of the Age. It gave us things we needed to know for the time we are living in. It is also the blueprint for how to live as followers of the ways of Jesus Christ and live free.

Before that angel touched me and told me to wake up in 2014, I had a vision of myself, I was floating above my lifeless body lying there as if I had died or in a deep sleep. I had left my body and was caught up in the air. Maybe I did die that day, or it was my time of visitation which makes me very grateful that I live in daily repentance and prayed for mercy every night.

Thinking about it, I was floating above, and I didn't descend to the depths of hell. I looked sleep, but I could tell it was a deep sleep. I was up there for a minute and I was being shown something, but I don't remember anything that was said. Then a mummy type figure, wrapped in linen cloths inched towards me slowly like he was coming from an ancient time, and tapped me on the forehead and said "wake up."

I was terrified. I saw this white image moving toward me slowly, and I was paralyzed and I couldn't move. After it tapped me, I was back on the bed and I sat straight up, and I was afraid. I was home alone, and I called my then boyfriend at work, who was living with me to tell him what had happened, but he didn't believe me. I understand now the Lord was showing me that I was in a deep sleep and the time had come for me to wake up. I understand why I was under strong demonic attack in October. The devil was trying to kill me to stop me from knowing my purpose. He was trying to delay the inevitable. The enemy was trying to silence the truth and kill the Holy Spirit, but unfortunately for him, the end has already been written. You cannot kill the Holy Spirit, it doesn't die. "The thief's purpose is to steal and kill and destroy. My purpose is to give them a rich and satisfying life." (John 10:10)

"In the third year of the reign of King Cyrus of Persia [the third year of Cyrus's reign was 536 B.C] Daniel [also known as Belteshazzar meaning God is my Judge] had another vision. He understood that the vision concerned events certain to happen in the future – times of war and great hardship. When this vision came to me, I, Daniel, had been in mourning for three whole weeks. All that time I had eaten no rich food. No meat or wine crossed my lips, and I used no fragrant lotions until those three weeks had passed. On April 23 [Hebrew April 24] as I was standing on the bank of the great Tigris River, I looked up and saw a man dressed in linen clothing, with a belt of pure gold around his waist. His body looked like a precious gem. His face flashed like lightning, and his eyes flamed like torches. His arms and feet shone like polished bronze, and his voice roared like a vast multitude of people. Only I, Daniel saw this vision. The men with me saw nothing, but they were suddenly terrified and ran away to hide. So, I was left there alone to see this amazing vision. My strength left me, my face grew deathly pale, and I felt very weak.

Then I heard the man speak, and when I heard his voice, I fainted and lay there with my face to the ground. Just then a hand touched me and lifted me, still trembling, to my hands and knees. And the man said to me, "Daniel, you are very precious to God, so listen carefully to what I have to say to you. Stand up, for I have been sent to you." When he said this to me, I stood up, still trembling. Then he said, "Don't be afraid, Daniel. Since the first day you began to pray for understanding and to humble yourself before your God, your request has been heard in heaven. I have come in answer to your prayer. But for twenty-one days [21 years] the spirit prince [Hebrew the prince] of the kingdom of Persia blocked my way. Then Michael, one of the archangels [Hebrew the chief princes], came to help me, and left him there with the spirit prince of the kingdom of Persia [Hebrew reads I was left there with the kings of Persia].

Now I am here to explain what will happen to your people in the future, for this vision concerns a time yet to come." While he was speaking to me, I looked down at the ground, unable to say a word. Then the one who looked like a man [something that looked like a human hand] touched my lips [my forehead] and I opened my mouth [eyes] and began to speak. I said to the one standing in front of me, 'I am filled with anguish because of the vision I have seen, my lord, and I am very weak. How can someone like me, your servant, talk to you, my lord? My strength is gone, and I can hardly breathe." Then the one who looked like a man touched me again, and I felt my strength returning. "Don't be afraid," he said, "for you are very precious to God. Peace! Be encouraged! Be strong!" As he spoke these words to me, I suddenly felt stronger and said to him, "Please speak to me, my lord, for you have strengthened me."

He replied, "Do you know why I have come? Soon I must return to fight against the spirit prince of the kingdom of Persia [Land of Horses, Land of Division, Land of Science] and after that the spirit prince of the kingdom of Greece [Hebrew of Javan meaning Ionians, Indonesia] will come. Meanwhile, I will tell you what is written in the Book of Truth. (No one helps me against these spirit princes except Michael, your spirit prince [Hebrew against these except Michael, your prince]. I have been standing beside Michael [Hebrew Him] to support and strengthen him since the first year of the reign of Darius the Mede [Obama] [meaning to possess good]. – Daniel 10:1-22"

Though I was terrified, I perceived it to be a visitation from heaven. Looking back now, I'm absolutely positive it was a supernatural encounter, and He was calling me and now I understand I was shown these things that Daniel saw. He was showing me where I was headed. I was dying in my sin and in that situation. I know the season. I was barely spending time with Him; I wasn't reading my Bible as I should. I was listening to the wrong voices. Sure, I prayed every night for mercy, but it was so generic and all about me. I didn't have a relationship with God the way I used to when I was a young girl. I was always talking to the Lord. I was always curious about the words in the book and wondered what they meant. I was always sharing about God, even when it wasn't popular, and no one wanted to hear it. I lived my life in the "against the norm" column.

It seems He had something important for me to do. I had become a slave to sin. After this, He sent me to a church to get cleaned up, washed in the Word, cleansing my heart and impregnating me with dreams again. Then I became His slave and He became my Master; and I would rather be a slave to Christ who is light of the world and author of life and live eternally with Him in peace and paradise, than to live in darkness and be a slave to sin and death and risk an eternity of darkness, hell on earth or an eternity in hell. I am a follower of the Way and I'm sold out for Jesus! I will not bow to man and He cannot make me, because the Lord God Almighty gave every man free will. God is the ruler of this earth and not man! Jesus came back to take back the title deed! He conquered death and the grave! He got the keys to the Kingdom! The heavens proclaim it! The Holy Spirit speaks!

"Then I said, "It's all over! I am doomed, for I am a sinful woman. I have filthy lips, and I live among people with filthy lips. Yet I have seen the King, the Lord of Heaven's Armies." Then one of the seraphim flew to me with a burning coal he had taken from the altar with a pair of tongs. He touched my lips with it and said, "See, this coal has touched your lips. Now your guilt is removed, and your sins are forgiven." Then the Lord asking, "Whom should I send as a messenger to this people? Who will go for us? I said, "Here I am. Send me." And he said, "Yes, go and say to this people, "Listen carefully, but do not understand. 'When you hear what I say, you will not understand. When you see what I do, you will not comprehend. For the hearts of these people are hardened, and their ears cannot hear, and they have closed their eyes – so their eyes cannot see, and their ears cannot hear, and their hearts cannot understand, and they cannot turn to me and let me heal them.

Then I said, "Lord, how long will this go on?" And he replied, "Until their towns are empty, their houses are deserted, and the whole country is a wasteland; until the LORD has sent everyone away, and the entire land of Israel lies deserted. If even a tenth – a remnant – survive, it will be invaded again and burned. But as a terebinth or oak tree leaves a stump when it is cut down, so Israel's stump will be a holy seed." (Isaiah 6:5-13) Adam and Eve continued to be deceived by the devil when they were kicked out of the garden, but when they would pray to the Lord, repent and fast, He would send His Word and forgive and save them. The angels would bring messages and gifts from the Lord God Almighty with instructions. This is happening again today. This angered the devil then, and he is still angry about it today and it's the reason he wars with the offspring of the woman, but God! We have Jesus, the blood and His resurrection power! It's a new day! Rise and shine for Christ, stand on His word, speak with resurrection power and believe what you decree and declare by faith. Faith without works is dead, you have to do something!

They had to listen to God's voice and the Lord always followed through with what He said He would do, but it wasn't the case with Satan. The devil would disguise himself and with his silver tongue he gave them promises of lies and when they came to receive what he said, he attacked and killed them over and again, because his promises are empty! To the contrary, Lord always sends His Word and saves and He's doing that same thing today. He sent His word and He sent me. It's the reason you are alive and reading this right now, because he chose you too! He sent His Holy Spirit to dwell among His people. He sent Himself and now He's sending us! We were born for such a time as this!

"The message is very close at hand; it is on your lips and in your heart. And that message is the very message about faith that we preach. If you openly declare that Jesus is Lord and believe in your heart that God raised him from the dead, you will be saved. For it is by believing in your heart that you are made right with God, and it is by openly declaring your faith that you are saved. As the Scriptures tell us, "Anyone who trusts in him will never be disgraced. Jew and Gentile [and Greek] are the same in this respect. They have the same Lord, who gives generously to all who call on him. For "Everyone who calls on the name of the LORD will be saved." But how can they call on him to save them unless they believe in him? And how they can believe in him if they have never heard about him? And how can they hear about him unless someone tells them? And how will anyone go and tell them without being sent?

That is why the Scriptures say, "How beautiful are the feet of messengers who bring good news! But not everyone welcomes the Good News, for Isaiah the prophet said, "LORD, who has believed our message?" So faith comes from hearing, that is, hearing the Good News about Christ. But I ask, have the people of Israel heard the message? Yes, they have: "The message has gone throughout the earth, and the words to all the world." But I ask, did the people of Israel really understand? Yes, they did, for even in the time of Moses, God said, "I will rouse your jealousy through people who are not even a nation. I will provoke your anger through the foolish Gentiles [unbelievers]." And later Isaiah spoke boldly for God, saying, 'I was found by people who were not looking for me. I showed myself to those who were not asking for me." (Deuteronomy 32, Isaiah 65)." But regarding Israel, God said, "All day long I opened my arms to them, but they were disobedient and rebellious." (Romans 10:8-21)

"Wake up, wake up, O Zion! Clothe yourself with strength. Put on your beautiful clothes, O holy city of Jerusalem [the Faithful City], for unclean and godless people will enter your gates no longer. Rise from the dust, O Jerusalem [Holy Mountain]. Sit in a place of honor. Remove the chains of slavery from your neck, O captive daughter of Zion. For this is what the LORD says: "When I sold you into exile, I received no payment. Now I can redeem you without having to pay for you." "This is what the Sovereign LORD says: "Long ago my people chose to live in Egypt [the United States]. Now they are oppressed by Assyria. What is this? Asks the LORD. "Why are my people enslaved again? Those who rule them shout in exultation. My name is blasphemed all day long [Greek version reads The Gentiles [unbelievers] continually blaspheme my name because of you].

But I will reveal my name [Yeshua Messiah] to my people, and they will come to know its power. Then at last they will recognize that I am the one who speaks to them. How beautiful on the mountains are the feet of the messenger who brings good news, the good news of peace and salvation, the news that the God of Israel [Hebrew of Zion reigns! The watchmen [we] shout and sing with joy, for before their [our] very eyes they [we] see the LORD returning to Jerusalem [Hebrew to Zion, the Holy Mountain]. Let the ruins of Jerusalem break into joyful song, for the LORD has comforted his people. He has redeemed Jerusalem [the Faith-full City]. The LORD has demonstrated his holy power before the eyes of all the nations. All the ends of the earth will see the victory of our God." [Isaiah 52:1-10]

"Then, after doing all those things, I will pour out my Spirit upon all people. Your sons and daughters will prophesy. Your old men will dream dreams, and your young men will see visions. In those days I will pour out my Spirit even on servants – men and women alike. And I will cause wonders in the heavens and on the earth – blood and fire and columns of smoke. The sun [Son] will become dark [skinned] and the moon [unbelievers] will turn blood red [become angry] before that great and terrible [Greek reads glorious] day of the LORD arrives. But everyone who calls on the name of the LORD will be saved, for some on Mount Zion in Jerusalem will escape, just as the LORD has said. These will be among the survivors whom the LORD has called." [Joel 2:28-32] Wow! Moses did a lot of work! All the prophets did too! "But in your great mercy you did not abandon them to die in the wilderness. The pillar of cloud still led them forward by day [good days], and the pillar of fire showed them the way through the night [dark nights]." Nehemiah 9:19"

I'm blessed and highly favored and fortunate enough to have all this technology at the disposal of my fingertips in combination with the actual books, and the leading of the Holy Spirit which has helped me greatly. I can't even to begin to imagine Moses' plight of having to do all the reading, researching and write it down? It was the Holy Spirit and the angels and the Lord God himself on that mountain with Moses, I'm for certain! I know for sure the Lord God Almighty was right by his side! Just like He is with me! Just like He's been with all the great men and women of God who risks their lives for the furtherance of the gospel. It was my mother's prayer for me, that I would use my gifts to further the gospel of Jesus Christ.

The great Apostle Paul said, "God raised Jesus from the dead, and we are all witnesses of this." (Acts of the Apostles 2:32) I am a believer! Amazing! I believe the spirits that are with me are all the prophets, from Abraham, Isaac, Jacob, Moses, Joseph, King David, John the Baptist, The Apostle Paul, The Apostle John, and Peter "the Rock", etc. I believe all of God's angels accompany me because the Lord is with me. I believe the four spirits going out to patrol the earth are the gospels, Matthew, Mark, Luke, and John headed North, East, South and John came blowing into the West. I believe we will see the greatest outpouring of the Holy Spirit and Great Tribulation on the earth in 2020, more than we've ever seen before because I truly believe we are approaching the end of Revelation. I can only pray, you make it out alive and I urge you to choose Jesus Christ, because He is the only one who can save you. To be continued…

Made in the USA
Columbia, SC
18 April 2021